Achieving Superpersonhood:
Three East African Lives

Achieving Superpersonhood: Three East African Lives

A novel by
William Peace

Strategic Book Publishing and Rights Co.

Copyright © 2018 William Peace. All rights reserved.

No part of this book may be reproduced or transmitted in any form or by any means, graphic, electronic, or mechanical, including photocopying, recording, taping, or by any information storage retrieval system, without the permission, in writing, of the publisher. For more information, email support@sbpra.net, Attention: Subsidiary Rights.

Strategic Book Publishing & Rights Co., LLC
USA | Singapore
www.sbpra.com

For information about special discounts for bulk purchases, please contact Strategic Book Publishing and Rights Co. Special Sales, at bookorder@sbpra.net.

ISBN: 978-1-948858-89-2

Table of Contents

Chapter: 1 The Migrant 1

Chapter 2 Mandrax Smoke 21

Chapter 3: Home Away 41

Chapter 4: Student Protest 61

Chapter 5: Abattoir 77

Chapter 6: The Prison 94

Chapter 7: Immam Arusei 111

Chapter 8: Intermediary 129

Chapter 9: Shepherds' Fields 149

Chapter 10: Training Camp 167

Chapter 11: Dhul Fikar 185

Chapter 12: Mine Ventures 205

Chapter 13 Atlantis Hotel, Zurich 224

Chapter 14 The Baobab Tree 244

Chapter 15 Refugee 261

Chapter 16 Baba 280

Chapter 17 Dr Wadaki 298

Chapter 18 Litigation 317

Chapter 19 Sword of Honor 338

Chapter 20 Attack 353

Chapter 21 Surgery 370

Chapter 22 Romance 390

Chapter 23 Ivory Poacher 413

Chapter 24 Marriage 433

Chapter 25 Combat 455

Chapter 26 Settlement 473

Chapter 1

The Migrant

Of the three roads leading out of Village, only the east road, eventually reaching City, can carry a cattle-shepherding black youth, seventh-born, toward his hopes; his dreams are still mist. Karimi is a desolate figure walking along the rutted dirt track, his third-hand Keds making coded geometric prints in the soft dust. The rainy season is over now, but the earth is still malleable. The air is warmer, and without a breeze, the sun and humidity are precipitating the beads of sweat on his forehead. He looks neither left nor right; his eyes are focused on the distant track as it narrows and disappears around a rocky hill. Karimi does not see the lone wildebeest standing dejectedly in the umbrella shade of a distant acacia tree to his left, nor does he take note of warthog piglet and his mother hunkered down in a fast-drying mud hole to his right. The thorny white skeletons of whistling acacias along the track, the bristling grasses to either side, and the pair of white-backed vultures drifting lazily overhead do not attract his attention.

Karimi is intent on reaching City, over two hundred kilometers ahead, down this and other east-bound tracks. His given name means "farmer" in the Kikuyu language, and he has been a shepherd for the last eleven of his eighteen years, but herding his father's goats and cattle and helping his uncles grow maize and beans have reached a dead end. As the youngest in a subsistence family, the life he could see ahead offers only suffocation. Besides, his oldest brother will succeed his father soon enough. Two of his older sisters have husbands and children in Village; his third sister left home three years ago, and her whereabouts are unknown.

The next eldest brother is very ill with *kangunyo* (AIDS), and the brother next to Karimi in age, Warari, went to City two years back. Three months ago, in a letter written in pencil on foolscap paper, Warari advised Kamiri: "You must come to City, brother. There is work and food, a place to live. It is hard work, but life will be better for you." There was no return address. Only a series of numbers which Kamiri assumes are a telephone number.

Kamiri's relationship with Warari has vacillated between respectful adoration and angry frustration: adoration of an older brother's assured competence, and frustration with his un-wavering selfishness. In spite of this ambivalent attitude, Warari's letter precipitated Kamiri's decision to leave Village, not with a plan or ambition, but with a determination to find an alternative to a village shepherd's life and to make good of it.

Kamiri's mother tried to forestall his departure. She pointed out several pretty girls in Village who might be prospective wives. One was the granddaughter of the affluent Village elder, but Kamiri doubted that she would say 'yes', and he found her showy self-confidence deflating. His father was principled, at first: "As a Kikuyu your place in life is here in the village, Kamiri. You can help your older brother with our livestock and our ground when I am gone."

"But Baba, my brother's sons will soon be able to look after the cattle. I am not needed and am an extra mouth to feed."

"Be wary, Kamiri, you are just eighteen, and the City is surely a bad place, without grass or kindness."

"Perhaps, but I will find my brother in City. He will show me how to make a different life of my own."

"Remember, Kamiri, when you're in City that you're still a Kikuyu, and that your blood rose here in Village."

Achieving Superpersonhood:

"I will surely remember that, Baba."

The One calls me the Other, so I am neither author nor narrator. I am a facilitator according to my own rules, and I have enhanced Kamiri's positive views about his prospects in City. I say that Kamiri is wise to go to City. Of course, there are risks; going to the City exposes him to homelessness, hunger and loneliness, but in City, with my direction, he can build a splendid, new identity that will be engraved with the name of the Other.

The sun in the west is only a palm-width above the distant trees. Kamiri sits cross-legged on an ancient termite mound in the shade of a candelabra tree. From this vantage point he can see westward down the track. *I must be alert for any passing vehicle which may be going to City.* In the last two days, there were several passing vehicles: three colorful but ramshackle private busses whose fares he could not afford, two tourist vans that blew their horns, and one rangers' jeep. There was no room in the jeep, and it was going to another assignment only eight kilometers down the track, but he was permitted to stand on the running board.

Kamiri removes a parcel wrapped in cloth from his basket. Inside there is a cake of cooked maize and beans held together with cane syrup. His mother keeps a small stand of sugar cane for family treats. The departure of her youngest child was surely an occasion which demanded the preparation of the special cake. His mother, overweight and suffering from gout, is always dressed in colorful gingham: sunflowers are her favorites, as is her Kamiri, who resides firmly in her mind as a loveable, shy but determined child, with an aptitude for school and a passion for football. *The best of them all, but a handful of respectfulness and rebellion.* For Kamiri, his mother's sanctity arises from her extraordinary example of principled, loving discipline.

I, the One, am fond of Kamiri's mother. Hers has been a hard life; a life without comfort, unencumbered health, or material reward. Yet she maintains her steadfast dedication to her family and uninformed commitment to Ngai (the Kikuyu deity) in spite of the many misfortunes which the Other has hurled at her.
And as to Kamiri, I have had a soft spot for him since he was a child. In fact, there is much of the child about him now that he is an adult. He has intelligence, a native kindness to others, and a willingness to persevere in the face of adversity. He is, however, somewhat gullible, and this vulnerability is a frequent target for the Other.

Kamiri considers his situation while eating his self-rationed portion of cake and observing the transformation of the western sky from yellow to gold to red. *In one more day, I should begin to see the edges of City. What will it be like? In the school, I have seen pictures of cities, but pictures don't tell you about the heart. Are the people kind, or like the tourists who blow their horn to warn you, and then wave at you from behind their dark glasses? How am I to find by brother?*
One might think that Kamiri would be worried or anxious – concerned already that perhaps he made the wrong decision to abandon Village. But Kamiri has a great reservoir of patience – learned perhaps from being the youngest and the last in the order of things. With his patience comes an optimistic sense: *Perhaps I am the youngest, but I am still here. I have learned some Swahili, mathematics and science in school. I am not stupid. I am not sick. I have had friends. I can care for myself.*

He trudges on until twilight. Ahead, on the right, he can see the outlines of several small dwellings, and hear the tenor bleating of the goats.

On the previous two nights, he found an elevated spot under a large tree near the track. While they are unlikely to attack, neither wild dogs nor hyenas can climb trees, and the elevation gave him

Achieving Superpersonhood:

the advantage of perception. He removed the old gray blanket that was strapped to his waist, and wrapped it loosely around himself. It represented a barrier against stinging ants. During the nights he slept intermittently, dozing to the questioning 'who' of a nearby owl and the barking of a distant zebra.

Now, he decides to approach the tiny settlement. *If there are friendly people there, perhaps they will let me stay the night. If not, I can settle for the night just on the other side, where predators would never dare.*

On his approach, a dog begins to bark. *The cattle dog.*

A burly man appears, heavy staff in hand. "Who are you?"

"My name is Kamiri, and I am going to City."

"Carry on then."

"Sir, may I bed down for the night with your cattle?"

The man roars a deep, prolonged laugh. "You are either a thief of kids, or milk, or rather stupid."

"I am none of those things, sir, but I have been a shepherd, and I dare not ask for the floor of your home."

"Where have you been a shepherd?"

"In Village to the west."

The man gestures toward a hovel: "You may sleep in the vacant place there, shepherd."

> When people use the word 'shepherd' in a figurative way, it always irritates me. For me, the Other, it conjures up thoughts of selfless care. In my opinion, reducing the priority of one's own interests is simply stupidity! All my friends put their own interests first.

Kamiri sleeps in the abandoned dwelling – one small room actually – the roof of which permits starlight to enter. With the dry skies, the derelict roof makes no difference, and in the unexpected absence of ants, Kamiri sleeps soundly. He wakes to the sound of the restless cattle, straps on his blanket and sets the basket on his head. Encountering the man, he wishes him a good day.

"Will you not have something to eat, shepherd?"

Kamiri hesitates. "You have been kind enough to me already, sir."

The man tilts his head. "Go inside. My wife has bread and milk."

The two-room house is built of a latticework of sticks and poles, covered with mud; the roof is palm-thatched: no materials from City. Inside, a woman dressed in faded fabric, a red bandana tied around her forehead, sits cross-legged on the bare earth floor. She nods and passes him a scarred plastic cup into which she pours warm milk from a brown earthenware jug. "From the cows this morning," she says.

"Thank you for your kindness."

She offers him a low, round basket; inside are crumbling pieces of corn bread. He takes one, murmuring his thanks.

"No, the cakes are for you," she says, gesturing toward his basket of essentials, which he has set on the floor beside him.

He repeats the Kikuyu proverb: "A man may be head of the home, but a woman is its heart."

She nods. "May Ngai (God) favor you in your travels. Let us hope that he has chosen a successful life for you."

"That is my hope as well."

I, the Other, say that the Kikuyu belief that Ngai chooses the destiny of a child before it is born is idiotic. They apparently like the idea of pre-destiny, which, of course, implies that one is powerless to change one's life. If one is poor, as most of the Kikuyu are, one can always hope that he is destined to be rich, and if he remains poor, it is not his fault. I, however, enjoy trying to meddle in one's destiny.

While I, the One, endorse the devotion to one god, I think that pre-destiny is defective philosophy: an excuse for laziness, or a conveyance of entitlement to the fortunate few. Although, when one of the Other's shortcut schemes for wealth or power succeeds, he will try to convince the beneficiary that it was pre-destined.

The woman says, "My husband says you are going to City. Is that true?" Kamiri nods. "They say that Ngai does not live in City."
"Why do they say that, wise woman?"
"Because no one provides him with a place to live, and they do not welcome him to City."
"But how can that be? Ngai is powerful and treats his people with kindness."
"They say that people in the City do not know Ngai. They say that he is not needed, because in the City there is pleasure and money. So they even say that Ngai is dead!"
Kamiri shakes his head, appalled at the very notion of the death of Ngai. "I am sure those people are mistaken!"
The woman cocks her head to one side in acknowledgement. "Be careful, young man! Stay away from the evil seducers in City!"

In case you are wondering who is right: the old woman or Kamiri, I, the Other, can tell you (off the record) that Ngai is alive. Of course, very few people in City have thought to inquire as to his health. This is as it should be, in my opinion. My friends have far more pressing priorities than to consider the welfare of an antique deity!

As he is leaving the house, Kamiri, sees a small brown lizard just outside the entrance, looking in. He calls to the woman, "There is a lizard here thinking of entering your house!"
"Ha!" the woman cries, and rushes out of the house, armed with a broom of twigs. She spots the lizard, and aims

a crushing blow at it, but it is too quick for her, disappearing around the corner.

"That evil thing! It will be cause of my death!"

Kamiri goes in search of the lizard, while she stands ready to administer a fatal blow, but the search is futile. He wishes her a good day, and placing the basket on his head, he resumes the track.

> I, the Other, am always amused by the antics which Kikuyu get up to in the presence of a lizard, which are, with the exception of some of their larger cousins, perfectly harmless. But many Kikuyu believe that Ngai sent a chameleon to tell the first man that he would have eternal life. But the chameleon had other priorities, and was delayed in delivering the message. A lizard had overheard Ngai's message, and out of spite, he delivered a contrary message: that man was to be mortal. As a consequence of this perceived perfidy, lizards are the great enemy of some Kikuyu. I appreciate this distraction from the identity of their real enemy. Some say it is I.

Kamiri comes to a T-junction. There are no signs indicating directions and there is no one to ask for guidance. He looks up at the sky. The sun is rising toward its zenith on his right. He takes the right hand, turning east. There are more junctions; some have direction signs, but they have names of towns and villages he has never heard of, and none indicate the direction toward City. Sometimes, there is a person within view. He asks, "Which way to City?" A man is puzzled by the request. He asks the question again, this time in Swahili, and the man points out the direction. Three times, he made the decision on his own, consulting only the sun, and later asked a person, "Am I going toward City?" And once, the woman pointed in the other direction. Disgruntled, he had to retrace his steps a thousand paces.

There is more traffic on the track now. There are people walking, carrying vegetables they want to sell, or kerosene they have bought for their lamps. There is a cart drawn by a bullock; it carries bags of cement. There is an old man on a bicycle: he wears a black cloth cap and a plastic sack is swinging heavily from the handlebars. Houses appear now on either side; many are larger, made of cinder block with corrugated iron roofs and glass windows set in wooden frames. Small markets with individual traders standing behind displays of bananas, pineapples, mangos. There is clothing on display, shivering colorfully in the morning air. He sees a bicycle repair shop with a man bending over an upside-down bicycle. General stores begin to come into view. They have fancy signs which he cannot read. *That must be English.* He pauses to stand at the back of a group of children longing for the sweets on display. Most of the merchandise on the shelves, he has seen before, but some items like sanitary napkins and facial tissues he does not recognize. He, too, has a longing for the sweets, but he has only the one hundred and ten shillings in coins his mother gave him from her secret store: enough to buy a cheap pair of sandals. He has resolved to keep the coins for an emergency or a life-changing investment.

The track has turned into a gray road with patches upon patches of tarmac. There are automobiles and small trucks making their way cautiously past groups of people walking at the edge of the road. Houses now are clustered together: some are identical with no space between them, and some are even two stories high.

The road slopes upward as it ascends a hill, a long gentle rise. At the summit, he lifts his eyes to the distance and stops, stunned by the scene before him. It is City. In the distance are the towers, clustered together and competing to reach the sky. They are surrounded by countless blocks of lower buildings, like ostrich chicks around their mother, and the chicks, in turn, are surrounded by a vast panorama of low buildings interspersed with green patches of trees. Off to his right he sees a solid mass of low, dark buildings without green patches, sliced by what must be roads: the dark mass of a huge slum. *How will I find my brother here? It will take days to find him and I don't know the telephone, but I must have money. I will go to the tall buildings. There will be work among them.*

His progress toward the center of the City is slowed by many unaccustomed sights: hundreds of white-skinned people dressed in new, fancy clothes; huge trucks with many tires; shops with grand glass windows behind which stand frozen people – then he realizes that the frozen people are not real but only there to show off the clothes they are wearing; delicious aromas coming from stores where people hurry in and out. Kamiri can smell chicken, and looking in one window, he sees pictures of chicken parts. In Swahili, the sign says: "Half chicken, fries, and a drink: 65 shillings". He feels stunned and hurt. *That is over half of the money I have!* He watches the patrons paying unconcerned with bank notes and leaving the shop with paper sacks full of food. *People must be very rich in City . . . and what are 'fries'? Maybe they are the expensive thing.*

As dusk is falling, he arrives among the tall buildings. In a small plaza, vacant except for a large metal man, he sits cross-legged, observing and thinking. Many people are leaving the buildings. *Perhaps they are going home, and they don't live in the buildings. What kind of work would there be in the buildings?* He cannot conceive of what the homeward-bound people would be doing in the buildings that he could do. *They seem so different. They must be doing something strange. But . . . but someone has to care for the building itself: patch it and sweep it. I could do that.*

He approaches a very tall white building; he pushes and pulls the door; it does not open. He stands back and sees that there are people coming out of doors that go around and round. A man goes into the building through the other side of the rotating door. *So that's how you do it!* He times his lunge and enters the building, his basket cradled in his arm. As he looks for someone to speak to, a middle-aged black man in a blue suit and cap approaches him. There is a disapproving look on the man's face. "Yes? May I help you?"

"I am looking for some work, please."

"I'm sorry, young man, but there's nothing here for you."

Kamiri is about to leave, but he asks, "Do you know where I can find some work?"

The guard pauses to take in the young migrant: impoverished, but handsome, polite and painfully earnest. "Do you speak any English, son?"

"No, sir, but I am a good worker."

The guard shakes his head. "This is a difficult time for people like you, son. There are thousands of you looking for work. I'm afraid I can't help you."

Thousands looking for work? How can it be? Kamiri searches the man's face for any sign of contempt, but all he sees is gentle sorrow. "Tell me, sir, is it true that Ngai does not live in City?"

"Sorry, young man, who is Ngai?"

"He is the one who made us what we are."

"Oh, I see." The man surveys the scene outside the tall glass windows. Carefully, he says, "I would say he comes here from time to time."

"But not always?"

"No, not always. He seems to come when people are kind to each other." He breathes a long sigh. "Which, I'm sorry to say, is not very often."

Confused and demoralized, Kamiri returns to the plaza. He sits with his back against the plinth of the statue. *But Warari said there is work in the City. He is here; he must know. I must use the telephone to call him, but I don't know how to do it. Tomorrow, I will find someone to show me how.*

The plaza is all hard surfaces: granite and concrete, and he feels exposed, even in the company of the statue. He finds another place to spend the night: a small grassy area with derelict palm trees and poinsettia bushes. On a secluded spot away from the sidewalk, he sets down his basket and spreads his blanket. In spite of his physical fatigue, he finds it difficult to sleep: there are the street lights, the sounds of motor engines, horns, the disagreeable odor of exhaust smoke, and the turmoil in his mind. He considers the words of the guard: "There are thousands like you." *There were perhaps twenty people like me I saw today. They were dressed in old, soiled clothing, and they seemed to have nothing to do, except for the three who were sitting beside a building with paper cups. Those beggars looked really miserable. I don't want to be like a thousand others, I want to be different. I want to be proud of myself in my future.*

Why did he ask about English? He seemed to be saying that speaking English would make a difference. OK. Somehow, I've got to learn English. I have learned Swahili; I can learn English.

There are sparrows squabbling in the poinsettia bush, and the sun has lit the palm tree trunk to just above his head. He can no longer sleep. After a dry breakfast of the woman's maize cakes, he walks around the center of City, keeping the tall buildings always on his left. He is seeking people, like him, who have lived in City, and who can tell him things: where to find water, how to use a telephone, where to use the toilet, how to make some money, where there is cheap food. *People like me are not in the center; that is for rich people.*

In a park, there is a fountain: a near life-sized elephant is spraying water on its back. He inspects the water; it is good. He relieves himself in overgrown bushes.

There is a chaotic bus terminal: a voice on the loudspeaker, hurrying people, dozens of gaudy busses, and the smell of diesel smoke. Beyond the terminal is an open area with some shade trees and benches. The people there – mostly men – do not seem to be waiting for busses. They are idle: sitting, talking, even dozing. Kamiri cautiously approaches a group of men clustered around a bench, basket in his arm. One of the men looks up, and their conversation halts; they turn to look at him. They say nothing.

He takes a breath. "Can someone show me how to use a telephone?"

There is general laughter. Kamiri clenches his jaw and compresses his lips; he stands his ground, but the hurt in his eyes gives him away. The men share quiet jokes. Slowly, he turns away.

"Come with me, boy." A gray-haired man in dirty coveralls is moving toward the bus terminal. Kamiri follows him. "You never used a phone, boy?"

"No, sir."

"It's not so difficult."

Inside the terminal, they stand by a wall-mounted pay phone.

"Here, now. You pick up the telephone and you use these buttons to dial the number. Then, you wait for the operator to tell you how much it is."

Kamiri pulls his brother's letter from his pocket and stares at the number.

"You have money?"

Kamiri nods and removes some coins from a sack in his basket. The old man prompts him as he dials the number and listens for a voice.

"Please deposit five shillings."

"Five shillings?" He looks with horror at the old man.

"Yeah, it's one of those special mobile numbers. Incoming calls give you credit for outgoing calls."

Kamiri hears the coins clatter into the phone and then he hears the ringing.

"Hi, this is Warari. Please leave me a message after the tone. Beep."

"Warari, this is Kamiri. I'm in City – near the bus terminal. Please come and find me."

"Was that family you called?" the old man asks.

Kamiri looks at his feet. "My brother."

"Well, I guess you'll have to stay with us and wait for him."

So Kamiri waits: for two days. He stays near the bus terminal with the vagrant men. He learns that there is food in the bins if one goes to the food markets just after they close, and he learns that there is work if one has 'connections'. "What are connections?"

"You know. You meet someone who knows someone who needs someone. But mostly it's shit work for no money."

This doesn't sound like what Warari said. Kamiri begins to think that the vagrant men he is with are ill or maybe lazy.

Kamiri is now worrying about his brother: is he still in the City? If so, why doesn't he appear? Maybe he doesn't want to be bothered. What should be done if he doesn't come? He can't go back to Village.

I know there is a reason for Warari not showing up, and I, the Other can confirm that my priorities had a hand in it. It is natural, I think, for Kamiri to lie awake at night and call on his great uncle, for whom he was named, to give him the wisdom he needs being alone in the City. According to the Kikuyu, the ghosts of their ancestors wander about on earth and can be called on for help. Some say there is no point in praying to Ngai: he is too busy with more important things. What important things? The Kikuyu religion amuses me!

It is late afternoon on the second day when a man wearing a clean white shirt and tan straw hat appears in the vagrants' area. "Any new arrivals here?" he asks.

"Yeah," the old man speaks up. "This one here," pointing to Kamiri.

"Where are you from?" the man in the hat asks.
"I'm from Village west of here."
"When did you arrive?"
"Three days ago."
"You have family here?"
"My brother is here – somewhere."
"You have work or a place to stay?"
"No, sir."
"Why don't you come with me, son?"
Kamiri turns to the old man for advice.
"It's OK, boy, you go with him."
The straw-hat man gets into a car. Kamiri approaches and stops: he has never been in a car. The man pushes open the door. "Get in, son. What's your name and how old are you?"
"My name is Kamiri. I am eighteen."
The sensation of effortless racing down the street is both exhilarating and frightening. "Where are we going?"
"We're going to Home Away. It's where people like you can have a decent meal and a place to sleep while you're looking for work."
"Why aren't the other men coming?"
"We have a rule: if you're offered work twice and you don't take it, you can't come to Home Away anymore."

To Kamiri, it is a large, dark, brick building: an abandoned warehouse which has been converted to a hostel. Inside, he is shown a living area, where a dozen men and three women are watching a television ten times larger than the one Kamiri has seen in the Village shop. Two other men are making a clatter with a game of table football. To one side is a long string of tables, placed end-to-end, and surrounded by chairs. "This is where you'll have your meals. Let's go upstairs and I'll show you where you'll be sleeping. This door is to the women's area. You're not allowed in there at any time for any reason. You understand?"

"Yes, sir."

He opens a door opposite. "This is the men's area. Women are not allowed in here. This bunk here is available. You can take it." Dutifully, Kamiri sets his basket on the bunk, first removing his small sack of coins. "In there," the man points, "are showers and toilets. All right?"

"Yes, sir. Thank you very much."

"My name, by the way, is Joseph, Joseph Maiyo. I am the manager of Home Away." He pauses to consider Kamiri for a moment. "You said you have a brother here in City?"

"Yes." Kamiri looks up at the ceiling, chin out but lips trembling. "Yes . . . but . . . he hasn't found me."

"Does he know where to find you?"

"I telephoned him. He wasn't there. I told him to meet me at the bus terminal."

"So, he doesn't know you're here now?"

"No, sir. Unh. No, Joseph."

"Well, you have his phone number. Let's go downstairs and call him."

"It will cost five shillings."

"That's OK. Let's call him."

Again, there is no answer and the call goes to voicemail. "Warari, I am Kamiri. I am now at the Home Away place. Please come and get me."

Another call is made to leave the address.

This place is very good! They give you a plate covered with potatoes, carrots, squash and some chicken! You can see right through the water you get. There's a big piece of maize cake, with white sugar on the top, and mangos! It's like it's your name day all the time!

At first, Kamiri has reservations about his bunk: it isn't hard, like the earthen floor should be, even with a woven palm-frond mat. And what was this 'pillow'? But on his second night, after watching two football matches (they said one was in

England and the other in Italy), he slept deeply, except there was something about an ancestor he had never met. Was it his great-uncle, another Kamiri, and did he offer some wisdom about life in City? He can't remember.

Nearly all of the people at Home Away are young: teens and twenties. Most of them speak Bantu tribal languages and Swahili, as well. There is no obstacle to comparing 'work appointments'. The best, and most difficult to obtain, are work appointments which offer training: security guards, kitchen helpers, rubbish collectors, gardener's assistants, cleaners. These 'appointments' (really interviews) are offered by companies and by the government. Work without training is offered by small companies and individuals.

At least once a day, Joseph holds a session called 'Getting a Job'. He gives a talk like 'How to Present Yourself', and then one of the residents will play the employer and another will play the candidate, practicing what they have heard. The play-acting is often very funny, but there is a serious side as well: learning what is expected of candidates and new employees. The learning goes on into the evening when experiences on 'appointments' are compared.

Late in the afternoon Kamiri is approached by a young woman: "You are Kamiri?" She has a shining halo of bushy, black hair; she is tall, confident, a couple of years older than he, and dressed like the people in the windows.

"Yes."

"My name is Dorothy. Will you come with me, please? We have to get some information about you." In the office, she sits at a scarred wooden table. He sits opposite her, hands under his knees. She takes out some paper and her dark eyes appraise him. She gives a dismissive gesture. "There's nothing to be concerned about. We ask for information from all our guests. It helps us find the right work for them."

He begins to relax as her questions take in his life, his family, his experiences and skills. *She is very pretty and smart. She seems to like me. I like her; she's better than any of the girls my mother wanted me to marry.*

"How much school have you had, Kamiri?"

"I finished the local school when I was thirteen. I was allowed to go to high school when I promised my father that I would milk the goats before I left and the cows after I got back. It was in the next village: about six kilometers each way."

"That's a long walk."

"No, I ran; I didn't have time to walk."

"Have you learned any English?" He shakes his head. "Would you like to learn English?"

"Yes, please . . . Dorothy."

She smiles at him. "I have a book here," she reaches around behind her, "you can study." She pauses, twirling her pen. "What kind of work would you like to do?"

He avoids her eyes. "I don't know. Can you tell me what I should do? My brother is here in City. He is supposed to come and get me. Perhaps he knows of work I can do."

"My father told me that you had called your brother. You haven't heard from him?"

"No. . . . Joseph is your father?"

"Yes."

"So you work here?"

"Just in the afternoons. I go to university."

"What is it like? To go to university, I mean."

She leans on her fist, pensively. "It's different than going to school. You have to read a lot, and you have to listen carefully to what professors say, and you have to do a lot of thinking on your own." She has the impression that he is thoughtfully weighing her words against his own experience.

"It must be difficult."

"No, it's just different." She leans forward. "Kamiri, I think that's all we can do today."

He nods. "What's that?"

She catches the little gold cross on its wisp of chain. "This?"

"Yes, it's pretty."
"It's a symbol of my religion – a symbol of Christianity."
"What does it mean?"
"Sometime I will explain it to you, Kamiri. Don't forget to take your English book."

I, the Other, think it's completely unnecessary the way some Christians go around flaunting their religion with crucifixes. Who cares? It's as if they want to say, "Now, let me tell you all about my religion!" Atheists don't wear gold zeros around their necks so they can say, "Now let me tell you what I don't believe!" I think Christians should not impose themselves, and, come to think of it, Jews should stop with that six-pointed star, which is not a uniquely Jewish symbol anyway, and the star and crescent long preceded the founding of Islam!

Dorothy is impressed by the tall, good-looking migrant she has just interviewed. He is unlike many of the migrants she sees most days: uncommunicative, unmotivated, hopeful of a handout. Here is one polite, open, who ran his way through high school, and was curious enough to ask what her cross means. He seems bright and eager, but naïve.

I, the One, can tell you that Dorothy, like Kamiri, has not found her life identity, which is fair enough: she is only twenty. Much as I am fond of her faith and her intelligence – abstract and social – she tends to be idealistic and stubborn, and paradoxically, a bit impetuous.

Kamiri has been on two unsuccessful appointments during his three days at Home Away, and is beginning to think his brother has lost interest in him. He is watching television when Joseph taps him on the shoulder. "Your brother's here." A surge of anger and relief grip Kamiri. Expecting to see his brother much as he had last seen him: faded checked shirt, second-hand trousers and worn out sandals, he is altogether different: shiny black shirt, tight new jeans and trainers. Is that a gold chain inside the shirt?

Warari snarls, "You ready to go?"

Kamiri glares at his brother. "Where have you been? I've been waiting for you for five days!"

Warari shrugs. "I've been busy. You coming, brother, or do you want to stay here with the riff-raff?"

Kamiri stifles a biting retort. "Let me get some things." He reappears moments later. "Joseph, thank you very much! You have a great place here!"

"Good luck, Kamiri. You know where we are if you need us."

With a snort, Wariri moves to the door.

Expecting a walk of some distance, Kamiri sets the basket on his head, and he is astonished to see his brother throw one leg over a motorcycle. "Get on and take that damn thing off your head. It'll blow away!"

Chapter 2

Mandrax Smoke

The speed is terrifying: Warari leans right and left as they weave through the traffic as if they were a cheetah chasing prey through the forest. Gripping his brother around his waist seems the only way to survive. He cannot cry out 'Slow down!'. That would mark him the weakest. The youngest OK, but never the weakest! Closing his eyes only escalates the fear of an unexpected, terrible collision. He focuses his vision to a single point over Warari's left shoulder and says, over and over, the Kikuyu prayer for a good life.

As the roaring subsides, they are surrounded by low, slipshod shacks. The street is narrow, unpaved and still pocked with puddles. Street children scatter at the roar of the bike, and Kamiri hears insults and sees gestures to slow, but Warari turns corners, weaves around puddles, brakes to avoid a large woman in the street and then accelerates savagely. They turn another corner, glide forward and halt. Kamiri slowly releases his grip when the engine stops and Warari shrugs himself loose. They are outside a low, weathered, wooden building with only one window. Next to it are similar structures – some painted white – most with rusty, corrugated iron roofs. The door to the house, like most of the others, is perhaps two meters from the muddy street. There is no space anywhere for a tree or even grass.

Warari removes a padlock from the door, and with a nod to his brother, steps inside. The single room is dark until Warari slashes aside the drapery over the window, and one can see thin mattresses on the uneven wooden floor, the table and two chairs, a chest, and the television perched atop a wheezing refrigerator.

"This is my place. Not bad, hunh?"

"Is it very expensive?"

"No, it's reasonable. I pay a guy four hundred shillings a week to stay here, but I'm not sure he actually owns it. I'm lucky to have electric; most don't. There's a shared shitter out back – just like home. I get water down the street; that's what these Gerry cans are." He pauses, looking around, and points to a mattress. "You can sleep here except when one of my girls is here."

"Oh! Well, maybe I ought to stay at that place where you picked me up."

"No, brother. How am I going to get you started in business unless you stay with me?"

"OK. Umm." Kamiri stands, playing with his hands, not knowing what to say or do; he has dismissed the idea of embracing his brother, of reminiscing about some old adventure. "Tell me about your job, Warari."

There is a broad smile on his face as Warari sits down and puts his feet up on the table. "I make a lot of money, brother."

"How did you get this job?"

"I met a man who introduced me to the business, which is supplying people with happiness."

Kamiri is skeptical. "How do you do that?"

"I'll show you, brother." From the bottom drawer of chest in the corner, he removes a mortar and pestle, an old briar pipe, a small sack and a brown bottle. One white tablet from the bottle is crushed in the mortar and pestle. He mixes it with green crumbs from the sack and stuffs it into the pipe. Lighting a match, he draws on the pipe until a bright flame and white smoke appear. There is an expression of great satisfaction as he tips his chair back, and draws the white smoke into his chest. "That's how you do it."

"So," Kamiri is biting his lip, "you sell the pipe and the other stuff to people?"

"Exactly, brother."

"How much do they pay you, Warari?"

"Depends on how much they want to buy. One pipe full costs about five hundred shillings. You buy more, you get more of a discount."

Wide-eyed, Kamiri stares at his brother. "Five hundred shillings is a lot of money! Only rich people can buy it!"

"Well now, Kamiri, this pipe is so, so good. It takes all your cares away! And lots of people like to have no cares. This is better than a bottle of good whiskey and believe me, I've tried 'em both."

Kamiri doesn't want to ask what 'whiskey' is. That would be naïve; he guesses that 'whiskey' must be something like beer because it comes in a bottle. "Who buys this stuff from you? Not just rich people, you say."

"No, not just rich people, brother. I got all kinds of customers: small traders, government workers, accountants, business people, and, of course rich kids. They call me, I tell 'em where to meet me, I get on my bike, make the delivery and collect the money."

"Where do you get the green stuff and the white pills?"

"I get 'em from a man I know."

"What would I do, Warari?"

"I think my business needs somebody to bring in new customers."

"You want me to bring in new customers?" A nod. "But I only know about twelve people here in City."

"You don't have to know a lot of people. You go out and meet 'em. You go to bars and discos, and . . ." He sees that Kamiri is puzzled. "A disco is where people go to dance, brother. And you have a pipe with you. You're looking happy and friendly and you give 'em a pull on it. When they enjoy it, you just tell 'em where they can get some more and you give 'em my phone number."

"Is that all you want me to do?"

"That's it, brother."

"How much money would I make?"

"I'm figuring to start you out on four hundred shillings a day. Naturally, you can stay and eat here – no charge for that – and the more customers you bring to me, the more money you'll make."

I, the Other, should point out that Kamiri has never seen four hundred shillings at one time is his life – poor wretch! I had suggested to Warari that he ought to make Kamiri a tempting offer. Well, it's to my advantage, also, that we get Kamiri on board. Now, I've got to convince the boy. So – next step – I suggest to Warari that he offer his brother the pipe.

Kamiri sits down at the table. He sniffs the white cloud of smoke. It smells of vegetation, sweet, with a bitter edge. *How is it possible to make so much money so easily and so quickly? Why haven't I heard about this before?*

"You want to take a couple of puffs, brother?"

Kamiri hesitates, then he puts his hand out for the pipe. He draws some smoke into his mouth, then, warily, having never smoked before, he inhales it. He is seized by a coughing fit.

"That's all right, brother. Take it slowly. You need to get used to it."

Kamiri remembers boys trying, surreptitiously, to smoke for the first time: they took tiny breaths. He tries the same strategy; the coughing has ceased. For a few minutes, he draws slowly on the pipe. His head is getting lighter; he feels pleasantly secure. He smiles. *This feels good!* He laughs.

"Good isn't it, brother?"

Kamiri nods and takes another puff, but the warm, blissful feeling alarms him. *I'm slightly dizzy; that's not good!*

Helpful as I, the Other, am, I suggest to Kamiri that he keep on smoking, but he doesn't seem to hear me, and he gives the pipe back to Warari.

"How often do you smoke the pipe, Warari?"
"Not often. I'm going to let it go out now."
"Why don't you finish it?"
Warari removes his feet from the table, and sits up straight, but he looks away from his brother. "Because . . ." He searches for words.

I make a suggestion.

"Because it would eat into my profits. Yes, it would eat into my profits."
Kamiri nods his understanding. "What is the green stuff, Warari?"
"Oh, that's dagga."
"What is dagga?"
"You know. It's like tobacco, but better."
"And the white pills?"
"They're called Mandrax. My man gets them from South Africa."
"Why don't you just take them with some water?"
"They work much better when they're smoked with dagga. . . . So, are we going to be partners, brother?"
"I don't know if I can convince people, but I will try. What do you call it?"
"I call it a Mandrax Smoke." Warari puts his feet back up on the table. "So what's the news from home?"
Kamiri shrugs. "Not much. Our parents are slower now; got aches and pains, I guess. Safiri is very poorly. The other three in Village are just the same, 'cept there are new nieces and nephews; not a word from Makimba since she left three years ago."

"I saw her the other day."

"Did you speak with her?"

"Nah. She was goin' about her business."

"What business is that?"

"Well, she was traipsin' down the street in a little black skirt, red vest and high-heeled boots; she was alongside this white man in a blue suit."

Kamiri flinches. "You don't suppose she's . . ."

Warari shrugs. "She had a big smile on her face, like 'look at me world'."

"Maybe she's married."

Warari gives a snort. "If she was married to that man, we'd have heard all about it!"

Kamiri stares gloomily into the distance. "That's too bad; she was a nice girl."

"What do you mean 'nice girl'?" Warari growls his dissent. "In the City you're just a girl.

Ain't no 'nice' or 'not nice'".

"How can that be?"

"That's somethin' you gotta learn, brother. City is not Village. People don't think about good and bad. They think about themselves – about money, and pleasure and havin' a good time."

"Maybe that's why they say that Ngai doesn't live in City."

Warari leans back, folding his arms across his chest. "Kamiri, let me tell you something: Ngai's been dead a long time, if he ever was alive."

"How do you know that?"

"Man! It's dead easy. You see all those poor people out there?" He delivers a broad, sweeping gesture. "They don't have enough to eat, or a place to live that doesn't have rats or rainwater or shit. Half of 'em are sick with horrible diseases, and if they don't croak tomorrow, it'll be the next day. What's Ngai doin' for them? I'll tell you what he's doin'! Nothin'! 'Cause he never was! And listen to this, Kamiri: there are lots of people out there with plenty of money, livin' in beautiful places, and havin' a grand time! Did Ngai help 'em get there? You ask 'em! They'll tell you they got there through their own hard work. Ngai didn't feature!"

"So, you don't believe in Ngai?"

"No, Kamiri, it's a nice little fairy tale."

"But, if it's a fairy tale, how do we know right from wrong? I mean, how do we know what we should do in life?"

"Like I say, Kamiri, it's very simple: you make yourself number one and you just go for it."

"Go for what?"

"Whatever you want: money, sex, a big bike, whatever."

"But, if you just go for it, as you say, you're bound to step on some of the poor people out there."

Warari shrugs his disinterest.

"OK. Then answer me this, Warari: when you're really old and about to die, what makes you better than a lion or an elephant? Somebody else gets the money and the bike and the big house. All you have left is your own memories – for a few more days. Nobody else will remember you. Why should they?"

"Well, I'll do some great things and I'll be remembered."

I find this kind of philosophical discussion useless. Lighten up, guys! Ngai doesn't feature. End of story. Get out and enjoy life. Warari is right!

I, the One, disagree! Philosophical discussion is essential, and Kamiri is right: what makes man better than a lion or an elephant? His conscience. And where does he get his conscience? Not from the Other.

Later that afternoon, Warari takes his brother to a shopping mall. "We have to get you kitted out, Kamiri." Kitting out involves the purchase of a pair of jean, two white polo shirts embroidered with lion logos, Adidas trainers, and gray felt, brimmed hat. "Yeah! The hat definitely makes you look a lot older." Kamiri studies himself in a mirror. *I don't know about older, but I look more like a City man: I look good!*

The next stop is a mobile phone shop. There are several counters full of smart phones, some with animated displays. Kamiri looks from one to the next, trying to decide which he likes best. Warari, however, settles on a simple pay-as-you-go model.

"But that's not a good one!" Kamiri protests.

"It's a good one, brother. I'll load up your SIM card."

"But I want a phone like yours!"

"Mine is very expensive, and I need the extra features in my business. Yours is just so you can call me if you need me."

Warari orders some business cards at print shop. One side is in English; the other side in Swahili. It reads: "Call Wahari for the best Mandrax Smoke. Discounts offered. 04417 563201."

While the cards are being printed, they go to a fried chicken shop. Kamiri consumes half a chicken, large fries and a large Coke; he announces that he is still hungry. Warari returns from the counter with another large fries. "Here, this will see you through until you get home tonight."

I, the One, haven't given up on Warari, but I am obliged to admit that he is very hard work: he just doesn't listen to any advice I try to give him. Whereas he seems to be all ears when the Other is whispering. But perhaps I am overstating the effectiveness of the Other's communication, or maybe he is reaching that part of the human mind which is susceptible to rash advice. Or perhaps Warari is more self-centered than most, and is temperamentally inclined to take shortcuts.

Kamiri enters the bar without enthusiasm. He remembers his brother's advice: "smile and be happy!". But he is an insincere actor. The place, packed with men, is noisy and smoky. There is a deep queue of customers – mostly in work clothes – along the counter to his left; he can see their faces in the mirror behind the counter. *First, he said I should get a drink, and then I should find a good spot where I can be seen. How can I get a drink?*

The three men behind the counter listen to instructions from the customers, handing out drinks in glasses and collecting money. *That's it.* He tries to catch the eye of a counterman.

"Here, young fellow, you want a drink?" a man at the counter has stepped back, allowing him access.

"Yes, thank you."

"Hey, Thomas! The young man here wants a drink!"

Thomas wipes his hands on a towel. "What'll it be young fellow?"

"I'd like a *stoney tangawizi* (very strong ginger ale) with no whiskey, please."

Thomas leans on the counter. "You mean you want a *stoney*, son?"

"Yes, sir."

The man at his side asks, "What happened to your whiskey, young fellow?"

This question is a complete surprise. "Well, sir . . . Umm . . ." He fingers the fifty-shilling note which Warari gave him. "I . . . umm . . . just have this money."

The man turns to Thomas. "I'm good for his whiskey, Thomas."

Kamiri places the fifty-shilling note on the counter as the drink is handed to him. The man hands the note back to him. "This drink's on me, young fellow."

Kamiri spots a vacant seat at a table. Nodding to the other men already seated there, he sets his drink down, removes the pipe from his pocket, and sits down. The flame and white smoke bursting from the bowl when the pipe is lit attract the attention of the others at the table. "Whoa! What's that you're smoking, mate?"

Kamiri draws gently on the pipe and puts on a beatific smile. He exhales a puff of white smoke. "This is Mandrax Smoke. It is so, so good," he explains.

"Smells a little like dagga to me," one of the men comments.
"It's better than dagga. You want to try some?"
"Yeah, I'll try a puff or two."
"Be careful, Henry, it may be illegal!"
"Ah shit! A puff or two in here ain't gonna cause no trouble." Henry exhales a long spume of smoke. "Not bad." He draws again causing mouth of the bowl to glow red. "Yeah. Not bad at all." He hands the pipe back to Kamiri.
"No, you're enjoying it. You keep it for a while."
When the smoker and his friends are ready to leave, Kamiri passes his brother's business card to Henry with the suggestion that he call to get a refill.

No one takes notice of Kamiri, with his nearly un-touched whiskey and *stoney,* puffing gently on the pipe. He stands up and moves to the end of the bar, but he can't seem to engage the men in conversation. He moves to different tables.

The bar is beginning to thin out.

In a loud voice, Thomas announces: "Closing in fifteen minutes!"

Kamiri looks up from his table and finds Thomas standing next to him. "What's that you've been smoking, son?"
"It's a Mandrax Smoke, sir."
"Smells like dagga to me."
"It's much better than dagga, sir."
"Well, that may be, but it's almost certainly illegal, and you can't smoke it in my bar, 'cause I could get in trouble. So I suggest you not come in here with that pipe anymore. You understand?"
"Yes, sir." Kamiri gets up and leaves the bar. *Damn! I was doing so good at first. Then nothing. Then he tells me it's illegal. That's bad. I'm not sure I like this job.*

He calls Warari and leaves a message that he is ready to be picked up.

I, the Other, want to get Kamiri feeling more positive about his new job: he had some success. I can help him in his new career. But he doesn't hear me. His mind is occupied with thoughts about 'illegal', and would he go to jail, and how hard it is for him to get people interested in the Mandrax Smoke.

An hour later, Warari appears on his growling motorcycle. "Hey Kamiri, you done great! You got me a new customer!"

Kamiri says nothing as he gets on the bike.

At Warari's place, he is grumpy. "The man at the bar said that the Mandrax Smoke is illegal. What did he mean? Would I go to jail?"

Warari is dismissive. "Oh, don't worry about that! He's just a spoilsport! I won't take you there again. . . . You did really good, Kamiri! A guy called Henry called me – said my brother gave him a Mandrax Smoke and could he get some? I said 'yes', met up with him and sold him a week's worth!"

"Is there anything to eat, Warari?"

"No, I'm sorry, brother. I been real busy. Here!" He pulls out a wad of notes, counts out four hundreds and hands them to his brother. "I think there's a little place just down the street where you can get something."

Kamiri glares at his brother. "But your deal was four hundred plus food!"

Warari retrieves another one hundred from his wad and hands it condescendingly to Kamiri.

The unlit street has only half moonlight and the leaked glow of some indoor kerosene lanterns. The dwellings are smaller, now, less well-cared-for, and packed more closely together. It is quiet except for the occasional barking of a dog. *It must be early morning. Is anything going to be open?* A rat skitters across the street in front of him. He comes to a crossing. To the left, there is a cluster of dim lights. He walks toward them and finds a stand with a string of lights above it. There is no one there, but on the shelf are some mangoes, bananas and two pineapples. The door at the rear of the stand is ajar. *Perhaps the owner is sleeping.* He knocks on the wooden stand. There is no response. In a loud voice, he announces, "I would like to buy some bananas!" There is a growl from inside. *That wasn't a dog; it must be the owner.* A hunched-over old man appears in the doorway. His downcast face is almost obscured by long gray hair. He is wearing what appears to be a dirty night dress.

"I would like to buy some bananas."

"I heard you the first time. Which ones?"

Kamiri selects a large bunch and holds them up.

The old man eyes the bunch. "They'll be twenty-three shillings."

"Do you have anything besides fruit?"

The man disappears into his dwelling. When he reappears, he holds up a whole loaf of dark bread. "This here is eight shillings."

Kamiri hands him the fifty-shilling note. The man studies it carefully, turning it over in the light. Apparently satisfied, he re-enters his dwelling and returns with a ten-shilling note and a handful of coins. Laboriously, he counts out nine shillings on the wooden stand.

Kamiri wishes him "Good morning" and, eating a banana, trudges off toward his brother's place.

When he gets there, he finds that the lights have been extinguished and the door is secured from the inside. "Warari, I'm back," he calls.

Wordlessly, the door is opened. He steps inside and finds that his brother is naked. But this is not unusual for a warm night after the rainy season. He places the partially eaten loaf and the remaining bananas on the dresser, strips off his shirt, jeans and trainers, and turns toward the mattresses. To his surprise, he sees that both mattresses are taken and there is another body hastily covering itself. He takes a step closer and sees that the body must be a woman, judging by the great mass of hair, though her body is turned from him.

Warari gestures toward the other side of the room, and lies down, facing the woman. *Damn! This isn't Kikuyu hospitality! My brother invites me to stay with him, offers nothing to eat, gives the only guest mattress to a stranger, and tells me to sleep on the floor.*

Kamiri finds his own blanket, and, spreading it out, lies on the floor, his back to the couple. He is tired and it is late, but sleep does not come. His mind is too busy with aggrieved thoughts and the formulation of childish retaliatory plans. He can hear the couple whispering, their re-positionings and fervent grunts. *They think I'm asleep. I think they sound like a boar and a sow!* Eventually, it is quiet, and in spite of himself, Kamiri falls asleep.

An ache in his shoulder awakens him, and Kamiri rolls onto his back. The room is still dark and quiet, but a narrow beam of daylight slips past the curtain. Slowly, he turns his head. Only his brother is there, snoring, his back to Kamiri. The woman is gone. The petulant thoughts return, and he lies there, savoring them.

He considers what to do. *I don't want to wake Warari – we'll just have a row. So no television. I'm hungry.* He examines the four remaining bananas and the two-thirds loaf of bread. *Something better for breakfast.*

At the door, he releases the latch and steps outside. Judging by the sun, it is early afternoon. He sets off down the street, which is alive now. Doors are open, dogs and children are playing in the street. There is bright color everywhere: the shop signs, the clothes of the women and children, even the dwellings themselves – here is a whitewashed shack; this one is painted yellow, there is one creamy purple. A gentle cacophony of vendors' cries, street music, children's shouts, and barking dogs fills his senses. Shops and stalls are open for business.

He spots an eat-in shop with mismatched tables and chairs under a tattered awning. He inquires as to what is available, and he sits down in front of a heaping plate of ugali, sakuma wiki, and kuku choma (cornmeal paste, green vegetable and chicken). It tastes particularly good, and is washed down with a bottle of warm orange soda.

When he returns to the dwelling, he finds that Warari is gone and the door is locked. He tries the rear without success, so he calls his brother.

After perhaps an hour, he hears the motorcycle approaching. Warari dismounts and unlocks the door. "How come you left the door open when you left?" he asks.

"Why would I lock it? You were inside."

"Kamiri, don't you realize that people know I have money – quite a lot of money – and Mandrax Smoke? People around here like to steal!"

"But they wouldn't steal when you're in the house."

"Oh, yes they would! When somebody knocks and the door is locked, I ask who it is. If I don't know them, I get out that machete from behind the chest. I've been robbed once already!"

"I didn't know that." He feels an upsurge of resentment. "Who was that woman here last night?"

"She's just a woman I know."

"I don't like sleeping on the floor when she's got the mattress."

"I told you that's the deal when you stay with me. Besides, how can we get cozy when I'm on a mattress next to you and she's over there on the floor?"

Kamiri tastes bile in the back of his throat. He swallows hard, suppressing the urge for a heated argument. *If I can just do this for a while, I can make some money, and learn about life in City. Maybe I can even find my own place to live. Warari is my brother and he's trying to help me get started, but . . . But he's doing it in a way I don't like – selfish and bossy. I would like it more if I had just one small room of my own*

"Where am I going tonight? Not to the same bar."

"No, I thought you could try a new disco over toward the center. I'll bet you'll be able to get a lot of customers, and I'll give you an extra fifty for everyone who calls me!"

The disco is subdued and nearly deserted when Kamiri enters. Perhaps half a dozen people – mostly young – are sitting at tables. One wall has a large window looking down on the vacant floor, and behind the glass, Kamiri can see a youthful man with black muffs on his ears nodding his head to an inaudible rhythm while arranging things. *Strange!* Along the other wall is a long bar. There are five men in black shirts and white aprons busily wiping and arranging glasses.

The disco is starting to fill with people. The bar is busy; tables are in demand. Suddenly, there is a very loud announcement: "Welcome! Welcome, all you beautiful people! Welcome to Nirvana, where you will dance to the best music in City!" Kamiri can see that it is the man behind the window who is shouting. "I am Music Man – your magic disc-spinner, and I'm going to get the evening started with a favorite of yours!"
With a thunder of drums, the music begins: insistent and thought-drowning. Lights begin to flash all around the enormous room: yellow, red and green. The tables are being vacated. The dancers crowd together under the window, flailing their arms about and twisting their bodies to the irresistible beat.

It is time to find an advantageous spot and light up. There are two tables pushed together, and it seems that four couples are sitting there. Kamiri walks over to the two couples who are there at the moment. His hand on the back of a nearby chair, he asks, "Mind if I join you?"
One of the men glances at him and shrugs.
Kamiri sits down on the fringe of the circle, puts on a face of deep contentment, and puffs gently of the pipe. The two couples ignore him.

The music stops momentarily, and a third couple returns to the table, seating themselves near Kamiri.

"Hey baby," the girl asks, "is that dagga you're smokin'?"

"No. Much better than dagga. It's a Mandrax Smoke."

The girl leans toward him to capture some of the smoke; he can see almost all of her breasts. "Let me try it for a minute, baby."

Kamiri hands her the pipe. The girl draws heavily and emits a long plume of white smoke. She considers the pipe and draws again. "Hey, this is pretty good! Where'd you get this smoke, dude?"

"You can get it from my brother. Here's his card."

The girl hands the pipe to her partner who takes a long pull on the pipe. He nods. "Pretty good."

"How much does he want for it?" she asks. She has a mobile phone in her hand and is copying Warari's number onto the keyboard.

Kamiri says, "It's five hundred shillings for a day's worth, and he gives discounts for larger quantities."

The girl is leaving a message. "He's not there." She retrieves the pipe from her partner, takes a big breath, and considers Kamiri. "Tell you what, dude. Why don't you sell me what you got? I'll pay you five hundred."

"But didn't you leave him a message? He'll be coming soon."

"If he's coming soon, you can get some more from him. Meanwhile, I'm having a nice smoke." She opens a small bag covered with blue sequins which was hanging over her shoulder. "Here's five hundred. Let me have your refills."

Kamiri hesitates.

"What's the problem, dude?"

He reaches into his pocket and removes a folded plastic pouch.

"Thanks, dude. You're a good man!"

Kamiri picks up his *stoney* and moves to a table near the entrance where he'll be able to intercept Warari when he comes in. But he can still see the table where the four couples are now sitting. They seem to be passing the pipe around.

Achieving Superpersonhood:

It has been a long while and Warari hasn't shown up. Kamiri decides to call him; as ever, the call goes to voicemail.

There is a commotion at the entrance. Kamiri turns to see what it is. "Cops!" somebody shouts. The music stops. Four policemen and two eager dogs surge into the room. "Nobody leaves!" one of the policemen shouts.

Kamiri stands up and looks toward the table with four couples. It is vacant. People are shouting and milling around, but no one is leaving now. There is a policeman at the entrance doors and by the double doors under the exit sign. *What should I do?*

I tell him to just look innocent.

One of the dogs is standing in front of Kamiri and barking insistently. A policeman comes over immediately. "You got any drugs?"

"No, sir!"

The officer pats him down. "What's this?"

"Those are some cards."

The officer studies them. "This Warari guy gave them to you?"

"Yes, sir."

The officer shakes his head. "Look, fella, selling or possessing drugs is illegal. If I had caught you with some dagga or other stuff on you, I would take you to the station and lock your dumb ass up, and then the judge would send you to prison for at least one year! You understand me?"

"Yes, sir, I do."

Kamiri sinks back down into his seat. His mouth feels very dry and his armpits are damp.

Oh Ngai, that was close! I don't want to go to prison: it would kill me; I love the sky and the open land. Maybe I should never have come to City. One thing is sure: I can't work for Warari anymore.

37

He debates how long he should try to find his way in City – two weeks? two months? longer? – without reaching a conclusion.

The police have left; Music Man announces: "Sorry for the interruption, beautiful people. There's one free drink at the bar for each of you. Now, let's start this evening just where we left off!" The music starts up and the dancing begins again.

Kamiri looks over at the table with four couples. There are only three. The girl with the important breasts and her partner are gone.

His phone rings. "No, I'm still inside. OK."

He goes outside and finds Warari across the street, astride his motorcycle. "You got the pipe, brother?"

"No, I sold it to the girl who called you – and the dagga stuff."

"How much did you get?"

"Five hundred." He hands Warari the five bank notes.

"You're not supposed to be selling! Don't do that again!"

Kamiri is taken aback by his brother's anger. "But if I hadn't sold it, the police would have taken me away!"

"What do you mean?" Warari snaps.

"A policeman searched me, but all he got was your cards."

At Warari's place there is a girl asleep. Is it the same girl or another one? The bananas and bread are gone. Kamiri walks to the all-night stand to get something to eat. When he returns, Warari is asleep.

In the morning – afternoon actually – after he has eaten some bread and bananas, Kamiri waits for his brother to awaken. The girl is gone.

"Warari, I've decided I don't want to work for you anymore."

"What are you talking about, little brother?" He reaches into his jeans. "Here's the four hundred and fifty I owe you for last night."

Kamiri shakes his head. "It's just too risky."

"You talkin' about last night? You handled that real well. There wasn't any risk!"

Kamiri's vigorously shaking head and pressed lips disagree. "If I had done what you wanted and insisted that the girl buy the drugs from you, I would be in prison right now."

"That's what I'm saying. You handled the situation real well."

"Sorry, Warari, it's not for me."

"Aw, come on! You're my brother!"

Kamiri feels a surge of heat through his brain. He restrains himself for only a moment. "I need to find a place where I can stay clear of the police, sleep on my mattress and eat the food I've bought."

Warari is angry now. "Get out, you ungrateful bastard! Get out!"

Warari is not just short-tempered and selfish in his dealings with his younger brother: he is jealous. Some of the origins of this jealousy arise from their mother's apparent feelings for the two of them. Much as she tried not to show it, she was often exasperated with Warari's willfulness and kindly disposed to Kamiri's flexible patience. In Warari's mind, his young sibling was his mother's favorite. Additionally, there is the issue of high school. Warari lost interest in further education by the time he finished the local school. Kamiri was feverish in his desire to go the high school in spite of the distance and the late hours that this choice entailed. Warari, as a fourteen-year-old, was at loose ends, and to keep him occupied, his father assigned him livestock duties, some of which might have fallen on Kamiri, who was occupied with his studies. Here, too, Warari, felt the unintended lash of favoritism, and when Kamiri caught the rapt attention of his family with gems of his new knowledge, Warari assumed that the listeners were convinced of Kamiri's superior intelligence.

I, the One, would like to observe that Kamiri's bad experience with this early employment is not uncommon.

There are situations where the involvement of others, family, financial or other pressures lead to hasty decisions. Finding the right path in one's life is what it's all about, and it is difficult! I will try to help him discover his path, but there will be diversions on the way.

Chapter 3

Home Away

Dorothy sits – somewhat ill at ease – in the professor's office. He is a placid, bald-headed man of her father's age with very long sideburns and a large knot in his loosened tie.

She looks over his shoulders at the white wall which displays two portraits: one of the President, Country and the other President, University. She distrusts the one and idolizes the other, but neither seems to offer her a hint of guidance.

"Umm... Professor, I wanted to speak to you about my field of study." She sits back and squares her shoulders. "I wanted your advice on a possible change."

"To what field, may I ask?"

"I was thinking about political science."

The professor purses his lips and turns the cover of a folder on his desk. "You are doing very well in the pre-medical curriculum. I see that you have an A minus average. If you keep this up, you'll have no trouble getting into medical school." He looks up. "What prompts your question, may I ask?"

She moves awkwardly in her seat. "Well, I'm just thinking that in politics I can exert some pressure toward honesty and openness. It seems to me that our government is too fractious and corrupt. We need women's influence."

Professor Kipsang is unable to suppress a smile. "So you would like to be the ninth female in our two hundred and fifty-four seat parliament?"

"Yes, I know it's difficult being elected over male candidates, but others have done it, and I was really impressed by Aristotle's thinking on governance in my philosophy elective last term."

"You know, Miss Maiyo, that every year we graduate about two dozen students with diplomas in political science?"

"No, I didn't know it was so many."

"Would you be interested in knowing what percentage of our political science graduates win an election to office?"

"Yes, it must be quite a high percentage."

"In point of fact, Miss Maiyo, it is less than ten percent in recent years." He takes in her open-mouth amazement before continuing: "So this means if you aspire to an elected office, your chances are, at best, one in ten."

"What happens to the other ninety percent, Professor?"

"Well, all sorts of things." He spreads his hands. "I haven't the statistics to hand, but a distinct minority remain in the political field – some as journalists, others as researchers and staff members. Many become teachers, and quite a few – perhaps the majority – find a career in business."

At this point, I, the One, suggest that he try – as a wise ally – to bring a personality dimension into the discussion.

"I wouldn't care to be quoted on this, Miss Maiyo," he continues, "but it seems to me that many of our elected officials have an air of the demagogue. They may choose to call it 'charisma', but I think there is often an element of sinister manipulation about them." He pauses, noting her frown of concentration, the chewing of her inner cheek. "And, from what I know of you, Miss Maiyo, there is very little sinister about you."

"Thank you, Professor. But perhaps what politics needs in our Country is a more honest, and less sinister approach."

"You are undoubtedly correct, Miss Maiyo. All I am pointing out is that our political system is biased against accepting people like you into influential positions. As reformers, they tend to dilute the power structure." He noted that she is still engaged in frowning and cheek-chewing. "To complete the picture, perhaps I should point out that about two thirds of our students who apply to medical school graduate, and of the graduates, about eighty-five percent become practicing doctors. So, to put it in simple terms, Miss Maiyo, there is a fifty percent chance of your becoming a doctor and a ten percent chance that you will be an elected politician."

"But maybe I could do more for the country as a politician than as a doctor."

"I think the probabilities are against it. There are several points to bear in mind. As a doctor, you can save or extend the lives of literally hundreds – perhaps thousands – of people. As a successful research doctor, the number of people benefitting from your career could be in the millions. I think you will agree that an adverse culture is at the root of our political malaise, and all I would add is that culture change on a national scale is an extremely slow, frustrating process. So, I think you know my recommendation, Miss Maiyo."

"Yes, thank you, Professor." Reluctantly, she gets up from the chair.

"To put our conversation into perspective, Miss Maiyo, I believe you – like many students – are exercising what the German philosopher Nietzsche called 'The Will to Power'."

"The Will to Power?"

"Yes. That expression may seem misleading. What Nietzsche wanted to identify is one fundamental driving force for all human beings. He concluded it isn't power, per se, sex or even money. He decided that it is the urge to forge a unique identity: a set of personal skills, attitudes and ideals that make each of us the best person we can be. He postulated that this process would lead to individual happiness, but he also said that the process would not be easy – that it would involve much of what he called 'self-overcoming' and that when one succeeded, one had power over oneself. Hence, the Will to Power."

"But, what must one overcome in one's self?"

"For Nietzsche, it was a contest between our reason and our urges or desires, facilitated sometimes by what he called an 'educator'. He took the view that there are only three categories of great people – artists, saints and philosophers – who could achieve the Will to Power. I must add that if he were alive today, he would add another category: scientists."

Dorothy is chewing the inside of her cheek again. "That list doesn't seem to include politicians, Professor."

"I'm afraid you're right, Miss Maiyo. Our politicians would qualify least of all as saints."

"And the list seems to exclude doctors, also."

"No, today, it wouldn't. After all, doctors are a special category of scientist."

Dorothy sits back in her chair, and considers Professor Kipsang. "Umm, do you qualify as a philosopher, Professor?"

"It's kind of you to ask, Miss Maiyo." His smile appears. "Someday, I may qualify as a philosopher, but not until I have made more progress in self-overcoming."

> I, the One, believe that the professor did an excellent job in that counseling session, though he didn't believe – correctly – he had convinced her. Still, I want to make him feel proud of good advice he gives to students, as an 'educator'.

Holding onto a strap in a crowded bus going across City, Dorothy searches for the best conclusion for her dilemma. Logically, it makes sense to continue her pre-med studies, and she is pleased to learn her chances are about even. She has heard stories – some of them first-hand – of people who didn't make it to the coveted MD suffix. Mostly, they failed or dropped out of med school, and a few decided that the blood and the clinical pressures were not for them. She isn't worried about body fluids or clinical urgency. She recalls the functioning stethoscope given to her by her aunt Rebecca, a nurse, and the shadowing sessions with her: blood being drawn, X-rays taken and babies delivered.

She walks the four blocks from the bus stop to Home Away, enters the office, and gives her father a kiss on the cheek. "How did it go?" Joseph asks.

She puts her book bag down and wakes her computer mouse. "OK, I guess. He thinks I have a pretty good chance of becoming a doctor, and that's what he recommends."

Joseph turns to take in the mood of his daughter. "He's right, you know. You'd make a splendid doctor."

She gives him a mournful look. "I just think I could make a bigger contribution to society in politics."

Joseph, not wishing to make a head-on tackle of her perpetual idealism, suggests an experimental approach: "Maybe you ought to do some political volunteering to find out what it's really like."

She sits down at her PC with a sigh. "Maybe." Glancing across at her father, she adds, "Professor Kipsang says I am engaged in the Will to Power."

"Nietzsche. That's appropriate."

"Is it? Have you read Nietzsche, Papa?"

"Yes, many years ago."

"So, what do I have to do to be self-overcoming?"

Joseph laughs. "I think you should read what the man himself says, but it's a complicated process: discovering talents and understanding vulnerabilities."

"Do you have a book of his philosophy?"

"He wrote many books. Let's see what I have when we get home. You know what else he's famous for?"

"No."

"He is the one who said. 'God is dead'."

"So he was an atheist?"

"No, not really. He said that he believed in God, however, he had a habit of exaggerating to emphasize a point. The words

'God is dead' suggest that God was once alive, and from there Nietzsche claimed that we have killed Him."

"What?"

"Nietzsche died over a hundred years ago, but in the late nineteenth century he observed that people were so engaged in and preoccupied with self-serving trivia: fashion, entertainment, making a good impression, etc., that God had been shut out of our lives: that we had killed Him."

Dorothy's frown is dissolving into acceptance and irritation. "Well, if people were busy killing God a hundred years ago, some of them are doing an even better job of it today!"

> This 'God is dead' business makes me laugh! I, the Other, can tell you, firsthand, that God is not dead, and that, in fact, he hasn't been dead for a long time. Nietzsche was right: God just gets neglected and peeved from time to time.

Joseph goes back to his computer screen for a few moments. "Oh, guess who's back!"

"Who?"

"Kamiri."

"When did he get here?"

"A couple of hours ago. He said the job with his brother didn't work out. You might want to find out some details."

"Where is he?"

"In the lounge, as far as I know."

Kamiri is watching a football game; there is a tap on his shoulder.

"Hi Kamiri, I'd like to hear about your brother. Let's get a cup of tea."

He stands up, a doubtful look on his face. "What kind of tea?"

"Chinese tea."

The frown recedes. "OK, I'll try some."

Achieving Superpersonhood:

In the small meeting room, she says, "I understand it didn't work out with your brother. Can you tell me about it?"

Reluctantly, he tells her that his brother wanted him to find new customers for his product.

"What was his product, Kamiri?"

"I'd rather not say."

"Kamiri, one of the rules we have at Home Away is that we are completely honest with each other. By being honest, we don't disappoint each other. But another rule we have, which is equally important, is that any information you give us stays within these four walls." She makes a sweeping gesture around the room. "So, for example, we would never inform the police about anything you tell us." He tips his head in acknowledgement. "Tell me, Kamiri, what was the product?"

"A Mandrax Smoke."

Dorothy sits back in her chair. "Kamiri, Mandrax is a very powerful drug. It is illegal in Country, because it is very addictive when smoked and has terrible effects on health. It can even kill you. Did you know that?"

Kamiri is emphatic. "No!"

"Is there any chance, Kamiri, that if you ran out of money, you would go back to your brother?"

"No."

"Why not?"

"Because I don't want to go to prison, and because . . ." He hesitates.

"Because what?"

"Because my brother didn't treat me very good."

"Did he hurt you?"

"No. He ate my food and he let women sleep on my mattress." Dorothy gave an involuntary smile. "It's not funny, Dorothy!"

"I'm not laughing at you, Kamiri; I'm laughing because it's so typical of men to deny their brother a bed so they can have comfortable sex with a woman."

"I wouldn't do that."

"OK, Kamiri, you know about our rule about refusing two jobs?"

He nodded. "Does it mean I get only one chance now?"

"No. You start with a clean slate – we're not going to count turning down your brother. You get two chances."

"Thank you."

For the next two hours, Kamiri completes psychometric and intelligence tests.

* * *

Dorothy is leaving the University to get a bus to Home Away. "Hey Dorothy, how are you?"

She turns to see Hassan Arusei waving at her. Hassan is a year older than Dorothy and in her elective sociology class. He is black, rather quiet, good looking and obviously from a wealthy family. Dorothy, however, is cautious, and treats him with reserve: one never knows what might be on the agenda of a very wealthy classmate.

She pauses. "Hello, Hassan."

"Say, Dorothy, can I interest you in a tea or a coffee?"

"I'm on my way to the charity where I work."

"I didn't know you were working besides uni. Is it a condition of your scholarship?"

"No, I'm just a volunteer."

Over tea, she describes Home Away.

Hassan says: "That must be difficult. A lot of these people are really lazy. Just looking for government money."

"Some people are lazy – even some wealthy people – but we eliminate them pretty quickly. We do get funding from the government, but it's based on successful placements, and the only cash we disburse is ten shillings a day so they can take busses to interviews."

"How did you get the job, Dorothy?"

"Nepotism. My father started the charity."

They talk for another ten minutes until Dorothy says, "Sorry, but I've got to go, Hassan."

"Dorothy, I've been meaning to ask you." He suddenly seems unsure of himself. "Would you like to go to a disco with me on Saturday night? We could have dinner before." He leans forward, hopefully. "There's supposed to be a really good seafood restaurant in the Life Mutual Building."

"Sorry, Hassan, I'm not much of a dancer, and I've been to a disco once. Too loud for me."

"Oh! Well . . ." He seems uncharacteristically flustered. "Would you just like to have dinner?"

She pauses for a moment. *Why not?* flashes into her consciousness. "Yes, Hassan, that would be very nice."

"Oh, that's great. I'll pick you up at about seven. Can you give me your address?"

"I can just meet you at the restaurant."

"It's no trouble. I've got a car."

I should have guessed he has a car.

At Home Away, Kamiri's test results have come back: high conceptual intelligence, above average in verbal, numerical and spatial reasoning. His personality profile shows high tendencies toward independence, self-sufficiency and tenacity; lower tendencies toward socialization and the need for recognition.

"Pretty promising young man," is Joseph's comment.

"So shall I start looking to place him?"

"Yes. You know, Dorothy, it occurs to me that he is a very good fit with the park ranger program."

"You mean because he likes independence, and he comes from a rural area with an understanding of animals?"

"Yes, but not only that. He has the intelligence to benefit from the ranger education program."

Dorothy adds: "And the program gives preference to people like Kamiri who are classed as rural poor."

"The ranger program takes quite a while to make a decision. Meanwhile, you can try to place him," Joseph suggests, "so that he doesn't go stale."

"OK."

"By the way, Dorothy, would you be able to work Saturday afternoon on the government reports? They're overdue."

"Yes, but I've got to be home by six."

"That's OK."

Dorothy senses that her father is curious about her plans after six, but that he is loath to probe. "Hassan Arusei asked me to dinner."

"Oh! Well! Is he part of the Arusei family?"

"I think so, Papa. He's in my sociology class."

For Dorothy, her father is her unconditional backer: she can do no wrong; but he is also an adoring, tactful observer who will invariably mention a misstep she might have taken, not as a critic, but as an 'educator', who, until recently, would not have recognized that title. Joseph spares no effort to help his elder daughter achieve what he now recalls as the Will to Power. With her mother, the relationship is less intense and in a different sphere: Dorothy and her mother have a loving, conspiratorial relationship focused on the issues, values and culture of womanhood.

I, the One, am not sure about Hassan Arusei. Of course, everyone is a work in progress, but Hassan's progress hasn't been brilliant; still, I have by no means given up on him. He is bright, good looking and not a bad football player, but insecure. His father has more money than he knows where to invest it. There are about two dozen companies under his umbrella: construction, housing, telecoms, food processing, and tourism. Nothing wrong with that, as such. The problem is: government decisions are too often facilitated in the Aruseis favor by large packages of shillings. In my view, growing up in a very fluid monetary environment can be a definite handicap. And I'm aware that the Other is attempting to exploit this. There is also the point that the Aruseis are Muslim, but I decided some time ago not to count the religion of birth against anyone.

At precisely seven o'clock on the Saturday the Maiyos' doorbell rings. Their modest house is stuccoed cinderblock, two stories, with a tile roof, on a narrow plot of land. It is located on the east side of the Town in an area with some mature trees, full utilities and macadam-surfaced roads.

Joseph answers the door. "Hello, you must be Hassan. Please come in. I'm Joseph, Dorothy's father. She'll be ready shortly."

Hassan follows Joseph into the lounge, where Helen, Dorothy's mother, and her younger sister Mary, are watching television. Mary offers a brief wave and a smile, causing Hassan to conclude, *Mary is even prettier than Dorothy.*

"What are you watching?" he asks.

Helen says, "Oh, it's just a silly quiz game, Hassan. I understand you are also at University."

"Yes, I am – not far from graduation. He hopes that this announcement of seniority would stir some interest from Mary. She, however, is leaning forward, her chin supported by her fist.

"And what field are you studying?" Helen enquires.

"Mostly liberal arts," he replies.

"Oh, for goodness' sake!" Mary slaps her hands together. "The dummy didn't know the capital of Canada!"

"Are you a geography student?" Hassan asks.

Mary glances at him briefly. "You don't have to be a student of geography to know that the capital of Canada is Ottawa!"

"Yes, I suppose you're right," Hassan concedes.

"I'm sure you knew that, Hassan," Mary says, making eye contact. "You liberal arts majors know all that stuff."

"I'm afraid I would wash out of a game show in the first round."

Mary shakes her head: "No you wouldn't – particularly if I were on your team."

My assessment of Mary is that she is what people tactfully call 'a handful'. She is beautiful, charming, willful and unpredictable. She can bend even inflexible people to her view of the world.

"Hi Hassan, shall we go?" Dorothy is in the doorway, wearing blue linen trousers and a white blazer. Her face is framed in a mass of shining black curls.
Mary calls out, "Don't do anything I wouldn't do, you two!"
Joseph frowns and shakes his head
Dorothy shoots back: "Well, that leaves us with a pretty open playing field."

A red Toyota sports car is parked in front of the house. Dorothy admires the black leather upholstery. "How long have you had this?"
"My father gave it to me for my birthday a couple of years ago."
"And you use it to drive to uni?"
"We live in City so it's not very far; there's no parking at uni," Hassan replies.
"So you take a bus?"
He glances at her. "We have a driver who takes me."
Dorothy laughs outright. "You know how I get to uni, if I don't get a ride with my father?
I take three busses. Takes between forty-five minutes and two hours, depending on the traffic."
"I like your hair like that, Dorothy."
"Thanks."

The twenty-second floor restaurant, Poseidon, is all windows and white tablecloths dotted with tiny floral bouquets and

Achieving Superpersonhood:

candles. Their table has a view over City to the west, where the dimming sun is partially masked by translucent gold clouds.

"This is very nice, Hassan."

"What would you like to drink, Dorothy?"

"What are you having?"

"Probably a gin and tonic."

"Aren't you a Muslim, Hassan?"

"Yes." Knowing what is coming, he is amused.

"But you drink anyway?"

"Yes – not much though."

It is her turn to be amused. "In that case, I'll have a glass of Chablis, please." She smooths a nearly-invisible wrinkle from the tablecloth. "I guess you know I'm a Christian, and I don't know much about Islam, but I thought alcohol is a no-no."

He tilts his head dismissively. "We are what I suppose you would call 'secular Muslims'. Which means that we go to Friday prayers, but don't necessarily pray five times a day. We haven't been on the Hajj – yet – and we may drink alcohol discreetly."

> I, the One, don't like the term 'secular Muslim'. I think the term is what linguistic scholars refer to as an oxymoron: a self-contradicting phrase. How can one be 'secular' and a Muslim at the same time? Perhaps it is a way of trying to position oneself on a non-existent middle ground.

> I, the Other, don't see anything wrong with term 'secular Muslim'. I coined the term, and I'm no moron! Anyway, there are lots of secular Muslims out there. There are secular Christians; are they a problem, too? I keep saying that everything operates on a spectrum: from the North Pole to the South Pole, for example. But the One seems to see things in polarized terms. I would also like to point out that many secular Muslims are real friends

– or potential friends – of mine. And I take care of my friends!

A waiter comes to the table to take their orders.
Dorothy says: "I'd like the prawn and avocado salad, and then the grilled king mackerel with French fries and a green salad."
"I'd like a dozen oysters to start and the grilled lobster with French fries and a green salad, also."
"You want the small, local oysters, sir?"
"No, the European ones. And can you bring us some Chablis?"

"Tell me more about the charity you work for, Dorothy."
"Well, the difficult part is the placement of the migrants in jobs, because the number of migrants we receive is greater that the number we are able to place."
"How do you go about balancing the numbers?"
"Some of the migrants don't like the jobs they are offered. If this happens twice, we put them back on the street. Other times, we are full, and can't take any more people. And, of course, some people leave for their own reasons."
"And the government pays you for every migrant you place in a job?"
"Yes. The problem is that we don't have enough private sector companies that recruit through us."
Hassan's mouth comes open involuntarily. "There are actually companies that recruit migrants? I can't believe it!"
"Most of our candidates are not just riff-raff, Hassan. The riff-raff ends up back on the street. The majority are eager to work, and just want a chance to show what they can do."
Hassan gives a hopeless expression with palms face up. "What can they do – apart from very simple manual labor?"
"Well, for example, one of our last year's 'graduates' (she makes quotation marks in the air) is the front of house manager in an Indian restaurant. And the owner is very happy with him. Most migrants just need a chance to learn."

Hassan frowns. "But most of these people coming from the countryside are barely civilized. They're just used to the tribal ways."

I, the One, whisper: Be patient, Dorothy, you're going to get there!

She cocks her head to one side. "This is a pretty common misunderstanding, Hassan, because 'civilized' is a misleading word. The main differences between migrants and City people (she makes a gesture around the room) are education and culture. Migrants have a hunger for education, and they can learn very quickly, because they're motivated. Culture is the way they do things. As you say it's different, often tribal. But what most people don't realize is that their values are the same as ours: family, and hard work are two of the things they believe strongly in."

"But culture, as we've learned in class, is not easy to change."

"True, but don't forget that here they are out of their familiar culture and suddenly immersed in a different culture. Human beings have a tendency to want to fit in. We try to make that easier for them by holding daily learning sessions. They learn what we do differently in a business environment and why."

Hassan sits back in his chair. "That is amazing." He is considering. "Does Arusei Industries use your services?"

The waiter arrives with plates.

She holds up a hand. "I've been meaning to mention that to you, Hassan."

There is a slight smile on his lips. "What do you charge per recruitment?"

"Fifteen thousand shillings."

"Oooh! That's pretty expensive."

"It isn't when you consider that you'd be hiring a known individual, who's got a track record with us, and has been profiled. You don't have to advertise, and you can interview up to three candidates."

"In what way have the candidates been profiled?"

"They have had intelligence tests and personality profiles; we also give our appraisal of them."

"And you collect fifteen thousand shillings from the government, as well. A total of thirty thousand!"

"Yes. We have to provide room and board, and, in some cases clothing, for these candidates, many of whom drop out. And don't forget: we're a charity: we don't make a profit."

"What is the drop-out rate?"

"It varies. Last year it was forty-three percent. Is this something you can mention to your HR manager? I'd be happy to show him or her around Home Away."

"Can you give me a real example of a candidate you currently have?"

"OK. Let's just call him K. We picked him up from a vagrants' area a month ago. He has an IQ of a hundred and twenty-two. Eighteen years old, good looking, youngest of seven, from Village west of here. High school degree, studying English on his own. Is always present for the training sessions. Very polite. Personality profile shows independence and determination."

"I'll have to talk to the HR people, Dorothy."

When their plates have been cleared and they have ordered dessert, she asks him: "What are your ambitions, Hassan? You want to join the family firm?"

His hands are in his lap and his head and shoulders suddenly down. "I'm the youngest of five children. My two oldest brothers are already running divisions; my sister is PR Director, and my next older brother has started as a manager in the telecoms business. I don't think there's room for me."

She frowns. "How many people work for Arusei Industries, Hassan?"

"I'm not sure – maybe about five thousand."

"And you can't find a space that suits you among those five thousand?"

"Well, I'm not sure that it's what I want to do."

Achieving Superpersonhood:

Again, I, the One, suggest to Dorothy: wait a moment, be patient.

Hassan continues: "My father doesn't think I'm cut out to be in business."

Dorothy's frown deepens. "What?"

"He says I'm more the artistic type."

"Are you?"

"I don't know, Dorothy." He looks miserable. "Probably not."

"I don't understand something, Hassan. You're a guy who seems to have everything. A rich family, a place at University, your own car – good looks. And you're even a pretty nice guy . . ." For the first time, she sees a slight, self-conscious smile. "But you don't know what you want to do with your life." He shrugs. "I don't get it," she adds.

Defensively, he asks, "Do you have your life all mapped out?"

"No, I'm trying to figure out whether I want to be in politics or medicine. But that leaves me with two choices; I haven't heard you mention any."

He demands: "And what does your father think?"

"Well, he would rather see me in medicine, but he wants the decision to be mine. Oh, and we talked about something the philosopher Nietzsche said." She explains the Will to Power.

"That's interesting. I wonder what I have to overcome in myself to be a great philosopher."

"Or a saint?"

"Not hardly; not an artist either."

"I suppose that's where the educator comes into it: pointing out which of our desires are impeding us." She pauses for a moment. "What does your father say about your career – other than it shouldn't involve business?"

"Nothing much; for me he's not really an educator."

"And what about the rest of your family? What do they say?"

Another shrug. "Nothing much."

"I don't get it, Hassan. You're the youngest in the family. I would have thought you'd get more advice than you know how to use."

"Not really."

More as a plea than a demand, she says, "Help me understand, Hassan."

I, the One, intervene, as a kind of therapist, and I say: "Tell her, Hassan!"

He is biting his lip and staring at the table cloth in front of him. "My mother said that I was a mistake."

I, the Other, don't think that Hassan should have told Dorothy that he was a 'mistake'. It just makes him look weak, and I'm against revealing any weakness! Besides, I made the arrangements for that 'mistake', so, from my point of view it wasn't a 'mistake' at all! I can usually communicate quite well with Hassan, but somehow the One got his message across quicker.

Dorothy is open-mouthed in horror. "What?"

He gazes at her through liquid eyes and nods.

"Oh Hassan, how awful! What a dreadful thing to tell a child!"

"I . . . I probably would have guessed anyway."

"How could you have guessed?"

There is a long pause. "I don't look at all like my father or any of my brothers or sisters."

"Well, that sometimes happens. Maybe you look like an uncle or grandfather."

He chews his lip. "I don't think that's what she meant by 'mistake'."

"Nobody is a mistake, Hassan! I'm sure of it! We are all God's children."

"I wish I could believe that."

Silently, their minds wrestle with the disclosure.

"Does your father know?"

"I think so."

Maybe, she thought, *that accounts for some of his father's behavior. Not wanting him to be part of the family dynasty while giving him the very visible car, so that no one will suspect.*

"Do you know who your real father is?"

"No."

They eat their desserts in silence, each lost in their own thoughts.

He looks up. "Interesting that you're thinking about politics, Dorothy."

"Oh, why do you say that?"

"Well, the newly re-elected government doesn't want to hear any criticism. They've already started to harass the newspapers."

"Yeah, I know; it's a bad sign."

"I think they'll be after the University newspaper next. You saw that letter to the editor of the student newspaper arguing that the defense minister should resign after all the rumors about corruption?"

"Yes, I saw it and I think the chances of him resigning are about . . ." Her right hand makes a circle of thumb and forefinger.

Suddenly, he seems ill at ease. "Dorothy, you won't mention . . ." His thought process seems to stall. "I mean . . . you won't mention about my family to anyone . . ."

"Of course not, Hassan. I don't like gossip."

"Thank you, Dorothy. It's good to have someone to talk to."

She offers a fleeting smile. *It must be terrible to live with a secret like that you can share with no one.*

"Can you talk to your mother, Hassan?"

"No. I think she feels too guilty."

Dorothy compresses her lips in frustration. "Do any of your siblings know?"

"I think my oldest brothers may suspect."

"If they don't know for sure, you can't very well talk to them."

"Exactly." He toys uncertainly with the handle of his coffee cup. "Is it all right, Dorothy, if I think of you as a . . . like a girlfriend?"

She smiles. "Well, you can certainly think of me as a friend, Hassan.   Tell me: why did you invite me out?"

"I don't know. I just like you and I wanted to talk to you."

"OK. Thank you for inviting me out, and thank you for the dinner." She pauses. "I think . . . that your situation will work out. I'll pray for you."

He is amused. "You will?"

"Yes, of course!"

"Would you like to go out next weekend – I mean we can go to a different restaurant?"

"I'll get too fat! Let's just meet during the week for a tea. You have my phone number?"

"Yes. Could you text me the title of that philosopher's book?"

Chapter 4

Student Protest

"You'll never guess what happened," Joseph announces as Dorothy walks into the office.

"What?"

"I got a call from an employment manager at Arusei Industries. He wants to meet with us, and the strange thing is he wants to meet a 'K', who he says is one of our candidates."

Dorothy looks out the window. "I suppose he's talking about Kamiri."

"How in the world does he know about Kamiri?"

"You remember last Saturday I had dinner with Hassan Arusei?" He nods. "Well, Hassan was asking me about where I work, and then he asked me to describe a typical candidate. So, I mentioned 'K' – Kamiri."

"I'm not sure that Kamiri is a typical candidate."

The following afternoon, Mr. George Mahati, the Employment Manager, Food Processing Division, Arusei Industries, arrives at Home Away.

Joseph shows him a presentation on the charity, and takes him for a tour of the premises.

Mr Mahati inquires, "About this fellow 'K'…"

"I can certainly show you his profile – which, as I've explained, is unique to Home Away – but perhaps first you can give me an idea of the job for which you'd like to consider 'K'?"

"In Food Processing, we have a large abattoir . . ." At the sound of the word 'abattoir', Dorothy, who is listening at the meeting, feels a chill in the nape of her neck. "The abattoir serves the general butchers' trade and also supplies our food preparation businesses. We process cattle, goats and sheep, and we serve the halal market, as well. In these facilities, our starting level jobs tend to be floormen. But employees at this level usually to go on to become cutters, tanners, and other specialties."

Joseph asks, "Do you provide training to these special positions?"

"Yes, we do."

"What are your requirements for floormen, and what are their duties?"

"The requirements are fairly simple: we need young men who are familiar with animals, are not squeamish about seeing them butchered, are willing to work hard, and are ambitious. The duties are general cleaning, routine maintenance, and portering."

Dorothy's face betrays her horror. "Are the floormen expected to kill the animals?"

Mr Mahati makes an easy gesture with his left hand. "Not initially, Miss Maiyo."

Joseph looks up from his notes. "Can you tell me: what are the pay level and working hours of your floormen?"

"The pay is four hundred and ninety-five shillings a week and we provide room and board. The normal working hours are 8am till 5:30 pm Monday to Friday and 8am till 1pm on Saturdays. I should point out, though, that the actual working hours are less than that because we tend to experience gaps in livestock deliveries."

Joseph reaches for a folder, from which he extracts a document. "Well, I think that 'K' is certainly familiar with animals, and our experience of him confirms that he is ambitious and willing to work hard." Joseph offers a slight smile. "We've never tested him for squeamishness."

"When can I interview him?"

"As soon as you sign the contract with Home Away."

Mr Mahati briefly scans the document which Joseph has given him. "As you know, Mr Maiyo, Arusei Industries is a big company, and we tend to hire quite a few starting level employees. Recognizing this, what discount can you give us from your fee of fifteen thousand?"

Joseph clasps his hands in front of himself. "Unfortunately, the government audits our books quarterly, and one of their requirements is that they will only match our fees from the private sector, and from their own departments. Before I was hired, Home Away did a lot of discounting. The word got out and the charity was almost bankrupted. So we don't give discounts to anyone. But we always give our best customers preferential treatment. Which involves giving them first right of refusal on our best candidates."

Mr Mahati puts on a disappointed face as he stands up to leave. "Well, in any case, I've got to run this contract past our legal people. I'll give you a call, Mr. Maiyo."

"What do you think, Dorothy?" Joseph inquires.

"I can't imagine anyone working in a slaughterhouse!"

"Well, I certainly wouldn't want the assignment, but I think we owe it to Kamiri to ask him, and so as not to bias him too much against the job, I suggest I ask him."

"So you don't think I can present the job 'objectively'?"

"No, I don't, Dorothy."

I, the One, have always been rather fond of animals, and plants – particularly lions, gazelles and yellow star grass. But there is a food chain, and, of course, it should be kept in balance – with minimum suffering. For me, Dorothy – much as I'm fond of her – is a bit of a paradox, being soft-hearted about cows yet occasionally unforgiving about people.

Kamiri, when asked about his views on the job at the abattoir, expresses considerable interest. "It sounds as if it offers a good chance to move into a better job. What is the pay of a cutter or a tanner?"

"I don't know," Joseph responds, "You'll have to ask about that if they call you for an interview, but I would think it's about a thousand shillings. . . . Can I assume that you're not bothered by working in a place where cattle are being slaughtered?"

"No. I was almost always asked to help when we slaughtered livestock in Village." He gives a dismissive wave. "It goes with tending animals."

Dorothy, who is sitting at the other end of the table, sighs in disbelief. *I guess it's just part of living in a village.*

Kamiri looks around the meeting room wistfully. "I will be sorry to leave this place, Joseph. It's very good here."

Dorothy is still trying to digest Kamiri's response as Joseph wishes 'K' luck and returns to the office.

"Do you think it will be good work, Dorothy?" Kamiri asks.

"I don't know; you'll have to find out if they call you for an interview. We'll certainly recommend that they call you."

"Thank you." Kamiri is pensive for a moment. "That necklace that you have about your religion – you said you would explain it to me."

"OK, Kamiri, I'll try. I am a Christian, and Christians believe that the son of God died on a cross a long time ago."

She goes on to explain the jealousy and myopia which led to Jesus' execution on the cross, his life and his miracles.

Kamiri is listening intently. "And the people loved him for his miracles?"

"Partly, and partly because they believed he was the son of God, and partly because of what he taught them."

"What was that?"

"He taught them that they had to do two things: love God and love all other people."

Achieving Superpersonhood:

"All other people?"

She nods. "Yes, I know. It's hard."

"Did he teach them anything else?"

"He said that if they did these things, they would have eternal life."

"And they believed that?"

"Yes. I believe that, and all other Christians believe that."

Kamiri stares at the ceiling in deep thought. "Dorothy, you said there is a book where all of this was written down."

"Yes. The Bible."

"Do you have a copy that I can read in Swahili?"

"Yes, of course."

I am rather proud of Dorothy. She explained the Christian religion briefly and clearly. Of course, if he does some reading, Kamiri will have a hundred additional questions. These things take time.

Dorothy's cell phone rings on her desk. "Hello Dorothy, this is Hassan. I thought you'd like to know that there are three police vans outside the campus newspaper, and we think they're going to try to shut the paper down."

"What are you going to do, Hassan?"

"I don't know. The editor of the paper is here, and he's asking for help in forming a barricade."

"I'll get there as soon as I can! Kamiri, you want to find out about university life?" she says, "Come with me!"

They board a bus to the University.

"Why are you in such a hurry, Dorothy?"

She explains the situation to him.

"What is the barricade for?"

"It's to prevent the police from shutting down the newspaper."

"How is it going to do that? The police are very powerful!"

"I don't know. We'll have to see when we get there."

As they approach the campus, the boom of the police loudspeakers becomes clear: "All students please disperse! The police have the lawful right to enter here! Disperse at once!"

Turning a corner, they enter an open area – ochre earth and worn grass – surrounded on three sides by three- and four-story brick buildings. A large crowd of students is milling about in front of one of the buildings. Three police vans are parked to one side, and a contingent of blue-uniformed police is facing the students.

One of the students shouts: "You do not have the constitutional right to close our newspaper! Freedom of the press!"

The crowd picks up the chant: "Freedom of the press! Freedom of the press! Freedom of the press!"

"Come on!" Dorothy takes Kamiri's arm and guides him obliquely toward the building and along its façade until they find themselves at the back of the crowd of students. There is a pile of randomly stacked chairs in front of a door to the building. "In there, downstairs, is the newspaper's office!"

> I, the One, am always in favor of people being able to express themselves. Of course, freedom of expression should not include intentional psychological injuries: such abuses only arouse anger and violence, and neither side wins. But truthful words, even if hurtful, can, if one is willing to listen, cause one to think differently. In my view, violence should always be avoided. Yet, I must admit that in history there are many instances of violence which was unsuccessful in defending freedom of expression, but later led to new protections of that freedom.

The shouting on both sides continues. The police are edging closer, raised truncheons in hand. The students crowd back, forming a tight mass around the barricade of chairs. "That's far enough!" a student at the front of the crowd shouts. "Come no closer!"

"That's Daniel Arap, the editor of the newspaper," Dorothy tells Kamiri.

"What's going to happen?"

"I don't know, but we have to stand our ground!"

The loudspeaker announces: "For the last time we tell you: Clear out of the way!"

Loud jeers from the crowd of students.

The police charge, beginning to strike at the youthful wall in their path. Students are shouting in pain and anger; some fall to the ground and are trampled upon. A student has wrested a truncheon from a policeman and is beating him with it. The weight of the crowd causes several police to fall, and the crowd, sensing its advantage, surges forward against the police. A whistle blows. The police who are standing retreat warily. Those on the ground are stripped of their truncheons and permitted to retreat.

Neither Dorothy nor Kamiri has been directly involved in the fray. Students are hugging and congratulating each other.

Daniel Arap shouts: "Listen up! The police are not leaving! They're getting out the tear gas and putting on gas masks. We have to be prepared! Soak your handkerchiefs in water! Cover your nose and mouth!"

"Hey, Dorothy, you made it!" Hassan shouts, approaching through the crowd.

"Yes, I was in the office and I brought 'K' along with me! Kamiri, this is Hassan Arusei."

The two young men stare at each other. "So you are the famous 'K'!" Hassan announces.

"I am not famous. Why am I famous?" Kamiri is puzzled. Then he adds, "Are you the owner of the slaughterhouse?" He holds out his hand. "Pleased to meet you!"

Hassan is amused. "No, my father is the owner. And your name is Kamiri?"

"Yes."

Kamiri's attention is attracted to several students making their way through the crowd. "What are they doing?"

Hassan calls to one of the students, "Hey Duke, what have you got?"

"You got a good throwing arm?" Duke responds.

"This guy here has a good throwing arm!" Hassan pushes Karimi forward. A paper sack half full of stones is thrust at Kamiri.

"Am I supposed to throw these?"

Dorothy shakes her head. "Not now!"

Across the open area, more police vans are arriving. Out of the vans pour more police, wearing helmets, gas masks and body armor. A sinister-looking black vehicle pulls up; it looks like a huge, man-made rhinoceros.

Hassan points. "Riot police and a water cannon!"

"What can we do?" Kamiri asks.

"We have to stand our ground!" Dorothy cries. There are fists in the air and the shouts of "Freedom of the Press!" resume.

> I, the One, offer advice to the students who will listen: when you can't win, go home. Little but martyrdom is to be gained against overwhelming odds, and one has to be certain that martyrdom will have lasting currency. Consider Tiananmen and Tahir Squares, for example. But very few are listening. For most, hot blood is flowing, and the herd instinct prevails: we are right and I am not a coward! I notice, however, that a few, more cautious souls discreetly move to the rear of the crowd.

"They're coming!" someone shouts.

There are popping sounds and trails of white smoke race across the sky, dropping black canisters of tear gas among the students. A few brave students pick up the canisters and throw them back at the charging police. A volley of stones arches out of the student crowd.

"Now, Kamiri!"

Kamiri can't actually see individual policemen involved in the charge from his vantage point in the rear. Instead, he hurls stones at the vehicles and police on the other side of the area.

The crowd begins to spread out, avoiding the noxious white smoke. But the inchoate rage of the crowd is almost deafening, encouraging one another and searching for weapons. A large rubbish bin is hurled through the air at the police. There are grunts and screams as the police attack the vanguard of the students, many of whom fall to the ground.

Now Kamiri can see individual targets and he delivers a stone at high velocity at a black-clad policeman, striking his face shield and knocking him off balance. With a shout of anger another policeman surges toward Kamiri, who is knocked off his feet by a powerful blast of water. Dorothy, Hassan and the surging policeman are also on the ground. Hassan seizes the policeman's truncheon and begins beating him with it. Dorothy tackles another policeman around his legs, bringing him down. Kamiri struggles to his feet and looks for a vantage point from which to throw his missiles. A group of five or six policemen have seized Hassan and Dorothy.

Kamiri continues to throw stones from a vantage point close by the building; the crowd has dispersed from around him. Two policemen mark him out and rush toward him, truncheons raised in readiness. Kamiri drops the stones, turns and sprints away. The soaked policemen, burdened by their body armor, give up the chase.

Concerned about what may have happened to Dorothy, Kamiri cautiously circles the area, taking advantage of any concealing shrubs and trees.

He is able to make out a group of wet and bedraggled students near the police vans. The group is surrounded by police. They are being handcuffed. Now they are being loaded into police vans. One of the students looks – at a distance – like Hassan. He cannot see Dorothy's yellow head scarf. *Could it have come off in the fighting?*

Three ambulances have come into the area. Police are herding several crestfallen students into the two of the ambulances; the third seems to be for two – perhaps it's three – injured police. Kamiri tries to see if Dorothy is among the injured. Faces are obscured. Two are women; neither has a yellow headscarf.

"Excuse me, Joseph."
Joseph looks up from his desk. "What is it Kamiri?"
"Something has happened to Dorothy."
Joseph is bolt upright. "What happened?"
"Well, sir, we went to the university. The police were trying to close down the newspaper. There was some fighting, and I think the police may have taken her away."
"Good God!" Joseph reaches for his mobile phone. Almost immediately, there are pictures on the small screen, and a voice says: "Late breaking news from the University. The government has closed down the University newspaper because of its unpatriotic criticisms. Students skirmished with police and several arrests were made. We go now to Winnie Ramongi at the site . . . Yes, Shaaban, police say that thirteen students have been arrested on assault and disorderly conduct charges. Three policemen and four students were injured in the melee – none seriously. . ."
"Damn!" Joseph picks up the office telephone and dials. "Yes, I'm inquiring about the students who were arrested at the University." There is a pause. "Yes, can you tell me if Dorothy Maiyo is among the students who were arrested at the University this afternoon?"
Another pause. "No? OK, thank you."
Joseph looks up at Kamiri. "You didn't see her before you left the University?"
"No, sir, I couldn't see her yellow scarf anywhere. Maybe she got in an ambulance, but I didn't see anyone with a yellow head."
Joseph dials his telephone again. "Can you tell me if you admitted a student from the University named Dorothy Maiyo? Yes, I'll wait. You did? OK, thank you!"

He looks up at Kamiri. "She's in the hospital." He gets up and moves toward the door.

"Shall I come with you, sir?"

"No, Kamiri, it's better if you stay here."

That evening, while watching the news, one of his fellow candidates shouts, "Isn't that you, Kamiri?" He points to the right-hand side of the screen. "There, in the back, throwing rocks!"

"I'm not sure. I can't see."

"Well, were you there, or weren't you?"

Kamiri concedes, "I went with Dorothy."

"So you were there, throwing rocks!" the tormentor announces. "I'll bet the police are looking for you!"

"Oh, come on, Kangol!" Mokalu interrupts. "The only people who can put a name and a location on that face . . ." He points at the screen. "Are Dorothy, Joseph and us."

"Well, somebody might turn him it," Kangol says argumentatively.

"Yeah," Mokalu snarls, "and that somebody will find his dumb ass out in the street for breaking the four walls rule!"

Next morning, Kamiri is watching television, but he has lost the plot of the soap opera; his mind is occupied with speculation about Dorothy's injuries, and trying to decide how much of the blame for those injuries should rest on his shoulders for what the news readers are calling 'the student uprising'.

Kamiri asks: "Isn't there a football game or something better than this stupid program?"

"Just because you don't understand drama, Kamiri, doesn't mean that the rest of us have to watch Manchester United or some Spanish team."

Kamiri sinks down into the beanbag sofa, resigned to his thoughts.

"Hello, guys. Are you studying English?" It is Dorothy with her left arm in a white sling and a matching white headscarf.

Kamiri leaps to his feet. "What happened to you?"

"Oh, I broke my right arm playing football at University."

"If Kamiri was on your team, how come you two didn't score a goal?" Mokalu inquires with a smirk.

"The other team was just too strong for us, weren't they Kamiri?" Kamiri nods. "And I guess you didn't have any trouble after the game?"

"No, I didn't. I came straight home." He pauses. "Did you get any . . . penalties . . . after the game?"

"Nope. I was taken to the hospital. They took some x-rays, put a plaster on my arm and sent me home. I guess the other team was kind of embarrassed that they had injured a female player."

She turns and strides to her office.

"So, you got something goin' with that booty, Kamiri?" Kangol nudges a colleague with his elbow.

"No."

"But you'd like to," Kangol sniggers.

"Sure," Kamiri concedes, looking at the others. "But you know what my odds – or any of your odds – are!" He makes a sweeping gesture around the room. "About a million to one. We're poor, uneducated country boys. She's a good-looking, college-educated woman from a good family."

"But that isn't stopping you from trying," Kangol persists.

Mokalu holds up a hand. "Give it a rest, will you, Kangol! He's right; it doesn't even bear thinking about. Besides, she's trying to help us. Why complicate things?"

* * *

Hassan is seated at a table in the same students' café.

"My goodness!" He asks, "What happened to you?"

Dorothy takes the chair opposite. "You remember when the water canon knocked us over? Well, there was a policeman trying to run right over us. I reached up and kind of tackled him.

He fell on top of me when my arm was in an awkward position. Broke my arm."

Hassan's face contracts in empathetic pain. "That must have hurt like crazy!"

"It did, and I was soaking wet, all covered in mud, and lost my scarf. At first, the police wanted to take me to jail, but they could see that I needed medical attention, and some sergeant or lieutenant said, 'Put her in the ambulance'. I think they were a little embarrassed that they had broken a woman's arm. At the hospital, they gave me some pain medication, set my arm and plastered it. Then my father came and picked me up."

"How did he figure out where you were?"

"I guess Kamiri told him."

"So Kamiri didn't get arrested?" She shakes her head.

"Lucky bastard!" he murmurs.

"What about you?"

"Well, I was put in a police van, and taken to the police station. There were about a dozen or fifteen of us. They checked our identity cards, took individual pictures of us and put us all in a large cell. They called us out, one-by-one, to be charged. In my case, there were two cops who said I was striking a policeman. One of them was the guy I hit. They charged me with assault on a police officer, and put me back in a cell. I tried to call my father, when they gave me the chance. He wasn't available, but the next day, he sent one of his lawyers to see me. The lawyer arranged for me to be bailed, so I'm one of the lucky ones. Quite a few of the others couldn't arrange bail, and they'll have to wait in jail until we're tried next month."

"How much was your bail?"

"A quarter of a million shillings."

"Oh, my gosh! The lawyer was able to raise that kind of money right away?"

Hassan shrugs. "My father doesn't have to raise money. He just signs stuff. But I got a message from him that I am <u>expected</u> to be wherever the lawyer wants me to be."

"Where is that?"

"Well, I'm <u>expected</u> to be in the lawyer's office next Monday at ten o'clock."

The Other has involved Dorothy and Hassan in a conflict with the police that they couldn't win, and look at the result! Dorothy has a broken arm and Hassan is in trouble with his father and the police. Of course, the truth is important: here, it's about a corrupt minister. But if you can't prove the truth and you've tried, unsuccessfully, to reveal it, you become the focus of a different problem – a problem that diverts attention from the truth itself!

"I'm sorry you're in trouble, Hassan."

"Actually," Hassan volunteers, "I'm more worried about what my father will do than I am about the police."

Dorothy lowers her tea cup to the saucer. "I don't get it, Hassan."

Pensively, he stares across the café and inclines his head. "With the police, the worst thing that can happen is I spend some time in jail. My friends would come to see me – I'd be a kind of hero, and eventually I'd get out. But with my father, I'd be made to feel bad – not worthy of the family name – a misfit."

Dorothy adds softly, "A mistake."

"Yeah, exactly."

She reaches across the table and touches his hand. "Hassan, you are <u>not</u> a mistake, you are God's child, and, you're right: you're a hero."

"That's very nice of you, Dorothy."

"I'm not being nice, Hassan, I mean it. You stood up for what you believe in: freedom of the press. Too many people in this country would look the other way. They think: *it's not my problem. I've got other things to worry about.* And what do they worry about? They worry about their bank account. Whether they can buy that new pair of shoes. About what clothes to wear on Friday night. Will they impress their friends? I don't think it was always this way!"

"What do you mean?"

"Think about a hundred years ago, Hassan. Only a very few people were rich. The rest didn't have bank accounts, or more than one change of clothes. If there was a party on Friday night, it was a tribal dance where everybody was dressed the same and it was about having fun – not impressing others." She pauses. "When I go to church, there are mostly two kinds of people: old people who've learned that life isn't just about pleasure and getting ahead, and poor people who are struggling to stay where they are and for whom pleasure is a kind word. These two groups of people lead different lives than most urban people under the age of forty."

"In what way are they different?"

"The old and the poor have different values and a different concept of who they are. For them, life isn't just about me. It's also about friends and strangers. They have tightly-held beliefs in concepts like justice, trust, and friendship."

For a moment, Hassan gazes at Dorothy thoughtfully. "I think you're a wonderful idealist, Dorothy."

She gives a shrug. "I can live with that."

Their eyes meet for several moments.

"Oh," she says, picking up her tea cup again., "I want to thank you for recommending Home Away to your personnel department. A Mr. Mahati came around and wants to interview Kamiri."

"Did he say for what job?"

"Floorman in an abattoir."

He shakes his head. "That's a hellish job."

"You ever been in an abattoir?"

He continues to shake his head in horror. "No, and I can't imagine all that blood and squealing animals!"

I am disappointed in Hassan! What's wrong with blood and squealing animals? It's the One who's always making a fuss about blood – always equating it with life. And as for squealing: 'there's no gain without pain'.

The Other talks about 'no gain without pain'! What a hypocrite! He's a specialist in pain, whose offers are sweetened with gratification that cannot hide the hurt when the pleasure evaporates!

"Speaking of Kamiri, Dorothy, do you know if he plays football?" Hassan asks.
"I haven't a clue. Do you want his number? You can ask him."
"Yeah, that would be good. He looks pretty athletic and we need a couple of new players on my Sunday team."

Chapter 5

Abattoir

The Arusei abattoir is well outside the City, at the edge of a semi-industrial area. Kamiri takes a 721 bus to its final destination, and walks a further three kilometers for his interview. In City, he has met with Mr Mahati, the Arusei HR manager, who was rather cool at first, but became warmer as the interview progressed. In fact, Mr. Mahati told Mr Kakuyu, the abattoir manager: "He seems like a good fit for your position. I just don't know how well he can handle the blood and gore."

The building, at the end of a dirt track, is tall, single-story, white-washed concrete block, which, together with the corral, covers just under two hectares. At the end of the dirt track are a parking area for cars and a livestock unloading area with a ramp. The cattle corral itself is sealed from view behind plywood sheets attached to the fence. As Kamiri approaches, he can hear the coughing and groaning of beef cattle. The sounds relieve him because there is no sign identifying the place, and he knows he has not made a wrong turn. He rings the bell beside the gray door. Moments later a burly man with a graying stubble of beard, dressed in coveralls, opens the door. "You must be Kamiri. Come in. My name is Kakuyu." Kamiri follows him into a small, undecorated room with a metal table and six chairs. There is no window; the fluorescent lights flicker slightly.

Mr Kakuyu seats himself at the head of the table. "Help yourself to the water. You've had a bit of a walk, I guess."

"Yes, sir, but the directions were very good."

Kakuyu opens a manila folder with coffee stains on the cover. "Judging by your surname, Kaiku, you, like me, are Kikuyu."

"Yes, I am Kikuyu." Kamiri feels his spirits lift: he is not a foreigner here.

"I don't know your Village: I come from an area farther north." He sits back, considers Kamiri and shifts into Kikuyu. "Tell me about yourself."

For the next five minutes, Kamiri reveals his family background, his work in Village and his reasons for immigrating to the City.

"As I understand it, you were hoping to find work with your brother."

"Yes, sir. It didn't work out."

"Why not?"

"My brother was selling drugs, sir, and I didn't like it."

"Tell me about your time at Home Away."

"It's been very good, sir. They teach us how to behave when you're working in a business, and I'm learning English."

"Do you have any experience butchering livestock?"

"Yes, sir; I helped my father and uncles butcher goats, sheep and cattle."

"And what did you do with the hides, entrails, heads and hoofs?"

"The hides were spread in the sun to dry. My uncles treated the hides, but I was not involved in that. The heart, liver, kidneys, testicles, pancreas and brain were given to the women to prepare; the rest was buried. Some of the bones were given to the dogs. The horns and hooves were sold separately."

"Would you like to see how we do it here?"

"Yes, I would."

They walk down a corridor, through a pair of rubber-edged swinging doors into a large space. It is cool and quiet. There are overhead tracks from which dozens of sides of beef are suspended. The floor, Kamiri notices, is large squares of white ceramic tile. The walls and ceiling of the space are also white.

"Let's start at the beginning," Kakuyu suggests, and he leads the way through a maze of carcasses. "Right now, we are doing beef cattle," he explains. "They put their heads through that opening there." He points to large rubber flaps. "We don't want them to see what's going on inside when they're in the queue." A brown cow's head appears, and immediately, a white-clad employee draws a large device down onto the cow's head. There is a loud thud and a hiss of escaping air. The cow's head droops, and its entire body is drawn into the space. Two employees attach steel cables to the cow's hind legs, and it is drawn upwards, suspended from the ceiling track. A black bull's head appears.

"We also process halal meat," Kakuyu continues. "This facility has been oriented so that Mecca is in that direction." He points down the conveyor line. "When we're doing halal slaughtering, a Muslim employee says a brief prayer over the animal after it is stunned, and then he slits the throat."

They move down the line. "Here, the cutters remove the head and tail of the animal. They also drain the blood into this trough. Tails are placed here, heads in there." He gestures toward two mobile bins.

"Do you make any use of the heads?" Kamiri asks.

"We probably do what you do. We remove the brains and tongues of animals under the age of two, and make them available to our distributors. Any horns are removed and sold separately."

Further down the line, a cutter is slicing the carcass open from tail to neck. The entrails are removed into a mobile bin. "One of the jobs of the floormen is to take these bins over to those tables . . ." He points to a line of stainless steel tables where a white-clad employee is working. "The floormen sort out the liver, heart and so on – from your list – and move them into cold storage. The remainder goes to disposal, which we'll see later."

"Here," he says, moving farther along, "the cutters are removing the hide."

"It's a lot easier to remove the hide when the animal isn't lying on the ground," Kamiri observes.

"All of our hides go to a separate tanning facility nearby, and they are picked up by distributors for resale. . . . Any questions so far?"

"No. It's the same as what we do, but also very different."

Kakuyu smiles. "How is it different?"

"It's like a car factory I saw on television once, and everything is so clean."

"Part of your job, if you come to work here, will be to keep it clean." He moves farther down the line. "At this station, the hooves are removed. They are sold to be made into glue. . . . And at this location, the cutters are cleaning and trimming the sides. You can see there is some additional waste here."

Kakuyu leads the way to where the track in the ceiling disappears through a wall, below which are double doors. He opens one of the doors; it is uncomfortably cool inside. "Here is where we store the meat ready for pickup." There are rows upon rows of red and white marbled carcasses, arranged by size.

"My gosh, I never saw so much meat! These rows are beef. These two must be mutton and this one is goat. How many animals do you do in a day?"

"It varies, depending on livestock deliveries, but the average is four hundred and ten a day."

"Do you ever have a problem where the distributors don't take enough?"

Kakuyu shakes his head. "That is my main job. I take and receive offers from the City Exchange for live cattle and carcasses. We negotiate prices to keep things moving.

"But suppose a farmer brings you cattle that are just skin and bones. Do you pay him full price?"

"No. There are only certain farmers that we do business with, and some of them have especially good animals that we can pay extra for, because distributors are willing to pay more for them. OK?" Kamiri nods. "Let's take a look at our disposal and recycling systems."

Kakuyu opens a door in the rear of the space. Across a concrete slab, there is a collection of large gray tanks: a whine of electric motors and the whirr of pumps. "This tank here receives all our waste liquids. Air and chemicals are recirculated through this tank, purifying the contents, which are periodically pumped into this tank, where they are allowed to settle. The sediment is moved to the solid waste disposal tank. The water from the top of the tank is filtered, treated and reused in the main building." He moves to the other side of the treatment facility. "This is the conveyor, which transports solid wastes into the digester, which is that large tank there. The grinder, here, is used to disintegrate the bones which we don't sell. The fragments go to the digester. Again, air and chemicals are used to treat the solid waste, which is compacted and dried. About three times a week, a truck comes to take it away to landfill – but it is inert enough that it can be used for fertilizer."

They move to another white, cinderblock building, which, unlike the main building, has many windows. "This is our residential building." On entering, they find the employees' lounge, with two large television screens and a random assortment of couches, chairs and tables. There are shelves along one wall with books and stacks of boxed games. Kamiri is puzzled. "It's cool in here. Why?"

"When this facility was built, it had to be out of the City. As you've learned, it's not an easy place to get to. Arusei decided that we would have to house our employees here. If we didn't, we would have a big absentee problem. So I argued that if we were going to build a residential facility, why not make it reasonably comfortable. Arusei agreed and it piggybacks on the air conditioning for the main building."

To the right, they enter the dining room, with its service line, neatly arranged tables and chairs – beyond is the kitchen.

"Are the employees served some of the goat or mutton that is processed here?" Kamiri inquires.

"Beef is served on Sunday nights, because we want to give the employees a good reason to be back here in time to start work on Monday. Meat is served two other nights: chicken, mutton or goat."

"So people can leave on Saturday afternoon as long as they are back for dinner on Sunday?"

"The married men all leave on Saturday afternoon, but anyone else can do the same."

He walks across to the other side of the lounge and opens a door. "Here is the bunkroom and in the back are the showers and toilets."

Kamiri takes in the rows of double-decker bunks down each wall. "How many people live here?"

"There are forty-three on site now and all but two of us stay here." He pauses and considers Kamiri. "What do you think?"

"I think it's very good, and you pay almost five hundred shillings a week?"

"Yes. I'll turn you over to our operations manager so he can sort out some details with you."

The operations manager is Daniel Arapa, in a white coat, tall and reed thin with a wispy gray moustache. He sits with Kamiri at a table in the lounge. At first, the conversation covers much the same ground as the initial discussions with Mr Kakuyu. Daniel also wants to know Kamiri's understanding of the process line and any questions he may have.

Kamiri says: "I think my main question is about the work I would do as a floorman."

Daniel opens a plan of the process line and points out which bins have to be moved and their destinations, inside and outside the building. "There is also the sorting of the sellable offal from the entrails. And once they are sorted, they have to be washed and packaged in the refrigerated room. Horns and hooves have to be packaged. Floormen also take readings on the disposal plant and add chemicals, as needed. Then there is the daily scrub down. You might also be asked to help a distributor load a shipment or a farmer unload a shipment. Sound like your kind of job?"

"Yes, sir, it does. Can I ask about the money?"

"You have a bank account?"

"No, sir."

"Well, you have to get one, because we don't pay in cash. On Monday mornings, our financial controller transfers the money you earned the previous week to your bank account. I'll give you a certificate of employment. You take that to a bank and they'll open an account for you." He pauses for a moment. "When can you start, Kamiri?"

"Tomorrow?"

Mr Arapa smiles in bemusement: "Let's say next Monday."

I, the One, am pleased with Kamiri's progress. He is out of bad and into good employment: a job for which he has the aptitude, and which removes him from poverty. Is it employment which nourishes the pride of fulfillment? We will have to see.

As he is walking back to the bus stop, Kamiri's phone rings. On the screen, it says "Caller unknown". He shrugs and presses the green circle. "Hello."

"Is that Kamiri?"

"Yes, I am Kamiri."

"This is Hassan. You remember? I was at the student protest, and I got your number from Dorothy."

"Yes, I remember."

"Do you play football?"

"I played on a team in my Village."

"Would you like to play on a team in the City?"

Kamiri is startled. "How could I do that?"

"You just come with me."

"When would that be?"

"Sunday morning. I can pick you up at Home Away at about eight-thirty. OK?"

"OK. Do I need to bring anything? I don't have football boots."

"That's OK. We're just going to do some training."

A rich guy that I barely know calls me on my phone and asks if I want to play football. Yes, I want to play football! But how does he know? Maybe my great-uncle told him, or maybe it was Joseph. Do they want money? Wait! Are they thinking of hiring me to play on their team? How much would they pay? Do I have to quit my job at the slaughterhouse? What if I turn up in these blue trainers? (He kicks a stone down the road.) *What if they're all rich guys and they laugh at me?*

These and similar worries usurp his attention. Joseph says that he hadn't said anything to Hassan, but perhaps Dorothy had. *That must be it!*

"I'm supposed to get a bank account," he confesses to Joseph, showing him the employment certificate.

Joseph leaps to his feet and shakes his hand. "Congratulations, Kamiri and best of luck!"

"Thank you. Can you tell me which bank I should go to?"

"There is the City Trust Bank over on West Street." He gives directions, and Kamiri sets off at once.

Kamiri is astonished at the size of the bank. He gazes through the wide glass front. Inside, there is another glass partition with busy employees behind it. Other people are coming and going. *This is nothing like the bank I have seen in the town near Village! The bank I know has two people inside. Mostly, they don't do anything.*

As he is leaving the bank, he looks at the many posters advertising the bank's services. *Gosh, they even help you buy a car! How many people in Village have bank accounts? Only* the rich ones! Does this mean that I am going to be a rich one, too? I hope so!

He considers calling his brother to inform him of the new job, but he decides against it. *He'll just laugh and tell me how stupid I am.*

On Sunday morning, Kamiri gets into Hassan's sleek, red sports car.

"So how much football have you played, Kamiri?"

"Not very much. We usually play just an hour or two every day."

Hassan glances in surprise at his companion. "Every day?"

"Yes. When the cattle have been brought home and before it gets dark."

They arrive at an open area with several football pitches, their limits marked by the white posts of the goals.

"We have the pitch over there. . ." Hassan points ahead to the right ". . . every Sunday morning. We'll do some training for a while, and when the other team and the referee arrive, you can watch."

Kamiri gives his companion a disappointed look. "I thought we were going to play."

Hassan shrugs defensively. "Well, we need to get to know you a little bit: know how you play. Maybe next Sunday you can get into a game."

They arrive at one end of the pitch. About a dozen young men are removing their jackets and putting on their boots, or are passing several green and white balls among themselves.

"Hey guys, this is Kamiri. He's going to try out with us."

There is a chorus of greetings. Some of the players come over and shake Kamiri's hand – including two young white men. Kamiri can't remember if he ever shook the hand of a white man previously. They are all wearing red and blue jerseys and blue shorts. Kamiri notices that Hassan has put on a pair of fluorescent orange boots. *I'll bet those were really expensive!*

"OK, guys, listen up!" a big man named Jacob announces, "The Buffalos team will be here in about an hour. Let's do some workouts."

The players begin assorted stretching, sprinting and keep-away exercises.

"Kamiri, why don't you come with me? You can warm up the goalkeeper by taking shots on goal."

At the edge of the penalty area, Jacob passes a ball to Kamiri, who scoops it up with his foot and examines it. *It's leather, a little lighter than our ball. But ours is old.*

He drops the ball to the ground, steps back two paces, and kicks the ball solidly with his left instep. The ball sails beyond the goal tender's reach into the top right corner. The goal tender retrieves the ball and rolls it out to Kamiri, who shoots it with his right foot into the top left corner.

"Hold on a minute!" Jacob holds up his hand. "Where did you learn to play football?"

"At home."

"OK. Would you try not to put the ball away? Just put it where the keeper has to work to get it, will you?"

"OK."

For ten minutes, Kamiri follows the keeper's instructions: "Hard ground ball – either side!" "Soft to the far left!" "Blast it right at me!" There is a loud smack as the ball, whistling in flight, strikes the keeper's gloves and rebounds away.

The keeper comes out of the goal mouth, holding the ball. "Where you from, Kamiri?"

"From Village west of here."

"So you learned to play football there?" Kamiri nods. "And what brought you to City?"

"Oh, I came to work here."

"What kind of work do you do, Kamiri?"

"I work in an abattoir – it's the one owned by Hassan's family."

"Is that a slaughterhouse?" Kamiri nods. The keeper smiles. "I think we're going to call you 'Killer'."

Achieving Superpersonhood:

Kamiri is introduced into one of the keep-away games, where he spends most of his time on the outer perimeter, passing the ball away from one of the charging players in the middle.

The keeper and Jacob are standing to one side, watching. "That kid, Kamiri, has a hell of an accurate shot off either foot," the keeper confides.

"His ball control and tackling are not bad either," Jacob says.

"You going to play him against the Buffalos?"

Jacob rubs the back of his neck. "I don't know yet. Apart from anything else, he hasn't got any kit."

The keeper shrugs. "He can use my regular kit."

"OK, but he doesn't have any boots."

"That kid doesn't need any boots!"

The Buffalos, in their yellow and green jerseys and green shorts, arrive and begin their warm-ups.

The referee, dressed in a white polo shirt and black shorts, blows his whistle, and after a brief conference, the play begins.

Kamiri stares in wonder at the colorful amateur game in front of him: in essence, so like the Village games, but so different: no bare chests or feet, no bare earth or indistinct boundaries, no self-appointed referee, no shouts of 'foul!'; instead there are a whistle and referee's hand signals, lush green grass and a net to catch the goals.

There is a shout from the yellow jerseys clustered at the far end of the pitch. The yellow jerseys are surrounding one of their players in a dancing hug.

"Shit!" a player on Kamiri's right announces.

"OK guys, let's get it back!" Jacob shouts.

Play resumes; the Eagles are more aggressive and determined, but five minutes later, there is another jubilant, hugging display by the yellow shirts. The keeper gives the ball a surly kick and shouts to Jacob: "Send in Killer."

A puzzled Jacob runs down the side line to confer with his keeper. When he returns, he inquires: "Where is the keeper's kit?"

"It's here, Coach."

Jacob rummages in a backpack, pulls out a blue and red jersey and blue shorts, and approaches Kamiri. "You want to go in?" he asks.

"Yes."

"Put this on then."

Kamiri, dressed in the blue and red of the Eagles and the trainers that Warari bought him, stands on the side line, awaiting instructions.

"OK, Kamiri. I want you to play left wing."

"Yes, Coach."

Kamiri is ready at midfield, watching the play in the Eagles' half. There is a shot on goal which the keeper blocks. He waves in Kamiri's direction and punts the ball. The ball, on its trajectory, and a yellow jersey are converging on Kamiri, who traps the ball with a thump under his right foot. The opponent is on him at once, trying to wrest control of the ball. Tapping the ball with his heel and spinning away from the yellow shirt simultaneously, Kamiri is suddenly free, and he is flying down the left side line, easily outrunning the frustrated defender. Two backs are intent on intercepting him as he approaches the penalty area. He glances to his right: there are two blue shirts there, and he slices the ball with his left foot. The ball in flight, the two strikers, and the Buffalos' keeper intersect. The ball flies off the head of the nearside striker and sails into the net. It is the Eagles' turn to engage in celebratory hugs, and Kamiri finds himself near the center of the pack.

Looking for more action, Kamiri has strayed into the center of the field when one of the Eagles' backs spots him and passes the ball. In evading the defenders, he finds himself on the right-hand side of the field with only one Buffalo defender ahead of him. Racing ahead, he is tackled but manages to shake off the opponent. There is only the goal tender, crouched and ready to spring, ahead. He feints to his left, taps the ball forward and drives it into the top right corner as the keeper falls away to the left.

Achieving Superpersonhood:

Embraced by a screaming flock of Eagles, Kamiri can scarcely believe his good fortune. Suddenly, he is aware that it is Hassan who is gripping him around the neck and shouting incoherently.

During half-time, Jacob lectures the Eagles about strategy. "We've got to tighten up on defense, guys! Let's go with the first team, but I want to see Kamiri at left midfield."

"Why don't you leave him where he is, Coach? He's doing great," someone objects.

"I said I want to try him at left midfield." He pauses. "Kamiri, I want you to mark their right wing. You know what I mean?"

"No, sir."

"It means that I want you to stay on top of him when he's in our territory. Keep harassing him; don't let him do anything with the ball. OK?"

"Yes, sir."

The whistle blows and the second half commences, with play surging back and forth between the opposing goal areas. But the score remains two all.

"Five minutes to play, guys. Let's do it," Jacob shouts from the sidelines.

The Eagles have the Buffalos tied down in front of their goal, their keeper frantically sidestepping from side to side as the play shifts. The ball is ejected weakly by a defender. Kamiri captures it and looks for an open Eagle: there is none. Warily, he dribbles the ball forward until suddenly a striker is clear. Kamiri's crisp pass reaches the striker; he races past a defender, and the ball, tapped forward by the striker, is under his feet. In a split second, Kamiri takes in the keeper's position and strikes the ball with his right instep. The ball curls gently across the goal line, hugging the right post. The keeper is stretched out, reaching for the left post.

There is a cheer of exultation as blue and red shirts envelop the goal scorer.

The ball is placed on the midfield line, and play is resumed with two minutes to play.

I, the Other, interrupt at this point, because this is exactly my kind of situation: where time is running out, and one team thinks they have the game in the bag. They tend to relax, don't they? They don't have to score any more goals. Just run the clock down! The other team, however, is high on revenge adrenalin, often inspired by the anger and cold frustration I stir up.

There is a misdirected pass on the right from an Eagle back to the right midfielder. A Buffalo striker intercepts it, pushes it forward to the edge of the penalty area, and blasts it out of reach of the keeper, into the net.

The game ends in a three-all tie.

"That's OK, guys. You played very well!" Jacob announces.

The team is milling around their bags, changing shirts or swilling water. Kamiri changes into his own clothes, and apologizes to the keeper for the damp condition of his borrowed shirt. "That's OK, Killer, we'll get you some kit."

Jacob approaches. "Kamiri, can you join us next Sunday – same time, same place?"

"Yes, sir."

"Just call me 'Coach', will you? Now, I want to tell you: you played very well. Only thing is: you were out of your position a little too much. You know what I mean?"

"Yes, Coach. I've seen on television how they play four – four – two or four – three – three, but I haven't done any of that."

"What have you done, Kamiri?"

"We just play football, Coach."

"Killer, you coming to have a beer?" Hassan calls. Uncertainly, the fledgling Eagle walks over to Hassan. "This guy is brilliant, isn't he?" His arm is wrapped around Kamiri's shoulder.

"Great game, Killer! Let's go get a drink!" someone shouts.

At the far end of the open area, there is a modest, wood-frame clubhouse serving ice cream, hot dogs and beer. The Eagles descend upon it, usurping nearly every seat at the weathered picnic tables. Kamiri finds himself seated between Hassan and the keeper, Sammy. A bottle of beer is placed in front of him. Thirsty, he takes a swig and nods his satisfaction: "This is a lot better than a *stoney*."

Sammy shakes his head. "Dog piss is better than a *stoney*, man!"

For two more beers, Kamiri responds to questions about his life prior to City, but he also enquires about Sammy, who turns out to be a carpenter, with a wife and two children.

"Time to settle up, guys!" somebody shouts. "The tab comes to a hundred and twenty-five shillings a head."

Kamiri reaches into his pocket and retrieves a battered hundred-shilling note.

Hassan shakes his head. "Put that away, Kamiri!"

"But I have to pay something."

"Anybody who scores two goals gets free drinks. That's a new rule from today," Sammy announces.

Inside, the restaurant is smoky with grilled meat. Tables and chairs are red plastic; there are ancient, scruffy animals' heads on the paneled walls.

A waitress approaches. "You want a beer, Kamiri?"

Kamiri runs a finger down the menu. "No, I think I'll just have some water."

Hassan turns to the waitress. "We'll have a large Dreadnought beer and a bottle of mineral water. You want a steak and chips, Kamiri?"

I, the Other, whisper to Kamiri: "Steaks are only for rich kids; poor boys have burgers!"

"No, I'd just like a burger and some chips, please."

"OK. You can bring us the five-hundred-gram T-bone, and the half pound burger, both medium rare, chips and salads."

Hassan leans back and contemplates his new friend. "Sammy says we're going to call you 'Killer' because you work in the slaughterhouse."

"I start work tomorrow." Seeking a change in topic, Kamiri asks, "You're studying at City University?" Kamiri asks

"Yes, I'm studying sociology, mostly."

"Sorry, but I don't know what sociology is."

"It's the study of the way human beings behave."

Kamiri nods. "So does that mean you'll become a sociologist?" He pronounces the word awkwardly.

Hassan smiles. "I don't think so. I'm not sure what I want to do."

"You'll probably be my boss – I mean, my way-up-high boss."

There is a chuckle from Hassan. "Why do you say that?"

"Because I work in your father's slaughterhouse, and you'll probably be working for your father, right?"

Hassan shakes his head. "I doubt if I'll be working for my father."

"I decided not to work for my father."

"So you ended up working in a slaughterhouse."

The waitress returns with their plates, and the conversation turns to football.

"Those orange boots you have, Hassan—I'll bet they're really good."

"Yeah, they're top-of-the-line Nikes." Hassan goes on to explain the kinetic and brand psychology benefits of the Nikes.

"Oh, I see! Umm… How much do bottom-of-the-line boots cost, Hassan?"

"You don't have any boots?" Kamiri shakes his head. "Well, we'll get you a pair on the way back to your place after lunch."

At the huge JCS Sports shop, Hassan inquires, "What size do you wear, Kamiri?"

"I think I'm about a thirteen." He is mesmerized by the endless display of football boots in every imaginable color, with decorations from stripes to polka dots. The prices are shocking. There is one pair, which Kamiri is careful not to touch, with a price tag of two thousand five hundred shillings!

"How about these?" Hassan asks, holding up a bright green pair.

Kamiri consults the dangling price tag – twelve hundred shillings – and shakes his head.

"Why not, Kamiri? These are good boots."

"They're too expensive."

"So what? I'm going to buy them!"

"Hassan, you are my friend. I can't let you spend a lot of money on me until I can spend a little bit of money on you."

The older man stands open-mouthed, amazed for a few moments. Then he nods. "OK, Kamiri, you pick 'em out."

A black pair with blue slashes and a price tag of five hundred and ninety-five shillings captures Kamiri's attention. Size thirteen fits exactly.

"Thank you very much, Hassan."

Having dropped Kamiri at Home Away, Hassan considers his new football friend, and he wonders whether all village people are as ignorant and self-effacing, but polite and athletic as Kamiri. *Dorothy says their values are similar . . . maybe that's why they're so polite, and I wonder if he feels inferior to us City people.*

For his part, Kamiri is genuinely shocked by the wealthy young man's attitude toward money: *it's not like he throws money around to show off; he just knows it's OK to pour money on your friends.* He senses also a whiff of insecurity about Hassan. *Maybe he feels better when he's spending money.* And he is surprised that Hassan does not look down on him as a villager. *He actually hugged me during the game.*

Chapter 6

The Prison

"Your father is expecting you in his office at 6 pm." The text message is from his father's PA. *Oh shit!*

At five-fifty-five, Hassan exits the elevator on the thirty-third floor of the Republic Building. To his right is a frosted-glass partition, in the center of which is a blue glass door on which the black lettering, Arusei Industries, stands out. Hassan presses the silver button and looks up to the CCTV camera. The receptionist's voice says, "Come in, Hassan." He presses the door open and steps into the white carpeted, floor-to-ceiling glass reception area. The gray-haired, white receptionist at her desk gives him a nod, and he turns right, down the corridor to the corner office. Beatrice, his father's PA, looks up from her monitor. "He has someone with him at the moment, Hassan."

The wood-paneled door to his father's office is closed. He sits cautiously on the edge of an upholstered chair opposite Beatrice. A piano concerto is playing softly from somewhere behind her.

Without looking up from her work, she asks, "How are your studies at University going, Hassan?"

He takes in her stiffly coiffed hair, the milk chocolate complexion, and her glossy mouth. *She's rather pretty.* "It's going pretty well, thank you."

"I have a cousin who will be starting at the University next year."

"I see." He pauses. "How is my father?" He had intended to add 'today', but he lost his nerve.

She looks up at him for a moment and sighs audibly. "Very busy, as usual."

The office door opens and a man in a charcoal suit backs out, says something, nods, and strides off. Beatrice gets up from her desk and hurries into the office. Moments later, she appears carrying several files. "You can go in now, Hassan."

He takes a deep breath and pushes himself to his feet. His father does not look up from his reading. "Close the door."

Hassan gently closes the door and steps closer to his father's heavy bubinga wood desk. The older Arusei is wearing an immaculate white dress shirt with an open collar. His gold-rimmed glasses stand out from his dark skin and curly hair. As he looks up at the youth, there is a puffiness in his cheeks and nose, as if he had been a prize-fighter. "Sit down, Hassan."

There is absolute silence in the room. *Doesn't he ever listen to music?* Hassan sits on a carved wooden chair with an upholstered seat and gazes at the curtains behind the older man.

"I am disappointed and angry with you, Hassan." The young man is giving tiny nods, but his eyes still avoid contact. "What possessed you to protest a legal government action and to strike a policeman?" Hassan considers the question. "Well?"

"I did not think it was legal."

"What?" And then more forcefully: "Where did you get your law degree?"

Quietly, Hassan offers, "It should not be legal to close a free press which is only telling the truth."

The older Arusei leans forward to emphasize his measured, categorical speech. "I want you to listen to me, Hassan! We do not live in some chaotic utopia where there is freedom of everything! We live in an ordered and orderly country where it is necessary to abide by the decisions of our elected leaders. It is necessary because we do not wish to become a poverty-stricken, basket-case of a country. Nor do we want to become a restrictive Islamic paradise where there is no freedom! Do you understand me?"

"Yes, sir, I understand you, but why was it necessary to shut down the student newspaper? It was only telling the truth?"

The word 'truth' is like a missile striking Kaddour Arusei. He stares at Hassan for a long moment. "Truth? Truth?" he asks.

"Yes, sir, it is well known that elements of the current government are corrupt."

"Rumors! Rumors are not the same as truth!"

"Yes, sir, I agree, but in this case, the student newspaper was about to publish evidence of the truth."

"And that evidence would have destroyed the credibility of a government minister! Is that what you want: the destruction of the government?"

"We aren't anarchists, sir, but we believe the law should apply to everyone, and that truth in government is important."

Kaddour looks away for a long moment of reflection. "Hassan, you are nineteen years old . . ."

"Twenty, sir."

"Twenty. I would have thought that by now, you would have learned that the Arusei family did not achieve the enormous success it has by following the academic theories of ancient philosophers. We have achieved that success by finding the most efficient means of pleasing powerful people. This success has benefitted you, as well, has it not, Hassan?"

"Yes, sir."

"Now, then, Hassan. At this juncture, you have a choice. You can divorce yourself from the Arusei family, and follow the instructions of the ancient philosophers – only Allah knows where that will take you. Or you can become a loyal member of the Arusei family, doing things the Arusei Way, and benefitting accordingly. Which path do you choose, Hassan?"

Hassan takes a deep breath. "The Arusei Way, Father."

Kaddour nods. "Then behave accordingly."

Achieving Superpersonhood:

In his bed that night, Hassan reflects: *I know I made the selfish, coward's choice. But did I really have a choice? I think the choice I had was to continue as I am – but being more careful – or being homeless and destitute – a lot like Kamiri. I could never do that. Strangely, my father did not say that the Arusei Way is the Right Way. He even mentioned Allah. What would Allah think of the Arusei Way? In the big mosque my father is known to be a devout follower of Allah. Is it true? And is Allah a follower of my father? Or are they dead to each other?*

The courtroom is noisy and confusing with people moving about. There is the high, paneled bench backed by the judge's chair on a raised dais. Hassan sits in an enclosed area behind the lawyers' tables. Amid all the noise and people, he feels isolated, even in the company of three co-defendants whom he barely knows. *Allah, please don't send me to prison!* he repeats to himself, over and over, omitting, though he barely knows it, the first ayah of the Qur'an with which every good Muslim begin his prayers. *I don't think I can stand it, being in prison with all those tough criminals.*

Apart from the one meeting with his father, his encounters with his siblings and his mother have been brief, curt and condemnatory. "How could you get yourself in trouble like that?" his oldest brother demanded.

His father's lawyer told him that, if convicted, the judge could 'award' him up to five years in prison. Five years! "You can get time off for good behavior," he added, unhelpfully.

"You want to come across as a very peaceful, young man, who was swept up in the emotion of your fellow students, and would never have joined the protest on your own."

There was a rehearsal of answers to questions which the prosecutor might ask, including advice on the most numbing wording to use, and when to say, "I don't remember." The lawyer concluded the meeting by announcing: "I think we're going to plead 'guilty'." Hassan hadn't the courage to ask what the sentence might be for a guilty plea.

"All rise!" a man in a brown uniform announces. "Judge Solomon Kibiwott presiding!" There is a crack as the judge hammers something on his desk. A cluster of lawyers gathers around the judge's elevated bench. The discussion goes on for some time until the lawyers sit down again.

The man in the brown uniform begins calling out names. "Hassan Arusei, stand please!"

Hassan pushes himself to his feet; his knees are trembling and the palms of his hands are damp. His father's lawyer looks back over his shoulder at him. "Hassan Arusei, you are charged with assault on an officer of the law, namely, Officer Oduya, on the twenty-seventh of March in the current year. How do you plead?"

He glances at his father's lawyer, who gives a brief nod.

"Guilty," he chokes softly.

"You may be seated."

This process is repeated for three other students in the dock, at the end of which, all four are commanded to stand.

"I find (the judge reads aloud the names of the four) guilty as charged. Sentence will be passed in this court in two weeks' time. In the meantime, you will be remanded in custody of the City prison. Prosecutor, please begin your next case."

Hassan is hauled out of court with the three others and pushed into a white van. He looks out the rear window of the van as it comes to a stop. He sees heavy doors swinging shut.

Dressed in a gray jumpsuit with a long number front and back, Hassan is photographed and fingerprinted again. He is escorted down a long, dimly-lit corridor with black doors on either side. His escort unlocks a door, pushes it open and says, "You're in here." The door bangs closed, and the lock turns behind him.

Raising his eyes from the concrete floor, he sees that there are three other men in the cell. One is leaning against an upper-lower bunk, one is sitting on the bunk opposite, and the third – a Goliath of a man – occupies one of the chairs below the high, barred window. They are all older: forties and fifties, unshaven and clad in the same gray. For some time, they say nothing, appraising the new arrival. Hassan is frozen: a hare cornered by three wolves.

"What are you in for?" one of them demands.

"For assault."

"What kind of assault?"

"I was wrestling with a policeman." This response draws loud guffaws from all three.

"Wrestling with a pig, hunh? What was you doin'? Tryin' it on with some bimbo or tryin' to nick some old crone's valuables?"

"I was trying to stop them from shutting down the University's newspaper."

There is a long, drawn-out "Oohhh..." from of the prisoners. "So you're one of them intellectual types what believes in freedom of speech! Well, by the time they let your dumb ass out of here, you won't believe in it no more!"

Hassan says nothing. There is oppressive quiet in the cell.

"Ain't cha gonna' ask what we're in for?" the standing prisoner demands.

"Yes. Well . . ." Hassan begins haltingly, "What are you in for?"

The standing prisoner, Charlie, announces, "I knocked over a liquor store. Could have got away, except the dumb ass behind the counter pressed the alarm button and all hell broke loose. Gave him a good slash across the face." He pauses and turns toward the prisoner in the chair. "Tabiz here has a fondness for the ladies, and he found one he liked on her way home one night. Trouble is, she picked him out to a line-up and there was a DNA match. And Angel, here – that ain't his real name, by the way – he came into the Country with a little too much heroin – a couple of kilos to be exact – in his suitcase."

Oh, Allah, I wish I were somewhere else! Clearly, that isn't possible. *Can I get them to focus on something else?* But there is nothing else of interest to the three prisoners; no view of the fields, no newspaper, nothing to eat. Hassan feels he has been stripped naked before a crowd of laughing thousands.

"What's your name, boy?" Angel demands.

"Hassan . . . Hassan Arusei."

Charlie leans forward with interest. "Arusei . . . Arusei. You're a rich kid! How come your daddy lets you rot in here?" He turns to the other two prisoners. "Mr Arusei owns half of Country!"

"No! No! I'm not from that part of the family. We're kind of poor relations. Sort of distant cousins."

"What's your father's name?" Angel insists.

"My father's dead!"

"And your brothers?"

"I don't have any brothers."

I, the Other, always tell my friends: if you have to lie, avoid saying something that can be easily checked, try to be as vague as possible, and be brazen!

He says, "If you have to lie . . ." as if lying is a normal activity! One may be <u>tempted</u> to lie, but there is almost never a <u>necessity</u> to lie.

Tabiz shifts with interest in his chair. "You say your name's Hassan?" The young man nods. "That's a Muslim name ain't it?"

"Yes, but we're kind of secular Muslims."

"What do you mean 'kind of secular Muslims'? You pray five times a day?"

"Not usually that often."

"That's not very good, is it, Tabiz?" Charlie says. "Tabiz here is a good Muslim. Ain't that so Tabiz?" Tabiz nods.

Angel says, "I think we can correct that situation. Tabiz, you can teach the boy to pray properly, right?"

"Yeah." Tabiz reaches under one of the bunks and drags out a red and yellow prayer rug. "Mecca is that way." He points diagonally across the cell. "First we start with Wudu. We wash our hands and face thoroughly and we wipe our feet. We begin standing by silently expressing the intention in our heart to be close to Allah. Next we say the first sura of the Qur'an. You know it, don't you?"

"I'm not sure."

"Well, repeat after me."

Haltingly, Hassan repeats. The words are familiar, and when he is in the mosque, they come into his mind and on his tongue, prompted by the clear words of the men around him, but under duress, and confronted by three experienced criminals, his mind is a vacuum. When he is at prayers in the mosque, the meanings of the Qur'anic words are never for consideration, but now, having to memorize the words, an understanding of them begins to take hold.

"You've got to memorize it. Then we say: 'He is God the One, God the eternal. He begot no one, nor was he begotten. No one is comparable to him.' At this point we kneel, we bend over so that our heads touch the floor. We say: 'Glory be to my Lord, the most High.' Then, we can offer our personal prayers to Allah. For example, you might say, 'Allah, I pray that you will forgive the sin for which I am imprisoned'."

Hassan repeats: "Allah, I pray that you will forgive the sin for which I am imprisoned."

Tabiz instructs: "Allah, I pray that Tabiz will keep me safe while I'm in prison."

For a moment, Hassan hesitates, then: "Allah, I pray that Tabiz will keep me safe while I'm in prison."

"Then," Tabiz continues, "We sit back on our heels, and usually we say to Allah that there is none worthy of worship but Him and that Muhammad is His Messenger. Finally, in this sitting position we look right and left and say to the people next to us: 'Peace be upon you and the mercy of Allah.' We repeat all of this two or three times five times a day."

Hassan rises from the floor, and he feels much better about himself: not quite so naked. He nods to Tabiz and says, "Thank you."

Tabiz extends his right hand. "Peace, brother."

Perhaps what Hassan feels is the acceptance of Tabiz, and, by extension, the acceptance of the other two prisoners, who have been watching silently. Or perhaps he feels that in approaching God he has cleansed himself and become less of an outcast.

I, the Other, think this cleansing business is unnecessary. I find all these phrases in Muslim prayers about 'the Almighty', 'Most Gracious', 'Most Merciful', 'Master of the Day of Judgment', etc. very boring. And they repeat all this repetition over ten times a day! Give it a rest! Why not keep it simple? I mean, if you're so inclined, you could say, 'I'm a pretty good guy. Thanks for your help. Keep it coming! You're my friend.'

The Other objects to certain phrases used in Muslim prayers. What is the harm in these phrases? It seems to me that the Other is jealous because these phrases do not apply to him! And as to repetition, it isn't the iteration of the phrase that is important; rather, it is the effect it has on the supplicant's heart.

Hassan is given the empty top bunk in the cell. Tabiz has demanded and received a threadbare, counterfeit prayer rug for him. Five times a day the prayer rugs are in use and Hassan is learning the prayers without prompting. Conversation with Charlie and Angel is sporadic, but frequent and relevant with Tabiz.

The prisoners are permitted an hour of 'recreation' in the 'yard', a dusty, square patch of ground enclosed within the four walls. Hassan walks beside Tabiz, and he learns that his mentor is from a city on the eastern seacoast, that he worked in construction, that he was married, and, in fact, at one time had three wives. He attributes his arrest to "a moment of madness for which Allah has forgiven me."

Achieving Superpersonhood:

Ten days have elapsed since Hassan's imprisonment. During a walk around the yard, Tabiz says, "You're like a changed man since you've been in prison. You know that, Hassan?"

"I've learned a lot and I thank you, Tabiz."

"When you first came here, you were a scared little rabbit. Now you're standing tall with a strong faith in Allah."

"Maybe so," Hassan concedes.

"And, if you want to keep standing tall, brother, you must pray hard, listen to the voice of Allah and do as He says."

He must be right, because I feel that Tabiz has been like an 'educator' to me: helping me to overcome my wayward self.

One evening, as he is pushing his tray through the chow line, the man in front of him says, "Hey, Hassan." As he looks at the man, he notices that Tabiz has gone ahead to find places at a table. The man stands close to him and whispers, "Be careful, Hassan, Tabiz isn't what he seems to be." And before Hassan can say anything, the man has gone.

The cell door is unlocked and a guard hands Hassan his backpack. "Here are your clothes. Get dressed. You're going to court." As Hassan is getting dressed, Tabiz reminds him again about standing tall with a strong faith in Allah, and adds, "Go to the Ibrahimi Mosque and speak to the imam there. Tell him that Tabiz sent you. He will take good care of you, brother!" Hassan is wrapped in a python's embrace.

In a court anteroom, his father's lawyer informs Hassan, "I think everything is going to be all right."

"What do I have to say?"

"Nothing. I'm going to tell the judge that you're a good boy and he ought to let you off."

Oh! Allah, let it be true!

In the courtroom, when Hassan's name is called, the lawyer stands and delivers an address which makes Hassan out to be a model student, a dutiful son, of excellent character, highly regarded by his imam, etc., etc. He concludes by telling the judge, "He is very sorry for the mistake he made, and he apologizes unreservedly to Officer Oduya."

Hassan is ordered to stand. The judge consults his notes and announces, "Hassan Arusei, I sentence you to two years in the City Penitentiary. Sentence to be suspended for two years pending good behavior and on the recommendation of your attorney."

Back in the anteroom, Hassan thanks his father's lawyer.

"Your father is the one you should thank, young Arusei. It cost him a sizeable amount of money, of which Officer Oduya got his fair share."

* * *

As Dorothy's arm heals, her thoughts are focused on the state of Country. *How can we profess to be a democracy when the very people we elect stifle our dissent? We must protest more loudly and take action!* She begins to search the Internet for organizations which oppose the government (apart from the opposition political parties, which she regards as ineffective and un-principled).

After dinner, Dorothy approaches her father. "Papa, I've been thinking that I should join a protest group."

Joseph sets the newspaper aside. "Is that because the government has closed the student newspaper?"

"Closing the newspaper is only the most recent travesty. Before that, there was the Defense Minister taking a big bribe for the helicopters, and the ballot box stuffing in the last by-election. You have to admit that this government is bent on exerting controls which fill their pockets and ensure that they remain in power."

Joseph's first inclination is to debate the veracity of his daughter's charges, but an insight suggests that contention is fruitless, and does nothing for Dorothy's development. Mildly, he asks, "So, you are thinking of joining an opposition party?"

"I might, if there is one which truly adheres to its principles."

"Then I think you may be left with half a dozen gimlet-eyed protest groups, each with its own agenda, from Trotskyites to Fascists."

Dorothy insists, "I think there must be some middle ground."

Joseph pats the adjacent sofa seat in invitation. "A wise political leader – I don't remember whether it was Mandela or Gandhi – said that the most effective, lasting change happens from within. What he meant was that rather than throwing stones at the police, it is better to win the respect of those in power by the force of your argument."

Petulantly, Dorothy remains standing. "I didn't throw any stones at the police."

Joseph shrugs. "Well, but you were part of a crowd that did. Do you understand what I'm saying, Dorothy? It is much more effective to be inside the system, arguing sensibly for change than to be outside the system demanding change."

"But how can I get inside?" She takes the seat at the other end of the sofa.

"Why don't you offer to be an intern for a member of parliament? In that position, you can learn how change actually happens in politics, and you may even get a chance to make policy suggestions."

"But how can I go to University, work at Home Away and be a political intern?"

"I think that Home Away can struggle along without you for a while. Besides, you've said you're interested in a career in politics. What better way to find out if it suits you than by watching it in action? Maybe even participating. . ." He grins. "Part of self-overcoming."

Dorothy begins by calling the offices of the most important parliamentarians: the Prime Minister, and ministers of the interior, justice, business, but overlooking the Minister of Defense with premeditated care. She is advised to send in her CV. Rather than rely on an old version, she updates it to reflect her work at Home Away, her involvement in the Political Union, the Debating Society, and the University women's tennis team. She emails them to the various offices, and waits with eager anticipation. Nothing. Not even a 'Sorry, we don't have an opening.' Being ignored only stokes her anger. *Probably, I've got to change my strategy. I guess the big cheeses have more than enough help. But how about the newly-elected members? And how about opposition members? I doubt that they have all the resources they need.*

Carefully she selects three new, opposition MPs whose websites and liberal views appeal to her. She emails each of the MPs directly. *There's no point in going through a jealous staff.*

The next day, she receives an email from a member of the Green Party: "Can you phone my PA, Hasina, and make an appointment to come in for an interview? With kind regards, Abdallah Ndungu, Member of Parliament, Green Party."

On arrival at the new parliamentary office building, Dorothy is informed that opposition MPs are still housed in the old building, across the street. "But isn't the old building going to be torn down?" she asks.

"Not just yet, miss. We don't have enough space in this building for all the MPs."

Then she remembers the two-year-old controversy about the various changes to the Constitution, including the addition of thirty MPs. This change was presented as necessary to serve Country's growing population, but careful gerrymandering by the United Country Party meant that the UCP's grip on power is likely to tighten. The relegation of the opposition MPs to the old building, without air conditioning and, reportedly, with a leaking roof further inflames Dorothy's conviction that government reform is essential.

Achieving Superpersonhood:

The Old Parliamentary Office Building is a brick and gargoyles structure dating back to colonial days. Its original parquet flooring is scarred and creaks to the step; the walls are off-white without decoration; and the doors have brass plates into which an engraved Bakelite nameplate can be inserted.

The Honorable Abdallah Ndungu's door does not have an engraved nameplate. Instead, it has what appears to be a piece of shirt cardboard on which his name and district have been written. Dorothy enters what seems to be an outer office with three metal desks occupied by two women, several four-tier filing cabinets topped by a dusty arrangement of plastic flowers and a poster portrait of the President on one wall.

"I am here for an interview with Mr Ndungu," Dorothy announces.

The older of the two women, hair done in an enormous flowered kerchief, gets up heavily from her desk. "Yes, dear, I am Mrs Ndungu, please come in." She gestures toward an open doorway behind her and calls: "Abdallah, your appointment is here."

Dorothy passes through the doorway and finds a smallish, handsome man with a sprinkling of gray hair rising from his desk. Behind him is the Country flag on a stand and another yellow and green flag. *Probably the Green Party flag.*

"You must be Dorothy. I am very pleased to meet you!" he declares, and flings himself into a monologue about the 'brilliant' contents of her CV, pausing only to ask about her interest in working there. Dorothy, amazed at his ability to remember details such as her current captaincy of the women's tennis team, and string them all together in an improvised speech, is forced to clarify that her interest is in a part-time, unpaid internship.

Ndungu expresses some relief that she is not seeking a paid position, because "funding for the staff of new MPs has not been released yet."

Rubbing his hands, he launches into a catalogue of help his office needs: dealing with queries and complaints from constituents, getting their issues resolved by various government departments, dealing with the media, liaison with Green Party head office, completing research projects on current issues before Parliament, and generally keeping the office tidy.

"That sounds very interesting, Abdallah, but what would I be doing that your wife and the other lady are not already doing?"

"Dorothy, since you'll be making a gift of your time, I think you should choose where you want to work."

"OK. I'd like to be assigned some of the constituent work and some of the research projects."

"Done! When can you start?"

"Next Tuesday at 2:30?"

On her way home, Dorothy is worried that she made a hasty decision to sign on with Abdullah immediately. *Maybe I should have asked more questions, or put him on hold until I see what response I get from the others. But I kind of liked him – in spite of his talking too much. I think he'd be a good person to work for.* She recalls the personal description on Ndungu's website: the youngest of six children from a farming village in the west; obtained a high school certificate while serving in the army; admitted to law school in Cape Town; joined a government-funded, small practice specializing in defense of indigents in criminal cases. He became a member of the Green Party, volunteering during election campaigns, because of his concerns about global warming. Selected as a Green Party candidate for Parliament, and won with a margin of ninety-six votes out of more than nineteen thousand votes cast. *He was obviously an underdog who pulled it off, and an idealist – global warming and defense of indigents – definitely my kind of person!*

On Tuesday, Dorothy learns that the other woman, Hasina, a single woman, with two children, worked on Abdallah's campaign with the hope of obtaining a job in his office. She tells Dorothy: "We worked hard, he got elected, I got the job, but no money!"

Mrs Ndungu, whose given name is Bahadia (but she likes to be called 'Baha') says: "Don't fret, Hasina. We're going to put you in for back pay."

After showing Dorothy her desk, PC and phone ("We didn't have to buy anything! That crooked old bugger that Abdallah turfed out left everything"), Baha calls an "organization meeting."

"Now, then. I suggest that Hasina and I will answer the phones, because we may know the person who is calling, or what he's calling about. We'll turn constituent calls over to Dorothy to handle and follow up. Now, Dorothy, if someone wants to see Abdallah, would you please refer him to me, because I keep his diary. And if you want to know who to call about a problem raised by the caller, you can ask me. Hasina has organized a database on the PC where we can put in everything we need to know about a constituent who calls: his contact details, his issues, how it was resolved or not, the dates and there is a follow-up system." She paused to take a breath.

Dorothy nods. "What kind of research will I be doing?"

"Well, that depends on what's going on in Parliament, and especially on any issues which come before the Parliamentary Committee on the Environment. Abdallah's just been appointed to the PEC – he's the junior member."

Dorothy nods. "May I ask about the remit of the PEC?"

"The PEC looks out for all our natural resources: land, water, air, beaches, mountains, forests, rivers, and so on. It deals with legislation that involves the Department of the Environment. Now, problems come in when another department wants to do something that it shouldn't be doing. Like Agriculture and Fisheries wants to turn government land over to a company that wants to plant these horrible palm oil plantations, or Business wants to grant some big foreign company the right to mine bauxite next to a wildlife reserve."

"I imagine there's a lot of controversy in cases like that."

Baha gives a snort. "Controversy is a polite way of describing a dicks-out pissing contest, if you'll excuse my language." Dorothy smiles in acknowledgement. "So we'd best leave it to Abdallah to decide when he needs your help with research."

Chapter 7

Immam Arusei

Kamiri has completed his first week of work at the abattoir. He is dressed in the uniform provided: white, knee-length coat, white cotton trousers, yellow rubber boots, and a round white sailor's cap. A fresh uniform is provided every other morning. He has been assigned to work with Koinet (the tall one), a young Masai who is nearly two meters in height. They are working at the sorting tables, removing the sellable organs from cattle entrails and placing them in gray plastic bins. They are speaking Swahili since their respective tribal languages do not always share the same words.

"Do you have a girlfriend, Kamiri?"

Kamiri places a liver in the appropriate bin. He shakes his head. "No, there were some girls back in my Village who were pretty, but they thought they were Ngai's gift to men, so I let them carry on pretending."

"OK, but how about a girl to have fun with – out in the bush?"

"Yeah, there were a couple of them. Trouble is they get kind of clingy after a while."

Koinet sweeps the remainder of the offal into the disposal bin. "I know what you mean. There is this one girl I'd ask to meet me outside the cattle corral after dark. She's very pretty but not stuck up, and she'd always tell me 'no'. But I kept askin' her until she said 'maybe', and I asked her 'maybe what?' and she said 'who are you goin' to tell about it?' and I said 'no one' then she said 'do you promise?' and I said 'on my mother's life'. And that night we met outside the corral."

Kamiri looks ruefully at his friend. "I wish I had a girl like that. Can you go to see her on weekends?"

"No, it's too far."

The two of them roll the disposal bin out the back door. "Do you have any family nearby that you can visit on weekends, Kamiri?"

"I have a brother here in the City, but we're not on good terms."

"Why not?"

"He's selling drugs."

"Did you ever work for him?"

"Yeah, it wasn't much fun."

"You think this is fun?"

"It's all right for now. This is a decent place, and we have a chance to get a better job. Besides when I worked for my brother, I had to sit around in bars and discos all the time."

Koinet helps Kamiri tip the disposal bin into the screw conveyor which feeds the digester. He asks, "Does your brother know you're working here?"

"No."

"How come?"

"I think he'll just laugh at me."

"So what if he does? You're the one who's got a legitimate job. Sooner or later, he's going to get in trouble. Maybe he could get a job here."

"Koinet, you don't know my brother. He's lazy, and he always wants to take shortcuts. He even laughed when I told him I was at Home Away."

"Kamiri, it seems to me, that you owe it to your brother and to your family to try to set your brother . . . what's his name?"

"Warari."

"To set Warari right. You're a smart guy and you're going to go places. Warari must know that, and he may be an older brother, but I think he may listen to you. Besides, Kamiri, you don't know how he's doing. He may be ready to get out of drugs and a little push from you would do it."

"I doubt it."

"OK. You doubt it, but what does it cost you to try? Besides, what would your father say if he knew his older son was in prison and his younger son did nothing to try to stop it?"

"That's a point."

Kamiri calls his brother; the call goes straight to voice mail. "Hi, Warari, it's Kamiri. I thought you'd want to know: I have a job now. Call me back so I can see you this weekend to tell you about it."

It is nearly ten that evening when Kamiri's phone rings. "So, what are you doin', Kamiri?"

"I'll tell you when I see you. Can I stop by your place at about four o'clock on Saturday afternoon?" There is a pause while Warari apparently considers. "If not four o'clock, any time on Saturday."

"No, four o'clock Saturday is fine."

Warari's place had impressed Kamiri when first he saw it. But now, when compared with Home Away and the domicile at the abattoir, it seems poor and shabby. *Maybe that's what he likes.*

The door is locked. Kamiri calls. Voice mail. He leaves a message and decides to wait for an hour. No Warari. *Damn him! Is he ever going to change?*

He takes the bus back to the abattoir, getting there in time for a beef stew dinner and several games of table football with Koinet.

"I think it's strange your brother stood you up and didn't call you."

Kamiri gives an angry shrug. "It's not strange at all."

"I think you ought to invite him to come here some evening," and trying to override Kamiri's shake of the head, Koinet adds,

"Hey, if he's going to keep you waiting, he might as well do it while you're here. Besides, you say he's got a motorcycle: it's no problem for him to get here."

"That's a point."

When Warari finally does call later that evening, Kamiri decides not to tell him on the phone about his job. Instead, he says, "You can meet me where I'm working." He gives Warari directions, ending with, "Follow the dirt track to the end and then call me. I'll come out to meet you."

Warari is sitting on his motorbike, frowning, when Kamiri comes out to collect him. "What is this?" he asks. "You workin' on some kind of a farm?"

"No, it's a slaughterhouse."

Warari's mouth gapes open as he stares at his brother, then at the building and the livestock pens. "I can smell the cow shit. How can you work in a place like this?"

"I don't just work here, I live here. Have a look." Slowly, Warari dismounts and locks the bike. "You don't need to lock it; nobody's going to steal it."

As they follow the path around the building to the residence, Warari says with a gesture, "So you work in there, killing cows, taking their guts out, skinning them and cutting them up?"

"Exactly what we did in Village."

"Yeah, but not ten hours a day, six days a week. What the hell do they pay you?"

"Five hundred shillings a week."

"You are some kind of stupid, brother! You used to make three times that much in a _day_ working for me!"

Kamiri opens the door to the residence and faces Warari. "No! I was lucky to get four hundred from you, and this job has some important benefits: I get room and board and training for a better position. But the main advantage is that the police don't bother you, and nobody's going to turn you in."

Warari runs his hand along the back of a couch and pauses to take in the La Liga game on the big TV screen. "Is that game on a DVD?"

"No, it's a live game."

"So it's satellite TV?"

"Yes, we have two screens."

"You allowed to have women here?"

"No. There are no women working here. The guys visit their wives and girlfriends on weekends."

"Well, that sucks."

"Warari, this is a slaughterhouse, not a whorehouse. Do you want a tea or coffee?"

"Do you have any beer?"

"No. There's orange or lime soda."

Warari shakes his head and sits down on the couch to watch the game. Koinet wanders over to sit at the far end of the couch. Kamiri introduces them.

"So, are you Masai?" Warari inquires.

"Yeah. What do you do in City, Warari?"

"Oh, I do various jobs, but it's goin' pretty good. Did you notice my new bike, Kamiri?"

"No, what is it?"

"It's a Kawasaki three fifty, set me back a chunk of change, but it's got the power I need."

Kamiri eyes his brother. *I suppose he means 'the power I need to get away from the cops.'* "And did I tell you I'm gettin' a new place – much bigger and better?"

"No, you didn't tell me that."

"Well, your old position is still open, Kamiri, and I figure you're due for a big salary increase."

Koinet asks, "What was his old position?"

"You interested?"

"I don't know."

"Well, it's like a pharmaceutical business, but now we're carrying some new lines."

"I'll talk it over with Kamiri and let you know."

"You do that."

There is a roar from the TV as Barcelona scores a goal, and for the next half hour, the conversation turns to football. When the final whistle blows, Warari, who has been fidgeting, stands up. "Well, I gotta get back to business. Let me know about my offer, will you?" Koinet nods.

Kamiri leads the way to the door. "I'll see you out, Warari."

As he unlocks the bike, Warari says, "With this new product I'm handling, I figure I can guarantee you five grand a week, Kamiri. Think about it."

"What's the new product?"

"Horse." (heroin)

"How do you sell it?"

"I don't sell any of it direct. It's all about building up a distribution network."

"I'll think about it."

Warari mounts the bike. It starts with a growl and goes hurtling down the dirt track, raising a cloud of dust.

Koinet shakes his head on hearing of Warari's new business. "Man, that is really risky." He is staring at the floor in silent concentration. "Is your brother always like that? I mean, does he always seem kind of edgy, not relaxed?"

"Yeah, he was in a bit of a hurry tonight. I don't know. Maybe he's got some deliveries to make."

"Including one for himself?"

Kamiri stares at his friend. "You think he's taking drugs?"

"I don't know, Kamiri, but I've heard that addicts get very up-tight between fixes. He didn't seem very brotherly or relaxed at all."

On Saturday morning, Kamiri and Koinet are loading solid waste from the recycling system onto a disposal truck. Koinet is maneuvering the Kaian mini front-end loader while Kamiri shovels the residue into the loader bucket.

"What are you doing tomorrow afternoon, Kamiri?"
"I'm going to play football. The Eagles have a game at one."
"Mind if I come along with you?"
"Of course not. Maybe you can get a chance to play."
Koinet dumps the bucket into the truck, and turns the Kaian back around. "I'm not any good; my legs tend to get tangled up, but I'd like watching the game."

They walk to the residence. "Tomorrow, if you're thirsty, maybe Hassan will buy us a beer after the game," Kamiri suggests.
"Who is Hassan?"
"The owner's son."
"The owner of the Eagles?"
"No, the owner of this." Kamiri makes a sweeping gesture. "The Eagles are just an amateur team."
Koinet, open-mouthed in amazement, stops Kamiri in mid-step. "You play football with Mr Arusei's son?"
"Yeah. He's a pretty nice guy. He's not cocky at all. I think he may have some family problems."

Koinet is introduced to some of the Eagles players at the pitch.
"You work with Kamiri?" Hassan asks. Koinet nods, and Hassan lifts his hands in wonder. "Every time I have a steak, I think of Kamiri!"
Koinet stands on the sidelines with the Eagles substitutes, watching the game unfold. A cheer bursts from the Eagles bench when they score: Kamiri twice, directly, and he contributes the assisting pass in two other instances. The game ends in a five – one rout for the Eagles.
Koinet notices that for most of the game, the coach has been standing next to an older man who is wearing a suit and tie. The two men point things out to one another during the game. *Strange that a man should come by himself to watch an amateur game in a suit and tie!* He decides to get closer to listen in.

Maybe the older man is the coach's father. He is able to overhear fragments of conversation.

". . . third game with us . . ."

". . . no formal training? . . ."

". . . works in an abattoir . . ."

". . . great left foot! . . ."

". . . we need a good left wing . . ."

The man in the suit departs as the final whistle blows. Kamiri and Hassan are gathering their street clothing when Jacob pulls Kamiri to one side. "Have you ever thought of playing professional football, Kamiri?"

"No, I haven't, Coach."

"Would you be interested in being a professional if you had a chance?"

Kamiri hugs his trainers, jeans and T-shirt to his chest and studies Jacob's face in search of understanding. "Well, I don't know. . . . maybe yes."

"That fellow I was talking to during the game is the scout for the Coast City Lions. They're interested in you."

"OK."

"I'll give you his phone number, and you should call him. OK?" Jacob removes a phone from his pocket. "Got your phone, Kamiri? I'll give you his number."

Kamiri puts his trainers on the ground and searches in his jeans. Extracting his phone, he nods to Jacob, and looks at the little screen. The name 'Hamidi Oduya' appears with a telephone number. "Thank you, Coach!"

As they walk toward Hassan's car, Koinet asks, "What was that about, Kamiri?"

Kamiri looks away. "Nothing much."

But Kamiri's friends will not permit him to escape confession during a beef and burger lunch for which an ashamed Hassan reveals he cannot pay. Koinet, eager to hear Kamiri's disclosure, slaps his thin wallet on the table and announces, "I'm good for it. Tell us, Kamiri!"

Kamiri relents. "You know that guy who was talking to Coach during the game? He's a scout for the Coast City Lions." He looks away. "...but I'm not sure..."

"What's not to be sure about?" Koinet demands. "You'll get buckets full of money, and you can have your choice of the girls. How much do you figure he'd get, Hassan?"

Hassan pulls himself back into the present. "Oh, I don't know. The Lions are a second division team so he wouldn't be getting the big money."

Koinet, refusing to be put off, leans forward. "What do you figure, Hassan? Maybe a hundred thousand a week?"

This optimistic assessment deteriorates under discussion, but Koinet evades discouragement. "Let's say they offered him five thousand a week. That's still ten times what he's making now!"

Their burgers arrive. Hassan has recovered some of his spirits; he removes the top of his bun and eyes the burger suspiciously. "How can I tell," he asks, with a faint smile, "whether you guys did this one?"

Koinet mimics Hassan's movements; he tests the burger with a fork. "Oh, yeah, I recognize this one! Kamiri, do you remember that brown and white cow we did on Thursday?"

Hassan slouches back in his chair. "Oh, please! I'm losing my appetite!"

Over coffee, they lapse into silence. Hassan is slouched in his seat, gazing at the table top.

Kamiri recognizes Hassan's mood of melancholia. *Something's bothering him . . . couldn't be football.* "You played fine, Hassan, what's eating you?"

"Oh, I just feel bad that I wasn't able to be a proper host."

Kamiri shrugs. "It's about time you let someone else pay. But something is eating you. Talk to us!"

"My father is really mad about my being arrested during the student revolt."

Koinet knows nothing about a student revolt, but he decides to pretend familiarity. "So your father won't give you any money?" Hassan nods. To Koinet, this seems an improbable situation: a rich man won't give his son any money. *Well, maybe if the son murdered somebody.*

"Have you spoken to your mother?" Kamiri asks.

Hassan bites his lip gloomily. "No, not yet. She's been busy."

Koinet is puzzled. *What does a rich man's wife do that keeps her so busy she can't talk to her son?*

Kamiri offers an optimistic gesture. "I'm sure she'll sort something out."

"I'm not so sure."

The house is quiet when Hassan returns; there is only the splashing of the fountain in the central courtyard. He looks up at the balustrade around the floor above: no sign of life. To his right are the double doors leading to the living area, the conservatory and the pool beyond. Cautiously, he peeks in: no one there. Turning to left are the double doors to the main dining room. On gently opening the right-hand door, he sees that the chandelier is lit. There is Damaris, one of the household maids, setting the big table. The embroidered linen cloth has been laid, and she is laying out the silver cutlery. "Hallo, Hassan, how was your game?"

"It was OK, Dami. Do you know where Mother is?"

"I think she's in her room, Hassan. I expect she's getting ready for the big dinner tonight. Said she didn't want to be disturbed."

"What's the dinner, Dami?"

"Oh, it's another one of those government dinners: Business Minister, Chamber of Commerce, some ambassador, bigwigs and their wives – eighteen people."

"What's the main course?"

"King mackerel with sea urchin sauce, white asparagus and that special green salad your father likes. Don't worry. There'll be some left over for you."

"Thanks, Dami."

Achieving Superpersonhood:

Hassan retreats, closes the door behind him and begins to climb the stairs apprehensively. His toes touch the brass rods which secure the long, blue Persian runner at the back of each tread: . . . seven, eight, nine . . . twenty. He has reached the first floor, and he pauses. Quiet. The hallway extends to his right and left; behind him, the stairs continue to the second floor, his room and the servants' quarters – without the blue carpet. Directly ahead are the double doors leading to his father's suite, and down the hall to the right is his mother's suite. He approaches the single door and listens. Nothing. Gently, he knocks. No response. He knocks louder; still no response. Slowly, he tries the door handle. The door is not locked. Opening the door a few centimeters, he calls, "Mother?" No answer. He steps into the room – a sitting room with English period furniture and pink silk curtains – and notices that the door to the balcony is ajar. Moving toward the balcony, he sees his mother in a dressing gown, apparently asleep on a chaise. "Mother?" She sits up and turns. Immah Arusei's well-kept face reveals the beauty she once was: large dark eyes, slightly upturned nose, rounded cheeks and sensuous mouth. "Oh, it's you, Hassan." She pulls the protective turban off her head, allowing a cascade of dark amber hair to fall over her shoulders.

"Mother, may I speak with you?"

She beckons, and he steps out onto the balcony with its view of the gardens below and the City in the distance. "What is it, Hassan?"

"I have no money, Mother."

She considers him for a moment. "I have asked your father to deposit some money in your account each month. He has agreed to the sum of three thousand shillings. That's to cover everything: your clothes, travel, meals away from home, and university fees." She looks away. "But no credit cards."

A wave of depression sweeps over Hassan. "But Mother, my university fees are thirty-eight thousand three hundred per year. How is it possible?"

"Well, you'll have to get a job if you want to stay at the university."

But I've never had a job! How could I get one? What would I do? He is overwhelmed with a terrible sense of isolation. Hassan falls to his knees and begins to weep.

"Come on now! Be a brave boy!"

Softly, Hassan asks: "Why am I treated like an outcast in this family?"

His mother hesitates. "Because you brought shame on the family by being convicted of a felony."

"And what about Daudi (his oldest brother) and that girl he got pregnant?"

"That was kept secret."

Hassan' cheeks are wet as he looks up at his mother. "So it's all right if things are kept secret?" he asks angrily.

Imman Arusei drops to her knees in front of him, and wordlessly embraces him. "I am so sorry, Hassan!"

Hassan struggles in her arms. "What are you sorry for, Mother? Sorry that you had me?"

"No, no, Hassan. I love you. I am sorry for your father, for myself and for you."

"For which father?"

She hesitates in shock, searching his face: *somehow he knows.* "Both."

He pushes her to arms' length, making eye contact. "What is the name of my father?"

"I cannot tell you, Hassan. I have promised that I will never reveal his name."

For several moments they look at each other, trying, perhaps, to read secret intentions. Hassan says, "Maybe I should drop out of University and become a vagrant."

"I can give you a little money every month, Hassan. I have no bank account or credit cards. My husband gives me some spending money each month."

"Why don't you divorce him?"

Achieving Superpersonhood:

"I have no grounds in Islam for a divorce. Besides, I would lose my other children."
"They aren't children any longer, Mother."
"And my place in society. Please be brave, Hassan!"

As he leaves the house, his oldest brother and sister arrive in a chauffeured Mercedes. They are talking animatedly as they push past him and enter the house without a word of greeting. From the side of the house, he collects his car and drives away, his mind a blizzard of contrary thoughts. *She says she loves me, but does she really? Why did she promise not to name him and who is he? Does her place in society matter so much? Being at a dinner with the Business Minister, the Chairman of the Chamber of Commerce and some ambassador's wife. Wearing a beautiful dress and an emerald necklace. Maybe she could sell some of her jewelry? But if she did, he would certainly notice and raise hell. Isn't she just a kept woman? But aren't all Muslim wives kept women? Their right to divorce is very limited. What am I going to do? I need someone to talk to . . . Dorothy, but maybe . . . what about that imam? Did I know his name? At the Ibrahimi Mosque. Tell him Tabiz sent me. Perhaps he will be a good one to talk with . . . listen . . . give me some advice . . . I feel lost.*

As I, the One, listen to Hassan, I must observe – much as I love him – that he will benefit from a little hardship. Those of my friends who have survived hardship emerge with a new identity, a new resilience and determination: self-overcoming. They are better able to distinguish what is important in life, and they tend to set aside the cotton candy. Unfortunately, as I was just talking, the Other whispered in Hassan's ear.

Sometimes, I, the Other, take advantage of the One's 'hardship first' technique, by persuading a potential friend that he or she can escape the misery of hardship with a taste of gratification. But usually, I favor a 'gratification first' technique, where my friend becomes addicted in the web of gratification and cannot disentangle.

The Ibrahimi Mosque is situated in an old, predominantly-Muslim sector of City, with narrow alleyways and only the main road suitable for cars. The small, gray mosque itself is huddled between two brick residential buildings, facing a fruit and vegetable market and fronted by a miniature courtyard with an ablution basin. The double doors and narrow windows are in the distinctive peaked, Islamic style. There is a single, cylindrical minaret topped with an array of loudspeakers and the crescent moon of Islam.

This couldn't be the main mosque for this area; it's too small. It could use a good scrubbing and some fresh paint. Hassan shrugs. *Oh, well.*

He finds that the doors are not locked, and they admit him to the dim prayer hall with its threadbare brown and beige carpet. There is no one in the hall. At the rear, a single open door leads to a transverse corridor. "Is the imam here?" he calls.

A door opens down the corridor, and a voice answers, "I am here."

Reaching this second doorway, Hassan finds a small office, barely illuminated by a single suspended light bulb. There is a wooden desk across one corner and a rear wall covered with shelved books. A man with a lined, dark face, gray beard, and eyes glinting in the reflected the light is seated at the desk. "Hello. I am Imam Kipyego."

"Tabiz suggested that I see you. My name is Hassan Arusei."

The imam spreads his arms in greeting. "Ah, yes, Hassan, you had some difficulty with the law during the students' revolt."

"How did you know?"

With a gesture toward one of the chairs, Kipyego says, "I keep in touch with Tabiz. He is a very good Muslim." The older man pauses to study his visitor, taking in the spiritless demeanor.

Achieving Superpersonhood:

"I sense that your day has not been without problems." Hassan nods. "Family problems, perhaps?" Another nod. "I believe Tabiz told me that you are the youngest of the Arusei clan."

"Yes."

"Having a little difficulty making your way in the world, perhaps?"

Hassan is chewing his lip. "I don't know how I can continue at University; my father no longer pays."

"A university is not for everyone. Did you know that our great Prophet – praised be his name! – did not attend University?"

"No, I didn't know that."

"But, he became the greatest theologian, general, politician, trader and leader that the world has ever known. Where is your path to greatness, Hassan?"

Hassan, gazing at the floor, says softly: "I do not have a path to greatness."

"Of course you do, Hassan! You are a member of the Arusei clan!" Hassan shakes his head. "So the family is standing in the way of your path to greatness?"

Hassan folds his arms across his chest. "My father doesn't like me very much."

"Would you like to prove him wrong, Hassan?"

"What do you mean?"

"Would you like to be someone he will look up to?" he pauses to smile. "Without attending University?"

"I don't think that's possible."

"Does your father look up to our Great Prophet?"

"Yes, I suppose so."

A smiling Kipyego beams his confidence at Hassan and stretches out his hands to him. "So there you have it!"

"But Imam, I am nothing like the Prophet."

Kipyego gives a dismissive shrug. "The Prophet is our example, Hassan, and all things are possible with Allah. What did Tabiz tell you?"

"He said I should stand tall with a strong faith in Allah."

"Exactly! That is your path to greatness, Hassan!"

"But if I were able to stand tall with a strong faith, how would I find my path?"

"The voice of Allah will guide you, Hassan." The young man gives a doubtful shrug. "Let us go and pray together."

In the vacant, darkened prayer hall, at the urging of Kipyego, they kneel in front of the *quibla* (indication of the direction of Mecca). "Great Allah," the imam intones, "here before you is your servant, Hassan – distressed with his family cares. Show him the path to strength. Let him be the man you always intended him to be. Let him feel your great care. Let him know the great glory of your paradise."

The imam is silent for a time. Hassan feels comforted by his anonymity in the gloom, by the mystery of prayer to Allah, and by the physical presence of the imam, who seems wise and helpful. In a whisper, he finds himself praying: "Great Allah, strengthen me. Show me my path to the future. Once I am on the path you have chosen for me, let me know the love of my mother and the respect of my father."

They are silent, still bowed, heads nearly touching the carpet.

The imam says, "Yes, Great Allah, your will be done! I will put him on the path you have chosen for him for your great glory and for the greatness of Hassan!" He whispers a further, unintelligible prayer. Reluctantly, he rocks back onto his heels, his head still bowed. Hassan follows his example. Wordlessly, Kipyego gets to his feet, and walks toward the rear door. Hassan follows him.

They are seated again in Kipyego's office. "Would you like a coffee, Hassan? I can make you one."

"Oh, no thank you, Imam. I couldn't trouble you for something like that."

"It's no trouble at all, I assure you." Kipyego takes in Hassan's anxious body language. "What is it, Hassan?"

Achieving Superpersonhood:

"Well . . . I was just wondering . . . did Allah speak to you?"

"Yes, of course."

"What did He say, Imam?"

Kipyego puts on a kindly face. "He mentioned some thoughts about your future."

"What did He say?"

"He suggested that you continue to come here for prayer."

"Yes, of course I will come here for prayer, but did he say something about my future?"

Kipyego nods. "He has a brilliant plan for you." There is a warm smile. "It is a plan that will transform your life. It will greatly elevate your stature in the eyes of you parents, Hassan."

"What is it, Imam?"

Kipyego cocks his head; the smile grows warmer. "Allah has not authorized me to disclose the details of his plan at this moment. He has directed me to help you grow in faith, so that you will be fully prepared to embark on the plan."

Hassan stifles his frustration. "I will return tomorrow to pray with you, Imam."

"Until tomorrow, then."

As he crosses through the prayer hall, Hassan's thoughts whirl through his head. *I did not hear the voice of Allah. But that is just the point! The imam will teach me to pray so that I can hear the voice of Allah, and when I can hear His voice, He will direct me to the path! What am I to do about University? It doesn't matter! What is important is for me to pray with the imam!*

> This is an endless problem for me, the One! I believe that religion should be kept clear of deviousness of any kind. Instead of black and white, when the two are mixed, you have black! It may look like gray, but it is black! More importantly, you are lost, and you can't tell where you are! Knowing that religion is important to me, the Other finds the most devious means of hiding falsehood within in it, so that my friends, relying on the purity of it,

sense a scorpion's sting, and turn away. Perhaps I should hide a redeeming bit of love inside the Other's hateful packages.

I don't think The One has anything to complain about. He invented 'religion' – to use his word for it. Why would I not want to make use of his invention for my own advantage?

Chapter 8

Intermediary

"There's a constituent call for you on line three, Dorothy."
"Hello, this is Dorothy. May I help you?"
"There's somebody digging under my land."
"Pardon?"
"I think it's that Mine Ventures outfit."
Dorothy grabs a ballpoint and begins to scribble notes on a pad. "What is it that Mine Ventures is doing?"
"They got a claim next to my property, but they're digging under my land!"
"How do you know they're under your land?"
"I can hear 'em."
"What are they digging for?"
"Diamonds."
"Are you digging on your land, too?"
"Yeah, but I haven't got any big machines."
"Can you give me your name and address?"
"Ma'am, if I gave you my name, the trolls would get me."
Dorothy shakes her head in confusion. "What trolls are you talking about?"
"I'm talking about the trolls that work for Mine Ventures."
"So you're afraid that if you complain about Mine Ventures, they would hurt you?"
"You got it, ma'am."
"Well, what would you like Mr Ndungu to do?"

"He should tell Mine Ventures to stay clear of my land!"

"But how can he do that if he doesn't know who you are?"

"I can give you my phone number. It's 2067364221."

"And where is your property located?"

"I'm in his district." Dorothy looks up at the ceiling in annoyance. The voice at the other end says, with equal annoyance, "You must know where Mine Ventures is working in his district!"

"Yes. OK. I'll have a word with him and I'll call you back."

When Bahadia ends a telephone call, Dorothy recounts the constituent call.

"Damn miners," Baha says with a slap at her desk. "You should go in and see him, Dorothy."

Abdallah shrugs. "I don't know what we can do. First of all, we've got to prove that they're doing something wrong. Not easy. But if we do, and we call the police, the police won't find anything."

"Why won't they find anything?"

"Because they'll be paid by the miners not to find anything."

Dorothy is indignant. "But we can't just let it go! They're stealing his diamonds!"

"If he has any."

"Even if he doesn't, they're still breaking the law: they're <u>trying</u> to steal!"

Abdallah gives another shrug. "OK, Dorothy, see what you can find out."

She rings the aggrieved miner back. "Mr Ndungu wants me to investigate."

"Very good!"

"Where is your claim located?" He gives her his site's GPS coordinates. "I'll call you again when I'm on the way for a visit."

On an official map of the district, Dorothy pencils a cross at the location given. According to the map, the area is listed as 'common grazing land', about thirty kilometers southeast of City. "Baha," she asks, "how did this common grazing land become a diamond mining area?"

"I didn't know there are any diamonds there. Perhaps you can check with the Bureau of Mines."

Dorothy is determined to get to the bottom of this constituent's complaint. After being shunted to and fro at the Bureau of Mines, Dorothy finds a young man, Gregory, who seems willing to help. "I am on the staff of Mr Ndungu, the MP, and he has a query about diamond mining in his district."

"What is his query, ma'am?"

She hands Gregory a slip of paper with the coordinates. "He'd like to know who has valid mining claims in this area."

The young man takes the paper, excuses himself, and returns with a large map. Laying it on the counter, he points to the coordinates given. "It looks like this particular area," his finger traces the circumference of a small plot of land, "is the claim of Shabaan Kemboi."

"And does Mine Ventures have a claim in this general area?"

Gregory consults the reference table on the map. "Their claim would be number seventeen." He studies the map. "Yes. That would be this large area here."

Dorothy peers at the map. "It looks like Mine Ventures is right next to Mr Kemboi."

"Yes, ma'am, it does."

"Are the boundaries of each claim marked on site?"

"Yes, Ma'am, they're marked with red metal stakes."

"And can you tell me whether there have been any finds in this area?"

"Well, each claimant is obliged to report any findings over one hundred milligrams, and must sell them to the government at a price of twenty-five shillings a milligram."

"How much is one hundred milligrams in carats?"

"Half a carat."

"But how do you stop people cheating on the rules?"

"There are random searches, rewards for whistle-blowers, and any miner caught cheating loses his claim and is prosecuted for theft. Besides, this area is not expected to be rich in diamonds. Before the claims were auctioned, there were only two cases of local shepherds finding small, poor quality stones."

Dorothy reports her findings to Abdallah, who says, "It wouldn't do any harm if you have another word with him."

"Abdallah, I have a bad feeling about this. Is it all right if I go and meet with him at the claim?"

He considers her briefly. "OK. There's a bus that goes down to that area from the main depot. You can put it on expenses."

This is a case where I, the One, enhanced Dorothy's doubts – what she calls her 'bad feeling' – through biasing her perception of the situation: not with facts, but with a sensation of gloom.

"Mr Kemboi, I can meet you Thursday afternoon at your claim."

"How did you know my name?"

"The Bureau of Mines gave it to me, based on your coordinates."

Dorothy is one of the last passengers to alight from the bus, at a point the driver suggests. When she consults Google Maps to her phone, after leaving the bus, it looks as if it's about three kilometers on foot. At first, there is a dirt track, which becomes a path. *I wonder how Mine Ventures gets their machinery here. They must come in from the opposite direction.*

To either side of her, there are foothills, beyond which are dark gray jagged peaks. *Extinct volcanoes.* The path covers flat, ochre earth, littered with living and dead whistling thorn bushes; large green acacia trees and solitary leadwood skeletons stand sentinel. There are patches of yellowing grass interspersed with the dark pellets of animal droppings. At four o'clock the heat is still oppressive, and there is no sign of humanity. Dorothy keeps her phone in front of her, walking so as to shorten the distance between the stationary red flag and the blinking blue dot.

Looking up, she sees the short silhouette of a man dressed in dark clothing. As she approaches, details of the silhouette emerge: palm thatch wide-brimmed hat, coveralls, rugged boots and bare arms. He turns to face her as she approaches: thickets of white beard shroud a large jaw and thin lips, and bushes of black eyebrows shade the dark eyes. "You must be Dorothy," he says with a slight nod.

"Yes, and you are Mr Kemboi."

"I am, and you are standing on my claim."

Dorothy looks around. There is a tiny shack, not much larger than a privy, with a pick and a shovel propped against it. "Where is Mine Ventures?"

"Their processing site is farther down, behind those trees."

She glances at him. "You said you can hear them."

A wide grin reveals his yellowing teeth. "You want to hear them, Miss Dorothy?"

She nods. Kemboi ambles over to his shed, unlocks it, and removes a heavy iron crow bar about two meters in length. "Come with me."

Briefly, he walks toward the distant trees, and, raising the crow bar to arms' length, drives it forcibly into the ground, so that about a meter and a half are protruding. He grasps the crow bar just under its flat, round handle and lowers his ear onto the flat handle. He listens and breaks into another smile. "Your turn, Dorothy."

She mimics him, pressing her right ear against the warm, rusty iron. There is a constant grinding noise, mostly in the bass register, but occasionally there is a higher pitched tone as the machine accelerates momentarily. "What is it?"

"It's rock mining."

Dorothy eyes him dubiously. "How do you know it's right under us here? Maybe the noise is coming from down there." She points vaguely toward the stand of trees.

"You want to try to listen to it down there? It's nowhere near as loud."

Dorothy squints, trying to see beyond the trees. "So what they're doing is cutting away the rock down here, and they're sending it back their plant, where they process it and remove the diamonds."

"Exactly."

"But why don't you have a machine like they do?"

Kemboi spits forcefully on the ground and glares at Dorothy. "That takes a lot of money. And it's a different way of mining. They're doing rock mining; I'm an alluvial miner."

"You're a what?"

"An alluvial miner. You see, diamonds were made long ago, deep down, under tremendous pressure. What brings them to the surface is a kimberlite pipe. Kimberlite was once a molten rock with diamonds inside it. A vertical pipe of molten kimberlite is squeezed to the surface over millions of years. When it gets to the surface, the kimberlite erodes, the diamonds are released and are washed away with the sand. What you're standing on was probably a river bed millions of years ago, and if there was kimberlite in the area, there are probably some diamonds here. Alluvial refers to the sand and gravel in an ancient river bed. So what I do is look for loose diamonds mixed in with the sand and gravel."

"Have you found any yet?"

"No, but I expect I will, what with the interest that Mine Ventures is showing."

Dorothy says, "But Mine Ventures is doing something different. They're not looking for loose diamonds, they're cutting rock."

"Yeah, I suspect they're cutting kimberlite."

"And you think they're cutting kimberlite below your claim." He nods. "Where are the boundary markers of your claim, Mr Kemboi?"

"Now, that's another problem. The markers have been moved."

"How do you know they've been moved?"

He turns around, facing away from the trees. "You see over there and there," he says pointing left and right, "those red pipes sticking in the ground?" Dorothy nods. "Now, I'll show you where those two used to be."

He walks about seventy meters toward the trees, then veers off to the right. "One of those markers used to be here," he says, pointing to a neat hole in the ground. "They didn't even bother to fill in the hole." Crossing to his left, he points to another hole. "And the other one was here."

Dorothy pauses to look around; the gently rolling landscape is largely barren. "What would you like the MP to do, Mr Kemboi?"

"I'd like him to stop Mine Ventures from stealing my diamonds."

"I understand, but how is he going to do that? They'll just point to the markers, and say that they're just working their claim."

"But you know it's not their claim."

"OK, I know it, but a judge in the City isn't going to know it until we have," she makes quotation marks in the air, "official evidence."

"So maybe the MP can order a survey to be done."

"OK, let's say he can do that. Let's say the survey's done, and you're right. What's Mine Ventures going to do?"

"They'll say they didn't move the stakes."

Dorothy shakes her head. "But that's not all. They'll stop mining under your land until the fuss blows over."

Kemboi glares at Dorothy. "What can I do?"

"May I ask, Mr. Kemboi: what did you pay for your claim?"

"I paid twenty-seven thousand, four hundred and nineteen shillings."

"And you've had the claim for how long?"

"About fifteen months."

"You might want to consider selling your claim to Mine Ventures for at least twice what you paid for it."

His frustration assumes an edge of anger. "But, Miss Dorothy, this mine was going to be my pension!"

"I'm sorry, Mr Kemboi. I don't know what else to say."

Having returned to the MP's office, Dorothy gives Abdallah a report. He stares at the ceiling for some time, then he seems to come back to the present. "So, you say that Mine Ventures is engaged in rock mining there?"

"Yes, I heard the machine underground."

"What are they doing with the spoil?" Dorothy is puzzled. "You know: the rock they've taken out of the ground. They've got to put it somewhere."

"I don't know; we didn't get close enough to their operation to be able to see."

His eyes flit around the ceiling. "I seem to recall that the government opened that area to alluvial mining only. There was to be no rock or deep mining, because the government didn't want a mess. It was a concession to the shepherds who graze their herds there, and they were given preference in the claims draw. Some of them had already started to dig. So, the idea was: let's get control of the situation, bring in some revenue, and make people happy, without destroying the land." His eyes return to Dorothy. "Would you check with the Bureau of Mines that my memory is correct about the alluvial mining only, and then give Mr Kemboi a call? Ask him to have a look and tell you what Mine Ventures is doing with the spoil."

Dorothy confirms that Abdallah's memory is correct: no deep or rock mining. After several phone conversations with Mr. Kemboi, she tells Abdallah: "He says that there is a large area next to the processing plant where they are stacking the spoil. He says there must be a couple of thousand cubic meters of it. And he says that Mine Ventures has put a two-meter high fence all around their operation to keep the shepherds out. He wants to

Achieving Superpersonhood:

know what you're going to do about it." *There. I've put the ball back in his court!*

* * *

Curiosity overcomes him, and Kamiri calls Hamidi Oduya. The call goes to voice mail, but Kamiri leaves a message, and two hours later his phone rings. He is in the midst of helping Koinet move hides to the shipping area. They both stop work as Kamiri responds, with Koinet's curious eyes catching every flicker of emotion on Kamiri's face.

Oduya can hear the rattle of the conveyor in the background. "Kamiri, have I caught you at work? Is this a good time to talk?"

"Yes, sir, it's OK."

"I guess you know that I'm a scout for the Lions football club, and I'd like to talk to you about a possible opportunity with the Lions."

"Yes, sir."

"I come to City frequently. When could we have a chat?"

"Well, sir, I have off from work Saturday afternoon and all day Sunday, but this Sunday the Eagles have a game."

"Could we meet some evening during the week – say for dinner?"

"Well, sir, we usually work until six o'clock. I don't think I could get to City before about eight o'clock, because I'd have to catch a bus and all."

"Suppose I sent a car to pick you up at seven tomorrow night?"

For a moment, Kamiri doesn't know what to say; he stares at Koinet. "Ahh . . . yes, sir. . . . Uhh . . . I can be ready."

"Let me have the address, Kamiri."

Kamiri explains where he is. "Sir, I'll be waiting just down the road from where I work."

Kamiri puts the phone in his pocket.

"Well?" Koinet demands.

"He wants me to come into City to meet him for dinner. He said there's a car coming to pick me up at seven o'clock."

Koinet bellows out a whoop. "He's sending a car to pick you up?"

"Ssshhh!" Kamiri presses a forefinger to his lips. "Don't tell anyone!"

"Why not?"

"Because maybe nothing will happen, and I'll look like a fool."

"But they'll see you getting into the car and want to know what's going on."

"No. I told him I'll meet the car down the road. I'll say that I'm going to check on my brother, who's in a bit of trouble."

Kamiri is standing several hundred meters down the dirt track, wearing his best pair of jeans, polo shirt with a logo and blue trainers. To his right, a large gray and rusty metal shop is still banging away. Intermittently, there is a tinkle of bells as a flock of sheep accompanied by their shepherd search for edible grass. Ahead, a plume of dust rises, and its cause – a black car – approaches and halts next to Kamiri. An electric window of the Mercedes sedan descends. "Are you Kamiri?" the driver asks.

"Yes."

"Get in. I'm taking you to the Life Mutual Building. Mr Oduya is waiting for you at the Poseidon Restaurant."

Before Kamiri has a chance to object, the car hurtles ahead, enters the abattoir parking area, makes a U-turn, and sprints off. Looking back, Kamiri can see an astonished Mr Kakuyu about to get into his car. *I hope he didn't see me!*

Dark maroon carpeting, paneled walls, piano music, and a white lady in a green dress at a podium: this is the entrance to Poseidon. Kamiri is distracted, taking it all in. "May I help you, sir?" the lady in the green dress inquires, expecting an 'oh-I'm-in-the-wrong-place' response.

"Yes. Umm . . . I'm supposed to meet Mr Oduya here."

"Right this way, sir. I'll take you to his table."

At a table next to the floor-to-ceiling windows, a burly, blue-suited man with close-cropped gray hair is scanning the menu. He gets up as Kamiri and the lady in green approach. "Hello, Kamiri, I am Hamidi. Glad to meet you."

"It's very nice of you to invite me here, sir."

Oduya looks around, feigning confusion. "No, I am Hamidi. Please sit down." They sit. Kamiri doesn't know where to rest his eyes: the view of City to his left, or on the warm, round face of his host. "I take it that you had no problems getting away from work?"

"No, s . . . ah, Hamidi."

"That's good. Now, I suggest that before we talk business, we order our drinks and our food. What would you like to drink, Kamiri?"

"May I have a beer, please?"

Oduya beckons to a green-jacket waiter. "What have you got on draft?"

"Heineken, Kilimanjaro and Stella, sir."

"Is a Heineken all right for you, Kamiri?"

He has no idea. "Yes, that would be fine."

Oduya turns to the waiter. "Can you bring us a pint of Heineken and Johnny Walker Black on the rocks with soda on the side?"

Oduya picks up his menu. "This restaurant specializes in seafood, Kamiri. Given your work, I thought you'd like something other than red meat."

"I don't know much about seafood, but I'd like to try some." He glances at the prices on the menu, and shakes his head. Oduya waits for his comment. "It's just that everything is so expensive!"

"It is a little expensive, but the food is very good. Would you like some grilled prawns to start?"

"Yes." *I wonder what prawns are.*

"And for your main course, Dover sole, sautéed?"

"Yes. That sounds good." *It probably doesn't mean a person's soul.*

Oduya places their order and their drinks arrive. The scout raises his glass to Kamiri. "To success!" Kamiri nods and raises his glass. "Yes. To success."

Oduya then recounts what he has learned from Jacob about Kamiri's football experience, and his own observations of Kamiri's playing skills. Then he asks: "How old are you, Kamiri?"

"I am eighteen, Hamidi."

The older man toys gently with his scotch. "There is a window of opportunity at your age when you can turn pro, because coaching staffs will consider you still young enough to learn. If you were an amateur at twenty-five, no pro team would touch you unless you were Olympic quality. Your competition for a starting position on a pro team will be kids who have come up through that club's academy organization from about the age of seven."

"I've been playing football every day since I was three."

"And you've learned a great deal from practice and experience. What you haven't had is the benefit of expert coaching."

"I think Jacob is a pretty good coach."

"Yes, he is, and he tells me that you've learned a lot."

Their first courses appear before them. Kamiri prods one of his prawns with an exploratory fork. "I know it's considered impolite table manners," Oduya suggests, "but I never try to eat grilled prawns with a knife and fork. Let me show you." He reaches across the table, selects a red crustacean, and snaps off the head. "This isn't edible anyway. What I do next is remove the shell, like this." He tears away the swimmerets from the underside of the shell, removes the shell and hands the naked shrimp to Kamiri. "If you hold it by the tail, that will come off when you put the prawn in your mouth."

"They're very good! I never had one before. What are those?" Kamiri suspiciously regards Oduya's plate of ice and gnarly flat rocks topped with gray slime.

Achieving Superpersonhood:

"Oysters. Would you like to try one?"

"No, thanks. I think I'll just stay with the prawns."

Oduya sets the last empty oyster shell down on the bed of ice. "Let me tell you a little bit about myself, Kamiri. I used to play football; I was a right back: played in Europe for a while – for Inter Milan – and for the Country team. I love the game. It's my life, and when my time came to retire at thirty-four, I hated the idea of selling insurance, or opening a car dealership, or even retiring to some nice resort. I had played for the Lions for a few years; recently, they asked me to become a scout. I know the club very well – their strengths and weaknesses – their character as a team."

Kamiri has been listening intently. "I knew there is such a thing as a scout, but I didn't know what they do, or how important it is."

"Would you like to play football at a high level, Kamiri?"

"Maybe so. I just don't know what's involved."

"Well, I can tell you the Coast City Lions need a good, young left wing. Their starter at left wing is thirty-one, and he doesn't have the speed he used to. They've got a kid your age who came up through their academy program. He's a great ball-handler with good instincts on attack, but he doesn't have your speed. So I could introduce you to the Lions' manager, with the intention that you would try out with them."

Their main courses arrive. Kamiri is presented with a whole, flat fish which just fits on the oval plate. "Would you take it off the bone for him, please?"

When the plate is returned to Kamiri, the fish has disappeared, and in its place is a mound of white flesh with a delicious scent, and spinach; French fries are overflowing a separate bowl. He tries a forkful of the white flesh, and shakes his head in wonder. "This is really good!"

"I'm glad you like it."

"Hamidi, what would happen after the tryout?"

"Assuming that they liked you, the Lions would offer you a contract."

"But I mean: what would I do if I signed with the Lions?"

"Well, you'd have training every day except one – it's usually in the morning – for about four hours. You would work on your physical fitness, on set piece training; there would be sessions with the coaching staff where they would go over videos of a game to point out what was good and what could be improved. Sometimes one of the coaches would work with you personally. Of course, you would watch all Lions' games from the bench to start, but I'd expect that, after a while, you'd get some playing time. Oh, and one of the things that the Lions do is a day or two before each regular game they have a scrimmage of the starters vs. the substitutes. In that scrimmage, the substitutes are supposed to play the same style as the team that the starters will face, and the coaches try different strategies with the starters to see what works."

"It sounds like I would learn a lot." Oduya nods. "And, I guess I'd have to move to Coast City."

"Yes. You have family here?"

"A brother, but we're not very close." Kamiri looks out over the lights of City for a long moment. "How long does the tryout take?"

"Usually about a week."

"So I'd have to get time off from work?"

"Yes." There is a pause. "How much are you making now, Kamiri?"

"Five hundred shillings a week, but I have free room and board."

Oduya offers a slight smile and says dryly: "I think you could expect to make at least five thousand a week as a sub for the Lions."

As he lies in his bunk that night, Kamiri is unable to sleep. His feelings surge back and forth between joy: *I can't believe that I might be playing for the Coast City Lions!* and apprehension: *If I don't make the team, people will laugh at me. Should I even be a football player? Am I good enough? Aside from the money, is this what I should do?*

The following morning, Kamiri approaches the operations manager. "Daniel, have you got a minute? I need to speak with you."

Arapa recognizes that a private conversation is intended and he leads the way to the office.

"Daniel, I have an opportunity to try out for the Coast City Lions."

Arapa frowns. "When did this come up, Kamiri?"

"Last night."

The general manager overhears the conversation and pulls up a chair. Kamiri looks from one to the other, trying to judge their reactions. Kakuyu says, "I thought you were being kidnapped last night, Kamiri."

"No, sir, I . . . "

"Just kidding, Kamiri. Have they made you an offer?"

"No, sir."

"Kamiri," Arapa begins, "how long have you been in touch with the Lions?"

"Well, I'm not really in touch with the Lions, Daniel. I met with Mr. Oduya last night and he suggested it."

Kakuyu asks: "How much time off do you need, Kamiri?"

"A week, sir."

What follows is an animated discussion between the two managers regarding the absence of Kamiri. Finally, Kakuyu says: "OK, Kamiri, we can give you the week after next off. Is that all right?"

"I'll have to check, sir, but, I think so."

"That will be one week off without pay," Arapa adds.

"No, Daniel, we can let him take a week's holiday."

"But, Boss, he's only entitled to holiday after one year."

"I'm prepared to make an exception in his case, Daniel, provided he can get us tickets to any games the Lions play here in City."

* * *

Hassan goes to the Ibrahimi Mosque every evening and for Friday morning prayers. There is at least an hour with Kipyego, followed by prayer together. Hassan's habits, his thoughts and his feelings have changed. After the *Fajr* prayer in his room, he steals down to the kitchen, where Damaris makes him a Spartan breakfast of *uji* (porridge) and tea. He is out of the house before any family members are about. He attends some classes at University in the morning and early afternoon, punctuated by the mid-day and afternoon prayers at the mosque nearby. There is an off-campus café where he can get a subsistence lunch of *sukumu wiki* (vegetable stew) and *ugali* (corn bread), with tea for eight shillings, fifty.

Slipping in the staff entrance to the house, he finds a plate of leftovers from the family dinner which Damaris has left for him on the counter, covered in foil. He takes the back stairs up to the second floor and his room, where he says the *Isha'a* (night) prayer.

It is not an easy life, but the imam says that I must cleanse my soul of its easy habits if I am to hear the voice of Allah. I am determined to be a person of stature – someone my father will admire, and my mother will love. I must live the life of a frugal scholar dedicated to Allah.

Hassan has very little contact with friends and none with his family. He waves distantly to Dorothy when he encounters her between classes. To Kamiri and Koinet, at the football pitch on Sunday, he seems pre-occupied, arriving late and hurrying away at the end of the game. Hassan is reluctant to engage his friends in conversation. *He seems a different person.*

Much of his free time at University is spent in the library reading items that have been suggested by Kipyego, with whom he says the sunset prayer. His thoughts return again and again to the Qur'an, the hadiths of Mohammad, and the commentaries of these 'Islamic scholars'.

Achieving Superpersonhood:

> *Where is my path to greatness? What would please mighty Allah?* He considers the writings of the teachers of Islam. *They say that a great revolution is coming – that a global Islamic Caliphate will be established – that Islam will triumph, and the unbelievers will be cast down into hell – that in the caliphate all Muslims will live in prosperity, justice and devotion to Allah and the Prophet. The blasphemies, false worship, exploitation, corruption, and lascivious drunkenness of the non-believers will be wiped clean from the earth. The poor shall triumph, and the rich shall be debased. Perhaps in this great upheaval, my path to greatness will emerge. My role might be as district governor in the caliphate, and my father will come to me for certain permissions! It is predicted that the poor and the rich shall exchange places!*

At one level, had he been sorely pressed, Hassan would likely have conceded that the outcomes predicted by these 'Islamic teachers' is unlikely fantasy, but he is engaged in self-overcoming, including the dismissal of contrary rationality. For Hassan, what is important is the creation of the new identity of power and confidence assured by Allah and Kipyego, and faith in their assurances must not be undermined by unnecessary doubt.

Hassan is feeling quite impoverished and resentful. Moreover, his stepfather and half-siblings are rich, powerful and oppressive: as such, they are naturally the opponents of global Islamic triumph.

> I, the Other, am certainly involved in the creation of Hassan's new mind set, using 'biasing of consciousness', where my friend becomes particularly aware of selective aspects of a situation and overlooks other aspects. The awareness of these special aspects influences my friend's decision-making, and, presto! I get the result I want! Yes, of course: the One uses the same technique. How do

we do it? Well, everyone knows that human awareness is incomplete, and sometimes flawed.

"Imam," Hassan asks as they are sitting in the semi-darkness of the spiritual leader's office, "can you now reveal my path to greatness which Allah has disclosed to you?"

Kipyego considers the question for some time. Then, he asks: "Have you read the essay by the great Islamic scholar of Buraydah, which I asked you to consider yesterday?"

"Yes, Imam."

"And what did he tell you, Hassan?"

"He says that the clearest path to greatness for any Muslim is to become Allah's soldier."

"Correct, Hassan!" Kipyego pounds his desk with a fist for emphasis. "And who does the great scholar say is the enemy of Allah's soldier?"

"Imam, he says the enemy is the non-believers."

"Why are the non-believers the enemy, Hassan?"

"Because, Imam, they do not believe the teachings of the Prophet, because they worship false gods, and because they debauch themselves in money, alcohol and forbidden sex."

"Very good, Hassan!" Kipyego stands up and theatrically paces the small room. "Are you ready to accept the assignment of Allah, Hassan?"

"Yes, Imam."

Kipyego turns, faces Hassan and spreads his arms. "It is to be Allah's soldier, Hassan! When we first met, Allah spoke to me. He said, 'Blessed Imam, you shall in good time reveal to my servant, Hassan, that I wish him to become my holy soldier. Tell him to prepare himself for conflict with the non-believers, so that, in his victories, he will be recognized for his greatness, and so that he may join me in Paradise!' Come! Let me bless you, Hassan!"

Hassan stands up and is swept into the embrace of Kipyego. He stumbles slightly. "Thank you, Imam!" *I didn't expect to be a soldier. I thought perhaps an important official. But if Allah wishes me to become his soldier, I am ready. I'm just not sure about paradise.*

"Let us go and pray together, Hassan. You will hear the voice of Allah commanding you to be his holy soldier!"

They kneel together, alone, ahead of the crowds, in the prayer hall. Kipyego recites the Maghrib prayer, beginning with the first two *rak'ats* which emphasize the obligations of all Muslims to Allah. During the third *rak'at,* which is said in silence, Hassan's mind wanders. *You are to become my holy soldier, Hassan!* The voice is clear. *It is the voice of Allah!*

In the *Nafl* prayer, Kipyego says, "Great Allah, bless your holy soldier, Hassan. Draw him close to you so that he may always attend to your commands on his path to greatness. And let him end his days in your embrace in Paradise!"

> I, the Other, must say that I did that very well. It is a kind of ventriloquism at which I have become adept. There is nothing wrong with it! After all, it is said that imitation is the sincerest form of flattery.

> Voices, voices, voices! When Hassan knew that no external person had spoken to him, and he was hoping to hear the voice of Allah – well, it was the voice of Allah! But, may I, the One, suggest that Allah does not usually tell us exactly what we want to hear? He may tell us something different. You have heard of cases where someone asserts: "God told me to kill that person!" But please, if a voice like that plays in your head, ask yourself: "Would Allah (who is kind) tell you to do something like that?" Ask yourself: if not Allah, who then?

They rise from the carpet just as worshipers arrive for the Maghrib prayer.

Hassan says: "Allah spoke to me, Imam. He told me that I am to be his holy soldier."

"Bless you, Hassan!" He takes Hassan by the arm. "When you are ready to take up your assignment, come back and see me."

Chapter 9

Shepherds' Fields

Baha appears in the doorway. "Tomorrow morning at eight-fifteen, Abdallah."

"That wily bastard! If I say I can't make it then, he'll say he hasn't got another time until next month." Abdallah turns to Dorothy. "I think it's important that you be there, Dorothy. Can you make eight-fifteen tomorrow?"

"My first class is at ten, so yes, but I may have to leave if the meeting lasts over an hour."

"We'll be lucky if he gives us twenty minutes."

At eight o'clock the next morning, they are waiting in an anteroom to be called for their meeting with the chief of the Bureau of Mines. Abdallah leans over so that his voice doesn't carry. "The guy we're going to meet, Mr. Kurgat, has some kind of connection to the president. I don't know what it is, but he doesn't know anything about mining. He owned a chain of department stores, retired, and worked on the president's political campaign."

At ten minutes after eight they are called into the chief's grand office. At the back is a large mahogany desk, flanked by two flags, and centered behind the desk is a life-sized portrait of the father of Country – its liberator from the colonial power.

A tall, older man dressed in an expensive suit, white shirt and striped silk tie gets up from the desk. "Hallo, Ndungu, you're right on time, I see." There is an edge of sarcasm in his voice. "Hallo, who's this?"

"This is Dorothy, my research assistant."

Kurgat moves closer to inspect Dorothy and wraps an arm around her shoulders, his voice dripping with syrup: "Welcome, Dorothy. Nice to meet you."

Deftly, Dorothy shrugs him off. "Hello, Mr Kurgat."

Kurgat moves toward a large, polished conference table with a high-backed chair at one end. Three men in similar attire as their boss enter the room and take up places to the right of the chief's chair. "These are some of my staff," Kurgat announces, pointing in turn, "Mr Jebet, Mr Lelei and Mr Bitok. Please be seated."

Kurgat's gray hair is drawn back in a ponytail; the bones in his face give it an angular appearance; his voice is deep and deliberate. "Now, what can we do for you, Ndungu?"

"It has come to our attention that Mine Ventures is violating the terms of their claim in the so-called Shepherds' Field area."

Kurgat leans back in his chair. "Oh, how so?"

"Mine Ventures is conducting rock mining operations in Shepherds' Field. As you will recall, rock mining is prohibited in that area."

"How did you come by this information?"

"One of my constituents complained that Mine Ventures is mining on his claim. Dorothy, here, went to investigate and found that not only was the complaint correct, but that Mine Ventures was engaged in sub-surface mining."

Kurgat leans forward, eyes gleaming, to consider Dorothy. "Do you have a degree in geology, Miss Dorothy?"

"No, it doesn't take a degree in geology to understand what is going on." Dorothy explains what she observed.

"Well," Kurgat extends a soothing hand palm down. "Perhaps your constituent is mistaken about the claims markers, and perhaps the noise you heard was agricultural machinery nearby."

"As far as I know, agricultural machinery does not produce rock spoil piles on Mine Ventures' land, Mr Kurgat," Abdallah says dryly.

"Oh? And, how did you come by the information that it was rock spoil, Mr Ndungu?"

"The spoil on Mine Ventures property is black – a characteristic of kimberlite. If it is not local kimberlite, it would have to have been imported into Shepherds' Field at considerable expense, as the earth locally is brown and yellow."

Kurgat extends his other hand palm up. "Well, perhaps Mine Ventures is processing kimberlite at Shepherds' Field from one of their other sites."

Abdallah is clearly annoyed. "Mr Kurgat, we didn't come here to listen to inventions about what Mine Ventures may be doing. We came here to request the Bureau of Mines to investigate the activities of Mine Ventures relative to their activities at Shepherds' Field."

"Well, of course we can investigate, Mr Ndungu."

"When?"

"Well, we are a bit short-staffed with the budget cuts you people have given us. Probably in the next month or two."

"Mr Kurgat, we are claiming that Mine Ventures has broken the law. Would you consider it satisfactory if I were to report to the police that my house had been broken into and my valuables stolen, but the police said they would look into the matter in a month or two?"

"That is only an off the top of the head estimate, Mr Ndungu. The staff here and I will see how soon we can organize an audit at Shepherds' Field and we will let you know."

Abdallah is a boiling thundercloud on the way back to his office. "That son of a bitch, Kurgat! I'm sure he's on the Mine Ventures payroll!"

Dorothy is startled. "I thought he was just lazy."

"Lazy? Lazy like a fox! And now I know why he wanted the Bureau of Mines job!" He punches an imaginary opponent with a right jab. "He was hoping we'd go away. Why? Because if he shuts Mine Ventures down, he'll lose that nice villa on the Mediterranean."

"So what should we do?"

"First of all, we've got to invite Mr Kemboi in to the office.

Kemboi is angry and discouraged by the apparent stalemate, but two days later he calls, and says, "There's something going on at Mine Ventures. There is a bulldozer at their site." He reports that it has flattened the spoil pile and seems to be covering it with local soil, and that the sub-surface mining has stopped.

"Do you think Kemboi would have told Mine Ventures about our complaint?" Abdallah asks.

Dorothy waves an index finger. "No, I don't think so. He's terrified of them."

"Ask Kemboi to check at night – when no one is around – whether there is really silence under his claim."

Two days later, Dorothy reports: "Kemboi said that the rock mining starts about an hour after sunset and ceases an hour before dawn."

"So at this point, if we went back to the Bureau of Mines and asked for an update, they would say something like: 'Our audit is complete. It shows that Mr Kemboi's claim markers are correctly positioned. Also, there is no kimberlite spoil pile; our audit shows that Mine Ventures is conducting surface mining only.'"

Dorothy clasps her hands in frustration. "So we just give up?"

"No, Dorothy, in politics survival depends on retaliation. There is a woman called Hetti Aguta. She is a news reader on channel 21 – late forties – with a passion for scandal. The only reason the government tolerates her is that lately she's been hunting in the opposition patch. If we can brief her and get her to Shepherd's Field some night, we can show her the misplaced markers, the midnight mining, and the buried kimberlite. Then we can sit back and watch the fireworks."

Achieving Superpersonhood:

That evening, Joseph asks Dorothy about her political internship.

"I'm learning a lot, Papa. I'm just not I enjoying it."

"What's not to enjoy?"

"There always seems to be a disagreeable side of things. Lots of constituents have problems – unnecessary problems – caused by unfair regulations or incompetent administration. And the big project I'm working on appears to involve some serious corruption."

"OK, Dorothy, but if you can solve those problems, the constituents should be pleased, and you should be proud."

"Maybe, Papa, but I'm not very keen on what the MP calls retaliation. Why not just call in higher authority? I don't like the deviousness."

"You've read Nietzsche?"

"Yes, he said that self-overcoming is long, hard process." Joseph folds his arms, "And I would add that for you, it will involve a few blind alleys."

> Rather than 'blind alleys', I, the One, would say this is a Sisyphean process. The higher you push the stone up the mountain, the more you learn about the mountain, the stone and yourself, and the grander is your view of the world below. In fact, many people stop well short of the summit just to enjoy the view.

Hetti comes to Abdallah's office the following Tuesday afternoon. "You know why I love this man?" she asks. Dorothy, glances at Baha, who is beaming with amusement. "I love this man, because when he sniffs a scandal, he doesn't keep it to himself! No! He passes it to Hetti, and Hetti can have a lot of fun with it!" She turns to Abdallah. "Do you remember the first juicy bit you gave me?"

"Was it the interior minister's house in Spain?"

"That wasn't a house, man! That was a sea-view villa with hot and cold – mostly hot – running women! And all that on a minister's salary of three hundred and ninety thousand shillings a year! I found out he bought it outright – no mortgage!"

Dorothy asks, "Where did the money come from?"

"We know, but I couldn't prove it. Anyway, he's out of the picture now. Sold the villa; retired to the hill country."

Dorothy finds herself admiring this brash, buxom woman with her dark, henna hair and her kaleidoscopically colored dress. *She's still rather pretty. I can see why she's popular on TV.*

I, the Other, dislike Hetti Aguta intensely. She's nothing but a vulture preying on other people's good fortune. If I ran things, there wouldn't be any whistle-blowers, tattle-tale newspapers, or people like Aguta!

Hetti takes notes in a small, spiral notepad during Abdallah's briefing. At the conclusion, she looks up. "I'll want to interview Kemboi on camera. Can that be arranged?"

"I'm sure he'd be happy to be interviewed."

"I'll get my cameraman to bring out a special microphone so we can pick up the underground machinery noise." She looks down at her notes. "I'll need a copy of the BuMines map showing Kemboi's claim with GPS co-ordinates on it."

"We can get that," Abdallah promises.

"Oh, and we'll need a GPS receiver to get the co-ordinates of the actual claim markers."

"We'll work on that."

"I'll need someone with a shovel to come with me when we dig out the kimberlite. Would that be Kemboi?"

"No, I'm afraid not. He's terrified of Mine Ventures."

Hetti looks up. "Oh, for goodness sake! You guys will arrange for somebody, OK?"

"Yes."

"And then, at some point, I'll need to interview you, Abdallah."

OK, I get it now, Dorothy muses, *this isn't really about retaliation; it's about unwelcome exposure.*

Achieving Superpersonhood:

"There are two action items I'd like to leave with you," Abdallah says, "get a GPS receiver and a man to do some digging. OK?"

"Yes. Is it OK if I go with her? I'm really keen to expose Kurgat and Mine Ventures for the cheaters they are!"

"Good for you, Dorothy!"

Where am I going to get a GPS receiver without spending a lot of the MP's money?

I, the One, provide Dorothy with a brainstorm in answer to her question.

"So what's the project you're working on?" Hassan asks with feigned interest.

Dorothy unfolds the story as if she is a police constable unraveling a murder mystery. She senses an initially disinterested Hassan has either become fascinated with her story-telling or is caught up in the crime resolution.

"Very interesting," he says with sincerity.

"I just need a little help from you, Hassan."

He looks at her and feels, rather than hears, the signals of a friend in need. "How can I help?"

"You still have that red sports car?" He nods. "Has it still got that fancy GPS receiver?"

"Yeah."

"Well, I'd really appreciate it if you can come with me to Shepherds' Field and record the actual coordinates of the markers: where they are now and the holes where they were."

"I can lend you my Garmin."

She shakes her head. "No, Hassan. I'm afraid I'll get it wrong and then our exposé will fall apart."

"How long will it take?"

"At most an hour on site."

"When?"

"About midnight tomorrow night."

The idea of being out 'in the bush' at midnight in the company of two women – one famous, the other pretty – to punish evil-doers overrides Hassan's rigid schedule. "It would be after prayer time?"

"Yes," Dorothy confirms, "it would be after your last prayer."

After the meeting, Dorothy feels slightly guilty for not telling Hassan that she also needs him to uncover the kimberlite, but she is afraid that trespassing on the Mine Ventures claim would put him off the entire project. *Besides, if Hassan won't do it, there is the cameraman, and maybe Kemboi.*

The moon is almost full, casting strange shadows from the skeletal trees. Dorothy, Hassan, Hetti and the cameraman are walking across the desolate landscape, avoiding the whistling thorn bushes.

"I didn't get your last name," Hetti says to Hassan.

"It's Arusei."

"Oh, now I understand the red Toyota GT86. You're working for your dad?"

"No, I'm at university."

"Studying journalism, by any chance?"

"I haven't really made up my mind yet." Feeling the need to change the subject, he asks, "How did you get your job, Hetti?"

"I slept with the producer. No, just kidding! They figured that if I was going to be a pain in the ass, it was better for me to be an external rather than an internal pain."

The solid black outline of the shack comes into view, then the nearby figure of Kemboi.

"Can you hear them mining, Shabaan?" Dorothy calls.

"Yeah, if you touch the ground, you can feel it tremble."

A faint, disagreeable, grinding noise can be heard. The cameraman drops to his knees and places his hand lightly on the ground. He nods. "Is this the place where it is loudest?" he asks.

Kemboi retreats several paces. "Over here."

The cameraman opens his back pack, removes a dark, heavy object, and twists it securely into the earth. He then connects it to a handheld recorder, activates a switch and observes a dial.

"What's the reading?" Hetti inquires, removing a notepad from her handbag.

"Seventy-six."

"OK, now, Hassan, what are the GPS co-ordinates here?"

He switches on the Garmin, looks up at the sky momentarily, and reads off two long strings of numbers. Hetti reads them back. He nods.

"OK, now," she says, "I want four more readings: about twenty-five meters from here." She points: "There, there, there and there."

The sound level readings and GPS coordinates are taken.

"OK," she says, "That shows that the mining is definitely taking place under (she stamps on the ground where the first readings were taken) here!" She turns to Kemboi. "Show us the claim markers that you say were relocated."

They move to the first marker. "OK, now, Hassan, you handsome devil, give me some coordinates."

When she has written down the reading, she removes a piece of paper from her handbag, and makes a comparison. "Yup! Not where it's supposed to be!" She turns to the claim holder. "OK, now, Kemboi, my love, can you find the spot where this marker was before?"

Kemboi walks for a while, shining a flashlight on the ground. "Over here."

She looks down at the hole lit by the flashlight's beam. "Hassan, more coordinates, please!"

Having written down the numbers which Hassan has given her, she makes another comparison with the paper. "You are brilliant, Hassan! Spot on!"

The process is repeated with the second, relocated claim marker. Hetti glances at the others with satisfaction. "OK, we've got the proof that the claim markers have been moved and that there is some infernal noise going on under Kemboi's claim. Now, we need the last piece of conclusive evidence. Kemboi, get a shovel and lead us to that covered spoil pile!"

Kemboi returns with a shovel and passes it to Hetti. She shakes her head. "Lead the way, Kemboi!"

"No, I ain't goin' there!"

"Why not?"

"I'm afraid of them trolls."

"But Kemboi, this is your claim we're trying to protect."

Kemboi backs away, dropping the spade on the ground. "I ain't goin' there!"

Dorothy glares at Kemboi in exasperation. *Damn! I should have known this was going to happen!* She glances at Hassan, who, sensing her anxiety, picks up the shovel and scans the horizon. "Where is it, Kemboi?"

Kemboi points. "Over there."

Hassan, Dorothy at his side, starts out in the direction indicated and waves to the others. "Let's go."

Hetti hurries after him. "Thank you, Hassan! I forgot that you are an Arusei!"

They approach the darkened shape of the grove of trees, and they pause to survey the scene ahead. There is a large, block of a building surrounded with single-story additions and outbuildings. A peculiar derrick structure protrudes through the top of the central building. There is the sound of machinery working: a steady hum with regular clanking.

"It looks like they've got a fence." Hassan says. "It probably goes all the way around."

Hunkered down, and moving together cautiously, they approach the fence. The cameraman is silently panning the scene. There is a single lighted window in the building.

"It's a three-meter chain link fence," Hassan comments. "Tough to climb. Probably barbed wire at the top."

"Maybe there's a gate somewhere," Dorothy suggests.

They edge slowly along the fence. "Look," Dorothy hisses, "there's a conveyor dumping stuff!"

"Where?"

"Just behind that bulldozer!"

"But the question is," Hetti whispers, "is it brown earth or black kimberlite?"

They stare at the dark cascade. "To me," Hassan says, "it looks darker than the earth in front."

As they approach what appears to be an access track on the opposite side of the site, they can see that there is a gate. "Looks like two meters high with a double strand of barbed wire," Hassan suggests. "Let me go look."

He creeps along the fence to the gate. "The gate is locked. There's a truck parked right next to the gate on the inside. With this kind of security on the outside, it would be impossible to go in, dig for a while, and expect to get out without being caught." For a moment he looks over the site. "Rather than dig, would a handful of whatever is coming off that conveyor be enough?"

Hetti and Dorothy are nodding. "But how can we get it?"

"I'm thinking that if you guys can boost me up on the fence right next to the gate, I can step on the barbed wire above the gate, jump down, make a dash for the conveyor, grab a handful, and sprint back here before their security can react."

Nervously, Dorothy asks: "You really think you can do that?"

"Yeah," Hassan nods affirmatively.

"It's the only chance we've got," Hetti says. "Let's go for it! You ready to shoot some pictures, Kimbi?"

"Not till after he's up," the cameraman replies.

Hassan claws his way up the fence, stands on Kimbi's shoulders, and, holding a fence post, transfers his weight onto the strands of barbed wire, which give way so that he is standing on the top of the gate. He glances back at the others, then jumps to the ground inside the gate. As he starts running toward the conveyor, a powerful light floods the scene. In the distance, an alarm can be heard. Hassan reaches the discharging conveyor, grabs handfuls and stuffs the pieces into his pockets. He sprints back toward the gate. A door of the building opens and a man shouts, "Hey you!" Hassan reaches the truck and vaults up into its bed. The man, brandishing a truncheon, races toward the truck. Hassan climbs onto the cab of the truck, and, gripping a fence post, steps back onto the gate. The man diverts toward the gate, but Hassan has already jumped to the ground. "Let's go!" he shouts and the four flee into the darkness.

"This guy did it!" Hetti informs Kemboi, emphatically, when they return to his claim. "He's a hero!" Beyond the trees, they can see that the area is brightly lighted; distant alarm bells are ringing, and an engine can be heard to start.

"They'll soon be coming for us!" Kemboi warns.

"Dorothy and Hassan, you better hightail it back to the car!" Hetti says, "Kimbi, Kemboi and I will walk back."

"Come with us!" Dorothy urges.

"Go! Damn it!"

Dorothy and Hassan are quite winded when they arrive back at the Toyota. Looking back, they can make out a low halo of light on the horizon.

"I can't hear anything – can you?" Hassan asks.

"No. Let's see what you've got in your pockets."

Hassan removes small chunks of dark gray rock, mottled with conglomerates.

Dorothy says: "That's certainly nothing like the earth around here." Hassan holds a piece up for closer inspection. "What are you doing?"

"Looking for diamonds."

The other three are striding back to Kemboi's claim. Hetti has to stifle Kemboi's urge to bolt. "You'll be safer with us, Kemboi."

A pickup truck approaches from behind, swings past them and stops, blocking their path. Four men descend: two from the

cab and two from the rear. They are all brandishing truncheons.
"Get in the truck!" a bull of a man orders.

"Start filming, Kimbi!"

Kimbi raises the heavy camera to his shoulder and faces the burly man, who is suddenly lit by a bright light. The light pans to the other three; they are all momentarily stunned.

"What the fuck are you doing?" the man demands.

"We're filming you for my show tomorrow morning on TV 21. You know: the Hetti Aguta show."

"Turn that damn thing off and get in the truck. You've been trespassing on Mine Ventures claim!"

"You have absolutely no proof that anyone was trespassing on your claim, while we have proof that you are – at this moment – trespassing on this man's claim."

"Shut your trap, and get in the truck!" He raises his truncheon threateningly as he advances on Hetti, who stands her ground.

A small, gray-haired man in dirty coveralls approaches the leader and says something to him. The only audible words are "Hetti Aguta". The leader lowers his truncheon.

"Let's go," Hetti orders, and leads the way, skirting around the men and the truck, and regaining the path.

Hassan has insisted, over the protestations of other students in the lounge, on watching channel 21.

"Hello, I'm Hetti Agunta, and have I got a story for you!" She picks up a piece of kimberlite from a table, and the camera zooms in on it.

"This particular piece of kimberlite – a diamond-bearing rock – happens to come from the discharge of Mine Ventures' deep mining operations in Shepherds' Field, where the government promised there would be no deep mining, and here's what the mining sounds like." The amplified sound of rock milling can be heard.

"Our measurements show that this sound is coming from right under here." She points to a spot on a map within red boundaries which she says mark the claim of a shepherd, Mr Kemboi, and explains that the claim markers have been moved.

"Here," (the image changes to a video of Hassan pointing out the hole in the ground, reading from his Garmin, and calling out the readings) "you can see my location expert, Hassan Arusei, taking the exact measurements and comparing them to the official Bureau of Mines claim map."

There is a cheer from the other watching students, as Hassan covers his face with his hands. *Oh, Allah, why did she have to show me and name me! I'm going to be in big trouble!*

"So there we have it," Hetti begins to summarize, "a big mining company that isn't supposed to be in Shepherds' Field at all is engaged in forbidden deep mining, and not only that, they're doing it outside their own allotted territory. But that's not the end of it. MP Abdallah Ndungu, who has Shepherds' Field in his district, complained to the Bureau of Mines about these violations. What was done about his complaint? (She makes a circle with her thumb and forefinger.) Nothing!"

Hassan is panic-stricken. *Mine Ventures know who it was that entered their premises and took the kimberlite. They'll go to the police, who'll arrest me, and find that I'm on probation. And I'll be sent back to jail.* He later realizes that the intruder could have been Kemboi, but he dismisses this possibility. *When the police question Hetti, she'll have to say it was me. I've gotta get out of here!*

Kurgat is watching a replay of the Hetti Aguta Show on his desktop, along with several of his department heads. "That bitch! That absolute bitch!" he snarls.

Later, his telephone rings; it is a familiar voice. "Hello, Norman."

"I want my money back!"

Achieving Superpersonhood:

"Now, Norman, let's think about this."

"What's to think about, Kurgat? You said we could go ahead with deep mining; I paid you for your <u>guarantee</u>. I've bought over a million dollars' worth of rock mining equipment, and what have I got for it? An invalid claim!"

"Well, Norman, it's not as bad as that. You've got some diamonds."

"But that just shows I was right to invest in this project. Let me remind you, Kurgat, that this is a <u>deep mining</u> project."

"Well, we'll have to get the law changed."

"Oh, come on, Kurgat, what are the chances of that? The government promised that this would be surface mining only, with riff-raff having first priority."

"Now that we know there are diamonds to be found in deep mining, the government will change its mind."

"Kurgat, I think it's time to start over on this project. You pay me the million you now owe me, and we can discuss how to restructure things."

"No, Norman, the million is a down payment. I'll prepare a plan to get the project through government as a deep mine."

"You are a son-of-a-bitch, Kurgat! And meanwhile, you're leaving me to deal with a media scrum!"

"May I suggest, Norman, that you throw as much confusion into the situation as possible. Say that the misplaced markers are due to a misunderstanding. You can say that the kimberlite is just the result of a test boring, which is normal practice in the mining industry. You could say that the test boring shows promise of a significant diamond find. That should whet the government's appetite to do a new deal! And you should prosecute the thief who stole your kimberlite!"

> Kurgat is definitely my man! Notice how he turned a disgruntled accomplice into a subordinate? He follows one of my key rules: when you get in trouble, raise the

stakes! Notice, also, how innovative he is: throwing in confusion, counterclaims and irrelevancies!

"Hassan, your father wants to speak with you!" It is the voice of his father's PA.

"OK."

"He would like you to be in his office this afternoon at five-thirty!"

"OK."

I wonder how the police are going to try to contact me. I can't stay at home tonight! I've got to turn off my phone and stay away from the university. Even my car is risky!

"It's good to see you, Hassan!" Kipyego's smile fades as he takes in the stricken face and body language of his tutee. "What's the trouble?"

Hassan softly rasps out his involvement in what is now the 'Shepherds' Field Scandal'.

Kipyego's grin returns. "Congratulations on bringing a corrupt instrument of Western capitalism into the disrepute it deserves!"

"But Imam, the police will be looking for me. My suspended sentence will be revoked and I'll be sent back to prison!"

"Don't worry, Hassan! Your greatness approaches!" Hassan is hunched over in despair, his mind unable to entertain any thought but the disaster he faces. "Hassan, listen to the good news I have for you. Allah is sending you out of City to assume your greatness in the company of Allah's chosen soldiers. You can leave at once, joining this holy Muslim army, which enjoys the great blessings of Allah!"

Hassan looks up. "Where is it, Imam?"

"Their holy camp is located near Coast City. When you descend from the bus this afternoon, one of Allah's leaders will take you to the camp."

Hassan considers the promised camp. In an immediate sense, it dissolves his fear of arrest and imprisonment, together with the shame of becoming an Arusei convict. Moreover, there is the realization that this development lies squarely on his plan – his plan to serve Allah and in doing so to become truly worthy of the name Arusei. He nods to Kipyego and agrees to text him the arrival time of his bus in Coast City.

But what am I to do with my car? I can't leave it at home: my father will sell it. If I leave it at the university, the police will claim it.

Hassan enters a lecture in human anatomy, and sits on the left in front. He ignores the lecturer's scowl, and turning, he surveys the ascending bank of student seats. There is Dorothy, alternatively intent on the lecturer, the screen and her notebook.

Brought back to the present by the noise of students leaving the lecture hall, Hassan springs to his feet, and waves to Dorothy.

"Hello Hassan, what are you doing here?"

They move down the corridor to a quiet spot.

"The police are going to be looking for me, and I've got to get out of City!"

Dorothy, suddenly aware of his agitation, places a calming hand on his arm. "Why would the police be looking for you, Hassan?"

"Because Hetti mentioned my name in her show this morning."

She shakes her head in puzzlement. "But you did a good deed last night, Hassan!"

Grasping her shoulders in frustration, he says, "But Mine Ventures won't see it that way. They will have identified me as the intruder, go to the police and press charges. The suspension on my sentence will be annulled, and I'll be back in prison!"

"But, it doesn't do any good to run away, Hassan!"

He grips her shoulders more fiercely. "Dorothy, I'm going! And I'm leaving you my car!"

She opens her mouth to protest – he interrupts. "It's on the second floor of the car park on Fifth of April Street. The registration is in the glove box. Here's the ticket. Here are the keys." He presses the items into her hands. "Goodbye, Dorothy." He turns and flees.

Shortly after eight that evening, Hassan steps down from the inter-city bus. He has no suitcase: only his phone, nearly empty wallet and the house keys. He pauses to survey the milling crowd: brightly dressed women balancing huge bundles on their heads; surly-faced men, lounging against the wall, casual cigarettes at their lips.

"Hassan Arusei?" It is a very large man with glistening ebony skin marked with the welts of scars.

"Yes."

"Come with me! I am Mujahid al Yemen." He gestures toward a battered, double-parked Toyota truck. "Get in!"

Chapter 10

Training Camp

Kamiri steps off the same bus that Hassan took two days earlier, but he is not expecting to be met. His bus tomorrow goes to a different training camp: Coast City Lions training camp, eight kilometers outside the city. He is not as empty-handed as Hassan. There is his blue canvas hold-all, with his football boots, Eagles uniform, and two changes of clothes. Also, he has ten one-hundred-shilling notes in his pocket. Tonight, he will sleep in a youth hostel.

He is impressed by the main entrance: two huge white elephant tusks intersect over the roadway. *They can't be ivory.* And suspended below the intersection is the massive head of a snarling lion. Inside, to the right, is a white, two-story building, with a sign: "Lions – Pride of the Coast", and farther down: "Administration, Operations, Public Relations, Shop, Tickets." To the left a great expanse of green grass stretches away; it is sectioned into individual pitches, marked with white goals, and, here and there, with moving arms of water spray. Kamiri pauses to take in the expanse. He wonders how he ever got to this particular point in his life, never having even imagined, as a barefoot village footballer, that he, boots in hand, could be at the Lions' camp. *How did it happen? Is life like that, or is it Ngai or God who somehow makes the arrangements, or is it luck? I could have said 'No' at any point and I wouldn't be here, so it's not as if I was predestined, but I didn't do it, so somebody must have done it!*

I, the One, think that Kamiri is often too humble: I know he did it – not all alone – but with some help from his friends, of whom I am one; and luck is too vague an explanation.

Just beyond the car park on the right, a group of men in yellow shirts and black shorts is emerging from another building. They lope eagerly onto a pitch.

Kamiri explains his purpose to a young woman, seated behind a counter and wearing a half headset. "There's a young man named Kamiri here for a tryout," she announces, seemingly to no one in particular. "If you'd like to take a seat, there'll be somebody here shortly."

Kamiri takes a seat on the lion-yellow leather sofa, and scans the magazines on the low table: some are in English, some in Swahili, but all are about football.

"You are Kamiri?" He looks up to find a mid-thirties white man with a neat moustache and dark eyes, dressed in gray shorts and a yellow Lions polo shirt.

"Yes. Yes, I am." Kamiri drops the magazine and gets up.

"Hi," the man says in Swahili. "My name is Jonathan. I'm on the coaching staff. Welcome to the Lions' Den!"

Jonathan leads the way to an office. "We are a first division team that was relegated last year, but the new owner, Mr Arusei, is determined to get us to the top of the second division, so we can re-join the first division next year. He has given Coach a budget to acquire some good new players, and I assume that's why you're here." Kamiri agrees. "Well, you'll be here for up to a week of tryouts. Do you have a place to stay?"

"No, not yet."

"There's a motel called Miriam's down the road. They charge between three hundred and six hundred a night – including dinner – depending on whether it's a single room or a dormitory. Will that be all right?"

"Yes, I think so."

"We expect the players to be here at 8:30 for breakfast. Then we'll train until 1:00. After lunch, which is also here, there may be another hour or two of training. The Lions' next game is on Saturday. It's a home game in the downtown stadium against the Blazers. If you're still here, you'll have a seat on the bus. Any questions?"

"Yes, umm, Jonathan," (he was about to say 'sir' and decided against it) "are there many other people trying out?"

"At the moment we have two others, but it's important to understand that the team situation is fluid now. There are no clear boundaries between the starters, the substitutes, and the candidates. Coach is in evaluation mode; he wants to see how various guys play in different positions and situations. I tell you, Kamiri, he's the best coach I've ever worked with."

"Have you been coaching very long?"

Jonathan smiles. "Two years. I played for the Lions about five years until I got hurt. Switched to coaching, and it's the best decision I ever made."

Kamiri emerges from the dressing room wearing the full Lions' kit: yellow from the waist up; black from the waist down, and his own boots. *Man, this is good!*

He lopes onto a pitch, with a dozen other players, where Jonathan arranges five-a-side scrimmages across the pitch, with almost constant instructions to a player to change position or to replace another player. There is barely time to catch one's breath!

Over the buffet lunch (*one of the best I've ever had*) Kamiri introduces himself to players he hasn't yet met, including the two other candidates. One, Daniel Arubo, aspires to be a central striker; he is short, with a Napoleonic ego, very quick, and very black. The other, Eddie Onyango, has the long arms and legs of a good goal keeper, and his scarecrow appearance belies his agility; unlike Daniel, he is pale-skinned and shy. Eddie, who was discovered by Oduya at a small-city, semi-professional club, is also staying at Miriam's. For an hour or two each afternoon, Eddie and Karimi practice together – even in the rain. Daniel rebuffs their invitation to join them. "No thanks, guys. I'm all set." And he goes off to the Palace Hotel, downtown.

"He's a cocky son-of-a-bitch," Eddie opines, watching Daniel get into his car and drive away.

"Maybe he thinks we're not good enough to practice with him," is Kamiri's view.

Toward the end of the week, Jonathan's charges are integrated into the larger squad, but now Coach Elim Wangari is directing the practice with Jonathan's help. Elim keeps mixing players: starters, substitutes and candidates – seemingly randomly – but now and then, he will call a player over to him. "Kamiri, that was good, but I want you to remember one thing: you are never trapped when opponents seem to surround you. When you feel trapped you make mistakes. So know that you can get out, by a clever move, by a quick pass, by lofting it over their heads, or, if you have to, by running over one of them. And it's OK if you try hard and lose the ball. OK?"

"Yes. Thank you, Coach."

The week has flown by. Kamiri feels a welcome responsiveness throughout his body, and his perceptions are more alert, sharper. *I feel like I'm really ready to play football.* He and Eddie have been nervously comparing impressions.

"I think I'm going to get cut, because Jonathan's always telling me something."

"You can't go by that, Eddie. If he really thought you weren't good enough, he wouldn't bother telling you much of anything."

"Well, that's my opinion. What about you, Kamiri?"

"I think I'm about fifty-fifty."

"Rubbish! You're ninety-ten!"
"Don't I wish!"

As they are eating lunch, Elim taps Daniel on the shoulder. The two disappear, and Elim returns. No Daniel. Elim taps Eddie on the shoulder. They disappear for a quarter of an hour. Eddie returns and sits down again at the table; he avoids Kamiri's eyes, but Kamiri notices that there is a thumb poking up from his folded hands.

"Kamiri, can I see you for a minute?"
"Yes, sure, Coach." He follows Elim to his office.
"Kamiri, I'd like to offer you a one-year contract to join the Lions' team. Are you interested?"
"Yes, Coach."
"OK. At the moment, you would be our second string left wing, but you have quite a lot of talent, Kamiri, and if you show the improvement you're certainly capable of over the next year, we'll offer you a longer contract with more money. OK?"
"Yes, Coach."
"I'm going to start you at six thousand five hundred shillings a week. OK?"
"Yes, thank you, Coach! When would I start?"
"As soon as you can in the next month. You're working now, aren't you?"
"Yes."
"Well, it'll be a slight change for you, Kamiri. I hope that now you'll be slaughtering our opponents."

That evening, Kamiri and Eddie compare numbers. Eddie was offered three thousand shillings a week more than Kamiri. "But I think that's because their back-up keeper may be leaving."
Kamiri asks, "What happened to Daniel?"
"He was cut."
"How come?"

"Mugo, the starting keeper, told me it was because Coach didn't feel he would fit in with the Lions: not enough of a team player."

"Well, I've got to go back to City and break the news to my boss."

"Kamiri, I've been thinking: shall we share a two-bedroom apartment?"

"Yes, but how much would it be?"

"I think I can find something – not downtown, but still pretty nice – for about four thousand a month."

"That would be about five hundred a week, each. Yeah, OK, but how about transportation?"

"I'm going to get at least a two-fifty bike. You can ride with me if you want to."

* * *

"Warari, this is Koinet. You remember? I'm your brother's friend working at the abattoir. Yes? Well, I was wondering if we could talk some more about that position you have.

OK, I'll see you there at eight o'clock."

Koinet has decided that he has to do something about Warari, the drug dealer, even if his brother is unable to take action out of a sense of loyalty. *He could kill others, and/or himself. Maybe I can get him to give it up.*

Koinet is sitting on a bench in an uninviting, litter-strewn park on the city outskirts. A vagrant is sleeping on another bench a stone's throw away. There is only the rattle of the wind in the dried palm fronds. The distant sound of a motorcycle becomes a bellow as Warari, clad all in black – leather jacket, trousers, boots and helmet – comes to a theatrical stop in front of the bench. He removes his gloves and considers Koinet silently.

"Hello, Warari."

"So, you ready to do some business?"

"Maybe. Tell me about the business."

Warari dismounts and stands in front of Koinet, hands on hips. "Well, I need someone to open a new territory for me. . . But I don't think there's much business where you work."

"OK, but what's the product?"

"My brother didn't tell you?"

"Well, he said it was kind of risky."

Warari gives a derisive snort. "For my brother, crossing the street is risky. I prefer to think of it as providing the golden hours of pleasure."

"Do you use it, Warari?"

"Sometimes."

"Don't you find it kind of . . . habit-forming?"

"Nah! Look, are you interested in the business or not?"

"What does it pay?"

"It pays very well. You can sell a hit for about two hundred and fifty shillings at a fifty percent profit margin. My good guys do at least a dozen a night and clear six thousand a week. . . . About ten times what you're making now!"

Koinet leans forward. "How would I get new customers, Warari?"

"Word of mouth, and you have to be in the right place at the right time."

"How about the police? Do you have trouble with them?"

"Not usually. Look, you have to be a bit careful; check around before you do a deal, and you gotta learn how the police cover your territory."

"Warari, I imagine that you do pretty well financially."

"Bet your ass!"

"So, I guess you've got a nice little nest egg built up. You ever thought of retiring?"

"What?" He glares at Koinet. "Hell no!"

"I was just thinking that with a nice nest egg you could buy a shop – go legitimate – get out of the risk."

"Bullshit! Are you some namby-pamby do-gooder?"

"No, I was just thinking that for six thousand a week, I could have nearly a million in three years, and I could buy a bicycle shop. A lot of people are buying bikes these days."

Warari shakes his head and gestures toward the machine behind him. "This bike here cost me forty-five thou."

Koinet gets up from the bench and surveys the Kawasaki. "Nice! Very nice!"

"Enough talk. Are you interested in the deal?"

"Yeah, but I need to think about it for a day or two, Warari."

In the bus on the way back to the abattoir, Koinet is uncertain. *There's no way I could talk Warari into quitting. Too money driven! He really ought to be reported. The question is: should I tell Kamiri first that I'm going to do it? No. Since he won't do it himself. Besides, who's to know who turned him in?*

In the bus depot, where the reception is good, he dials 999. "May I speak to the police, please?" He recounts the sense of his earlier meeting while insisting on anonymity. "His name is Warari, medium height and build – a Kikuyu – clean shaven – wearing black motorcycle clothes and helmet. He rides a Kawasaki 350, license GD40157F. No, I don't know where he lives, but if you arrest him there, you'll find heroin."

* * *

"I can't pay you at the moment, Warari. Give me a couple of days!" The young man is pleading in the shadow of a derelict warehouse on the outskirts of the city.

"Time's up, Rosco! You gave me that same story twice already!" He advances menacingly on Rosco. "I know what your problem is, Rosco. You've been shooting up my horse. How am I gonna make any money like that?"

"No, no, Warari, I swear to God, it's nothing like that. It's just there're a couple of guys who owe me."

"You got a bike or a laptop, Rosco?"

Achieving Superpersonhood:

"No, nothin' like that, Warari. All I got's this little phone here." He holds up a small Nokia mobile phone. "Hey, I just had a call from a hype. We can go and you can get your money."

"But you ain't got the horse."

"No, like I say, I'm out."

"Gimme that phone." Warari snatches the phone and hurls it against the pavement; black bits fly. He draws back his fist and strikes Rosco powerfully in the belly. Groaning and doubled over, Rosco cannot shield himself from Warari's haymaker to the side of his head. The young dealer crumples to the ground, motionless. Warari stares sullenly at his victim for a moment, then administers several severe kicks. "Worthless bastard!"

Why is it that desperate people blurt out "I swear to God" as the preface to an obvious falsehood? Not only does it fail to convince, but it only enrages the intended convincee. I, the One, think it would have served Rosco better had he admitted a transgression, begged forgiveness and offered a solution. It seems to me that bringing God into bad behavior is bad practice.

Warari retreats to his flat, nursing his anger and his sore hand. *I probably broke some fingers on that asshole.* He stamps around his disheveled flat. *I probably need a bit of cake.* He lifts one corner of the stained mattress and withdraws a folded manila envelope. Sitting in the ancient armchair, he spills a small pile of white powder onto a glass plate. He hurriedly scrapes the powder into parallel rows. The rows disappear up a glass tube which he inserts alternatively into each nostril. He leans back in the chair. *Damn, this stuff is good! And it's not dangerous like horse. That's why the celebrities use it.* He chuckles. *Maybe I'm becoming a celebrity! Well, I guess I need to find a new dealer to replace that worthless fuck Rosco. Maybe Koinet. Came to see me last week. I should give him a call later.*

For a time, he lapses into a listless reverie.

There is a hammering on the door. *Who the hell is that?* He peeks out the window. *Holy shit! A police car!* His mind whirls through the possibilities.

There is a shout: "Police! Open the door!"

Best if I am charming and innocent. He opens the door, blocking the entrance. "Yes?"

"Are you Warari?" asks a powerfully built man in police uniform. Warari notices that the policeman has lowered his hand to his holstered revolver.

"Yes, I am. How can I help you, officer?"

"That your motorcycle?" The officer half-turns to gesture toward the Kawasaki parked nearby.

"Yes, it is, officer. Something wrong with it?"

The officer ignores the question. "We have a search warrant for these premises."

"On what grounds, officer?"

"Possession of class A drugs."

"I don't do drugs, officer."

"We'll find out, won't we?"

Warari stands resolutely in the doorway. "I have to go in and tidy up a bit."

"That won't be necessary. Step aside!" The officer removes his revolver; two colleagues press close behind him.

Reluctantly, Warari steps aside. *Who's the fucking rat that turned me in? Probably Rosco.*

Warari stands mute by the window watching two policemen and two other men in dark track suits and baseball caps ransack his flat, going through every drawer, opening books, looking inside shoes, examining medical bottles. Each find is placed in a lockable box, and each find intensifies the search. There are five hundred and seventy-two carefully-wrapped, miniature sacks of water-soluble heroin hydrochloride, and an envelope containing two hundred grams of cocaine. The apartment, messy before the search started, now looks like it was visited by the funnel cloud of a tornado.

"OK, Warari, you come with us. Is this your money?" The armed policeman is holding a wad of shilling notes.

"Yeah."

"We'll put it in safekeeping."

Warari is charged with possession of a class A drug and is confined in City prison. He is permitted one phone call.

"Kamiri, this is Warari. I'm in a bit of trouble."

"What kind of trouble?"

"I've been busted by the police."

Kamiri's voice is flat: "Why?"

"Possession of class A drugs."

"I'm not surprised."

"OK, but you gotta do two things for me. You gotta take my bike away and you gotta get me bailed."

"Warari, I live in Coast City now."

"What the hell are you doin' there? Milkin' cows?"

"I've signed with the Coast City Lions."

"As what? As a waterboy?"

"As a left wing."

There is a long moment of silence, unbroken by Kamiri.

"Listen, brother, I really need your help. Can you come over and do these two things for me?"

Kamiri thoughts are overwhelmed by a surge of anger; he is tempted to say 'No!' and hang up. For some moments his mental processes revolve around resentment and 'I told you so'. But then there is a strange moment of calm, the anger evaporates and his thoughts clear. He recalls what Koinet said about helping a brother: "What would your father say if he knew?"

"I'll see what I can do."

Warari is admitted to cell 137 in block B, where three men are already asleep. He climbs into the remaining upper bunk and lies there in the semi-darkness, staring at the ceiling. There is a kick from below. "Hey you, up there, what're you in for?"

"Possession of class A."

"Recreational or business?"

"Business."

"How much?"

"That's my business, not yours."

"Well, I used to be in the business. Used to be an importer."

A voice from the other bunk: "You ever have anyone try to cheat you?"

"Not often."

"And if someone was to cheat you, what would you do?"

"Beat the crap out of 'em."

It was silent for a time.

"Say, you know about the kid who got beat up real bad? They think it was a drug deal."

"No."

"Well, like I say, he was beat up real bad – is in hospital with a coma. Yeah, it was on TV."

Warari remains mute.

"The kid's name was Rosco. They say they're lookin' for the guy."

The quiet resumes. Warari fidgets in his bunk. *Rosco ...in a coma...looking for the guy...did I leave anything? No, nothing ...but what if Rosco recovers and talks – or what if he don't recover? Hurry up, Kamiri, I want outta here!*

In early morning, the breakfast trays are passed through the door. One of Warari's cellmates is kneeling on a prayer rug; he is muttering, and his head touches the floor. *Probably a Muslim.*

"You been in prison before?" a cellmate asks.

"No. First time. My brother's gonna get me out."

"Kind of in a hurry to leave are we?" The Muslim is seated on his bunk and he is staring intently at Warari.

"Yeah, I got a business to run."

"You ain't a Muslim, are you?"

"No."

"But you're a hard man, ain't you?"

"If you say so."

"Kind of like a fight, don't you?"

"From time to time."

The Muslim pauses to consider. "So your brother's gonna bail you and you're gonna fly away?" He makes flapping motions with his arms. Warari silently returns his inquisitor's stare. "Sounds like you're gonna need a place to lie low. Somewhere they won't come lookin' for ya."

"Maybe."

"You ever feel like the world dealt you a shit hand? And you'd like to hit back?" Warari responds with a tilt of his head. "Place I have in mind is full of guys like you. They're tough and they're lookin' to punish." Warari's eyes narrow with intensity. The Muslim suddenly asks: "What's your name?"

"Warari."

"Mine's Tabiz." Warari nods. "You got anything against Muslims, Warari?"

"Nah. Muslims are OK."

Tabiz offers a slight smile. "Do you believe there was a Prophet Muhammad?"

Warrari shrugs. "I dunno. Probably. You want me to become a Muslim, or somethin'?"

Tabiz' shoulders edge forward. "That's for you to decide. I've got an offer for you."

"Which is?"

"I'm offering you a hidden camp. It's a camp the police don't know about. People there are tough; they're warriors, and they fight for a better world. They would welcome you."

"Yeah? How much does it cost to get in?"

"Nothing, Warari. Nothing at all."

"What's the catch?"

"You just join."

"Do I hafta become a Muslim?"

"Like I say, Warari, that's for you to decide. They'll tell you about Islam."

"I'll think about it." Then, after a pause, "How do I get to this secret camp?"

Tabiz fumbles in a knapsack at the foot of his bunk. "Here, Warari, the guy to call is Mujahid. His number's there on the card. Just tell him Tabiz sent you."

I know. False advertising. One of the Other's favorite inventions: telling a potential friend what he wants to hear; not mentioning that there is fine print, or a few of the 'catches'. The problem with Tabriz' smooth pitch is: "It's for you to decide." If Warari decides that the camp isn't for him, what then? That's probably covered by their covert fine print.

I wouldn't call Tabiz' pitch to Warari 'false advertising'. It's more like 'the-way-I-see-it advertising'. Anyway, I have plans for Warari, and I don't want to see him sitting in jail. He has a lot of potential! Notice how I got him in the same cell as Tabiz?

Kamiri arranges with Jonathan for one day's absence from the Lions' Den. His first stop is the police station where Warari was charged. He is given the name of a bail bondsman, and he inquires about his brother's possessions.

"We're holding some money and some keys," the desk officer says, "but we're not releasing anything until he gets bail – if he does."

"How much of his money are you holding?"

The officer consults a sheet on his desk. "One hundred and eighty-eight thousand, four hundred and twenty-five shillings."

The bail bondsman informs Kamiri, after a call to the police station, that the bail has been set a half a million shillings.

"How much do you want to pay the bail?"

"Fifteen percent, and his signature on a piece of paper."

"OK. Now here's my proposal: my brother has a hundred and eighty-eight thousand being held by the police. If you pay his bail, he'll turn over the hundred and eighty thousand to you."

"And if he doesn't?"

"He will, but if he refuses, he goes back to jail."

The cell door opens. The prison officer signals Warari with a jerk of his head. "Your bail has been paid."

"Don't forget, Warari," the Tabriz says, "You'll be in good company at the camp. Call the man!"

Warari is escorted to the police desk where Kamiri and the bail bondsman are waiting.

Kamiri says: "Before we complete this, I'd like a word with my brother."

The desk officer signals his assent. Warari and Kamiri can be heard in whispered conversation.

"No!" Wariri shouts.

Angrily, Kamiri turns to the bondsman. "Let's go."

Warari seizes his brother's arm. "OK. Yes. I agree."

The bondsman places a certified check on the counter. He and Warari sign a document, copies of which are given to the desk officer, the bondsman and Warari. The desk officer hands Warari a plastic envelope, which the released prisoner opens and begins to count the money.

"Don't bother counting, Warari. Just hand him the money," Kamiri says.

Meekly, Warari complies and the bondsman departs.

Outside the police station, Warari pauses to take in a hemispheric view: the cityscape around him, the dirty pavement at his feet and the cumulus clouds above. He draws a deep, appreciative breath, then, with a start, he comes back to the present. "Thanks, brother. I gotta go."

"You said something about your bike," Kamiri reminds him.

"Yeah, yeah. It's at my place. Come on."

They find the motorcycle still parked outside Warari's flat. "There's my beautiful machine. You want to buy her?"

"Well," Kamiri concedes, "it'd be better if it weren't in your name with a court case pending against you."

They argue over the price. "I haven't got the cash to give you; I can only pay you about four thousand a month."

"How much are the Lions paying you?"

"That's my business."

They finally agree that Kamiri will pay four thousand shillings a month into an account he will open in Warari's name for eight months.

Warari signs the owner's certificate and turns toward his place. "OK, brother, take care."

"Don't forget. You have a court appearance next Wednesday."

"Yeah, I know. There's a helmet in the compartment under the seat."

The road between City and Coast City is two-lane, nearly-straight, paved macadam. At one hundred and thirty kilometers per hour (somewhat above the legal speed limit), the ride is exhilarating: the feeling of power beneath him, the steady roar of the engine, a fresh wind in his face, and the constantly changing one hundred-and-eighty-degree panorama of rolling hills, coverlet of yellow grass, flying green trees and intense blue sky.

*   *   *

I really like this car! Dorothy has collected it from the garage and is driving it home. *Actually, I can't drive it very much because if the police will be looking for Hassan, they'll probably be looking for his car. Where to keep it? Somewhere out of the public view. No garage at home.*

Joseph is suitably impressed by the car, but increasingly skeptical when he hears Dorothy's narrative.

"Maybe, you ought to just tell the police you have it," he suggests.

"But, Papa, that would be a violation of a friend's trust. Besides, it's not stolen, and nobody is searching for it. If the police ask me about it, I'll tell them."

"Well, it needs to be stored someplace where it's out of the way, pretty much invisible, and pretty soon."

I, the One, confess that I gave Dorothy a little help with this dilemma: I put Kemboi's name into her awareness.

Kemboi!! There's an idea! I couldn't store it on his claim – which is out of the way, but I wonder where he lives.

She calls him. He says, "I live in the shepherd's settlement at the end of the dirt track. Why do you ask?" She explains her need to hide the car. "Well, it'd be safe enough here. There's no garage, but the other guys would help me look after it. It probably should be covered with a tarpaulin."

Dorothy and Joseph move the car to the shepherd's settlement, where it is left behind a fenced corral, wrapped in sand-colored tarpaulins.

I really should tell Hassan what I've done with his car. She presses his number, and is surprised to hear: "The number you have dialed is not a working number." She tries again with the same result. *Maybe he's changed phone numbers. Kamiri would know.*

But, Kamiri doesn't know, nor does he know about the Shepherds' Field scandal or Hassan's involvement in it.

"Hassan always seems to get hurt trying to do the right thing." Then he adds, "I have a new job, Dorothy, but still working for the same guy."

"Who is that?"

"Mr Arusei. I was scouted by the Coast City Lions, and I've signed a one-year contract with them. So I'm in Coast City now."

"I thought you were still at the abattoir, Kamiri. We had a note from the Parks Commission telling us that they would like to see your application to be a ranger; we told them you already had a job."

"Funny how things happen. If they'd approached me before the abattoir, I would have gone with them, but then I wouldn't have been scouted by the Lions."

"Kamiri, will you be coming here to play any time soon?"

"There's a game with the City Rhinos next month. I don't know if I'll be playing."

"Can you get me a ticket? I'm sure Papa would like to go, too."

"I'll see what I can do, Dorothy."

At home, Joseph looks up from his evening newspaper: "This guy, Warari: wasn't he Kamiri's brother?"

"What are you talking about, Papa?"

"I'm talking about this guy, Warari." He taps a page of the newspaper. "Apparently, he put that fellow, Rosco, in a coma."

"I thought they didn't know who attacked Bosco."

"That's right, but Rosco is awake now, and he's talking to the police."

Dorothy nods. "I'm pretty sure Kamiri's brother's name was Warari and that he was a drug dealer. Do you remember? He came to Home Away to pick up Kamiri. He was impatient and disagreeable; I didn't like him at all."

"Well, the police are looking for him; he is out on bail. I think I ought to tell the police about the relationship. Maybe Kamiri knows where he is." He listens to Dorothy's news about Kamiri's new job. "That's all the more reason to call the police. Maybe Warari's gone to Coast City, too."

Chapter 11

Dhul Fikar

Dorothy is filing constituent paperwork when Abdallah looks in. "Can I see you a minute, Dorothy? This Shepherds' Field business is getting hot again." In his office, he continues: "Kurgat has drafted an amendment to the law that makes deep mining in the area legal."

"That's terrible: just what Mine Ventures and Kurgat want." Dorothy bites her lip. "Will the amendment pass?"

"I'm afraid it has a good chance. If the Environment Committee approves it, the Business Committee certainly will – after all, it's good for business. And when it gets to the floor of Parliament, the government will whip it through."

"But you're on the Environment Committee; can't you kind of veto it?"

Abdallah smiles. "Don't I wish. The problem is that the committee chairman controls a majority, and if he wants it to pass, it will pass."

"But the chairman must be aware of the Shepherds' Field Scandal. Why would he want it to pass?"

Abdallah holds out his right hand: his thumb is caressing his four other fingers.

"No! A committee chairman would take money?" Dorothy suddenly recalls the scandal of the crooked helicopter purchase, and her own fury about government corruption. She sighs heavily. "Who would provide the money?"

"Mine Ventures, of course."

"What are we going to do?"

Abdallah studies the ceiling. "I would like you to be involved, because you're tough, bright, and you know all the history. We'll probably want to involve Hetti, also, but later."

"OK, Abdallah, but what do you want me to do?"

"Well," Abdallah hesitates, searching for the right words, "I'd like you to get close to Joshua Wangai, the committee chairman."

Dorothy gives the MP a doubtful look. "But you're on the same committee; you know each other; shouldn't you get close to him?"

"The problem for me, Dorothy, is that since I'm not a New Republic party member, I tend to be viewed as the enemy. What's needed is a woman's touch."

Something urges Dorothy to be cautious. "What do you mean, Abdallah?"

"Well, I mean that Wangai likes women."

Dorothy blurts out her shock. "And you want me to become his mistress!"

"No! I would never ask you to do that! What I was thinking is that you could become somebody he likes and trusts."

"And lusts over?"

"Yes, possibly, but nothing further."

Dorothy glances up at the framed print of a lioness crouching in long grass, stalking an alert Thompson's gazelle. *Which am I? The lion or the gazelle? Perhaps, if the gazelle thinks it's a lion, and the lion pretends to be a gazelle, this would work.* Her inner smile creeps across her face. "Yes, OK, let's give it a try."

I, the Other, like the way that Dorothy has been maneuvered into this 'relationship' with Wangai, whom I agree is a proper dirty old man, but, of course, he would say, "I just like young, good-looking women; what's wrong with that?" A man who has my genuine affection!

Achieving Superpersonhood:

There is always the possibility that things will carry on in the dirty direction I have in mind.

Dorothy follows Abdallah into the parliamentary dining room. It is busy: groups of men in dark suits; a scattering of women in long, colorful dresses, many with head scarves; dark paneled walls set with historic portraits; white tablecloths and an energetic buzz of conversation. For a moment, Abdallah halts, surveying, then he moves toward the bar at the far end of the room. He pauses frequently to respond to greetings, and at each instance, he introduces Dorothy. It proves impossible to reach the bar itself; Abdallah calls an order to a barman over the heads of others. White wine in hand, Dorothy finds herself hemmed in by loquacious parliamentarians, who ignore her presence after a phrase or two of polite acknowledgement.

"There you are, Ndungu!" The voice is commanding, and as its owner pushes his way into the encirclement, it continues: "I have a table for the EC over there."

"Joshua, I'd like to introduce Miss Dorothy Maiyo. She is my parliamentary researcher. Dorothy, this is Joshua Wangai, Environment Committee Chairman."

Wangai turns, looks Dorothy over and announces: "And a very good researcher I'm sure she is – very good indeed! Will you join us for lunch, my dear?"

Dorothy finds herself the lone woman at a table originally laid for eight, with eight men, but she is scarcely left alone. Sitting on Wangai's right, she is the center of his attention: "Are you working full time for Ndungu, my dear?"

"No, I am studying medicine at the University."

"And which part of the body will be your specialty, if you don't mind my asking?"

"I haven't reached that decision yet, but probably I would like to be a general surgeon."

"Excellent! So if I require a heart transplant, I will be sure to ask for Doctor Dorothy Maiyo."

Surprised that he remembers her name, she decides, nonetheless, to humble herself. "But Chairman, I am sure cardiology is a specialty far beyond my capabilities."

"Please, my dear, call me 'Joshua', and then, if you don't mind, I can call you 'Dorothy'. But as to your capabilities, I'm sure you should not underestimate them."

A waiter sets plates of soup in front of them. "Dorothy! Is this soup all right for you? There is also melon."

"The soup is fine, Joshua."

He takes several spoonfuls of the tomato soup and turns to Dorothy again. "Now, I suppose that the research you are completing for Ndungu is environmentally related?"

Should I lead him onto the subject of Shepherds' Field?

I, the Other, whisper: "Yes!"

"Yes, Joshua, it is environmentally related. Lately, I have been looking at the issues around mining in Shepherds' Field."

"And what conclusions have you reached, my dear?"

"None as yet. On the one hand, there is the possibility of considerable revenue for the government. And on the other hand, the government may wish to avoid taking a U-turn on its promise not to leave ugly spoil piles, and its promise to give the shepherds priority to any diamond finds."

Wangai nods wisely. "Has your research revealed to you the potential size of diamond finds from Shepherds' Field over – let's say – the next twenty years?"

"No. I'd be most interested in the numbers you have heard."

"Well, Dorothy, I have asked the Bureau of Mines for their estimate, and they have told me a million carats."

"Very interesting, but have they made any forecasts of weight and quality of individual stones?"

"They are working on those figures at the moment."

"And tell me, Joshua, have you consulted any industry sources, as well?"

Achieving Superpersonhood:

"Industry sources, as you know, my dear, tend to keep their cards very close, and, in any case, any figures that they may quote publicly will be very conservative indeed."

A waiter clears away the soup plates.

"So, Dorothy, can you tell me which way Ndungu is intending to vote on the Mining Amendments Bill?"

"He hasn't decided yet, Joshua. There is so much to weigh up."

"Yes, of course, and you spoke of a government U-turn. Fortunately, there is no government U-turn involved. Shepherds who wish to dispose of their claims will be fully reimbursed, and the landscape will be returned to its original condition, complete with trees."

I'm not sure the shepherds can opt not to sell, as he implies.

Dorothy and Wangai's plates of chicken and lamb, respectively, are set before them.

"Dorothy, you lead a very busy life: studying medicine at University, working as a researcher for a prominent MP, and you must have a whirlwind social life as well, with a very attentive boyfriend."

"Actually, Joshua, you are correct about my being busy. In fact, I haven't time for a boyfriend."

"Oh, dear, some poor fellow is missing out on a splendid woman. Or perhaps I should say a man is missing out – a man who could shower you with presents, take you to glittering events and totally adore you!"

Boy! He sure does know how to lay it on! She says, "I suppose, Joshua, that one should always be open to the possibilities, and ..."

"Indeed one must always be open to the possibilities!" he insists.

"Well, perhaps I should make more time for myself by giving up the volunteer work I do." She continues, "I am wondering, Joshua, whether you might be able to introduce me to an industry source in connection with the research I am doing?"

"Yes, I can probably get you an appointment to see the chief mining engineer at Mine Ventures."

"Oh, that would be splendid, Joshua!"

"And in that connection, perhaps you and I can have lunch at Poseidon next week so that we can compare our research findings?"

The only research he's going to be doing will be on me!
"Yes, that sounds lovely!"

"Excellent! Would you be so kind as to give me your phone number?"

"I can be reached most weekday afternoons at Mr. Ndungu's office."

"Yes, of course, but it may be more convenient to exchange mobile numbers."

She removes the iPhone from her handbag and they exchange numbers.

Abdallah shakes his head with amused incredulity. "The Chairman is unctuous, polite, intelligent, and a dirty old man: just as I told you. But you handled him extremely well, Dorothy. Now . . ." He pauses to take a deep breath. "As to the 'research' he alleges is being done by the Bureau of Mines, do you think there is any substance to it?"

"Well, there certainly isn't any physical research being done. As I understand it, physical research would require test borings, and Kemboi would surely have mentioned the presence of a large boring rig when I saw him last week. Alternatively, I suppose BuMines could be using figures they got from Mine Ventures."

"But Dorothy, businesses tend to be very precise in their estimates. A million carats is a very round number – the kind of number which would impress the general public. I doubt that figure came from Mine Ventures, but when you meet with their chief mining engineer, you can get a feel for the origin of the figure. Besides, if there is corruption involved in the passage of the amendment – as we suspect – why would Mine Ventures want to give the Bureau any figures? If they gave a low figure, the amendment may not pass, and if they gave a high figure, it's likely that Wangai would demand a heftier pound of flesh." He pauses for several moments to consider. "I think we should have a chat with Hetti."

Twenty minutes later, Hetti is on the loudspeaker and has been briefed. "I've had dealings with Wangai before, and I can assure you he's as crooked as a snake. I'd suggest you try to drive the two sides apart: make Wangai think the project is going to be a bonanza for Mine Ventures, and Mine Ventures doubt the economic value of the project. They'll waste a lot of time arguing about the size of the bribe. For example, I can probably arrange a live interview of Kemboi during which he'll complain that if somebody is going to harvest a million carats of diamonds, the shepherd claim-holders are going to want to be paid some real money for their claims. That should make Mine Ventures a little nervous. And Dorothy, when you have your meeting with the chief mining engineer, you could have your research hat on and remind him of some kimberlite pipes around the world that turned out to be complete busts."

Abdallah says: "Hetti, I'm a little worried that with Dorothy's involvement with you in the earlier sting at Shepherds' Field, she'll be recognized by the Mine Ventures people."

"I wouldn't worry about that, Abdallah. Any CCTV pictures they may have will be indistinct. The people they'll remember about that sting are me, Kemboi, Arusei and a cameraman. They may recall that there was another woman, but pretty as she is, they won't remember her face. Besides, the chief mining engineer almost certainly wasn't involved then, but if he was and he recognizes Dorothy, is he going to file a complaint about trespass? I doubt it. They haven't filed one against me."

"OK Hetti, what about Dorothy's lunch with Wangai?"

"Well, the most important point is that you, Abdallah, should call her about halfway through the lunch and insist that you need her back at the office. That way she doesn't have to make up any excuses for not going with him to the Excelsior Hotel."

"Good point. What else?"

"I think it would be great if she could give him a report on a really successful kimberlite pipe – a bonanza. That will get his mouth watering. Besides, he'll sense that she's on his side. And I think that you, Dorothy, should try to get a feel for his relationship with Mine Ventures."

"Hetti, this is Dorothy. All that makes sense, but it doesn't answer my key question: how are we going to catch the actual financial transaction?"

"Right! Let me say a couple of things about that. First of all, I doubt that Wangai would want an electronic transfer of funds to any account which he controls. That's just too easy for the Anti-Corruption Tsar. Wangai will want to receive cash in a hard currency that he can deposit in a secret foreign account. Secondly, it will be enough to find Wangai with the money. How can he explain a windfall of that size? A loan? A great aunt who died? An unexpected lottery win? Then to reduce his term behind bars, he'll want to give evidence against Mine Ventures."

"Should we tell the Anti-Corruption Tsar what we suspect?" Dorothy asks.

"Heavens no!" Abdallah shouts. "We might as well publish it in the newspaper."

Dorothy remonstrates: "But I thought the Anti-Corruption Tsar was supposed to take action in cases like this!"

"Dorothy, you haven't yet understood the nuances of politics in Country. On issues which are quite sensitive to the public, like this, the president naturally wants the people to believe that all is clean and aboveboard. But the president depends on the support of the senior people around him; without it, he is finished. So, he expects the senior people to be secretive in any shady deals, and he can turn a blind eye to them. As for the Tsar, he would never uncover a big, secret shady deal without the president's OK."

Dorothy gazes despondently at the floor. "That is really depressing. How can you be in politics with that kind of thing going on, Abdallah?"

"Dorothy," Hetti interjects, "without people like Abdallah, who try to clean up our politics, we would be living in a kleptocracy."

Dorothy nods her acquiescence. *I just have to see how this works out.*

I, the Other, don't think this is depressing at all. It's fun! I enjoy helping my smart friends – they tend to be the greedy ones – boost their bank accounts. The One is so simplistic and narrow-minded that life would be suffocatingly boring if he were completely in charge!

I disagree, of course, with the Other. The sad part is that when all the elaborate planning and deception is completed, and his friends get caught playing the double game, he just laughs.

* * *

Hassan has been transported blindfolded for about half an hour by Mujahid and another man in the pickup truck, the last third of the trip over increasingly derelict roads. He is uneasy about the blindfold, expecting to be welcomed as a soldier of Allah. *But maybe it's necessary: a secret place. Is this good or bad?* Hassan is ordered out of the truck, his blindfold is removed, and he sees that he is in a narrow valley with steep rock faces on either side. The valley floor is covered by a canopy of tall, thick-rooted trees interspersed with tan tents. In the air is the odor of wood smoke and balsam. It is quiet now that the truck has been parked alongside half a dozen similar vehicles.

Mujahid announces: "This is the training camp for Dhul Fikar (the Prophet's sword). You are assigned to the large tent over there with the other soldiers in training. You will be here for about ten weeks, and when you are assigned to another location by DF, you will be one of the most feared and competent of

Allah's warriors." *Competent: yes, I like that. Feared: I'm not so sure.*

Mujahid escorts Hassan along a narrow path, pointing out the various tents. "That one is where you take your meals. That is the mosque. This one here is the armory. That one in the back is the latrine. Over here is the office. This is the living quarters for the instructors." He consults his watch. "We will go now to the mosque, as it is almost prayer time."

As Hassan enters the flap of the mosque, he notices the stenciled lettering on the side of the tent: UNHCR The UN Refugee Agency and beside it a logo consisting of two laurel branches around a shelter composed of human hands protecting a solitary figure. *I wonder whether these tents were somehow leftovers.*

Within the tent is a stained and threadbare carpet which stretches nearly from wall to wall. There is no other decoration. Ahead is the qibla blue arrow affixed to the tent wall and pointing the direction to Mecca. Immediately to the right is a makeshift lectern for the imam: the *minrab*. Hanging from the center of the ridgepole is a single incandescent bulb.

The space begins to fill with young men of about Hassan's age; all of them have full beards and are dressed in loose-fitting, dark camouflage garb; many are black-skinned like Hassan, but most have the lighter skin of the coastal Arabs. There is even one tall white man with a russet beard and brown hair. *I wonder where he came from.*

He hears snatches of Swahili and other languages, but when the imam utters the call to prayer, it is in Swahili.

Hassan finds himself between two large men who make no secret of their enthusiasm for the prayer, throwing themselves forwards and backwards, and repeating the words as if the world were hard of hearing.

The prayer itself isn't as Hassan remembers it. There are new, militant phrases, and some of Allah's generosity seems to have disappeared. *Maybe that's the way this sect does it.*

Achieving Superpersonhood:

At the conclusion of the prayer, Hassan is sitting back on his heels, looking ahead at the qibla arrow so as not to draw the attention of either of his neighbors.

"You get here today?" the man to his left inquires in a powerful, bass voice.

"Yes, I got here just before prayer time."

The man's dark face is dominated by cheekbones and huge eyes beneath a sloping forehead. "Where you from?"

"I'm from City. My name is Hassan."

"OK, Hassan. My name is Wassim, but they call me Wassy, as in Wassy the Magnificent. This here is Raouf, but we just call him Bad Ass."

Hassan turns toward Raouf who responds with a gap-toothed smile and a casual salute.

"Does everyone here have special names?" Hassan inquires.

"Yeah, most do," Wassy says, "but most gets their name after they've been here a while, and we get to know what's good and bad about 'em."

From the prayer tent, Hassan is called to the office, where he is given a four-page form to complete: one page of personal history including family, education and language skills, half a page of health data, and the balance are essay questions probing military experience, religious commitment, reasons for joining Dhul Fikar, special skills of interest to Dhul Fikar, and willingness to make personal sacrifices for Allah. *I wonder what personal sacrifices are expected of me – I'll just say 'willing to give myself to Allah'.*

From the office, he is sent to the storage tent, where he receives two sets of camouflage, a pair of lace-up boots, two sets of socks and underwear. The black baklava he is given attracts greater attention than the boots to ensure a good fit. He is asked: "Is it tight enough? You don't want it slipping down. Can you see all right? How is your peripheral vision?" He changes into the fatigues; his civilian clothes are removed. His mobile phone and wallet were previously placed 'in safekeeping' at the office.

From the storage tent, he is sent to the food tent, where the evening meal is to be served. On arrival, there is already a queue of ten men waiting for the tent flap to be opened. Wassy and Bad Ass are toward the front of the queue. He falls in behind the red-bearded white man. "You're the new guy, hunh?"

"Yes, I just arrived today; my name's Hassan."

"My name's Mabrouk, but they call me Irish."

"Are you from Ireland, then?"

"Yeah, partly. My mother's Irish and my father is Syrian. They split up when I was in high school, but I was raised as an Irish Catholic kid. My father went back to Syria; I joined him and became Muslim. When he was killed, I decided to come here. For a while, I lived in City; I understand that's where you're from, Hassan."

Feeling the intensity of Irish's focus, Hassan decides to abbreviate his answers: "Yes."

"Attend University?"

"Yes."

"On scholarship?"

"No."

"Rich kid, hunh? What's your surname?"

Hassan hesitates, weighing his options: *refuse – leads to a bad start; invent a name – will be found out.* "Arusei."

"Ah, we were expecting somebody like you. I think we're gonna call you The Heir."

"Except that I'm not."

"What do you mean?"

"My father has disinherited me."

"Why would he do that?"

Hassan recounts, briefly, his problems with the police.

"Yeah. Welcome to Dhul Fikar."

The meal is served on stainless steel trays from the cooking station: chicken-rice curry and collard greens with flat bread which is used as a scoop in place of utensils. There is coconut water and sweetened bean curd.

There are about twenty-five trainees at the camp, arranged along both sides of trestle tables. Hassan listens to the banter, which is mostly about the day's events. "Mourad, you were supposed to jump over that ditch, not fall in it!" and "No! I had a higher score than he did on the killing range!"

After the meal, Hassan is called back to the office, where a man dressed in green fatigues, with three gold stars on each collar, is waiting. "I am Major el Hashem, your commanding officer." He has a piercing stare and a mouth that turns up and down at opposite ends.

"Yes, sir."

"Why are you here?" The question has an accusatory tone.

"I am here because Imam Kipyego sent me."

"But what is the real reason you are here, Arusei?"

Possible responses whirl through Hassan's brain. He decides on: "I wish to get closer to Allah."

"What does that mean?"

"Well, sir, until now I have lived a spoiled, secular life, and the imam has taught me that I can become a better person if I dedicate myself to Allah."

El Hashem is sitting on the corner of the desk; he reaches down for a folder which he opens and peruses.

"It says here that you are the stepson of Kaddour Arusei."

"Yes, sir."

"Tell me, Arusei: since Dhul Fikar would welcome a cash injection, and since your father is rich, why shouldn't I hold you hostage until your father sends me a hundred million shillings?"

"Because he would laugh at you, sir."

A flash of anger crosses el Hashem's face; he leans forward aggressively. "He would dare laugh at Dhul Fikar? We could kill him tomorrow before breakfast!"

"He would laugh at the situation, sir. My father and I are not on good terms. He would give you nothing on my behalf."

El Hashem's lower jaw protrudes. "Explain!"

Hassan describes his assault on the police officer, his suspended sentence, his trespass at Shepherds' Field, and his father's lecture.

"So, Arusei, to answer my earlier question, you are here to avoid a prison sentence."

"In part, yes, sir, but I believed the imam when he said that if I came here, I would become Allah's holy soldier."

"And what does Allah's holy warrior do, Arusei?"

"He fights for the Islamic caliphate and against the infidels."

For a long moment, el Hashem stares coldly at Hassan. "What you say is correct, Arusei, but make no mistake. At Dhul Fikar there is no theoretical or motion picture fight. This is a <u>real</u> fight where people, many people, are killed, and where you, Aruesi, will watch them – including your friends – die. There is no turning back, Arusei; you must fight with all your strength and all your will if you are to become Allah's holy warrior. Do you understand?"

"Yes, sir."

"Go then, and obey the commands you are given!"

Hassan has a nauseous sensation deep within. He overrides it with a commitment: *I've got to be tougher!*

The evening prayer is said. The young men move to the sleeping tent, where narrow cots are arranged in three tight rows. There is little talking. Boots are removed, and bodies are stretched out. Hassan is physically tired, but his brain insists on processing the events since his arrival at Dhul Fikar. *This is not what I expected. What did I expect? Did I expect an isolated military camp with men who are serious about killing? I think I expected a camp where people come and go, and where there is much dusty marching. The food is not good: the little chicken was tough as vulture. My boots don't fit right, and I have never slept on a cot. But . . . perhaps this is the trial I need to become the person I want to be. The person that my father will truly respect.* His thoughts are interrupted by persistent snoring.

There is a loud metal clatter. Groans are emitted. "Reveille, reveille, reveille! Get up, you lazy bastards!" A short, stocky, bearded man dressed in sand fatigues and a black beret strides through the cots. "Assemble in the prayer hall in five minutes!"

Hassan looks at his wrist. Then he remembers: his watch is also in 'safe keeping'. He buttons his shirt, pulls on his boots and follows the others to the prayer 'hall'. Outside, there is only a hint of dawn.

Prayers completed, the black beret man, Sergeant Kingali, orders the recruits into two columns, and calls out the cadence as they begin to march down the valley. About every hundred meters, he orders them into a trot, then into a disorganized sprint, and back into an orderly march. They are out of the valley now and crossing a plain densely covered with brush and stunted trees. There is only the dirt track: no sign of humanity. The sun has risen; it is burning the morning mist into high humidity. But no one – certainly not Hassan, whose shirt is soaked with perspiration – complains.

After another sprint, the sergeant announces: "All right you little boys, it's time to show me some strength! Carry the poles!" There are brief anonymous groans from the recruits, but they gather around four telephone poles which have been left by the side of the track. One group of five recruits lifts a pole to their shoulders and moves into the center of the track, facing the direction from which they came. Other teams do likewise. Hassan hesitates until one member of a team waves him to join them. "No! Get on the other side!" And Hassan realizes that the team has taken up positions on alternate sides of the pole. "Otherwise, we can't control it," the recruit behind explains.

"Ready?" the recruit at the head of the pole calls out. "Right, left, right, left!"

"Get in step!" the recruit behind admonishes.

Even in synchronous steps, with the weight of the pole on alternate shoulders, it is a heavy burden. Hassan's team begins to sing a dirty ditty in time to their steps. It is a poem Hassan has never heard before, but after the fourth repetition, he has learnt it and joins in the singing. There are constant criticisms from the black beret, who is marching alongside. "You, there, pick up your feet!"   "Eyes forward!"   "Backs straight!" "Are you men or babies?"

On and on they go.

The hard pole is causing Hassan's shoulder to ache; his legs are beginning to burn with fatigue, and he is panting for breath. *How much farther? I'm afraid I'm going to faint!*

Someone in another team stumbles and there are cries of alarm as his team struggles to retain control of the pole.

"One hundred meters farther!" Black Beret announces.

The lead team has stopped.

Hassan's team leader shouts: "On the count of three, down to your waist! One, two, three!" The pole is brought halfway to the ground. "On the count of three, drop it and jump! One, two, three!" Hassan releases the pole and it thuds to the ground, narrowly missing his foot.

"You have to jump back when you release the pole," the recruit, now on his right, shouts.

"Sorry, I didn't know."

"Well, it's your foot, not mine!" He is young, with only the wisp of a beard, brown eyes and light skin. "You must be the new one."

"Yes, I came yesterday. What's your name?"

"My name is Wadam, but they call me Baby Face. So, you must be The Heir."

Hassan stifles a chuckle. "Don't I wish."

"Don't you wish what?"

"I'll tell you later."

Black Beret is forming them into marching columns again for the return to camp. They swarm eagerly into the food tent, where their trays are loaded with hot, sticky porridge and flat bread, smothered in black treacle. There are mugs of strong tea.

Hassan sits next to Baby Face, who asks, "So, what's your story?"

The young man chews thoughtfully on his bread as Hassan tells him.

He can't be any older than fifteen!

He glances over at Hassan. "Well, at least you had a chance."

"A chance for what?"

"A chance to make something of yourself!"

The response reverberates in Hassan. *I have a chance now, and I must seize it even if I don't much like it.*

I, the One, know that Hassan is preparing a rebuttal. Gently, I cool his anger, and I whisper: "Listen!"

"So what's your story, Wadam?"

"I grew up on the northern edge of Coast City. My mother is from Lebanon – from a wealthy family. My father is from around here – very handsome. He went to Lebanon, where an uncle lived, to look for a wife. He found my mother, married her – and her dowry – and came back to Coast City." Hassan nods with interest. "By the time I was two, the money, my father and the interest any other men had in my mother were all gone. My mother works as a street sweeper; there's something wrong with her breathing."

"What is it?" Hassan asks.

Wadam shrugs. "I've been workin' and stealin' what I can. Like you, the police are looking for me. I decided to join Dhul Fikar. Once I pass the training, they'll pay me, but now my mother has only herself to feed."

"Do you see your father anymore?"

"Nah. He's probably dead – or should be!"
"And your mother: why doesn't she go back to Lebanon?"
"Are you kidding? She is damaged goods. Nobody would want her."
"You're a Muslim, Wadam?"
"Yeah, when you have to hustle, you can fake most anything."

I, the One, am angry at the way some Muslim men treat women: worse than cattle. And this in spite of what the Prophet said in his farewell address near Mount Arafat: "So fear Allah in respect to women, and concern yourselves with their welfare. Have I given the message?—O Allah, be my witness."

The One says he is disappointed at the way some Muslim men treat women. In his farewell sermon the Prophet said that women, "have the right to be fed and clothed in kindness." He didn't mention anything about forgiveness if they marry the wrong man, or equal treatment in general. In my opinion, if the One isn't happy with the way men treat women, He should have done something about it a long time ago. It is well known that women are the 'weaker sex'. I have never wrestled with a woman, but I find them intellectually, emotionally and spiritually stronger than men. However, I must confess that equality and strength are not my areas of interest. I prefer exploring vulnerability!

The recruits move to the 'killing range' where four AK-47s are issued, and each man is provided with five cartridges. Single shots are fired at paper bull's-eye targets by each standing recruit in turn. Each shot is scored zero to ten and tallied on a slate board. Black Beret comments on each shooter's posture and technique. There are loud jeers for each score 3 or below, and Hassan begins with a 0, missing the target altogether, but

Achieving Superpersonhood:

he ends with a 5 for a total score of 17. Bad Ass scores 38 and leads in the overall scoring. From the banter, it becomes clear to Hassan that there is intense competition to achieve high scores. *I wonder if there's some reward at the end of training. I've got to do much better than 17 next time, but I've never done it before, and the gun is heavy. It's hard to keep it pointing at the target. Would it be hard if I am pointing at a man who is trying to kill me? Or if he is running away? The gun really hits my shoulder. BB says I should squeeze the trigger and accept the hit: difficult! He says when you're firing a burst, the muzzle tends to rise. I wonder when they're going to give us more ammunition.*

Next is Knife Skills. Irish seems to be a particular favorite of BB in rushing at a dummy, turning him and slitting his throat.

There is hand-to-hand combat in pairs using rubber knives and judo skills. Hassan dies eight times at the hands of Baby Face. *I just don't know any judo; he seems to be good at it.* There is a special training for Hassan and three other recruits that afternoon in judo.

After prayers and the midday meal comes tactical skills: setting up a sniper position; finding and killing a sniper; street fighting: offensive and defensive; anti-tank operations; setting booby traps.

Then there is working with explosives: how to use IEDs. And, naturally, another two hours of marching and physical training: a complex obstacle course.

The days pass quickly for Hassan, The Heir. He has little in common with the other recruits, and his natural reserve keeps him at arm's length. But he is alert to the macho, competitive culture of the camp: to the put-downs, the sparring, the jokes about women, the foul language, and the devotion to an Islamic state. For Hassan, who came to the camp seeking a personal relationship with Allah, he finds the fervor for a pure Islamic state difficult to understand. *Are they that much ahead of me in faith that they have already achieved a relationship with Allah and are longing for the next step: bringing Allah, the Prophet and his teaching alive on earth?* But when he mentions Allah or the Prophet in casual conversation, the response is typically an oral shrug: "Is that so?" or "You sure about that?" or "Who are People of the Book?" (Those who profess an Abrahamic religion.) *Their faith compared to mine seems quite shallow.*

From brief asides and reading between the lines of what the major, BB and the older recruits say, Hassan has formed another impression: one joins Dhul Fikar for life and not for one's convenience. An 'Othmane' is mentioned. He 'deserted camp' after three months, and has not returned. His family has 'paid a price'. The nature of the price is not clear, but 'security has been tightened' since Othmane's departure.

There is also talk about the 'missions' they will go on after their training is complete. To Hassan these missions sound like vivid video games. *And maybe that's the way they think of them: wreaking havoc, death and destruction with casual ease, while they are immortal, or at least, through the mission, they have earned immortal souls. I'm not so sure it works like that.*

But Hassan is also feeling the benefits of the rigorous training. His physical fitness has much improved. He has achieved a 34 on the killing range. His team has jogged a full kilometer with a telephone pole, and BB has complimented him for his innovative ideas for booby traps and the use of IEDs. *Perhaps the hardship and uncertainty are good for me.*

Six weeks into the training, a new recruit is introduced: a man named Warari.

Chapter 12

Mine Ventures

Kamiri and Eddie Onyango have rented a two-bedroom, furnished flat in a refurbished building about four kilometers from the Lions' training ground. Kamiri still can't believe that it's his – at least partly. There are large windows, a sliding glass door onto a ledge of a balcony; there is a tall, white refrigerator which also makes ice; there is a stove with <u>four</u> gas burners; the brown leather couch faces a television which is at least a meter wide. The shower pours down clear water at the temperature you like, and his bed is twice as wide as the television! *I wonder what my father would think of this! I know my mother wouldn't believe it.*

Most days, Eddie and Kamiri take their separate bikes to the training ground. When the scheduled training is over, Eddie rides in to Coast City to see a girlfriend, while Kamiri stays on to practice with anyone who is there, or he works out in the gym: his ambition is focused on the starting left-wing position. Kenny Mambola – known as Mambo – is the incumbent. He is thirty-three, and surprisingly – at least to Kamiri – he has taken on the role of coach/mentor. *I would think Mambo would want to play as much as he can while he is still able. That means he should view me as a troublesome nuisance who might end his career.* But Mambo sees it differently. "Look, Kamiri, I've got maybe another two years to play. There will come a time when Coach says to me, 'Mambo, I think it's time for you to retire', and he'll make that decision when I get beaten too many times by defensive backs. So my body will make that decision on his behalf. I can't influence the decision by being nasty to you."

To which Kamiri replies, "OK, Mambo, but I wasn't expecting you to help me improve."

"Well, I joined the Lions fifteen years ago, and I was a little like you, Kamiri: fast, skillful and ambitious. At that time there was a great left wing named Dumo ahead of me; he was in his early thirties, and the fans loved him. He taught me a lot, and he did it because he said, 'I don't want to leave a hole where I was. The crowd wouldn't like it, and, besides, I'm thinking about coaching when I retire. If I can't develop my replacement, how can I develop a team?'"

"Are you thinking about becoming a coach, Mambo?"

"Don't know yet, Kamiri but Dumo had a point."

In my opinion, Dumo is a dunce. He owns a little restaurant in City called 'Dumo's Place'. Very original name. Instead of wallpaper there are a couple hundred photographs of footballers: some on the playing field, a few with an arm around Dumo. The only ones he coaches are waiters. When he tries to coach the chefs, they just tell him, "Yes, Dumo", and carry on just as before. People go there to bump into a favorite player, to collect an autograph, and for the surf and turf. He's just hanging onto his past. I, the Other, tried to get him to do something new, like buying into a very lucrative sports betting syndicate.

If neither of them is involved in the training session, Mambo, gesturing enthusiastically, nodding and offering observations, can often be found standing next to Kamiri.

"You see: he didn't look up when he made that cross? His head was down on the ball, and it was intercepted."

"Yes, but it's hard to see both the man and the ball at the same time."

Achieving Superpersonhood:

"It is, and usually knowing where the ball is takes priority, but often it's necessary to know where the man is before striking the ball. It that case, don't drop your head completely. Look five meters ahead, where you have awareness of both the location of the man and the ball. The challenge is that you, the man and the ball are all in motion. Your brain has to take all three into account."

Typically, Kamiri climbs aboard his motorcycle at about five-thirty in the afternoon: an hour or two after the formal training session has ended a seven-and-a-half-hour day. Within fifteen minutes, he is home, exquisitely fatigued, and ready to flop down on the leather couch. At first, he would turn on the television, but at that hour there is nothing of interest, except football and the news. The news and weather he watches at ten o'clock before turning in. Football? Well, enough is enough. *Something to get my brain going before I make myself dinner.* He gets up and wanders around the flat.

I hear the One making a quiet suggestion. I suggested that he try the adult channels, but apparently Kamiri didn't hear me.

His eyes light on the beige spine of a book on the shelf below the TV. *That's Dorothy's book.* He selects it, opens the cover and begins flipping through the pages. He sits on the couch. There is a bookmark with handwriting on it: "Kamiri, if you want to know what Christianity is about, I suggest that you read first this Letter from James, whom we think was the younger brother of Jesus Christ. The letter was written about two thousand years ago. Dorothy"

Kamiri finds that the letter is only five pages long, and the introduction says it includes 'practical wisdom' about riches and poverty, temptation, patience, judging others, quarrelling, pride and humility, use of the tongue.

He sits down and begins to read: "The rich will pass away like the flower of a wild plant." "Every good gift and every perfect present comes from heaven." "Be quick to listen but slow to speak." "Love your neighbor as you love yourself." "So then, as the body without the spirit is dead, also faith without action is dead." "Come near to God and he will come near to you."

This seems to me to be very true. The world should be this way! I like it! I will read some more. Where to start?

He decides to start at the beginning: Genesis, but the Outline of Contents doesn't mention Jesus Christ. *Maybe he comes later.* Suddenly he recalls his eighth grade Reading class: *Index! There is an index. Here is Jesus Christ. On every line there is 'NT'. What does that mean? Oh! New Testament.* He turns to page one and begins to read in Swahili.

> I, the Other, don't know why anyone would want to read the Bible. Everyone knows that the Old Testament is about fairy tales, kings, prophets and rules. Fairy tales like Adam and Eve and Noah. There are hundreds of rules about things you should and shouldn't do. What good are all these rules? They just make your life more complicated! And the New Testament is all about Jesus, and it's told mostly by people who never met him, at least fifty years after he died. It's all full of magic miracles and word-for-word quotations. How much of that is worth reading? Actually, there is one line in the Bible that I rather like: Satan says, "I have been walking here and there, roaming around the earth." (Job 1:6)

Eddie finds him stretched out on the couch, snoring. A book has fallen to the floor beside him. "Hey Kamiri, wake up! It's time to go to bed."

"Oh! I guess I dozed off." Slowly, Kamiri sits up and recovers the book from the floor.

"What were you reading, Kamiri?"

Achieving Superpersonhood:

He pats the book. "It's called the Bible. It's about Christianity."
"Oh yeah, I've heard of it. Any good?"
"Very good."
Eddie pops open a can of orange soda. "Nshulubi has a girlfriend who'd like to meet you, Kamiri."
"I don't think so, Eddie. Thanks anyway."
Eddie sits down at the table and regards his friend thoughtfully. "You studying to be a religious football hermit, Kamiri?"
Kamiri sets down a plate with a grilled, gently-bleeding steak and an enormous, steaming, microwaved potato. He plucks a bag of prepared salad from the counter and sits down. "I <u>have</u> thought about it, Eddie, and I think I'm not ready for a serious girlfriend."
"It doesn't have to be serious, Kamiri."
"I know, but if one of us did start to get serious that would be a problem for me." Eddie has a puzzled frown. "I don't think I have the time, or the energy, or – I don't know – the will to involve myself with a girl right now. I just want to focus most of my time and energy on becoming a better footballer." He notices that his friend's curious frown has moderated only slightly. "Look, Eddie, I'm trying to make up for lost time. I've had professional coaching for less than two years now. You've had – what is it – eight years of professional coaching . . ."
"Ten."
"And you know what it takes to be a good keeper. I'm still learning, Eddie!"
"I'm still learning, too, Kamiri, but I take your point."

It is Saturday afternoon, partly sunny, quite humid. The stadium's 27,000 seat capacity is already buzzing with a crowd that will fill it by kick-off. There is a brass band practicing an out-of-step march behind the Lion's benches. The spicy aroma from the *smokie* (local sausage) vendors drifts across the pitch. Most of the customers will have their *smokies* with the breathtakingly hot *kachumbari pili pili* (a tomato, onion and chili garnish), and a Kilimanjaro beer.

Kamiri, dressed in black and yellow like the rest of the team, has been going through the stretching routine. He has heard that Mr Arusei had the artificial turf replaced with natural grass when he bought the club, and that this project alone cost over one million shillings because of the complex irrigation and drainage systems. The transition to grass is an important milestone for Kamiri. *In Village, I used to play on natural dirt (and stones); for the Eagles, there was plastic grass; for the Lions, it is the real thing!*

Now, the players begin assorted passing and ball-handling drills under the watchful eye of Coach Elim, who paces restlessly on the side-lines. At the far end of the pitch, the Lake City Leopards – dressed in red and green – are similarly occupied.

Eddie nudges Kamiri: "He's here today," and gives a nod toward the stands behind them. Glancing up at the top, center-field row of windows, Kamiri can make out the head and shoulders of a man in a white shirt. "That's him," Eddie adds. "I know that's where he sits when he's here."

Kamiri shrugs and asks, "You starting? I see Karoko's on the bench."

"Yeah. Last minute change. Still a problem with his right shoulder."

"Good luck, Eddie!"

The Leopards kick off; the partisan crowd whistles when a Leopard has the ball and shouts in outrage when a Lion is fouled. The ball surges back and forth from one end of the pitch to the other without either team having an obvious advantage, and the half ends in a nil-nil tie.

In the dressing room, Elim lectures the team on second-half strategy: "Look guys, I want to see more alert, aggressive play. Don't hold the ball so long. Move it forward. Let's try to avoid the east-west passes. Keep the ball moving south. And let's test their left side backs. We know they're strong in the center and they've been double-teaming Mambo. Get creative!"

Ten minutes into the second half, the Lions' right fullback clears a long ball down the right sideline. The left side defenders

Achieving Superpersonhood:

are caught out of position, and the Lion's right wing gets possession just short of being offside. He races toward the goal as the last opposing back converges on him. Feinting right and moving left, he shakes off the defender and slams the ball into the upper left corner. The stadium thunders to thousands of dancing feet.

Fifteen minutes later, the Leopards exact revenge. The Lions' right fullback makes a long pass intended for the central striker. It is intercepted in Lions' territory. Three precise and crisp passes later, the ball squeezes inside the right post just out of Eddie's lunging reach.

The stalemate resumes during the next ten minutes. Mambo is being double-teamed whenever he receives a pass. Elim is rubbing the back of his neck on the sideline. He turns and says something to Jonathan, who beckons to Kamiri: "Coach wants you to get ready to go in." Immediately, Kamiri sheds his bench vest and begins to jog and stretch his legs on the sideline. He glances down at his three-thousand-shilling fluorescent green boots. *Now we find out how good you really are.*

Play is whistled dead for a free kick. Mambo strides toward the waiting Kamiri. For a second, they embrace: "You'll need your afterburner, Kamiri."

For several minutes, Kamiri trots up and down the pitch, keeping even with the play on the far side. Sensing a favorable flow in the direction of play, Kamiri drifts into Leopards' territory. The left back has the ball. He glances up, sees Kamiri and lofts the ball ahead of him. Kamiri sprints after it, taking in the position of the right defender who has given him too much space. There is another defender converging to his right, but Kamiri hurtles past him. Fifteen meters to the goal line. There is a yellow shirt in his peripheral vision racing toward the goal. *He'll have a better shot.* His left foot taps the speeding ball to the right. *Five meters ahead: ball, man.* A step later, his left foot lofts the ball into a pass. The central striker heads the ball between the outstretched arm and leg of the keeper and into the net.

Kamiri finds himself in the enthusiastic, dancing embrace of Joram, the central striker, and seconds later most of the Lions on the pitch pile in.

The final whistle blows and he heads for the tunnel to the locker room. He is intercepted by Elim: "Well done, Kamiri! That's exactly what we want from you!"

"Man, we got the strategy now!" Mambo announces to the crowded locker room. "I go out there, get double teamed and can't score for shit. Then we bring in this Killer guy, but the Leopards don't know. They pay him no attention, and they get burned. Hot damn!"

I'm a believer in strategy! You have to be a believer when you're up against someone who has the upper hand. My opponent's weakness is that he's inflexible; he always wants to play the ball straight down the fairway. My strength is flexibility: 'do what it takes' is my motto. If a ball lands in a sand trap, I'll put it on the green. After all, the object is to win, and when I win, I have a new friend who likes to play by <u>my</u> rules.

Kamiri takes a phone call from Koinet. They chat amiably about football and what's going on at the abattoir (not much). "Kamiri, did you know that your brother has jumped bail and the police are looking for him?"

"No, I didn't know that. We don't speak much nowadays."

"Well, his picture's in the paper here."

"I'm not surprised."

"So the police haven't been around to ask you about him?"

"They probably don't know I'm his brother." A pause. "Did you mention it to them, Koinet?"

"No, I wouldn't do that, Kamiri. I just thought you ought to know. By the way, are you coming to the City any time soon?"

"Yeah, I think there's a game next month."

"Be sure to give me a call, will you?"

Achieving Superpersonhood:

Kamiri is torn. *Should I call Warari? Should I let it go? He'll probably ask to stay with me. He'll be thinking, 'Kamiri can hide me!' I don't want that! Even if it wasn't hiding a fugitive, I don't want Warari in my flat. What would Eddie think? What do I think? He would be like a wild baboon with his drugs, his women, no money, TV too loud, and eating all the food.* He grimaces. *What would our father think?* For a time, he avoids the question, but eventually: *He would say, 'You're his brother, Kamiri, you must call him!'* He sits and ponders. *I could call him and tell him he can't stay here. He should turn himself in – or go back to Village. What would Baba say then?*

Kamiri calls. The phone rings for some time and then goes dead. He tries again; no answer. *Maybe he threw the phone away. Like he did that time when the police raided the disco. That's probably it. Well, I tried.*

Actually, I, the Other, happen to know where the phone is. It hasn't been thrown away. It is in safe-keeping. Major el Hashem has a collection of phones, each neatly labeled with its owner's name, for 'safekeeping'. He has a system where he monitors incoming voicemail on each phone. Tonight, for example, he will record: "Warari: Kamiri @ 19:07 and 19:08 726-518306 no voice mail" Prior to final assignment, the major will have a discussion with each trainee about each call: Who? What? Why? I'm rather proud of this system which I helped the major to set up.

* * *

Dorothy is wearing a gray trouser suit, with wide lapels, and a ruffled-collar blue satin blouse. She hopes this outfit conveys a sense of business-like femininity, without being ordinary or flirty. The Mine Ventures reception area is dominated by a huge color photograph of an open-pit mining operation: enormous piles of brown overburden, gigantic trucks and power shovels at dusty work, contrasting strata of the pit walls, and lighter ramps and roads. *Is it coal or is it ore?* she wonders, and walking over to take a closer look, she decides. *It's coal. They're definitely digging coal.* "Where was this picture taken?" she asks the lone receptionist, who is busy at her PC.

The receptionist looks up. "That's the Black Thunder Mine in Wyoming, America, dear."

"It certainly is big, and . . . a little bit messy, I think."

The receptionist gives a shrug. "It keeps the lights on over there." She returns to her work. "Mr Akunyili will be with you shortly, dear."

Dorothy resumes to her seat behind a low table littered with mining journals. The reception area is quiet: the faint chatter of the receptionist's keyboard is muted by the deep beige carpeting and the heavy drapery in a tan savannah perspective covering the wall behind her.

"You can go in now, dear. Through the door there, down the corridor to the end."

What's he going to be like? What's he going to say?

She takes a deep breath and opens the door. Inside, directly across from the door is a massive, ornate desk, and behind it is a small man, wearing a denim shirt and a gray flat cap. He looks up suspiciously, removing the steel-rimmed spectacles from his dark eyes. "You can have a seat," he says, gesturing toward a heavy oak chair.

Dorothy takes the uncomfortable seat offered, and for a long moment the two stare at each other. He adjusts the nameplate holder on his desk so that it is facing her: Chief Mining Engineer.

"You are from the MP's office," he announces in a slightly accusatory tone.

"Yes, sir, I am."

"And you're looking for information about the Shepherds' Field mine."

She nods. "Yes, sir, the MP would like to know your assessment of the probable diamond production from Shepherds' Field."

"It's too early to say."

Dorothy looks past him to the windows where the Venetian blinds have been drawn.

I hear the One whispering to her, suggesting an aggressive approach.

"Excuse me, Mr Akunyili, your deep mining operations in Shepherds' Field are a matter of public record, and your lobbyist, Mr Tinibu, has been urging the MP to vote in favor of the amendment to the Shepherd's Field Mining Act. Your company must have some idea of the potential benefit of continued deep mining."

"I'm not aware of any public record of deep mining by Mine Ventures at the site."

"Perhaps, sir, you have forgotten that Hetti Aguta presented evidence of your deep mining on her television program."

Mr Akunyili adjusts the cap on his bald head and looks away momentarily. "What does the Bureau of Mines tell you about probable production?"

There is another whisper from the One.

"Excuse me, sir, but the Bureau of Mines is part of the government which is proposing the amendment. The MP is a bit concerned that BuMines' estimate will be high to encourage passage of the amendment, and he would be very interested in a corporate assessment."

Mr Akunyili picks up his spectacles and polishes them energetically. Dorothy notices a tick in his right cheek. "Well, Miss Maiyo, I could give you a rough estimate of the production if you will promise to confine its disclosure to the MP."

"Yes, I can promise that." *He didn't mention a specific MP.*

"There is another condition . . . which is that you disclose to me the Bureau of Mines estimate."

Dorothy says, "With the same conditions about confidentiality, of course." She waits for his disclosure.

In a low voice he says, "Our <u>confidential</u> estimate of production over twenty years is half a million carats, and BuMines?"

"A million carats over the same period."

Akunyili scratches his chin, frowning. "Do you know how BuMines' estimate was derived?"

"No, sir, I don't, but if I'm able to find out I will let you know."

"Excellent."

"And do you have an estimate of the size and quality of the individual stones?" Dorothy asks.

"I can speak to that in general terms." He places a sheet of paper on his desk in front of her, and leaning forward, he begins to draw. "This vertical axis is the number of stones of a particular weight, and the horizontal axis is the weight of individual stones. We tend to have a distribution that looks like this." He draws a line which slopes down steeply to the right and becomes asymptotic to the horizontal axis. He marks off weights on the horizontal axis: 0.1, 1.0, 10.0. "Like that."

Dorothy studies the chart. "Your curve starts at a tenth of a carat. What happens below that?"

"Stones smaller than a tenth are generally too small for jewelry. If they can be separated out – which can be costly – they are of industrial use only."

Dorothy traces her finger along the line. "It looks like stones one carat and larger represent less than five percent, and above ten carats is non-existent."

"That's about right. Above ten is rare."

"So if the average stone is one third of a carat, you're estimating about one and a half million stones over twenty years, or about two hundred a day." He shrugs. "And if the wholesale price of an average-quality, third-of-a-carat stone is three thousand shillings, your daily turnover will be about six hundred thousand shillings."

"Any estimates of that nature should not be discussed publicly."

Dorothy nods. "I understand. What can you say about clarity and color?"

"Clarity follows this same type of curve: flawless is out here to the right. Stones with more inclusions are more common and to the left. Color can be estimated from the chemistry of the pipe. Shepherds' Field tends to be a little yellow, but a clear yellow can be more valuable than an icy white."

"Mr Akunyili, you're estimating half a million carats, but it could be a lot less, right?"

"We don't think so."

"I've read about a pipe in Russia called Thunder Flash that was supposed to be a great find, but it turned out to be uneconomic."

"Yes, but that was a long time ago. We've learned a lot since."

Dorothy looks up at the ceiling. "Still, Thunder Flash might be worth mentioning in your discussions with Wangai."

The reply is instantaneous and sharp: "What discussions with Wangai?"

Dorothy makes an off-hand gesture. "Oh, I just meant in case you run into him."

In Abdallah's office, Hetti is proposing how Dorothy should approach her meeting with Wangai: "Make him think that you've got all the inside dope on Mine Ventures, and that even though you're on Wangai's side, you made a promise to Akunyili to keep his info secret. That will increase your value to Wangai and the value of the information he is able to tease out of you. You need to come across, Dorothy, as bright, sweet and honest girl, who is smitten with this committee chairman, but you're also a little scared of him."

Dorothy says, "That last part won't be hard."

Dorothy arrives a little late, and still apprehensive. She is dressed in a cream satin blouse and a thigh-length, light blue skirt. Her legs are bare and the top two buttons of her blouse are unfastened. "I'm to join Mr Wangai," she informs the Poseidon's receptionist, and she is led to a corner table.

Wangai hurries to his feet and appraises her; "You look lovely, my dear Dorothy!"

"Thank you!" She smiles as he seats her.

"Would you like a cocktail, Dorothy? They make splendid cocktails here."

"I think I'll have a Chablis, please."

Wangai beacons the sommelier. "The lady would a large Chablis and I'll have the usual." He turns his sunniest smile on Dorothy. "And how is our young doctor, or should I say our geologist?"

Dorothy tilts her head to one side, and looking down at the tablecloth, says, "Thank you, Joshua, you are very kind, but, in reality I am just a lowly student."

"Ah, but you are destined for great things! I know it!"

A waiter sets down a glass of white wine ... *My goodness! If I drink all of this, I'll surely be under the table!* ... and for Wangai, a cut-glass tumbler filled with clear liquid, ice cubes and an olive. After a consultation, Wangai places their luncheon orders.

"Well," she begins, "I met with Mr Akunyili last week."

Wangai nods vigorously. "Ah, did you? As it happens, I met with his boss, Norman Garfinkle. We had a very pleasant dinner here, in fact."

Dorothy says, "Did you? That's excellent! I suppose you chatted about Shepherds' Field."

"Yes, very amiable." He takes a generous sip of his martini. "So, what did you learn from Akunyili, my dear?"

Dorothy shifts in her chair. "Well, he gave me quite a bit of information, but he made me promise that I could reveal it only to the MP. I suppose it's very confidential!"

"One mustn't forget that I am an MP, my dear."

"Yes, of course, how silly of me! He said that the information should not be made public in any case."

"I am the custodian of vast quantities of secret information, my dear Dorothy. His secret is entirely safe with me!"

"He said that he is estimating the twenty-year yield from Shepherd's Field at half a million carats. But I think that his real estimate may be a lot higher."

Wangai glares at the tablecloth. "Aha! So, Norman is playing games with me! He even mentioned some Thunder Flash mine in Russia which was a complete bust."

Dorothy furrows her brow. "What kind of games is he playing, Joshua?"

"He wants me to believe that the output from Shepherd's Field will be well below the BuMines estimate."

"Do you suppose that Norman has been talking to Akunyili?" she asks. *Or more likely, that Norman and Akunyili have decided to undermine the BuMines estimate.*

"Yes, that's probably it. Mine Ventures' internal estimate is half that of BuMines! It seems that they're trying to get this project approved on the cheap!"

"Well, Joshua," Dorothy begins innocently, "it's only natural that Mine Ventures wants to save money."

Wangai stares at her for a moment. "What do you mean, Dorothy?"

"Oh, I just meant that they probably want to reduce their royalty payment to the government."

"Yes, that's probably it." Wangai takes another long sip from his martini. "They're a clever bunch, all right, but . . ." He smiles at Dorothy. "They've met their match in Joshua!" He holds up his nearly empty glass in a toast.

During lunch, they discuss the political outlook for the amendment to the mining bill. "Well, as I'm sure Ndungu can tell you, we are lining up support for the amendment. I will have to do some favors for several of the opposition MPs."

Dorothy asks hesitantly, "What favors were you considering for Mr Ndungu?"

"You name it, my dear!"

"Would it be all right if I ask him and then give you a call?"

"Yes, of course, an excellent idea!"

Dorothy gazes past Wangai for a moment. *This is becoming an increasingly dirty business; I don't like it at all.*

Their plates are cleared away and the dessert menu is considered. "They have a splendid French brandy here, Dorothy dear. They say it is produced by the same cellar that provided brandy to the Emperor Napoleon. May I offer you a glass?"

"Yes, that would be lovely!" *I don't have to drink more than a sip.*

Their brandies arrive and Wamgai makes a toast to "the loveliest and brightest girl in Country!"

Gosh, I've got to respond with something! Doesn't have to be sincere. "To the kindest and most attentive man I've ever met!"

He reaches across the table and takes her hand. "May our great friendship continue to blossom!" She nods vigorously.

"Dorothy, a question for you."

She struggles for an appearance of enthusiastic interest. *What's coming?*

"Dorothy, have you ever been to Europe?"

Her face relaxes into a smile. "No, Joshua, I haven't. Why do you ask?"

"Well, as it happens, I expect I'll have a business trip to Europe, and I'm inviting you to come with me. We would fly first class. . . . Have you ever flown first class?" She shakes her head. "Altogether a different experience than economy: excellent food, wine and service; seats that become beds for a delightful night's sleep; some airlines even have private staterooms for two." *I have absolutely hypnotized her,* he thinks. "We'll stay in a five-star hotel, where everything is absolutely glorious! What do you say, Dorothy?"

"It sounds heavenly. Where would we go?"

"Probably to Switzerland and most likely to Zurich – the financial center."

"I suppose you have business there." *This must be it! Where he gets his payoff!*

"Yes, I expect to."

"And when will we go?"

"I expect we'll go within the next couple of weeks."

"I can't wait!"

"Neither can I!" He reaches for her hand again. "Dorothy, would you like to see my bachelor's apartment here in City? It's very nicely decorated, and it's where I reside when parliament is in session. We can have our coffee there."

Suddenly feeling quite ill at ease, Dorothy takes a gulp of brandy. "Excellent! I just need to make a stop in the ladies' room before we go."

"Yes, of course."

Dorothy is gone for two minutes. She sits down, smiling happily while he is paying the bill.

Her phone rings. "Hello…Yes?" There is a long pause. "Oh no! Can't your wife handle it? But Mr Ndungu, you gave me the afternoon off!" Another long pause. "All right, I'll be there right away. I'll take a taxi."

She puts the phone back into her handbag and looks up at Wangai, her face attempting anguish. "Bad news! I've got to go back to the office right away."

"What's the problem?"

She sighs. "Mr Ndungu has an emergency back at the office. It's a private matter, but he desperately needs my help. I'm awfully sorry, Joshua, but I won't be able to see your place this afternoon." She stands up. He rises also. Giving him a quick embrace and a kiss on the cheek, she backs away. "I'm sorry about this afternoon, but I'm really excited about our trip to Switzerland together. Please call me when you know when we're going!"

Abdallah Ndungu listens to Dorothy's tale of the luncheon. "Dorothy, you were fantastic! Have you ever thought about being an actress?"

"No, I guess I'm still undecided between a doctor and a politician."

"Well, politicians sometimes have to display theatrical skills."

"You mean when they have to back a program they don't really like?"

"Yes, much as you did today."

"I didn't like it very much, Abdallah."

"Of course you didn't! But don't forget, it's the end result that matters!"

Dorothy looks up again at the lion and gazelle. "So, Abdallah, what's the present you want from Wangai in exchange for your vote?"

The MP frowns. "I don't think I want to sell my vote."

Dorothy suppresses a chuckle. "Don't lose sight of the end result, Abdallah!"

"Well, OK, but it has to be something that will cost him. Maybe a line item for funding to clean up that landfill in my district."

"So . . ." Dorothy eyes the ceiling for a moment. "So, Norman Garfinkle gets the mine he wants, Wangai gets the money he wants for the villa in France, and Abdallah gets the landfill cleaned up. Everybody wins!"

The MP's face turns sour. "But a few people had to break the law to get there. That's politics in this country, I guess."

> I find Ndungu's attitude irritating. Everybody wins! Let's just leave it at that! Why carp about the law? If bribery is part of the process that takes everyone where they want to be, make it legal! Nothing's perfect! Except the One, and he's suffocatingly boring! Imperfections and chaos are what make life interesting!

Achieving Superpersonhood:

The Other thinks I am boring. I am an advocate of peace. When is peace boring? Well, it is boring when one has a hankering for conflict. I am also a believer in love, and when is love boring? Probably love can be boring when one becomes impatient investing in peaceful satisfaction. The Other is a change junkie: do it now! For me, time is unimportant, and I am not opposed to change as long as it is peaceful.

Clinging to the grab rail on the bus home, Dorothy is smiling secretly with pride in her performance at lunch with Wangai, but apprehension lurks in the back of her mind: *How am I going to handle this trip to Zurich without having sex with him?*

Chapter 13

Atlantis Hotel, Zurich

"Hello?"

"Hello, Dorothy! Have you got your passport ready with a Swiss visa?"

"Yes, of course I do, Joshua! When're we going?"

"We're going next Thursday morning, so I'll meet you at the Swissair counter at ten o'clock."

Forcing herself to be enthusiastic, Dorothy says: "I can't wait! Where are we staying?"

"We'll be staying at the Atlantis. It's a little bit out of town, but it's the best hotel, and it has all those fabulous amenities in the perfect setting."

"Wonderful! How long will be staying?"

"Unfortunately, I have to be back in City on Monday, so we'll take the flight back on Sunday night."

There is an uncertain, queasy feeling in Dorothy's stomach as she hangs up, but she tells herself: *We have a plan. There are lots of contingencies, plenty of back-up. Hetti says she'll support me fully. . . . but what if . . .*

"The Atlantis?" Hetti exclaims. "That place must be seven or eight thousand shillings a night! He's got to be anticipating a big payday! But channel 24 won't put me, a cameraman and my assistant there for three nights. We're going to stay at the Best Western!"

"Is the Best Western very far away?" Dorothy wonders.

"No more than a kilometer. Zurich is pretty compact. Don't worry, sweetheart, we'll be there for you!"

"Where are the security men going to be staying?"

"They're all local, darlin', don't worry!"

The flight is delightful: a glass of champagne before take-off; a glass of Chablis in the air; a linen, silver and crystal setting for lunch right in front of her; smoked salmon and caviar; lots of choices of bread; tender, juicy roast beef with wonderful little potatoes and salad; a delicious chocolate roulade stuffed with raspberries and whipped cream; coffee in tiny cups and brandy in huge round glasses.

Wangai is a kind and attentive companion, telling her stories about his childhood in a poor section of City. His father died when he was four, the youngest of six children. His mother worked in a laundry "six – sometimes seven – days a week. My oldest brother – he was nineteen when dad died – helped me a lot through school and university. He died last year." Sharing his sorrow in the loss of his brother, his love for his mother, and his adolescent memories so openly with Dorothy gives her a view of a Joshua Wangai who has a soft side and is genuinely interested in her as an individual. She begins to think, *Well, it wouldn't be the end of the world if . . .* She dozes off.

The lobby of the Atlantis is glossy, modern, Art Deco with a welcome gas fire set in a burnished gold wall. Dorothy sits on one of the sculptured brown sofas, her back against an enormous blue silk pillow. *I could definitely get used to this!* The atmosphere is hushed and deliberate: no one is in a hurry. Wangai is standing by the reception counter. He is speaking on his mobile phone.

Across the lobby from Dorothy, there is another woman – a black woman – sitting, apparently reading a newspaper. *Something about her is familiar. Oh my gosh! It's Hetti!* Hetti is not wearing one of her usual flamboyant outfits; she is wearing a simple black dress, sunglasses, and beautiful black dreadlocks instead of the usual auburn bob. Hetti looks up from her newspaper and gives Dorothy a casual nod.

The hotel room is a suite with separate living and sleeping areas, and there is a balcony with views toward the city and the Zúrichsee. The bathroom is a marvel: bathtub, shower and walls covered in black, white and gray stratified marble. There are fresh lilies, orchids and carnations on every table. She surveys the soft comfort of the bedroom. *This bed would sleep four people comfortably.* She turns to Joshua. "It's amazing. I think I'd like to look around the hotel for a little while, Joshua."

"OK, sweetheart, I have to meet someone here at the hotel, then I have to go out for a while. I'll see you back here at the hotel about six?" She nods. "You can charge anything you want to the room."

Picking up a book, Dorothy goes down to the lobby, anxious to know what is going on there. As she gets off the elevator she pauses; Wangai is sitting on a sofa with his back to the rear windows and speaking with a white man at the far side of the lobby. The white man, early thirties, has a blonde crew cut and is wearing a gym suit and a New York Yankees baseball cap. Hetti, on a nearby sofa, is observing surreptitiously from around her newspaper. A familiar black man, well dressed in a dark gray suit, white shirt and striped tie appears; a black leather handbag is slung casually over one shoulder. Dorothy draws in a breath involuntarily. *It's Kimbi, the cameraman!* Kimbi goes out the rear door onto the terrace, turns and, like a casual sightseer, looks back into the lobby.

Mesmerized, Dorothy takes a seat near the elevators and opens her book.

The white man passes a brown leather briefcase to Wangai. They appear to be discussing it. Kimbi, behind them, is holding his handbag awkwardly at his waist. *He must be filming them.* Wangai opens the briefcase, glances at the contents and closes it. The white man passes him a sheet of paper which Wangai signs, briefcase on his lap, and passes the slip of paper back to the white man.

Wangai rises, nods to the white man, and strides toward the entrance. *Now they're going to arrest him!* Dorothy stands up to get a better view. The doorman opens a car door, Wangai gets in and the car drives away. *Shit! They let him get away!*

A horrified Dorothy turns to chastise Hetti, and she is astonished to see two uniformed black police officers escorting the white man to the elevators. *What in the world?*

Hetti takes Dorothy's arm and steers her, also, toward the elevators. "What's your room number, Dorothy?"

"Four twenty-three. Why?"

"We're going to use it for a few minutes."

Hetti closes the door and faces the white man, who stands uneasily between the two policemen.

"OK," Hetti flashes an ID card and announces aggressively, "you have violated a corrupt practices statute in Switzerland. If you're convicted, you could face ten years in a Swiss prison. I assume you'd rather avoid that." The white man nods vigorously. "In that case, we're prepared to overlook your crime if you can produce four documents for us now."

He is trembling with nervousness. "We want to see your passport, your employee ID card, the document which you asked Mr Wangai to sign, and any document which instructs you to make that delivery to Wangai."

Frantically, the white man searches his pockets.

Hetti asks: "Kimbi, you got your still camera?" Kimbi holds it up.

The white man produces some papers and hands them to Hetti, who spreads them out on a table.

Strange, Dorothy thinks, *that the Swiss have black policemen.* She studies the uniforms of the policemen. *Oh my gosh! They're not Swiss, they're Country police!*

"So," Hetti announces, "you are Willem De Vries, a South African citizen, employed by Cape Courier Services. And this says you were to deliver a dispatch case on today's date to Mr Joshua Wangai at the Atlantis Hotel, Zurich. Who hired your company to make this delivery?"

"It says there: Mr Jeffery Sanderson."

"And who is Mr Sanderson's employer?"

"I believe it's one of the mining companies."

"And this document with Wangai's signature says 'dispatch case containing quantity: two thousand, five hundred Euro notes. Is that right?"

"I don't know. It wasn't opened until I gave the key to Mr Wangai."

There is a lengthy but dead-end discussion about the identity of Mr Sanderson's employer.

"You got your pictures, Kimbi?"

"Yeah, I got 'em, Hetti."

"OK, DeVries, you're free to go." Hetti hands him his documents. "I would advise you to get on the next plane back to South Africa. And if you want your name kept out of the newspapers, you can send me an email or a text with the name of Mr Sanderson's employer." She hands him a business card. He hurries out the door.

"Hetti," Dorothy pleads, "why did you let Wangai go?"

"I didn't. I'll explain later. He may be back soon, and before he gets here, we need to search his suitcase."

"What for?"

"He wasn't going to go back with you, Dorothy. He was going to Nice, and then back to City."

"Why was he going to Nice?"

"To buy that nice apartment on the Riveria."

Tucked in the back flap of Wangai's suitcase is a brown manila envelope containing brochures of apartments for sale.

"This one looks nice", Hetti reads, "Saint Jean Cap Ferrat: in a small residence, very rare apartment with private swimming pool and sea view close to the beach. The apartment has been modernized with quality materials from renowned designers.

Air-conditioning, alarm system, parking place, landscaped garden. Two bedrooms, two baths, eighty-seven square meters. To be seen!"

Dorothy asks, "How much is it?"

"Eight hundred and ninety-five thousand Euros."

There is a knock on the door. "Come in!" Hetti shouts.

There is a burly white man with a blonde crew-cut, wearing a gray suit. "I'm to collect Mr Wangai's suitcase."

Hetti gestures toward the case. "It's right here, Davis. Everything went OK?"

"Yeah. He's in the car. Wants to go to the airport. We got pictures of the deposit receipt."

"OK. Off you go."

Dorothy is frowning and chewing on her lip. "Hetti, can you please tell me what's going on? Why are you letting Wangai go?"

"Sit down, Dorothy." Hetti flops down on the sofa. "When you first told me that Wangai was going to Zurich, I did some checking. Ideally, we would have liked the Swiss police to arrest him, but we realized that if we told them that we were expecting an illegal funds transfer, they would have raised queries with Country through diplomatic channels. If that had happened and the government had understood that one of their MPs was about to be busted on a bribery charge, you can guess what would have happened."

Dorothy grimaces. "Wangai would have been tipped off."

"Almost certainly. So we thought about springing the problem on the Swiss police at the last minute. The trouble was: we couldn't predict their reaction. Would they react quickly enough? Would they gather the right evidence? What would they do with the evidence? Would they turn it over to Country?"

"I'm with you."

"So we decided we had to do it on our own."

"But why the uniformed police from Country?"

"Because impersonating a police officer is a crime in Switzerland, and we figured that the courier wouldn't recognize that he'd been stopped by other than Swiss cops. He was nervous, and when the cops grabbed him, he assumed that they were Swiss. So when I made him the offer to go, he assumed that we were after Wangai, not him."

"Who was that man that was here collecting Wangai's suitcase?"

"He is part of our limousine team. When our MP left the hotel and asked the doorman for a taxi, the doorman recommended the shiny Mercedes limo. The driver and the blonde guy informed Wangai that they had been hired by Mr Garfinkle to make sure that the delivery was transferred in full and was successfully deposited. They said that Mr Garfinkle had previous experiences where the delivery was 'misplaced'." Hetti makes quotation marks in the air around the last word.

"OK, so he made the deposit, and they took a photo of it, but why didn't Wangai come back here?"

"Because the limo guys told him that the courier had been arrested and they were afraid a sting was in process; they were going to the airport right away, and didn't he want to go with them? Yes, but could they get his suitcase?"

Dorothy is pensive. "Maybe he's going to France to buy that apartment right away."

"Maybe, but I doubt it. He'll be feeling that City is the safest place to be – that he'll be protected there. Besides, he doesn't have to be present in France to buy property there."

"Is he going to be able to keep the money?"

Hetti waves her right index finger dramatically. "Lawyers from Channel 24 are going to call the Anti-Corruption Tsar, tell him the evidence we have, and demand that he take action to freeze the funds in the bank."

"So who'll get the money?"

"Good question! I doubt that Mine Ventures will come to the surface and claim the money as theirs. Wangai can't get it. Probably it'll remain on the bank's balance sheets as . . ." she makes quotation marks again . . . "miscellaneous assets".

"Hetti, what do you think is going to happen to Wangai?"

"Well, it's really going to hit the fan after my show on Monday. The President will be 'outraged', and he'll talk about the pristine values of the United Country Party. He'll tighten some loose anti-corruption screws here and there, won't have any direct contact with Wangai; he'll dust off his hands and declare: 'fixed!' Wangai will lose his chairmanship, and later may lose his seat in parliament, but I doubt that he'll go to jail. Any case against him will eventually suffer a loss of momentum and peter out."

Dorothy squeezes her eyes shut. "That's depressing!"

"That's how it is in Country!" Hetti gives an elaborate shrug.

"Don't you get frustrated? Your job is like . . . well, it's like throwing snowballs at hell!"

Hetti guffaws. "I hadn't thought of it that way." She pauses to reflect. "I guess I feel . . . that if I didn't dig up the snow, make snowballs, and throw them, that hell would get that much bigger and hotter."

Dorothy laughs. "You're amazing, Hetti!" She turns away to look toward the Zurichsee, taking in its deep tranquility. "You planned and worked this sting perfectly. I didn't have to do anything."

"No, on the contrary, this sting was only possible because of you. In fact, you had the hard part: getting Wangai to want to take you here to Zurich with him. You gave me the vital information: Zurich, Atlantis Hotel, and the date."

Dorothy turns back to Hetti. "You aren't going to mention me in your show on Monday, are you?"

"No, in fact, the internal report I've got to write for Channel 24 will mention a 'Joanne' who played your role, and nobody else at Channel 24 knows who 'Joanne' is. By the way, I've pretty well decided not to go after Kurgat. If he hasn't already got his money, he and Garfinkle will both be pretty scared on Monday."

Dorothy chuckles. "What's going to happen to Mine Ventures?"

"They'll probably get their amendment – not in this session of parliament – but eventually. In the meantime, they'll have a miniscule profile, or, if they're visible, it'll be in a painter's smock with a large pail of whitewash."

"What are you going to do now, Hetti?"

Hetti glances at her watch. "I'm going to try to make the nine-fifty Swissair flight. I've got some work to do to get ready for Monday."

"Maybe I ought to change my flight to go with you."

Hetti shakes her head gently. "Why? Stay here; enjoy yourself! You're covered by Wangai's credit card until Sunday. Have some good champagne! Try the caviar! Have breakfast in bed! Take a tour of Zurich! Maybe you'll meet a rich banker!"

Dorothy giggles and then looks down at her pink polished fingertips. "Hetti, what should I do if Wangai calls me?"

"He probably won't try to call you till after Monday when he's feeling sorry for himself. If he does, you can stifle any discussion of his illegal financial transaction by saying you feel sorry for him and that it must be terrible to be criticized and hated by so many people."

"Actually, I don't feel one bit sorry for him, but what if he wants to see me?"

"Assuming you want nothing more to do with the scumbag, you could say that you'd like to see him but that your father has absolutely forbidden it."

"Papa knows nothing about Wangai and me. He thinks I went to Europe with some girlfriends on a special travel offer."

Hetti considers the young woman opposite her for a moment. "When I was about five, I said something to my brother – he's two years older – that got him very upset. I can't even remember now what it was. Anyway, my mother introduced the concept of 'white lies' to me. She said that sometimes white lies are necessary when one doesn't want to hurt or upset someone, and the lie isn't a <u>big</u> lie. She told me that God will forgive white

Achieving Superpersonhood:

lies if you put your right hand behind your back and cross your first two fingers. So Dorothy, I suggest that when you give your father your report on your European trip, and if Wangai calls you, remember my mother's advice."

That is ridiculous! Believing that God will forgive you for telling lies if you cross your fingers behind your back! He is such an insufferable goody-goody that he believes lies are a sin. You don't have any room to maneuver with him! My philosophy has always been to be very flexible with my friends. Make things easy!

* * *

There is nothing remarkable about the village to a casual observer: about fifty round wattle and daub huts clustered together and protected by a barrier of thorn bush. From the village, with its back to the first hill and its foot washed by an intermittent stream, one can spot approaching visitors a hawk's view away. Near the center of the village is an open, communal area and a livestock corral with its own prickly barrier. What is unusual about this village is that it has become a base for Dhul Fikar. Selected by Major el Hashem for its remote, unmemorable location, it has now become the home for about half of the now-dispersed graduates of the training base. Several changes have been made to the infrastructure. Four vehicles, including two pickups with heavy machine guns, are parked under what looks from the air like a large, palm-thatched cattle shed. Behind the village, and invisible from the savannah, are three tents camouflaged with palm fronds: the mosque/dining hall, the armory/officers' quarters, and a storeroom. The soldiers of Dhul Fikar have been assigned in groups of three or four to conscripted huts, whose residents have been evicted to other shelters.

New disciplines had to be installed by Dhul Fikar. The Marshal for Women is Wassy the Magnificent, whose job it is to enforce 'Islamic behavior' from the women. The brightly colored dresses are gone; in their place are dark, full-length abayas. A niqab, showing only the eyes, is required outside the hut. The Marshal for Men is Irish, who demands that all men have beards. He has outlawed smoking, alcohol and bright-colored clothes. There is a Marshal for General Conduct: Bad Ass. His remit is to forbid any frivolity: drums or flutes and dancing. Permission must also be sought from the marshal for any travel beyond the savannah. (In cases where permission is granted – for the purchase of provisions or the sale of livestock or craft items – two Dhul Fikar soldiers provide an escort.)

When the jihadists first arrived at the village the headman told them they were not welcome. The response of the major was, "You don't understand, nigger, we're going to stay here and you lot will do what you're told."

"This is our village! You bad men are not welcome here! Go away!"

The major, turning away, ordered his men: "Unload!"

The soldiers began pulling bundles and boxes off the trucks.

A tall male villager, naked to the waist and wearing a dark blue flowered sarong, grabbed one of the unloading soldiers and threw him to the ground. For a moment of shock, no one moved. The major walked over to the villager, and drawing his sidearm, shot him in the chest. The man staggered, his eyes fixed on the major. Blood poured from his gaping mouth and he crumpled to the ground. There was a scream of despairing disbelief. A woman wearing a belted shift of the same fabric flung herself on the fallen man.

The major turned his back on the pair. "Carry on unloading," he ordered. He strode over to the headman, brandishing his pistol. "You will do what we say! You understand?"

The headman looked at his feet. "Yes."

"Then tell your men to help us unload!"

The order was given.

Achieving Superpersonhood:

"Now," the major continued, addressing the headman, "we will require about a dozen houses for my men. You and I will go and select them!"

There were no further executions, but there were periodic canings for willful disobedience. A woman was caned for appearing on the common ground in a pink shirt, orange skirt and a blue headscarf. Two boys were caned for playing with a football.

No attempt has been made to convert the villagers to Dhul Fikar's version of Islam. The presumption is that they are hopelessly inferior beings unworthy of Allah's consideration.

Hassan is disturbed by the competing thoughts occupying his mind. There is disgust at the treatment of the villagers, though at a rational level he understands the need for Dhul Fikar's security. On the other hand, he admires the major and many of the soldiers. *They are dedicated to the cause of Islam; they support each other; they are tough!* Irish has become his good friend. Five prayers a day in the tent mosque, in the company of his brothers at arms, have forged a commitment and loyalty to Dhul Fikar, and the major's daily lectures on the strategies and tactics of Islam in the modern world have opened his eyes to injustice and the intense need for Islamic justice and a universal faith.

The accommodation, the food and the hygienic facilities are, in spite of his erstwhile preferences, acceptable to Hassan. He must live down the moniker 'The Heir' by showing that he is indeed one of the soldiers, and not some callow prince. The dirty, dark, discomfort of the hut he shares with Irish and two others is normal. A stew of peppers, beans and goat is tasty, particularly when supplemented with cornmeal cake and molasses. At least once a day, Hassan can wash his face and hands; his underclothes are washed weekly and his fatigues fortnightly by the village women.

Still, he wonders, *Where is this taking me? This was to be my path to greatness. Well, I didn't really believe I am destined for greatness, but perhaps distinction, or at least someone who is worthy of the name Arusei. Perhaps it is just that nothing is happening yet.*

Warari, the new arrival, arouses suspicion in Hassan. But 'The Heir' considers it prudent to observe with minimal interaction. Warari's 'native', uneducated background is plain enough, as is his aggressive, oversized ego, but his commitment to Islam seems – at least to Hassan – dubious. Glances at Warari during prayers or one of the major's lectures reveal a detached, disinterested figure who might actually be sleeping behind lowered eyelids. *So what is he doing in Dhul Fikar? The rest of us are Allah's Muslim warriors. Does he not believe? Is he, like the rest of us, really committed to Islam?*

> I can feel Hassan's tensions: I am creating small events which prompt questions about the destination of the path he is on. The Other is whispering confirmations of prior commitments to the path. It is Hassan's choice which of us will succeed.

Hassan is startled when Warari sets his metal tray down next to him during the noonday meal. "How's it going, mate?"

Hassan glances at Warari's tray, awash in dark brown 'gravy'. "OK, thanks. How are you?"

"Couldn't be better, mate! And ya know, I was thinkin' that I've been derelict in my duties not to really make the acquaintance of The Heir!"

Hassan nods semi-agreeably, his eyes still on the tray.

"So tell me, what's it like to be The Heir of the Aruseis?"

Hassan chews the inside of his cheek; he murmurs: "I'm not an heir; my father disinherited me."

Warari slaps him on the back. "Oh, come on now, mate! I heard there was a little scuffle with the police and you spent a few days in jail. You don't mean to tell me that the great Kaddour Arusei would disinherit his beloved son for something as small as that?"

Hassan glances briefly at Warari. "Yes, he would."

There is a scowl on Warari's face. "So now you're a member of Dhul Fikar: what're you going to do? Take him out? We'll help you."

"No, I don't think so." Hassan nudges a piece of goat with his fork.

"You know something, man? You remind me of my brother." Warari is shaking his head. "He's just like you: always believing in doing good!" He spat out the last word as if it had a foul taste.

"You have a brother?"

"Yeah. In fact, he used to work for your old man."

"Where?"

"In one of the slaughterhouses."

"There's only one in Arusei Industries."

"Whatever. He's a football player now."

Hassan turns in surprise to face Warari. "Kamiri?"

Warari shrugs is disgust. "Yeah, that's him. He sits on the bench with the Coast City Lions now."

"No, Warari, you got that wrong." The voice of a new recruit, Kukulo, comes from across the table. "He's first team now." Warari shakes his head in denial, but Kukulo continues: "Yeah, he is. The fans call him 'Killer'."

"That's because he used to kill cows," Warari snorts.

"No. He's a killer on the pitch. Almost every game he's involved in at least one goal. The Lions are top of their league now, Warari."

"Kukulo," Hassan asks, "are you saying that Kamiri is based near here?"

"I don't know about 'near here', but he's based at the Lions' camp in Coast City."

Warari digs his fork into a pile of stewed kale in disgust.

Warari's sudden memory of his brother is my, the One's, prompt of consciousness, and Kukulo's revelation of Kamiri's whereabouts may be important for Hassan. Scraps, seemingly-worthless bits of information can change a thought process and a life.

Major el Hashem puts his thumbs in the waistband of his fatigues, the fingers of his right hand draped over the butt of his sidearm. "I'm going to send some of you on an important operation. This operation has two objectives: first, to raise the profile of Dhul Fikar; we want global recognition! Second, to contribute to our funding. You all are receiving stipends. There are also living, recruitment and armament expenses!" The major pauses to take in the nods of agreement. "So, I'm putting Wassim (Wassy) in charge of the operation. He will be supported by Raouf (Bad Ass), Mabrouk (Irish), Hassan and Warari. There's room for two more." He surveys the forest of raised arms. "OK, you two can go. We will pray now for the success of this team to the great glory of Allah! After *Dhuhr* prayers there will be a planning meeting for the team in my quarters!"

"Pull in up there," Wassy instructs, pointing to a dirt track leading into the dunes to the left. The pickup truck has just passed the Royal Coast's entrance with its marble columns and archway of bougainvillea set in what is otherwise a nearly impenetrable wall of gorse, buckthorn and stunted pines. Only the roof of the club house is visible from the narrow macadam sea road. All of them are wearing civilian shorts and T-shirts of various descriptions – all but Hassan and Kukulo, who are wearing the matching white polo shirts, knee-length navy blue shorts and brown flip-flops which are reported to be the attire of the resort maintenance crews. Hassan suspects that he and Kukulo – both freshly shaved – have been selected as beach sweepers for their fluency in English.

Achieving Superpersonhood:

"All right," Wassy announces, "Irish, have you got the binoculars?"

"Yeah."

"All right. You and Bad Ass go up there into the dunes and look the place over. Don't get seen; stay flat on the ground. Look the place over, see who's on the beach and give us a report."

Irish and Bad Ass disappear into the dunes to the north.

"All right. Warari, turn the truck around so that it's facing out. Then I want the rest of us to move brush so it can't be seen from the road."

With the truck partially hidden, Wassy turns his attention to weapons, inspecting the four AK-47s and ammunition which are stowed in old grain bags on the bed of the truck. He also pats the coil of rope, and assures himself that his knife and the bundle of fabric to be used for gags and blindfolds are in the cab.

"OK, Wassy, we checked it out," Irish reports. "There are two couples at the pool, and three on the beach. One couple is out there on the ski boat." He nods toward the Indian Ocean and adds, "Nobody is playing tennis."

"All right. Which ones are good candidates?"

"Well, we looked for gray hair, and there's one couple at the pool and two at the beach with gray hair. The ones on the ski boat are too far away. Don't know about any others."

"Are these couples all men and women?"

"Yeah."

"All right. Hassan and Kukulo, I want you to start sweeping the beach, and each of you work your way toward one of the gray hairs. Look 'em over and have a chat with 'em if you can. See if you can figure out how rich they are. If somebody from the resort management approaches you, pretend you're a halfwit sweeping the beach and go when they ask you to leave. Irish and Bad Ass, go back up and watch which cottages the grays on the beach use."

There isn't much seaweed on the beach. Hassan and Kukulo default to sweeping up piles of sea shells. It is at least thirty meters up the beach from the piles of shells to where the grays are sitting on beach loungers. *This isn't working,* Hassan thinks. *There's no seaweed and few shells up the beach, so how can we get up there to talk to them?* He is looking idly out to sea when there is a voice behind him. "Hello. Are you boys sea shell collectors?"

Hassan turns to find a chubby older woman in a dark green, one-piece, bathing suit surveying him with a half-smile. She is wearing a straw hat. Something in her facial expression and her manner remind him of his mother.

"Umm, no ma'am, we're just cleaning the beach."

"Oh, that's a shame. Many of these shells are so pretty." She stoops and selects one. "I particularly like these little pink and white striped ones. My granddaughter would love these." She holds out the shell in her open palm. "But the hotel tells me that it is illegal to take them out of the country."

"I didn't know that, ma'am."

"Well, I must say that it doesn't make sense to rake them up and dump them back in the sea when a little girl in England would love to have a few."

Hassan nods. "Is that where you live – in England – ma'am?"

"Yes, we live in London, but every year at about this time, I insist on getting away into the sun for a couple of weeks. English weather's not so nice now, you know. And it's good for my husband, too. His health hasn't been the best."

"What does your husband do ma'am?"

"Oh, he's retired now, but he was a senior manager in banking." Hassan nods. She gives him a brief smile: "Well, it's time for my afternoon swim."

He gazes after her as she wades out through the miniature surf. *Such a nice lady. I wonder if she has a son.*

"So, the people I was talking to are from Belfast," Kukulo reports. "I think that's in Ireland."

Achieving Superpersonhood:

"Are they rich?" Wassy demands.

Kukula shrugs. "I dunno. They ain't broke."

"Well, did they have any jewelry on?" Wassy persists.

Kukulo considers. "The lady had a gold ring; the man was wearing a watch."

"All right. We'll take Hassan's ones. At least the man was a big banker." Turning to Irish, he asks, "Which house are Hassan's in?"

"We think they're in the one that's the second from the far end."

"All right, go watch some more and make sure."

At twilight, they all relocate to Irish's vantage point to look down on the resort. Couples emerge from the cottages – ladies in colorful dresses, men in long trousers and pastel jackets – and stroll along the boardwalks to the club house, from which music spills though the open doors. Faint snatches of laughter and conversation can be heard. Wassy shakes his head. "These people are seriously rich!"

"You want to be like them?" Warari asks. There is a long pause. "Well, do you?"

"You have to look at it this way, Warari: they are all non-believers who are going to hell. So, am I tempted? No."

Three couples emerge into the exterior deck where a violin and a clarinet have begun to play. They dance. The laughter and talk are clearer now.

"See what I mean, Warari? That man in the white jacket looks like he's drunk. That's what happens to non-believers: they drink alcohol, dance to music and have sex!"

"You against sex, Wassy?"

"Everything in its place, Warari; everything in its place!"

The music stops and couples drift back to their cottages. Lights begin to go out.

"It's one-o-six," Wassy announces, "an hour to go."

Only a few lights along the boardwalks remain lit.

"All right! Baklavas on! Hassan, Kukulo, Irish and I are going in. The rest of you wait on the beach. Have your AKs ready, but don't fire unless I tell you. You got the flashlight, Irish?"

"Yeah."

"Ties and gags?"

"Yeah."

Hassan feels the rapid beating of his heart. *I want out of this! What if I just ran for it? But where? The club house. Sure as hell there'd be shooting. Somebody killed.* He grimaces. *Got to stick with it for now.*

The four approach the cottage. Wassy moves silently along the board walk. He grasps the door handle and pushes it down, then pushes the door. It doesn't give. He tries again. Nothing. He waves the others to join him. "It's locked!" he wheezes. They confer in whispers. "No other door." "Only windows." "Got to break it in."

"I'll kick and then we'll rush."

There is a splintering crash as the door flies open. The four surge inside a living room, picked out by Irish's wayward beam. A door ahead is open. Sounds of fearful protest inside. Irish leads, his beam flickering about. Two beds. Someone is sitting up and shouting. Wassy throws himself on the person. Muffled cries. Someone in the other bed is trying to sit up: "What?" Kukulo pounces and claps a hand over the mouth. Irish produces a wad of cloth. It is stuffed in the mouth. On the other bed, the woman is growling and thrashing as Irish inserts the gag, then leans on her to tie her feet. Wassy pins her arms behind her and ties her wrists. Her husband is already tied.

"Explain to them, Kukulo!" Wassy demands.

"Do not resist! You will not be hurt. We are the Sword of the Prophet. We will take you to our camp where you will be held for ransom."

Outside there is the sound of shouting and running feet on the boardwalks.

Wassy throws the woman over his shoulder and is out the door. Kukulo has her husband.

"What's going on?" someone shouts.

"Fire a couple of air bursts!" Wassy yells. He is running along the beach, closely followed by the others.

The loud clatter of automatic weapons shatters the night. None but the running men are visible, but lights are coming on.

Panting, they reach the truck. The hostages are dumped immediately in the back. Irish's beam shows that the woman is dressed in a pink cotton night gown; her husband in light blue pajamas.

Warari drags the brush away from the front of the truck.

"Let's go!"

The truck surges onto the coastal road and speeds away into the darkness.

Chapter 14

The Baobab Tree

"Very well done!" the major announces, as he inspects the contents of the truck bed. "You can remove their gags, now, Wassim."

The woman coughs and blinks as lights are shined at her. Her husband raises his head and drops it again with a sorry groan.

"We are the Prophet's Sword. What are your names?"

"I am Mrs. Eleanor Pritchet, and this is my husband, Jonathan; untie us, please!"

The major ignores her request. "Who is your next of kin?"

Mrs Pritchet's lower lip is trembling and her eyes are brimming. "That would be our son, John."

"His telephone number?"

The major dials the number, puts the phone to his ear and waits. It rings for some time. He is about to press the end call button when there is a female voice at the other end. "I want to speak to John Pritchet."

In Battersea, South London, Julia Pritchet hands the phone to her husband, who is struggling, quizzically, up on one elbow in bed. "Somebody strange wants to speak to you, John."

Frowning, John takes the phone from his wife. "This is John Pritchet."

"I am the Sword of the Prophet. We are holding your parents – Pritchet – hostage. For their release, we require the sum of one million dollars. Do you understand?"

"Unhh . . ." John makes desperate gestures to his wife for a pen and paper. "Unhh . . . who did you say you are?"

"We are the Sword of the Prophet."

John is writing frantically. "Yes, but what is your name?"

"I am the major in charge."

"Yes, but I didn't get your name."

"My name is unimportant. What is important is one million dollars if you want your parents to remain alive."

"May I speak to them, please?"

"No. They are uninjured. I will call you in twenty-four hours to arrange the transfer: one million dollars for two old people."

"I can call you back when arrangements are made."

"No, I will call you."

John glances at the phone screen: 'no number'. He begins to protest: "But . . ." The line has gone dead.

Eleanor Pritchet has been listening. She is lying on bare earth on her side, her hands behind her back, her night dress dirt-stained and the hem torn. She raises her head to look for her husband; he is out of sight. "Jonathan?"

"I'm here," comes the labored reply behind her.

"You all right?"

"My ribs are sore." A pause. "Eleanor?"

"Yes."

"I don't have my medication."

Eleanor shouts: "Major!" She can hear talking among the soldiers. "<u>Major!</u>"

"He's not here right now, ma'am," Hassan replies, "What is it you want?"

"My husband needs his medication!"

"He must have left it back at the resort."

Mrs Pritchet strains unsuccessfully to sit up; there is bile in her mouth. "<u>He</u> didn't leave it! <u>You</u> left it! My husband <u>needs</u> medication for his heart and his diabetes!"

Hassan fetches the major, who demands, "What is it you want?"

"My husband," Mrs. Pritchet spits out each phrase emphatically, "<u>must</u> have his medication! Without it he will <u>die</u>! And <u>you</u> will get <u>nothing</u>! Do you understand?"

Major el Hashem considers. "You will have to make the medication part of the ransom deal."

She cannot see the major, but she knows his face is cold. "Let me speak to my son!"

"No! Wassim, put the captives in an empty hut, and place an armed guard on them!"

"There is no empty hut, Major."

"Oh, for fuck's sake, Wassim! Make one empty!"

"Yes, sir!"

A dozen villagers are standing silently watching. One of them touches Wassim's sleeve and points to his hut. A woman approaches Hassan, and says in broken Swahili: "Woman need clothes. I get."

The captives are moved bodily to the hut. A soldier armed with an AK-47 stands at the entrance. Another soldier sits inside, cradling his weapon, watching the captives.

"What are we going to do, Eleanor? I need my insulin."

"I know, Jonathan, I'll try to talk to them."

"Maybe the hotel could bring it here."

She says nothing, but she is thinking: *These pirates would never go for that; they'd be afraid the hotel would bring the army. Could the hotel drop it off somewhere? No. In making the pick-up the pirates would be captured. John has got to deliver some insulin with the money.* She thinks about alternatives: *Maybe the army can figure out where we are; maybe they even know where the pirates are hiding.*

Hassan, too, is thinking: *She is not black like my mother, but in other ways, she is like her: a woman of importance who is determined and can be kind. I don't like the way they are treated – but what can I do?*

Eleanor says, "Major, do you understand the word 'diabetes'?"

He glares at her sourly. "Of course."

"My husband has acute diabetes. He takes insulin injections four or five times a day. Do you know what happens when he doesn't get the injections?"

"He dies."

"Yes, and do you know how soon he will die?"

"Within two weeks."

"No, major. In two or three days."

The major studies her, trying to make out how much is bluff and bluster.

"I suppose, major, that a live hostage is more valuable to you than a dead one." She pauses. "Particularly later in a court of law where the judge is deciding whether to just lock you up or hang you."

With a sneer, the major spits at her and leaves.

"Eleanor, I have to pee," Jonathan announces. He gets the guard's attention, points to his crotch, and gestures. The guard shakes his head. Jonathan reaches into his pajama trousers and removes his penis, and the guard, offended, shakes his forefinger vehemently. In desperation, Eleanor makes extravagant gestures from her own crotch to the ground. After a moment of puzzlement, the guard grunts his understanding, and shouts something to the outside guard.

Nothing happens. Jonathan and Eleanor repeat their pleas. The guard shrugs. Finally, Jonathan rolls onto his side, removes his penis and releases a copious stream of urine onto the floor of the hut.

A woman with an arm load of clothing enters the hut, with Wassim, who tells the guard: "It's OK if she helps them get dressed, but kill her if she does something you don't like."

The woman sets down the pile, and gestures Eleanor to select from it. Eleanor picks out a dark blue shirt and a pair of brown trousers. The guard objects when the woman tries to shield Eleanor from his eyes when she removes her night dress. Eleanor brushes the woman aside and stares fixedly at the guard during the disrobing process, and the guard – humiliated – allows Eleanor's bound feet to be temporarily unbound to permit the trousers to be pulled on.

John is on the phone from just before eight that morning – first to the Foreign Office, then to MI5 and MI6. The latter two agencies – domestic and international security, respectively – listen, ask questions, but promise nothing. The Foreign Office promises to contact its counterpart in country. No one seems to know anything about 'Sword of the Prophet'. John's contact at the Foreign Office, a Charles Weybridge, reminds John that it is British policy not respond to overseas ransom demands with money.

"Are you saying that I should just tell these people to fuck off – that they're not going to get any money?"

"No, I'm not saying that. I'm saying that paying ransom in poor countries where law enforcement is weak only encourages more hostage-taking, and more distraught families."

"Frankly, Mr Weybridge, you're not being very helpful. Do I have to go to Country to try to get the police and the army interested? We're talking about the lives of two very kind and good British citizens."

"I quite understand how you feel, Mr Pritchet. We have already alerted the Country police and the army, so there is no need to go. Believe me, this situation is best handled through diplomatic channels."

"What about the British SAS?"

"We have been speaking to the people at Defense. The major problem is that we have no idea where these hostage-takers are located. They may not even be in Country."

Julia has located the spare keys to the Pritchet senior's house, gone there and found that Jonathan's desk is locked. With some coaching from John, she finds the key, and begins to search the files. There is one fat file full of financial data marked 'RBS'. She relays the information to John, who calls the broker.

"I'm sorry, Mr Pritchet, but your father transferred his assets to Morgan Stanley last year." He does not, however, recall the name of the Morgan Stanley broker.

While Morgan Stanley is searching for the Pritchet account, Julia finds the Morgan Stanley file, which shows total security and cash assets of one million, seven hundred and thirteen thousand, two hundred and eighty-eight pounds.

John calls the Morgan Stanley broker and explains the situation to him.

David Feldman, the MS broker says: "I'm very sorry to hear about your father's situation, Mr Pritchet, but I'm sure you'll understand that the only way we can release funds to you is via a legal power of attorney from your father and identification for yourself."

John shouts into his mobile phone: "God damn it, Mr Feldstein, my father is being held by terrorists somewhere in East Africa! Do you really think he can execute a power of attorney in front of terrorists?"

"No, sir." (apologetically) "But we have certain security procedures."

In frustration, John hangs up. His mind searches for an alternative. *Maybe . . . maybe, we could borrow the million dollars from the government.* He calls Weybridge, who is distinctly cool to the idea: "I'm afraid that would require the approval of the prime minister."

"Well, damn it! Go and ask for her approval!"

Maybe there's another way with Morgan Stanley. Maybe we could get Dad on the phone, and he could answer security questions to prove who he is.

The front page of the *Evening Standard* says: LONDON OAPs (old age pensioners) HELD FOR RANSOM IN AFRICA!

The story itself is reasonably accurate, and includes a neutral statement from the Foreign Office, and an up-beat, we-will-get-them quotation from Country's foreign minister. At first, John's spirits are lifted by the words from the foreign minister, but then he realizes that one vital issue hangs in the balance: Country's important tourist trade.

The phone rings at eight twelve that evening. The major's voice demands: "Are you ready to deliver the million dollars to save the lives of your mother and father?"

"I am working on it as hard and as fast as I can," John assures him. "There are complex procedures which have to be followed to get money out of my father's account. I need to speak with him."

"No! He is all right. You have to send his medication with the money, or he will die."

"Let me speak with him."

"No! Time is running out. I will call tomorrow night. Get the money and the medicine!"

The line goes dead.

The next morning John calls Weymouth. "Is there anything new on your end?"

"Well, Country army and police are trying to find these guys."

"How do they do that?"

"They're listening to the same conversation and trying to track the phone; calling on local sources of human intelligence; and sending out surveillance aircraft."

"Eleanor, I'm very thirsty. Can't we get more water here?"

She is worried. Jonathan stands up at least once an hour to urinate in the jug, and he has been drinking water greedily.

"Yes, I know what this means: my body is trying to get rid of the sugar, but I'm not eating any carbohydrates or fruit. What can I do?"

Achieving Superpersonhood:

"You're going to be all right, Jonathan. I'll speak to the major." She turns and gestures: "Guard, call the major."

The major stares at her acidly and says nothing. "Major, my husband is very ill; he needs insulin urgently. If you want your money, you had better find a chemist who will sell you some – very soon!"

He glances at Jonathan. "Your husband is all right." He turns to go.

"Major," she shouts. He half turns. "In one day, he will lapse into a coma, and in two days, he will be dead."

Calmly, he asks, "How do you know this?"

"Because I have rushed him to a hospital twice before, major. The disease is not forgiving at his age and as long as he has been fighting it. Send one of your men to get at least ten milliliters of rapid-acting insulin and a dozen syringes."

The major sits at the desk in his hut. *If she's not playing a game, and if what she says is true, I could lose the ransom money. If she's playing a game, what is the game? Insulin is not an explosive; needles are not weapons.* "Send Hassan and Warari to see me!"

"Soldiers! I want you to go into Coast City and obtain ten milliliters of fast-acting insulin and twelve syringes from a chemist."

Hassan glances at Warari to determine whether he has understood.

"Is this for the male hostage?" Hassan asks.

"Yes."

"But Major, one has to have a prescription for insulin. Wouldn't it be better to go to the hotel, and get what the hostage left?"

"Don't be an idiot, Hassan! The hotel will be crawling with police." He opens a desk drawer. "Give the chemist this thousand shilling note, and tell him it's for your sick grandmother who lost her prescription."

A crew is setting up for an interview with Chris Shipley of ITV News.

"Tell me a little bit about your father, John."

"Dad is a lovely man. He worked in personnel with Barclays most of his career. He is a people person with a great many friends. He and my mother decided to take that holiday in Country. I told them it would be better in the Caribbean, but they wanted to try a new place."

"When you were growing up, what kinds of things did you and your father do together?"

"We used to go fishing on weekends. He took me the first time when I was nine years old." John clasps his hands under his chin. "He taught me how to cast. He taught me where the trout like to hide." There is a snuffle; John's lips are compressed. "He taught me patience and that it is important – sorry." John retrieves a handkerchief and wipes his eyes. "It's important – he said – to be kind to people. Sorry." The tears run down John's cheeks. "He has severe diabetes and no medication."

When the phone rings that evening, John begins at once. "Major, the only way I can get money for you is if my father speaks personally to his banker. Do you understand? I <u>cannot</u> get any money if I ask for it. The bank <u>requires</u> my father's authorization. Do you understand?"

Major el Hashem's mind searches the situation for a trap, but he finds none. "Give me the number of the banker. We will call tomorrow evening."

Jonathan is complaining of stomach cramps and headaches. He seems to be breathing very rapidly.

Eleanor, nearing panic, demands to see the major. "Where is the insulin, major?"

"We could not obtain any. Your son will have to bring it with the money."

Eleanor is shouting with anger and frustration.

The major ignores her, focusing his attention on her husband, who is lying on his side on the floor, shivering and covered with blankets. There is a small greenish puddle of what must be vomit in front of him. *How long can he last? There have been two army helicopters searching the vicinity. The money had better come soon!*

"Our embassy has been advised that two men in military fatigues tried to obtain insulin without prescription from three pharmacies in Coast City," Weybridge informs John. "They became abusive and the police were called, but the men disappeared before an arrest could be made. The army has received information that some Sword of the Prophet jihadists may have taken over a native village northwest of Coast City. They are making aerial searches to try to identify which one."

"If the village is identified, are the SAS ready to go in?"

"The SAS are in position, but the prime minister will decide whether to deploy them."

John considers this. *I guess that's fair.* "Has the prime minister decided about whether to lend us the £1 million?"

"What is the status of obtaining money from your father's account?"

"The terrorists are supposed to call the Morgan Stanley number tonight and let my father speak to them."

"Let's re-visit the subject of the loan tomorrow. You may not need the loan."

At eight sixteen pm, the phone on Mr Feldman's desk rings. He is put through to Mr Pritchet, whose voice is hardly recognizable: slow and slightly slurred. Multiple identity questions are asked and answered correctly.

"OK, Mr Pritchet, how much money do you want?"

"One million dollars to be given to my son ASAP."

"All right, sir, we'll have the money tomorrow."

The authoritative voice comes back on the line: "Let me speak to young Pritchet." Feldman passes the phone to John. "Tomorrow, when you bring the money, I will call you on your mobile number and tell you where to leave it. If you want to see your parents again, do not disclose the location to anyone. Come alone to deliver the money, and leave immediately. We will be watching you. Understand?"

"Yes."

"I will tell you tomorrow what kind of container to put the money in. When we have the money, I will call you and tell you where to pick up your parents. Do not be later than seven pm; we do not do transactions in the dark."

"What time tomorrow morning can I have the money, Mr Feldman?"

"Not before about ten. It will take us at least an hour to round up a million dollars in US cash."

John begins a search on his mobile phone. "The British Airways website says to flying time to City is eight and a half hours. That means that if I leave tomorrow with the cash, I can't make the seven pm deadline."

The banker gives an apologetic shrug. "I don't know what I can do Mr Pritchet. What is the earliest direct flight?"

"British Airways: leaving at 10:30 and arriving at . . . " He gasps. "21:00! My God! That means I can't make the delivery until the day after tomorrow!"

"But it also means that you'll be in the air at the time he tries to call you if you fly BA tomorrow."

John is staring intently at the ceiling. "The only way I can do this is to leave on a private jet, stop somewhere on the way to take his phone call, and continue on the next day."

"Mr Pritchet, I want to relay to you the Home Office recommendations on this matter, which have been agreed by the prime minister."

John regards Weybridge suspiciously. "Yes?"

"And that is that you deliver less than the one million requested." John is about to interrupt, but Weybridge continues hurriedly. "About four hundred thousand – mostly in one-dollar notes, which will make the delivery package large – but with some five, ten and twenty dollar notes mixed in. That will make the counting process difficult and time consuming. I can tell you, also, that the Country army believes they have identified the village where your parents are being held. They are reluctant to go in unless there is a direct threat to your parents' lives. They say there is no way of mounting an attack with an element of surprise, and they are concerned about loss of life: your parents and the villagers. Instead, what they propose is to send two military helicopters on a search of a shepherd's settlement about two miles away. The terrorists will certainly see this, and be concerned that the army is about to attack. They'll want to drop the hostages, take the money and run under the cover of darkness."

"You don't think they'll want to count the money before releasing my parents?"

"In the scenario I've described: no. Four hundred thousand in small, used notes will fill a good-sized suitcase and look like a hell of a lot of money. You have been very compliant and there's no reason to suspect you. Don't forget that one million was their asking price. If you had haggled, you could have gotten them down to half that."

At two-fifteen pm, the Global Executive Citation jet is rolling down the Biggin Hill runway, bound for Catania, Sicily, where it will spend the night, and where John will receive the call from the major. With him are the large suitcase full of US dollars and a small overnight bag containing insulin. At six am tomorrow the Citation will depart for Cairo and then Khartoum where it will make brief refueling stops. The pilots, Andy and Bob (John didn't get their last names), expect to arrive in Coast City by five pm local time.

Eleanor is desperate. Jonathan was sleeping fitfully last night, and, amid spasms and loud cries of stomach pains, he wet himself. Now, he is lying on his back, mouth open, panting and failing to respond to her queries, even her attempts to wake him. "Damn you people, you are the absolute scum of the earth!" she shouts. "You have killed my husband! I will see the lot of you hanged! He did nothing to you! In your greed, you have killed a kind, intelligent man! I hope the devil drags the lot of you down to hell!" She flings herself, sobbing convulsively, onto Jonathan.

Hassan hears her shrill diatribe in his hut thirty meters away. He approaches the captives' hut and listens. *I've got to do something – this is awful!* He approaches the major. "Is there nothing we can do, Major? If he dies, we only get half the money."

"What the hell are you talking about Hassan? If he dies, they're not going to know he's dead until they leave the money. Besides, they are coming tonight with the money."

Hassan enlists an elderly village woman to go and comfort Eleanor, and instructs the woman to say, "Your son is coming now."

Eleanor listens to the fractured message delivered several times, shaking her head. The woman sits on the floor and tries to embrace Eleanor. "It's too late, I tell you!" Eleanor shouts. "It's too God damned late!" The woman touches Jonathan's neck. There is some warmth and a feeble, rapid pulse.

"No! No!" the woman protests, and points to the pulse. Eleanor, still shaking her head and weeping in great shudders, throws her arms around the woman. Softly, she repeats: "It's too late."

John has spoken with the major and explained the one-day delay, that he has the money, is coming by private jet, and expects to arrive in Coast City by five pm the next day. "I will call you tomorrow," the major says.

There is a brief squeal as the tires touch the tarmac at Coast City Airport. A black Mercedes sedan with obscured windows draws up to the parked Citation. Four men get out. One is a local driver in a suit, white shirt and chauffeur's cap. Another is an official-looking black man in a dark suit and blue tie; he presents himself as George Kambuli, "from the Country Interior Ministry." The other two are fit, young white men dressed in jeans, trainers and bulky jackets. They introduce themselves as "Mark" and "Tommy, Special Air Service."

Once the baggage and men are in the car, George sets out the plan. "We will wait for the terrorists to call you, Mr Pritchet. They may have special requirements for packaging the funds, because they are probably concerned about booby traps. After meeting their requirements, we will take the funds to the location indicated. We recommend that only you get out of the car, but if anyone approaches you, these gentlemen will intervene. OK?"

"Yes, but how do we pick up my parents? There's isn't much room in this car and both of them are old and may be ill. In fact, my father will need urgent insulin treatment."

"Yes, Mr Pritchet, we have made arrangements for a private ambulance to be on standby. The ambulance will meet us at the pick-up point and take your parents to Victoria Hospital in Coast City."

Their wait seems interminable.
Finally, John's phone rings. "Pritchet?"
"Yes."
"You must put the funds in a clear plastic bag. Make sure it is a clear bag; we must be able to see what is inside. You must deposit the clear plastic bag at the base of an old baobab tree." He gives directions. "We are presently observing the

tree. It is in open country. If anyone attempts to interfere with our pickup, we will kill your parents immediately. Do you understand?"

"Yes."

"What kind of vehicle are you in?"

"A black Mercedes sedan."

"Do not send any other vehicles into the area. Do you understand?"

"Yes."

"He's a careful son of a bitch!" Tommy says.

"Most plastic bags are white or colored, where can we get a large clear one?" George inquires of the driver. The driver scratches his head. "Sir, what about one of those bags that the dry cleaners use? They might have a little writing, but that's all."

Twenty minutes later they are parked outside a dry cleaner at the end of a strip mall on the outskirts of Coast City. The boot is open. Mark and Tommy remove their C8 assault rifles and magazines, taking them into the car. It takes about twenty minutes for George and John to fashion the clothing protectors into a large sack, fill it with the money and seal it with cello tape.

George replays the recording of the major's instructions. The Mercedes moves slowly down the dirt track. Twilight is approaching. "There's the tree." Mark is pointing ahead to the right. The car stops opposite the tree, some thirty meters away. John gets out and looks around: nothing in sight except flat grasslands, shrubs and the occasional tree; he hears a faint whirr and the car's electric windows are lowered. *The SAS want a clear shot if somebody comes for me.* He is trembling slightly. The driver has popped the boot. John lifts the sack and carries it toward the tree. He sets it down against the trunk and looks around again. There is nothing and only the muted clatter of a distant helicopter.

He gets back into the car, and the driver pulls away.

Achieving Superpersonhood:

Half an hour later, his phone rings again. "Your parents are by another baobab. Go back down the track, cross the road and three and a half kilometers ahead, on the left is a large baobab."

The driver accelerates. George calls instructions to the ambulance.

"I think it's that one." Mark points to a tall, shadowy shape to the left.

John leaps out and rushes toward the tree; the two SAS men are behind him. He sees a light-colored shape at the base of the tree. "Mother!" He falls to his knees and embraces her. "Are you all right? There's an ambulance coming!"

She puts her arms around his neck and begins to weep. "I'm all right, but your father is dead."

"Oh, my God! Are you sure?" He moves to the other shape to her left. "Dad? Dad?" His hand finds a face. It is cold. Frantically, he searches for a wrist. Cold also. The throat is cold and there is no pulse. "Oh my God! Those absolute bastards!" An avalanche of feelings bursts inside him: fury, love, hatred, and the abatement of acute tension. He puts his head on his father's chest, weeping incoherently.

His mother is saying something. He looks up. "Will you untie me, please?"

Tommy and Mark are working on her bound hands and feet. Eleanor sits up. "Thank you, John. Thank you all."

"Mrs Pritchet, there will be an ambulance here in a few minutes to take you to Victoria Hospital for a check-up."

"And my husband?"

"He will go with you, Mrs Pritchet."

I, the One, am so sorry for the Pritchet family. They have lost a truly good man.

The One says he feels very sorry for the Pritchet family. For my part, I don't particularly care about them: they're not my friends. They're his friends. The question that everyone (well, almost everyone) asks is: how can he let bad things happen to his good friends?

This is just posturing from the Other. He is often involved (as in this case), but never admits it. If he were never involved, nothing bad would ever happen to my good friends. He would have no friends, and they would all be mine.

Hassan is in the Mosque tent praying when the major interrupts him. "This isn't prayer time, Hassan. Get your butt into my tent; we've got to count the money."

He is given a pile of US currency to sort by denomination. *The Prophet said, "You who believe wrongfully consume people's possessions and turn people away from God's path."* (Qur'an 9:34) *This is what is happening here, but not just wrongful consumption, murder!*

The major is outraged at the final tally: four hundred thousand and four dollars. "That bastard Pritchet cheated us!" he shouts.

Hassan looks down at his hands. *I've been handling this money. All but the six hundred thousand that represented the life of the old man. This cannot be on my path to greatness.*

Chapter 15

Refugee

"Kamiri, someone wants to see you." He kicks the practice ball aside and follows the Lions' ballboy, who looks up at Kamiri apprehensively. "He looks sort of like a beggar, Kamiri, and they were going to send him away, but he says he knows you very well and he's a friend of yours. He even said he used to play football with you!"

Kamiri frowns in puzzlement. "He's in the office?"

"No. They wouldn't let him in the office. He's outside by the gate."

There indeed, under one of the gate tusks, is a dark figure with disheveled black hair. Kamiri strides forward, trying to make out who this is. *Probably somebody from Village.*

The dirty face turns toward him. "Oh my God, it's you, Hassan!"

"Yes." Hassan spreads his arms in abject confession. "I'm sorry I'm such a mess, but I need to see you." He lowers his gaze to the ground.

Kamiri sweeps his friend into his embrace. "Where have you been? What have you done?"

Hassan withdraws. "I have escaped from Dhul Fikar."

Still holding his friend's shoulders, Kamiri asks: "What is Dhul Fikar?"

"It is a terrorist organization." Seeing the relief on Kamiri's face, he adds, "I wasn't a captive. I joined."

Kamiri is horrified. "You joined?"

"Yes." Hassan looks around. "Is there someplace we can talk, Kamiri?"

Kamiri glances at his watch. "Let's go to my place. Let me get my bag and my bike."

"Do you want some tea, Hassan? Please sit down."

Hassan stands in the doorway to Kamiri's living area, taking it in. "Yes, I would like some tea very much." He steps forward toward the immaculate couch and halts. "I'm sorry, Kamiri. I'm too dirty. I've been on the run for the last week – sleeping in out-of-the way places – scavenging for food." His eyes turn to Kamiri. "Dhul Fikar has been trying to find me." He pauses. "They kill deserters, and ordinary people want to report me to the police." He grasps the front of his dirty shirt. "This is a combat jersey. People think I've deserted from the army."

Kamiri's mind races to catch up with his friend's situation. *I've got to be patient and try to understand; after all, he is my friend.* "Why don't you take a shower while I'm making you some tea?"

"But I haven't any clean clothes."

"Don't worry about that. We'll find something of mine or Eddie's that fits you."

"Who's Eddie?"

"He's the Lions' goal keeper. The bathroom's through there."

Hassan offers a faint smile. "Are you trying to hurry me into the shower?"

"Well, as a matter of fact, you do smell a little ripe."

"This tea is so good – and the biscuits."

Kamiri winces at his own hospitality. "You need a proper meal, Hassan. How about a steak, a big potato, and some collard greens?"

"Kamiri, I just want to talk."

"We can talk while you're eating."

Hassan gives a start of recollection. "You remember after you came to play football with me, I had a steak, and you insisted on a burger?" Kamiri nods. "Well, have you got any burgers?"

"No. . . . Well . . . there may be a couple in the freezer."

"May I have one of them?"

"No! You're going to have a five hundred gram, medium-rare sirloin."

Hassan gives a shrug of acceptance; he pauses. "What does it mean: this conversation about steaks and burgers?"

"It means that we are friends and neither of us – out of politeness – wants to impose, but this time it's different: I was only broke; you're broke and in real trouble."

"Yeah. I was stupid. . . . I wanted so much to believe that by serving Allah, I would be a better person, and I let myself get pushed into Dhul Fikar, and once you're in, you can't get out."

Kamiri is taking things out of the refrigerator, including a large bottle of beer. He pours a glass and hands it to Hassan, who shakes his head. "Oh, sorry, I forgot! Mind if I drink it?"

"No, of course not."

"What made you decide to quit?"

"It was a lot of stuff. They didn't really read from the Qur'an. The major gave lectures about what the Qur'an says, but I've read the Qur'an, and I don't remember it saying anything like that; they just made up things that they believe in."

Kamiri peers into the broiler. "Like what?"

"Like: Christians and Jews and Shia, and most everyone else, as far as I could tell, are infidels and Allah will reward anyone who kills them."

"Where do they get ideas like that?"

"I don't know. Some of them barely completed elementary school, and didn't know any better. Quite a few of them are poor and want to blame their poverty on someone else. Most of them were really macho but underneath are insecure, so they act real tough as a cover-up. I think that made all of them susceptible to brain washing: 'You're going to become a great hero!' or 'You'll be one of Allah's favorites in Paradise!"

"All of them except you."

"Well, that wasn't the only thing." Hassan goes on to describe Dhul Fikar's treatment of the villagers, and the capture, ransom and death of Mr Pritchet.

Kamiri, seated opposite Hassan, listens, his chin in his hands, his expression shifting between horror and pity. "How can people behave like that?"

Hassan says: "In the Qur'an, the Prophet speaks about evil-doers: 'Satan has gained control over them and made them forget God. They are on Satan's side.'(Qur'an 58:19)"

They sit in silence for a time.

"This steak is wonderful, Kamiri! Thank you!"

"I'm glad. How did you get away?"

"About a week ago, Warari and one other guy and I were sent into town to get some stuff, and . . ."

"Did you say Warari? My brother's name is Warari!"

"I know. Your brother's in Dhul."

Kamiri slams his fist on the table. "Oh my God! Are you sure?"

"Yes, I'm sure, and he's trying to prove he's a really tough guy – like he's ready to take over from the major."

Kamiri grimaces and shakes his clasped hands in front of him. "That's terrible! Really bad for everyone!"

"Yeah," Hassan agrees. "In the last week, I've had three close encounters with Dhul Fikar. Twice, I've had shots fired at me – most likely by Warari."

Kamiri expels a huge breath. "Why do they care if you quit?"

"It's like the army, but a whole lot worse. Deserters are shot as cowards, and they want to discourage anyone else from deserting, because deserters tell their secrets."

"Do you think they're still after you?"

"Yeah, they'll still be looking for me – probably in City."

"Will they hurt your family?"

"I don't think so. They like to talk a big game, but they know that if they killed an Arusei – other than me – the entire army would be mobilized."

"And does anyone in Dhul Fikar know that I'm your friend?"

"Well, Warari and a couple of others know. Oh, Allah! They'll be looking for me here!"

"Maybe. Maybe not. If you're really worried, we can put you up someplace." Kamiri paused to study his friend. "Right now, you need some rest, Hassan. I have some ice cream and another cup of tea for you."

"OK, that couch looks great."

"No, I'll take the couch! You sleep in my bed."

"No! If you won't let me sleep on the couch, I'll sleep on the floor!"

When Eddie comes home he finds what looks like a bearded refugee, dressed in an assortment of his and Kamiri's clothes, sleeping on the couch. And next morning, over coffee in the kitchen, Eddie complains to Kamiri.

"Sorry, Eddie, he's an old friend of mine and he's in big trouble."

"But Kamiri, you told me that you wouldn't even let your brother stay here when he was in trouble. How can you let in a destitute friend?"

"He's not just destitute, Eddie, my brother wants to kill him."

And then the whole story comes out.

At lunch in the Lions' club dining room, Eddie puts his tray down next to Kamiri's. "I've been thinking, Kamiri; this is really complicated." Kamiri, recognizing the issue he's been avoiding, gives a nod. "I mean, he can't very well stay with us," Eddie continues, "because, sooner or later, the terrorists will find out where you live and look for him there. But also, he can't go back home because of his relationship with his father. Maybe he could stay with a friend in City, but he's well known in City, and if the terrorists manage to catch wind of that, he's done for. So what he needs is a longer-term place to stay that the terrorists would never think of, and where he can earn enough money to live, because you say he's broke."

"I guess you're right. I'm reluctant to kick him out, because it may sound like I'm afraid of a terrorist attack. . . I know he won't turn himself in to the authorities because he'll be afraid they'll send him to prison. Let me think about it, Eddie."

During practice that afternoon, I hear The One whispering to Kamiri. Why doesn't the One keep his ideas to himself? Well, I guess that doesn't prevent me from offering my advice, if Hassan will listen.

That evening Kamiri and Eddie sit down with Hassan in the kitchen.

"I'm sorry, guys, I don't want to put this burden on you, and you're right, Kamiri: I don't want to turn myself in. I'm pretty sure I'll end up in prison. Maybe what I ought to do is go to a town in the northwest, and see if a mosque there can put me onto a job and a place to stay. The trouble is, I'd have to borrow some money."

Kamiri said: "I can certainly lend you the money, Hassan, but going away sounds like starting your life all over again."

"Yeah, I don't like that idea either, but I can't put people in danger because of my screw-up."

"I have another suggestion which will give you a job, and a well-hidden place to stay, and you can be in touch with your friends. I know you're not going to like this suggestion at first, but think about it."

"OK, try me."

"Hassan, do you remember where I was working when I first met you?"

"Yeah, you were working in an abattoir." Hassan closes his eyes in pain. "Oh, no! I could never cut up a cow!"

"You get used to it, Hassan. Besides, Koinet is there; you remember him. You get a free bed, good food, TV, you'll be with other guys and you'll earn a little money. It would just be for a couple of months until you decide what you really want to do."

"They're not going to want to hire me, Kamiri."

"They might if Koinet and I recommend you – otherwise it probably is your northwest option."

The next morning, Kamiri is on the phone with his old boss's boss: "Mr Kakuyu, the Lions are coming to City next month – on Saturday the twenty-third. Would you and Mr Arapa like to go to the game? I should be able to get pretty good seats for you."

"Yes, we would be very pleased, Kamiri."

They talk briefly about how various teams in the league are performing and then about how things are at the abattoir.

"Mr Kakuyu, is there any chance you need a new floorman?"

"Yes, we're short two at the moment, which means a lot of overtime and one of the cutters has to work down. Pain in the neck. You know of somebody good? Home Away has nobody right now."

"Yes, I've got a good friend – he's a few years older than I am, he's a good worker from a good family – studying at university."

"Why would he want to work in an abattoir?"

"Because he got himself into trouble. He was caught up in a bad gang of people, and he needs to get away from them for at least a couple of months until it blows over. He can't go home because he's afraid the gang will come after him there."

"Who are these people?"

"They're a bunch of illiterate law-breakers. He realizes now that he was stupid to get involved with them."

"Is he on the police wanted list?"

"No."

"You say he's from a good family. Tell me more about that."

"Brace yourself Mr Kakuyu. He's the youngest Arusei."

"Oh, my fucking word! Let me think about this! . . . How would Mr Arusei react if he knew I'd hired his son to work in his abattoir?"

"Well, actually, I think he'd be rather pleased. Hassan has earned the old man's displeasure by making some bad choices in his life, so I think Mr Arusei would be quite pleased to see that his wayward son has willingly taken on a hard, honest job without asking for financial help from his old man."

"OK, Kamiri, I'll talk to him. Send him in."

This is ridiculous! Did the One give Kamiri the script for that conversation? It's just plain fraud! Most of the facts have been withheld or misrepresented. And he accuses me of misrepresenting things! I'm going to try to make this backfire on the two of them!

The Other is too quick to cry, 'Fraud!' – a technique at which he is particularly skilled. There was an inducement to listen, and not all the circumstances were revealed, but no lies were told and Kakuyu can make his own judgment.

Kamiri informs Hassan of his conversation with Mr Kakuyu. "You didn't tell him that I was a terrorist, Kamiri."

"Did you ever think of yourself as a terrorist, Hassan?"

"No."

"Is there a chance you might behave like a terrorist at the abattoir, Hassan?"

"No."

"All right then. I didn't tell any falsehoods. You can correct any 'misunderstandings' during your job interview."

"When is the interview and how do I get there?"

"Tomorrow's my day off. I'll take you on my bike."

On arrival at the abattoir, Hassan is taken on a tour by Koinet and Kamiri, beginning with the living quarters. During the lunch break, Hassan has a chance to sample the food, note the quality of the beds, and observe the widescreen TVs. Koinet's positive, off-hand manner in describing the abattoir operations helps to ease Hassan's queasiness. "Well, it doesn't seem all that hard," is Hassan's summary.

"It isn't hard," Koinet agrees. "You're busy all the time and you don't have opportunities to think about how the cows might feel about it. Besides, they're never in any real pain."

During the interviews with Mr Arapa and Mr Kakuyu, Hassan is asked whether he is in any trouble with the police. He explains his two-year suspended prison sentence.

"How long ago was that?"

"Just over a year ago."

"Well, we've got half a dozen ex-cons working here, so you'll feel right at home."

Hassan seems to be a sincere, naïve young man, eager for the job. He is hired.

Kamiri takes Hassan into the city to buy some clothes. (He is still wearing borrowed clothing.)

"Let me have the receipts, Kamiri, because this is a loan and I'm going to pay you back."

"Jesus said that if somebody wanted your coat, you should give him your shirt, too. So I'm going to follow his advice."

The bits of receipts float to the ground outside the abattoir. Hassan impulsively embraces his friend for a long moment. "Thank you so much, Kamiri!"

"You are welcome, Hassan. Please stay in touch." He holds up his mobile phone as he mounts his motorcycle. Hassan stands gazing at the slowly diminishing figure on the bike.

* * *

Dorothy and Joseph have picked up their tickets, as arranged by Kamiri, at the stadium ticket booth, and they join Messrs Kakuyu and Arapa in the bright sunlight, at midfield and five rows back from the visitors' team bench, watching the players warm up on the pitch. A cluster of small boys is leaning through the railing below, shouting, waving programs and pens, trying to get the attention of favored players.

Kamiri, dressed in black shorts and a yellow shirt, is running back and forth on the near sideline, exchanging long crosses with a Lion on the far sideline. He waves to his guests as he crosses the pitch to join the Lions' huddle by their bench, signs several autographs and disappears into the melee of players.

The game, in which the Rhinos are the technical favorites, owing to their higher position in the first league, is close. Neither team has more than a one-point advantage throughout, and at eighty minutes, the score stands at two all.

"This is quite a game!" Kakuyu says.

Joseph, who, as a source of floormen to the abattoir, is on a first name basis with Kakuyu says: "Do you think it will go to overtime, Dani?"

"Hard to say. The pressure is really on both teams now."

"I'd like to see Kamiri score a goal."

"Miss Maiyo, I understand how for sentimental reasons, that might be desirable," Arapa says, "but, as a Rhinos' fan, I hope they score the next goal."

The four watch with nervous intensely, and the roar from both sides of the stadium increases. The Lions right fullback clears a ball from his own penalty area to his center midfield, who then turns and fires the ball down the left sideline. Kamiri sprints after it. The Rhinos' right fullback is caught out of position and is forced to chase the ball and Kamiri, who suddenly cuts right with the ball, threatening the goal. The Rhinos' back suddenly sees that Kamiri will have a clear shot at the goal, unless . . . He makes a sliding tackle and brings Kamiri down in the penalty area. The referee blows his whistle, brandishes a yellow card and points to a spot on the pitch in front to the goal.

Kamiri is back on his feet and shaking his head at a gesturing teammate; he points to one of the central strikers, who points back at him. The Lion forwards turn toward the sideline and look toward Elim, their coach, to settle the disagreement. Elim points at the central striker, who carefully positions the ball on the spot indicated by the referee. Standing to the right of the ball, and four paces away, he pauses to study the goal keeper, who is bouncing up and down, arms widespread. The referee's whistle shrieks; the striker begins a powerful lunge at the ball; the goal tender surges to the right, in anticipation. But the striker lofts the ball to the left, into the top corner of the net.

Dorothy takes a sip of her white wine, smooths the white table cloth in front of her, and fastens her eyes in Kamiri for a moment. "I can't get my head around the fact that Dad and I are here at Poseidon for dinner with you and that you are the host! I can easily remember when you barely had a shilling to your name!" Kamiri gives an amused shrug. "And now look at you! You're a professional footballer, with a bank full of shillings, and probably being chased by half – no, probably all – the pretty girls in Country!"

There is an embarrassed look from Kamiri. "I'm not being chased by any pretty girls."

"You're not? Why not, for goodness sake?"

Kamiri gestures earnestly. "I just haven't had time with all the training."

Dorothy scowls.

"No, really, Dorothy. I believe that it takes time to have a relationship with someone. I've seen too many of the guys who are disappointed – even hurt – though they pretend not – in casual relationships."

Joseph says: "I think you're right, Kamiri."

They are interrupted by a waiter who takes their orders.

"So, is football going to be your career, Kamiri?" Joseph inquires.

Kamiri gives a wistful smile. "I certainly thought so when I signed my first contract with the Lions. But now I'm not so sure."

"What's changed your mind?" Dorothy asks.

"It's not that I've actually changed my mind. I enjoy the games and the company of my teammates, and the money's nice, but I don't actually spend much money. I feel like I'm missing something; like it's not the real me."

Joseph asks: "You'd like to use your brain a little more?"

"Yeah. I mean I have a body, but I have a brain too, and it's not being challenged very much. I don't care about being famous."

I hear Dorothy's thought: *Yeah! It's some body! Very nice!* I, the Other, am trying to persuade Kamiri not to change his mind. He should stay with football, where's there's lots of money, and money is fertilizer for my kind of opportunities.

"If I'm honest with you, Kamiri, I don't see you as a football player."

"Papa! How can you say that? He is a successful football player!"

"Yes, Dorothy, but I'm talking about the future – what comes after football, more football? Kamiri isn't a loud, self-promoter like most footballers. Could there be something that demands a little more intelligence and less ultimately pointless competition?"

Kamiri's eyes are squinted in concentration as he looks across the room. "So what kind of thing do you see me doing, Joseph?"

"Well, for me, you have several characteristics which stand out. You're intelligent, and you get along well with people. That we know. But I was watching you on the football pitch this afternoon, and it struck me that you're also a leader. Your teammates listen to you and they watch for your hand signals, and . . ."

"But," Kamiri interrupts, "I'm not the captain."

"Maybe you will be, but that's not my point. I think you have the basic capabilities of a good manager."

"Manager of what?"

"I don't know. We'll have to see, won't we?"

The waiter brings their first courses.

"What I really want to know, Kamiri," Dorothy prompts, "is why Elim chose the white striker to take the penalty, rather than you."

Kamiri gives a brief laugh. "Well, José is a very experienced player. He's over thirty, and he's played in Country for at least eight years. Knows all the goal tenders and their tendencies. Scored against all of them. Elim wanted to win the game. Mr Arusei wanted to win the game, so Elim picked the best guy to win it."

"Well, I think you could have just as easily scored that goal, Kamiri."

"Maybe – maybe not, Dorothy. If I'd tried and failed, I'd be feeling pretty low right now."

The waiter returns to refill their glasses.

"I wanted to have some time with the two of you not just to thank you for bringing me in off the street, for giving me my first chance and introducing me to Hassan, but also to ask you for some advice."

Joseph pushes his knife and fork into alignment on the plate. "OK."

"Well . . . I've been reading the Bible you gave me, Dorothy, and I believe that it is telling the truth about Jesus, and what he told the people to do." Joseph and Dorothy share smiles of agreement. "And I'm feeling like a deaf man who has just started to hear. It's as if I can hear a little bit of music that I like, but I don't know the tune, and I'd like to be able to sing it."

I feel sorry for Kamiri! He's been completely misled by that stupid book of old fairy tales! And to hear him say he'd like to sing along with it! How can he do that? It's all dissonance! And they're probably going to volunteer to give him singing lessons! It's ridiculous!

When the Other speaks about the Bible and musical dissonance, he, himself is tone deaf and always has been.

Joseph and Dorothy begin asking questions about what church he is attending; has he been baptized, what is he reading (apart from the Bible), has he begun to pray? In short, their advice is to go to several churches, picking out the one that best suits him. He should get baptized in the church, and Joseph promises to send him the titles of several books which Kamiri would find interesting. "There is a book by C. S. Lewis, called *The Joyful Christian,* that is a good insight into what being a Christian means, and there is *People of the Lie,* by M. Scott Peck which is about the influence of evil in the world, and then there is a whole series of books published by Barclay that help one fully appreciate each book of the New Testament."

Kamiri holds up a hand. "But Joseph, why should one read about evil?"

"Because in Christianity, and in other monotheistic religions – Judaism and Islam – God has opposition: the force of evil; in Christianity and Islam that force is controlled by Satan. Satan and God are inimical to each other. Christians love God, and we try to understand and obey his teaching, but I believe it is also important for us to realize that there is also the opposite polarity: evil. If we understand the force of evil, we can understand why bad things sometimes happen to good people. We can also see that between good and evil, God gave human beings the power of free will – to make our own choices, without His interference. An awareness of Satan will also sharpen our sense of God's teaching and the reasons for it."

"OK. I get that. How about prayer? I don't know that much about it, except that I've learned the prayer that Jesus recommended."

Joseph says, "Prayer is just an honest attempt to communicate with God. One can express questions, doubt, love, fear, or worry as long as it's honestly seeking a response from God."

"Yes," Dorothy interrupts, "but don't expect that there will always be an answer."

"There may not be a discernible answer," Joseph continues, "but I often feel more at peace after I've prayed – not that I have the answer, but I feel more comfortable about the situation, and that somehow God will guide me."

"How does God guide you, Joseph?"

"I don't know, Kamiri. I may have thought about a particular problem and prayed about it for some time: should I do this or that? And then, I'll suddenly feel comfortable with this choice – it's a feeling, an intuition – not logically driven."

"Sometimes," Dorothy adds, "I find it very helpful to ask myself, 'What would Jesus do?'"

They compare main dishes, and there are some tastes exchanged.

"This is really delicious," Joseph comments on his fish stew. "It's got oysters, clams, white fish and even some lobster. Really good!"

"You know, Dorothy, that I've seen Hassan?"

"No, tell me about him."

Kamiri recounts Hassan's flight from Dhul Fikar, his employment at the abattoir and his apparent commitment to a new, reformed life.

Dorothy says, "I suspected he was in some kind of trouble when he disappeared."

Joseph frowns. "I wonder why Dani didn't mention that he hired him."

"Come on, Papa! You have a connection to the Aruseis. I'm sure Dani is nervous about having hired Kaddour Arusei's son."

"I guess you're right. You know, I think that if Hassan is ever going to be able to stand up to his father, he'll have to find some kind of work that the old man would admire."

"Well, it's certainly not working in the abattoir!"

"You say that, Dorothy, but I think Kamiri is right that if Kaddour does find out, he'll have to give the boy some grudging respect for taking a disagreeable job to redeem himself."

"What's going on with your brother, Kamiri?"

"Well, Dorothy," Kamiri begins with a sour face, "Hassan told me Warari has joined Dhul Fikar."

"Oh boy! That's real trouble! You know the police are still looking for him, Kamiri?"

"I'm not surprised, Joseph."

"I think the police ought to be told."

Kamiri gives a shrug. "Just please don't mention Hassan."

Joseph leans back in his chair. "You know, Kamiri, Dorothy, has given up her ambition to be our prime minister?"

"He likes to tease me; I never said I wanted to be prime minister. I just wanted to make Country a better place."

"You could certainly do that, Dorothy."

She sticks out her tongue at her father. "Thank you, Kamiri. But, I worked for a while in the office of a Green Party MP, and I began to realize that politics is not for an idealist like me. You have to cut too many corners to be a successful politician. I'm not saying they're all corrupt, but they all have to compromise, and I hate compromise."

Joseph says, "We've been talking about the theory, called the Will to Power, of a German philosopher. It's about how to become what he called a 'supermensch'.

"What is a supermensch?" Kamiri asks.

"The literal translation would be 'superman'," Dorothy explains, "but Nietzsche had a tendency to exaggerate. What he was talking about was how to be the best you can be."

Kamiri is glancing back and forth at his two guests. "How did he say one should do that?"

"His answer would be self-overcoming," Joseph replies. "What he meant by that was more than self-discipline. His prescription would have included identifying and overcoming any weaknesses we may have."

"And for me," Dorothy adds, "my main weakness in becoming a politician is my idealism, and I don't intend to stop being an idealist."

Joseph reaches across the table to pat his daughter's arm. "She can be just a bit stubborn, too, which is an uncommon political trait, but fortunately, Nietzsche did not include politicians in his list of supermensch."

Dorothy scowls at her father. "So, I've decided to continue my medical studies and become a doctor."

"That's good, Dorothy. What do you have to overcome to be a doctor?" Kamiri asks.

"My tendency to enjoy sleeping late. It's hard work, long hours, Kamiri. We're expected to be in the hospital by seven in the morning to do ward rounds, then we attend lectures from ten until three, and we have to be available on the ward from four till eight. We have a good three hours of reading to do every day, and three times a week, we're expected to shadow someone for a full shift."

"What kind of doctor are you planning to be?"

"I haven't made up my mind yet. Probably general medicine. I don't want to get so specialized that I lose contact with the whole patient. I like diagnosing illnesses, and it seems to me that this is what the people of Country need. I've seen too many cases of people who come to hospital when they're gravely ill, and at that point, their chances of survival are low. If they had just had access to a doctor earlier, the disease could be identified and treated sooner."

Joseph adds, "I think what Dorothy is saying is typical of the developing world: emphasis is placed on hospital care in an effort to demonstrate that 'we are not backward'. But this neglects primary care, which is much more cost effective but less glamorous."

"So, where will you end up working, Dorothy?"

"I don't know, Kamiri. If I decide to go into general medicine, I'll probably be working in some small town somewhere."

The waiter clears their plates. "Kamiri, you've mentioned your brother, but how about the rest of your family. How are they?"

Kamiri gives a shrug. "They're OK, Joseph – getting older. I've been back a couple of times. There are only three or four mobile phones in Village, so I can't really call. I did write to my father a few months ago."

"Did he write back?"

"He can't write, and he would never ask someone else to write. He would think it is too personal."

Joseph is pensive. "Family is important, Kamiri. They are usually the ones who outlast friends when times are tough. They are the ones who best know and respect the person each of us is."

"I should go back again. You know that in my village, a lot of young people have left, and sometimes their families don't hear from them again."

"That's a shame. Staying in contact doesn't have to change the kind of person we've become."

"I think that's my point. I dislike going back to Village to hear everybody say, 'Look there's Kamiri, the great football player! He used to live here!' And having a celebration and making a fuss." He shakes his head. "I'd just rather sneak into my family's little home and have some beans and lemongrass tea and talk for a while. I do miss my parents."

Joseph gazes into the middle distance. "Would your father like to see you play a game of football?"

"Yes, I suppose he would, but he would never travel here."
"Suppose you sent a car to pick him up?"
"Oh, he would really like that! He would feel very important in the village."
"So why don't you arrange it?"

Chapter 16

Baba

I've timed it just about right. It's late but not too late. Not many people are out and it's getting dark. Kamiri parks his motorcycle, with which he had walked silently the last four hundred yards, alongside the mud brick wall of his childhood home. There is the yellow glow of an oil lamp behind a curtained window. The wood paneled front door is closed. He pauses, taking a deep breath, knocks on the door and calls out, "Kamiri!"

He hears a scuffle and voices inside; the door opens, and there in her blue and red shift is his incredulous mother. "Kamiri!" She flings her arms around him and looks up into his face. "It is really you! Come in!" Clinging to him, she escorts him into the living area to the left. It is all as it was: mud brick walls decorated with colorful woven pieces, handmade carpeting on the earth floor, two oil lamps suspended from the rafters. His father is seated at a low table on the floor next to Faraji, his brother-in-law. His third sister is standing nearby, and their two small children are playing in a corner.

"Sit down, Kamiri. Are you hungry? Would you like some stew?"

"Yes, Mama, that would be very nice."

His sister embraces him formally. "How are you, Kamiri?"

"I am well, Asha, thank you."

Faraji, on his feet now, nods a greeting. Eshe takes two steps forward and smiles bashfully, but Kibwe, dressed in a green

Achieving Superpersonhood:

Rhinos t-shirt and blue shorts, rushes forward and shakes Kamiri's hand. "I saw you play football, and Mama says you're my uncle!"

"Yes, Kibwe, I'm your uncle. Do you play football?"

"Yes, but I play right back, and some day I'm going to play for the Rhinos." Suddenly, he, too, turns bashful. "Or maybe the Lions."

"Here you are, Kamiri: vegetables, potatoes and a little chicken. Not what you're used to, I expect, but it's what we have."

"It's fine, Mama. Can you make me a little lemongrass tea?"

Kamiri sits next to his father and begins to eat. "How are you, Baba?"

"Well enough for my age. I am seventy-two, you know."

"You're not working the fields."

The old man shakes his head.

Faraji says, "Your older brothers and I work the fields, including the three small plots from people who have left." He asks: "How long were you in City?"

"I worked in an abattoir for some time."

Asha says, "That's a damn sight better than some of the places I worked! I was working in a bar and a few other places – none of them good." She adds bitterly, "City is a horrible place!"

Faraji asks, "Where's Warari?"

"He's somewhere near Coast City."

"What's he doing?"

"I don't know, exactly."

This is annoying! Kamiri knows exactly what Warari is doing: he's a terrorist. He should just say so! It's not like Warari has testicular cancer, or some other secret disease! The only things that should be kept secret are intentions. If a friend of mine wants to commit adultery, for example, that is completely confidential information.

The conversation continues: family, football, the state of the rural economy.

His mother asks, "What are your plans for tomorrow, Kamiri? Will you stay with us for a while?"

"Unfortunately, I have to be back at training camp late tomorrow. I just had the inspiration to come and see all of you."

"You'll come back in the off-season, won't you, Kamiri?" Faraji inquires.

"Yes, of course."

That evening, Kamiri sleeps on a bedroll with six other people in the old home. *I can remember when there used to be eight other people in this room. Snoring isn't quite so bad now, and Asha and Faraji have taken over the screen Baba and Mama used to use.*

Breakfast is bread, pickles and tea with milk.

"Are you going to come and watch us play this afternoon, *Mjomba* (uncle)?" Kibwe asks.

"No, Kibwe, unfortunately I have to get back to Coast City. We have a game on Saturday."

Kamiri finds his father sitting on the old bench at the front of the house, watching the to-and-fro of passersby.

"Baba, do you feel like taking a walk?"

His father studies him for a moment. "You want to talk, Kamiri?"

"Yes, I'd like that, if you feel like it."

The old man gets to his feet, and rests a hand on Kamiri's shoulder. "I suppose you want to tell me that I was wrong to advise you not to go."

"No. You and Asha are right; City is not a friendly place."

"What then?" He shuffles forward.

"I don't miss Village, or most of the people here, or the work. What I find I have been missing is you, Mama and the family. It is very good to be back."

"You have Warari."

He turns to face his father. "Baba, I did not want to say so last night, but Warari has joined a banned organization."

The old man stops and gazes at his son. "What sort of organization?"

Kamiri takes a deep breath. "It's a terrorist organization, Baba."

In his anguish, the old man clasps his head in his hands. "Oh, Ngai, why have you led my son astray? He will bring shame onto our family and our village." Bitterly, he bites his lip.

Kamiri murmurs, "I don't think Ngai had anything to do with it Baba. He was in trouble with the police."

"What kind of trouble?"

Kamiri says nothing for some moments. "He was selling drugs; he got into a fight; and the police arrested him, but he got away."

"Have you seen him?"

"Not for some time."

"The police were asking about him a while ago. I couldn't tell them anything. How can I live this down?"

"It's nothing to do with you, Baba."

The old man smiles bitterly at Kamiri. "It's everything to do with me."

They walk slowly on, his father pointing out areas that the family has under cultivation, and where the livestock are corralled. "Faraji seems all right; doesn't work very hard, but he's pretty good doing palm thatch. Asha was like a lemon when she first came back – less so now. Your older sisters and brother – well, they're as good as can be expected."

"Baba, would you like to see me play in a game?"

"Well, I seen you play not long ago – on the television that they have at the shop."

"No, I meant in a live game."

"I thought you had to leave this afternoon."

"No, Baba, I meant in the stadium at Coast City."

There is a look of rebuke on the old man's face. "How am I going to get to Coast City?"

"I can send a car to pick you up."

The old man searches his son's face for understanding. "So you can order up a car just like that?" Kamiri nods. "Why would you want to do that?"

"Because I'd like to spend some time with you. You - and Mama - are the only people in Village I really care about. And because I'd like to know what you think about the world I live in now."

His father shakes his head. "I wouldn't think much about it."

"Baba, you've never seen it. There are two worlds, actually. The world that Asha and Warari lived in, which is where I started out, and then there's another world, an artificial world with a lot of comfort, but where you don't know what people really believe in." His father frowns his disapproval. "Baba, you're a wise man. I respect you, and I need to hear your advice. Please come to Coast City – just for a couple of days."

"I gave you my advice before and you didn't listen."

"I did listen and I understood the risk I would be taking. Now, the risks I'll be taking are much less clear."

The old man gazes into the distance. "All right, Kamiri, when is this car coming?"

"Let's say on Thursday, next week." There is a pause. "Shall I ask Mama if she wants to come, too?"

His father frowns. "She will never leave Village."

Kamiri finds his mother shoving pieces of wood into the outdoor oven. "Mama, I have to go now."

She turns, clapping the dust from her hands, and embraces him. "Good bye, sweet Kamiri, come back soon."

His hand finds one of hers. She steps back to look in her hand. A five-thousand-shilling note. "Oh Kamiri, what am I going to do with this?"

"Save it, Mama, save it."

Kamiri's father stands in the center of the living room, slowly surveying the place. "So this is where you live."

"Yes, Eddie, my teammate, sleeps in there and I sleep here."
"I've heard that these beds are quite comfortable." He passes his hand over the foot of the bed and moves to the window. "What is that?"
"It's a golf course, Baba."
The old man nods. "That's for people who don't work." He moves on to the kitchen. "This here must be a stove. Shop owner's got one of these – and a refrigerator. What's this?"
"It's a dishwasher, Baba." Kamiri opens the machine and his father peers inside. "You can put dirty dishes inside – a little soap goes in here, and when you start it, hot water is sprayed around and it cleans the dishes."
"Where's the hot water come from?"
"There's a heater in the closet over there."
Kamiri's father looks inside the closet. "There are two things in here."
"The other one is the air conditioning unit."
"We haven't got anything like that in Village – too expensive. What else?"
"This is the bathroom."
"This here is what they call a toilet?" Extra emphasis on the last word. Kamiri nods. "I sure would like to have one of these – in the house – rather than that damned chamber pot. But I'm told it takes a lot of pipes and water. Where're we gonna get that?" He studies his son for a moment. "How much does this place cost you?"
"It's a little over fifteen thousand shillings a month, but Eddie and I split it."
The old man shakes his head in disbelief. "And you have some left over?" Kamiri nods. "I heard that there's a lot of money in football." He looks around. "Where do you want me to sleep? On this thing here?" He gestures toward the large leather couch.
"No, Baba, you should be comfortable. You and I are going to stay in a hotel."

"There's no need for that, Kamiri. I reckon I can sleep pretty well on this here."

"Baba, the people back home are expecting a full report from you. You know that. They want to hear about your car ride and how you stayed in a hotel, and ate in a restaurant, and went to the big stadium and saw the tall buildings in Coast City. You aren't going to disappoint them, are you?"

The old man considers. "How do we get to this hotel?"

"On my bike."

"I never rode one of them."

"Is this one of these fancy restaurants I hear about?"

"No, this is just a Golden Hotels restaurant. There are probably several hundred just like this around the world."

"And they all have this white cloth on the table, and the music playing, and these little flowers, and a young woman who lets people in?" Kamiri nods. "Well then, what is a fancy restaurant like?"

"We can go to one tomorrow night."

There is a pained expression on the old man's face. "I don't think I'd like it."

Kamiri picks up his father's menu and explains the various choices. "You mean I can have *all* these things?" His hand makes a sweeping gesture.

"It means you can decide what you want to eat first and second and third."

"And whatever I choose, they will cook it for me?"

"Yes, of course."

"But Kamiri, suppose I don't choose this thing here." He points to the menu. "Whatever it is, and nobody else chooses it. What happens to whatever it's made of?"

"Baba, they don't put things on the menu that people don't like, but if the fish they bought this morning doesn't get used in the next day or two, it will end up in a soup."

"Ah. Same as we do." He picks up another folder. "What's this list here?"

Achieving Superpersonhood:

"That's the list of drinks." He points to the categories. "These are wines, here are beers, soft drinks, juices, spirits, and cocktails."

"Are cocktails something to do with chicken?"

"No, Baba, they are strong drinks made with spirits and juices."

The old man shakes his head in disgust. "And these are the prices? One hundred shillings? Crazy!"

After a consultation, Kamiri places their orders.

"Baba, I want you to know that I have become a Christian."

The old man is skeptical. "Isn't that the white man's religion?"

"No Baba, most of the people at my church are black. Maybe you're thinking of the missionaries who came to Village."

"Why have you done this?"

"Because there was nothing for me in our religion."

The old man is exasperated; he makes a sweeping gesture. "Everything in our religion is for you: Ngai, the sacred mountain, Kirinyaga, your ancestors!

Go on, Mchumba, give him a piece of your mind! You know what Kikuyu should believe!

"I didn't explain that very well. What I mean is that Christianity is a religion about relationships: between a Christian and God or Christ, and between a Christian and all other people. A good Christian has to be involved. He has to <u>do</u> some things, be active, care about other people, love them, love God. A Kikuyu can't get involved with Ngai; he is too remote and he has already decided about us."

"Well," the old man said tartly, "Ngai has apparently decided that you're going to be rich football player!"

"You say 'apparently decided' and that's my problem. We don't know what Ngai decides and there's nothing that we can do about it. The Christian God gives us the chance to decide what we want to do with our lives. He loves us and cares about us, and I can feel that."

"Kamiri, you're a rich football player. What difference does it make if Ngai decides or God lets it happen?"

"There's a huge difference, Baba! Ngai decides and then he doesn't care what happens to us. God lets us decide how to live, and he loves us and cares about us. God is like a father to us. Ngai is indifferent to us."

"Well, if God is our father, why does he leave so many in poverty; why can't he just get rid of poverty?"

"If He did that, would there be any doubt that God is real and does exist?"

"I suppose not."

"And if we all believed in God, could we all live our lives as we wanted?"

"Why not?"

"Because, if God abolished poverty, wouldn't he also abolish war, and slavery and drugs and sickness, and crime and . . ."

"OK, OK. So he lets us decide whether to start a war or commit a crime . . . what's in it for him?"

"I don't know exactly. What I believe is that God is not alone. There is also an opposite that the Christians call Satan, and he's the one who starts wars; slavery was his idea, and he believes in crime."

"How does Satan start a war? It's pretty obvious that idiot leaders start wars!"

"I'm not sure how he does it, but he is powerful, and his voice – the voice of temptation – can be heard. I've heard it; you've heard it: 'just do this; it will be fun and nobody will know!'"

The old man laughs. "I thought that was just me being bad."

"But where does the bad come from?"

"So you think it's like this…" The old man leans over and whispers gibberish in his son's ear.

"Yes. Like that, but real."

Achieving Superpersonhood:

Mchumba stares into the distance. "You mentioned someone else besides God. Who is that?"

"Jesus Christ, his son."

The old man gestures toward the ceiling. "And he is up there, somewhere, with God?"

"That's where he is now, but a long time ago, he was here alive on earth."

"How do you know that?"

"There is a book called the Bible, and part of it tells the story of Jesus' life on earth."

"Have you considered that this Bible may be something that some men wrote just to tell people what they believed?"

"The part about Jesus was written by different people in the same century that Jesus lived. One was Jesus' brother; others knew a lot about him, or had seen him in person."

"And what's so special about this Jesus fellow?"

"Several things. There are many miracles he performed – like bringing dead people back to life. He said it was God's power that permitted him to perform miracles. He was an amazing teacher. Just reading what he said to people gives me goose flesh!"

"Give me an example."

"He said there are only two things that Christians have to do: love each other and love God."

Mchumba chuckles. "Well, if we could all really do that, the Satan fellow would be out of work."

"Yeah."

"So that must be God's method for defeating Satan. . . Anything else about Jesus?"

"Yes. He came back to life after he died and joined his father in heaven."

"How do you know that?"

"People who saw it happen tell the story in the Bible."

For some moments, the old man sits considering the far wall of the dining room. "Well, after you explained it to me, I can't see anything wrong with this Christianity, but it's going to be hard for you to love all these other people." He makes a sweeping gesture taking in the room. "Some of them are idiots, and others are just plain <u>bad</u>."

". . . and then the next day I went to the Lions' training camp. A dozen pitches like the best green carpet with a man to attend to each one." Mchumba is holding forth to a score of men seated on the ground in the shade of an umbrella acacia tree. "And I shook the hand of Elim the coach."

"Isn't he a white man?" someone asks.

"Yes, he is a white man, but if you close your eyes and listen to him, you would think he is black. And that afternoon we went into Coast City to look around."

"Did that same car pick you up?"

"No, we went on Kamiri's motorcycle and then we got on a strange bus that had a stairway up to the roof. There were chairs up there, so as the bus drove along, you could see everything. There were wires you put in your ears to hear someone tell you what you were watching. If you turned a knob, she would speak to you in a different language."

"How come Kamiri has a motorcycle instead of a fancy car like most big footballers?"

"He says he wants to save his money and he doesn't need a car." He pauses to judge the attentiveness of his audience. "Coast City is a wonder of the world. You have never seen so many buildings that make you strain your neck to see to the top of them. And the people – all of them in a hurry and no one dressed like us. They dress like they're on television. When you see into the shops – many big and fancy – you can see all the things that people buy and how much they cost. I mean it's like there is a rainstorm of money every day: people spend that much."

"Did you go to the game, Mchumba?"

"Yeah, I went to the game. I sat next some businessmen who were speaking another language and they exchanged a lot of money at the end of the game. Did you see that Kamiri got a goal?"

"Yeah, we heard about it."

"Then I went down to the home team dressing room. Mr Arusei came in to congratulate the players, and I shook his hand, but I don't think he remembers me. This morning we woke up very early, because Kamiri had something he wanted me to see. In the dark, we went right through the city until there wasn't any more city. Kamiri told me, 'this is the beach.' I didn't know what he was talking about; it was really dark, but we walked along the soft earth and I could hear a strange sound like 'whoosh' 'whoosh' 'whoosh' and my feet were wet. I realized that we must be standing on the edge of the ocean. When a cloud moved away, I could tell that the ocean went as far away into the dark as one could see. We stood there for a while, and then, in the distance, I could see where the ocean meets the sky. The sky began to turn a little bit pink, and then orange and brighter yellow. All of a sudden, I saw the sun come up out of the ocean and it seemed to light up the whole world. It was wonderful!"

"You seen a sunrise lots of times, Mchumba."

"Yes, but never like that!"

"Did you have a chance to talk to Kamiri about what he's going to do after football?"

"Yes, he mentioned some wise old man from Germany – wherever that is – who wrote about improving yourself by correcting yourself."

"We don't need somebody from Germany to tell us that."

Mchumba is silent and reflective. "It is difficult for Kamiri."

There are murmurs of disagreement. Someone says, "What's difficult? He's making more money than the whole lot of us put together!"

Mchumba ignores the comment. "I told him, 'you come from a simple land where the weather, like everything, is known. Now, you find yourself on a perch high up in a strange land with great winds and unpredictable storms. Much effort must be spent on maintaining your perch, sometimes taking actions that are against the kind of bird you are. Perhaps, Kamiri, you should be on the lookout for another land with more predictable weather – one which offers you a perch where you can sing your song in peace'."

* * *

Dorothy is bending over the male patient lying on the gurney. She palpates his swollen stomach. *This is not fat; his stomach cavity is full of fluid. I can barely feel his liver.* She moves her attention to his lower legs. "How long have your legs been swollen like this, Mr Nagumba?"

"Quite some time. Since I started feeling tired. I just figured I'm retaining water and that makes me feel kind of logy."

She notes the yellowish cast to his black skin. "Do you drink alcohol, Mr Naguma?"

"No Doctor, can't afford it. May have a beer once or twice a year."

"Are you married, Mr Nagumba?"

"I was married until about five years ago."

"Do you have a partner now?"

"Yes."

"Did you ever have a pretty severe attack of fever, tiredness and feeling generally unwell which went away after a while?"

"Yeah, there was something like that a while back. Doctor couldn't find anything wrong."

"Did your wife or partner have a similar attack?"

"My wife had something similar after the baby was born."

"OK, Mr Nagumba, we're going to run a blood test to see if we can find out what this is."

"What do you think it might be, Doctor?"

"Well, we won't really know until we get the results of the test, which will be tomorrow. I think we're going to keep you in the hospital overnight."

She goes to the nursing station and fills out a blood test form. In the comments section she writes 'Hepatitis B?', and hands the form to a nurse. "Would you take some blood from Mr Nagumba, Carole?"

She scans the nurse's triage form for the next patient: 'Mrs Lupinu – aged 82 – fell outside her house this am – very confused – may have a broken arm'.

"Hello, Mrs Lupinu, I'm Miss Maiyo, one of the doctors. I understand you had a fall?"

The reply is halting. "I told the other . . . person . . . I fell down." Dorothy notices that there is a lack of symmetry in the patient's face. The right eyelid is markedly lowered and the right corner of her mouth is immobile.

Dorothy turns to an attending nurse. "Blood pressure?"

"One-o-nine over seventy-six."

"Has she had an anti-coagulant?"

"Yes."

Dorothy turns back to the patient. "How did you fall, Mrs Lupinu?"

"I don't know. . . . I just found myself . . . on the ground."

"Did you hit your head?"

"Yes, I hit my head. It hurts!"

"And did you hurt your arm, as well?"

"Yes!" She places a protective left hand on her right shoulder.

"Where does it hurt?"

Mrs Lupinu reaches behind her head with her left hand. "Here." Then, she gestures toward her upper right arm. "And here."

"Would you lean forward, Mrs Lupinu, so I can see the back of your head?" *Significant swelling and abrasion, some bleeding.* Mrs Lupinu would you move your right leg for me?"

The patient seems to be making an effort but eventually shakes her head.

"OK, Mrs Lupinu, I'd like to examine your right arm." The patient makes a protective gesture. "I'll be very gentle, Mrs Lupinu. I just want to see if your arm is broken."

Major bruising. The humerus may be broken. Dorothy holds up a finger. "Try to follow my finger, Mrs Lupinu."

The patient's eyes do not follow to the right.

The question is: did she have a stroke and fall or fall, hit her head and have a concussion?

"Mrs. Lupinu, I'm going to send you for a CT scan of your head, and while you're waiting for that, we'll x-ray your arm."

"Am I going to be all right, Doctor?"

"I certainly hope so, Mrs Lupinu. Have you had a stroke before?"

"Yes. I fell down before."

Does she know what a stroke is? "Have you had to go to the hospital after a fall?"

"I don't think so."

Dorothy fills out a radiology referral form, ticking 'Brain' under CT Scan and 'Humerus' under X-ray. In the comments box she writes: 'Ischemic stroke? Fractured humerus?'

From the case box, Dorothy picks up the next triage form: 'Desta Okeke – aged 7 – temperature 40.2° C – chills – has vomited – perspiring' *Oh dear! Is this flu, pneumonia or malaria? Or cholera or even diphtheria? I remember what Professor Ojukwu said: "It takes evidence – not hunches – to rule things out. When your list of possibilities gets short and doubtful, consult your memory bank and rule something strange and possible in."*

Dorothy examines the little girl. *Blood pressure and sats OK; temperature elevated; perspiring but chilled under a blanket. Throat is normal. Heartbeat OK. No sign of a chest infection; sinuses are clear; liver slightly enlarged.*

She turns to the mother: "Mrs Okeke, has your daughter had diarrhea?"

"Yes."

"And is she very thirsty?"

"Yes, more than normal."

"Do you have a headache, Desta?"

"Yes, ma'am."

"Do other people in your village have the same symptoms now?"

"Doctor, as far as I know, nobody right now, but in the past, yes."

"And can I assume that the water in your village is good, Mrs Okeke?"

"Yes, we have used the same well for many years, doctor."

"Is malaria a problem in your village?"

Mrs Okeke compresses her lips in anguish and begins to cry. "I lost my first son to malaria! It's horrible! What can you do for Desta, Doctor?"

"The first thing we want to do is to test her blood. That will tell us whether she definitely has the disease. If she does, we can give her drugs.

"My son had drugs but he died, Doctor."

"Some forms of the malaria parasite are immune to some drugs, but we can try different drugs or a combination of drugs."

In a barely audible whisper comes the question, "Is she going to survive, Doctor?"

"Mrs Okeke, at this stage, I feel positive. Your daughter seems to be in good health; keep your hospital appointments and follow the doctor's instructions."

Dorothy bends down and kisses Desta on the cheek.

Directly across from the hospital Accident & Emergency Department there is a small park where bare earth has overtaken the grass, a grove of African Oil Palms, and three wooden benches. Normally crowded at lunch time, at eight pm, and halfway through Dorothy's shift, she can find a seat near a streetlight, where she can watch the comings and goings at A&E while she eats her sandwich and drinks her coffee.

I really like working in A&E. You get to see all kinds of injuries and diseases, and you can make a huge difference to patients by coming up with the right treatment. Hard work and long hours. Horrible injuries, pain and blood. I don't really mind all that. What I like is having to think and communicate under pressure. Getting it right is so important – so challenging. What are the downsides? What does Papa say? 'You're a stubborn idealist.'

I guess the thing that bothers me most is so many of the injuries and illnesses are self-inflicted. I'll bet that Mr Naguma doesn't use a condom or made some other stupid mistake – that's how he got Hepatitis B. And Mrs. Lupinu wasn't being careful when she fell. Ideally, these things shouldn't happen! It makes me impatient sometimes, and I want to tell them off. So my self-overcoming project is to become more realistic and patient – more forgiving. It's not easy; Nietzsche was right.

Dorothy is on the phone to the sister on Ward 3 when there is a tap on her shoulder. She turns to see that it is her superior in A&E, Consultant Anesthesiologist Benjamin Wadaki. "I'll be with you in a second, Dr Wadaki. Sister, this is Dr Maiyo. Do you have a bed for a child with acute appendicitis? He's scheduled for an op tomorrow morning with Dr Okonjo. That's great! I'll send him up. His name is Danni Awela; he's 10. Thanks! Sorry, Dr Wadaki. You wanted to see me?"

Wadaki is a big man in a light green surgical gown; his round, unsmiling face is topped by a matching green cap. "When the doctor calls, Miss Mayo, other business must be set aside."

"Yes, I'm sorry, Dr Wadaki."

"Miss Maiyo, I'd like to review the cases you've handled on this shift. I haven't heard from you about any of them."

"They've all been pretty straightforward, Dr Wadaki."

"What about the appendicitis case?"

"I called Dr Okonjo to confirm my diagnosis."

Wadaki's eyes narrowed. "Okonjo is just a general surgeon. I am a department head and your superior on this assignment. Therefore, I am the one who will grade your performance."

"Yes, Dr Wadaki."

He picks up a sheet of paper and studies it for a long moment. She recognizes it as a radiology referral. "You say here that Mrs Lupinu had suffered an ischemic stroke."

"Yes, I thought she might have."

"In fact the scan shows an ischemic event <u>and</u> a concussion. Did you consider the concussion, Miss Mayo?"

"Yes, I did, but I thought the ischemic event was more important, and that if there is any pathology from a concussion, that will show on the scan."

"You <u>thought</u> the ischemic event to be more important than a concussion. Why did you think that?"

"The patient was exhibiting more symptoms of a stroke – slurred speech, distorted face, inability to move her left leg."

"So you didn't think it was more important; you thought it was more <u>likely</u>. Isn't that correct?"

"Yes, I suppose so."

"Good doctors do not 'suppose' things, Miss Maiyo." Dorothy fastens her eyes on a slowly-turning ceiling fan to the right of Wadaki's head. There is a long pause. "Miss Maiyo, I think we should have a review of your progress next week."

"Yes."

"I'll let you know where and when."

God, he's a bastard! Always critical. I don't think he likes me at all. What kind of grades am I going to get? This is one thing that worries me about being a doctor: how much politics do you have to play?

Chapter 17

Dr Wadaki

Monday evening. The end of the noon-until-eight shift is approaching. Dorothy is cleaning up her shift paperwork.

"Miss Maiyo, shall we go?" It is Dr Wadaki.

"I beg your pardon, Doctor?"

"I thought we might have our review this evening, and to make it a little less formal, I suggest we have it at the nice Indian restaurant just down the street."

"Oh. . . . All right."

He strides along purposefully, informing her of several 'difficult cases' he had dealt with during the day. ". . . so the man's heart stopped in the midst of surgery. We had to shock him back to life, but I was able to switch him to an oxygen-anesthetic mix, and he came out just fine."

Why is he telling me what a great doctor he is? Everybody knows that.

The Indian restaurant has maroon plastic booths down one side and eight tables covered with brown paper. The sitar music is a bit too loud and there is an intense smell of garlic.

"We'll take one of the booths," Wadaki announces to an Indian youth in a black apron. *I wonder why he wanted to come here; he didn't speak Hindi with the waiter.*

"Shall I order for you, Miss Maiyo, or would you prefer to look at the menu?"

"I think a mild curry and some rice would be fine for me."

"Oh, but you must have the chickpea fried dumplings!"

"OK, I'll try them."

He gestures for the waiter. "We'll have the chickpea dumplings and then the green chicken curry with steamed rice; we'd also like a bottle of the spicy red wine and a basket of papadums." He offers Dorothy a long, appraising smile. "Now then, Miss Maiyo, you are, I think, a very promising student; patients seem to like you and we all appreciate your good looks. I have found that to be successful in medicine, one needs a top-class mentor – one who can steer you along and make sure that you get the good grades you need to achieve the next favorable posting. You see what I mean?"

"Yes, you're saying that if I have a mentor, I could benefit from his or her experience."

"Yes, but it's not if you have a mentor but when you attach yourself to one. And it would not be appropriate for a bright and lovely person such as yourself to be attached to a female mentor. In this competitive world of medicine, Miss Maiyo, male doctors are the lions of the jungle! And, I should add that if you attach yourself to me, Miss Maiyo, you will find that I can offer you much more than my experience. I have the position and the political clout to push aside any barriers that may be in your way!"

"I see."

"What do you say, Miss Maiyo?"

"I'd like to think about it, doctor." *Somehow, he reminds me of Wangai.*

"What's to think about, Miss Maiyo? One has to seize an opportunity when it presents itself!"

I've got to stall him! How can I do it? "Doctor Wadaki, can you tell me about your mentoring experience with another junior doctor?"

"Yes, of course!" And the rest of the dinner is largely a monologue in which – in glowing terms – he describes the advancement of a junior doctor named Joyce to a consultant surgeon. This is followed by several examples of "my favorable connections with board examiners and other influential people," interspersed with tales of his own medical prowess.

Dorothy sits in a state of tension – unperceived by her host – braced for any curve ball that may be thrown at her, and offering "oh, really!" or "and then what happened?" or "my gosh!" as the situation demands.

Wadaki's soliloquy is fuelled by a second bottle of red wine with minimal participation by Dorothy. *The Indians certainly know how to corrupt their red wine.*

At last the bill arrives. "Now then, Miss Maiyo, let us retire to my flat which is just around the corner, where we can savor some of my excellent Napoleon brandy, inspect my collection of bronze sculptures, and begin our partnership."

"Oh, I'm sorry, doctor, I have to get right home tonight."

"Oh, come now, Miss Maiyo, it's still early, and you will find my flat both convenient and comfortable!"

'Make up a creative excuse involving your father,' I, the One, suggest hastily.

"I'm sure it is, doctor, but you see, my situation is a bit difficult. My father has a very firm rule that he must meet any man before I go out with him. I'm sure he would allow tonight's dinner on the basis that it is a business meeting. But if I am later than expected in returning home, he would insist on knowing all the details and he would make major problems for both of us."

Well, I don't think she had to be quite that creative!

"In that case, Miss Maiyo, I will devise an alternative arrangement for our partnership."

The following Tuesday, before beginning the night shift, a porter approaches Dorothy with a message: "Doctor Wadaki would like to see you in Theatre No. 7, doctor."

"Thank you, Tomi." *Why Theatre 7? It's a small eye-surgery theatre. Perhaps he has just been involved in a procedure there.*

She pushes through the series of double swinging doors leading to Theatre 7. Inside, the space, with its reclining theatre couch, suspended imaging and banks of diagnostic apparatus, is dimly lit. She can make out Wadaki dressed in a green surgical gown.

"There you are, Miss Maiyo, come in! This is the perfect location to cement our partnership – in working hours and away from Daddy's fussing. Nothing is scheduled tonight for this theatre, so we have some privacy. There is even a comfortable couch for our use!"

Dorothy begins to back away. "No! No! This is not at all what I want!"

He shrugs the gown off his shoulders, grips her left arm. He is naked, and she sees with horror that he is erect. "Oh, come now, Miss Maiyo! This is just a pleasant initiation ceremony."

"No! No! Let go of me!" She slaps him with all her strength across his face.

Immediately, he punches her, and seizing her in his arms, he presses a wet cloth to her face. She struggles, gasps and loses consciousness.

There is a misty vision of ceiling lights. An acute pain in her groin, and an oppressive weight on her. The weight is removed, but as clarity returns, her head aches fiercely.

Wadaki is standing over her, indifferent and spent. He leans down, his face close to hers. "Maiyo, if you breathe a single word to anyone of what happened tonight, I can guarantee that your career in medicine is over! You won't even be able to get a job as a nursing aide! Do you understand?"

The sense of vile degradation, humiliation and agony is overwhelming. She turns away, and raising herself on an elbow, she sees that her trousers and knickers are gone. Her shirt is torn open and her bra ripped so that her breasts are naked. *Oh, God, how could you let him do this to me? I am finished!*

Wadaki pulls on the gown, steps into his Crocs and leaves. The room is silent.

I've got to get out of here! Please help me, God!

She pulls on her trousers: buttons are missing, and her knickers are shredded. She retrieves a patient's gown from a bin and pulls it on over her torn shirt. Briefly, she looks around.

'Evidence!' I, the One, say.
What evidence?
'In front of you!'

She spots the bright red stain and wet spot in the centre of the couch. Taking a step forward, she considers it; then she strips the fitted cotton cover from the couch. In one corner of the cover is a white tag: Property of City Hospital. Bundling the cover under her arm, she picks up the sharp-smelling scrap of Turkish toweling.

Quickly she makes her way to the female medical staff changing room. *Fortunately, there's no one else here. I desperately need a shower – to scrub myself from this filth I feel!*

Again, I whisper: Evidence!

But am I going to make a complaint to the hospital? Am I really going to say 'this is my blood and his semen, you see? He'll say, 'It was consensual!' Then I'm finished! Complain to the police? Maybe, but I doubt it.

Just in case!

Maybe I ought to get evidence just in case. Where? Certainly not here! There is the City Women's Crisis Centre.

To the consultant who is the shift leader, she says, "Doctor, I'm sorry. I've got a terrible stomach problem. I need to go home."

"OK, Dorothy. Do you need some medication to take with you?"

"No, thanks." *I'll get it at CWCC.*

The taxi comes to a stop in front of a single-storey brick building in a residential sector of City. The white sign in front says only 'CWCC' in blue letters. There is a light over the door. Dorothy presses the lighted bell-button. At first, there is only silence. *Maybe they're not open at night.* Then, she hears footsteps, and someone calls out 'Coming!'

The door is opened by a middle-aged woman in jeans and a white polo shirt with CWCC in blue. "May I help you?"

"I'm sorry it's late."

An anticipatory smile. "That's all right, dear."

"I've been raped."

"Oh, I'm so sorry, dear! Come in, please!" A consoling arm around Dorothy's shoulder. Dorothy starts to sob. "We're going to take good care of you, dear. Come in and sit down. My name is Beverley; our nurse, Naomi, will see you shortly." At the desk in the hallway, Beverley assembles a form with a clipboard and pen. "Now, do you mind filling this out? It's just for our records, and no one outside CWCC sees it."

Dorothy scans the form, considering. "Yes. OK."

Beverley glances at the completed form. "Do you mind if I call you 'Dorothy', or do you prefer 'Miss Maiyo'?

"I'm actually 'Doctor Maiyo', but please call me 'Dorothy'."

Beverley glances at the form again. "Oh, I'm so sorry, Dorothy; let me take you to Nurse Naomi."

Naomi is also middle-aged, dressed, like her colleague, in jeans and an identical white polo shirt. Her hair is braided into neat corn rows, and Dorothy notices the nursing affiliation pin just above the CWCC. "I'm very sorry for what's happened to you; please sit down. . . . Now what we're going to do is to take a sample for evidence. We will not release the sample to anyone until you tell us to. It is usually a good idea to examine you for any physical injuries, and I can take photographs, if that's all right?" Dorothy nods.

"OK. First things first: are you using contraception?" Dorothy shakes her head. Naomi reaches into a drawer and removes a gray, playing-card-size piece of plastic with a single white pill in the middle. "Take this now, and try not to vomit during the next forty-eight hours. Sorry, it will make you feel less than perfect for a few days." She pauses. "Now, you can tell me what happened, and I'll make a recording of it. Same rules apply: we don't release anything without your agreement. Is that all right?"

"Yes."

Dorothy feeling miniscule and sobbing violently, sits, naked, on a chair in front of Naomi, who has been listening to Dorothy's story. Naomi places a small vial on the table next to her and carefully labels it. "And there is any reason in the world why he would have thought you wanted a sexual relationship?"

"No reason at all! Except that he kept insisting we should form a partnership."

"And by that you understood he was talking about a mentor-mentee relationship."

"Yes, exactly."

"Men! A lot of them have their pea brains inside their testicles!"

"Naomi, is there a shower here? I am dying to scrub myself!"

"Yes. There's a shower through there. But can you wait a minute, Dorothy? I need to examine you for cuts and bruises." Dorothy stands, and Naomi inspects. "This looks like a bite here." Dorothy looks down at her breast where there is a curved line of livid red marks. "There are bruises on your hips, front and back, a pretty nasty scratch mark on your back, and this bruise on your cheek. . . . You smell of ether, Dorothy!"

"No, the odor is probably coming from the piece of cloth. I put it in my handbag."

Naomi steps closer and sniffs. "No! The odor is coming from your face. Definitely from your face! You aren't, by any chance, an ether-sniffer, are you?"

Involuntarily, Dorothy gives a slight smile and shakes her head. "No."

Naomi begins to take close-up photographs of Dorothy's injuries. "What else did you put in your handbag, Dorothy?"

"I have the cover from the theatre couch."

"May I see it?" Dorothy unrolls it for Naomi's inspection.

"May I suggest two things about this cover?"

"Yes."

"First of all, if I were you, I would call the housekeeping department at the hospital, and tell them that you have borrowed the cover from the couch in Theatre 7, and that you suggest they should put a new cover on the couch."

"Why would I do that?"

"Be sure you get the housekeeper's name. She'll remember an unusual phone call from a doctor, and that will provide independent evidence of time and place."

"But I'm not sure I want to complain to the hospital. He'll claim it was consensual, the hospital will back him up, and fire me."

"Maybe – maybe not. You don't have to decide now."

"But what about the housekeeper: won't she want the cover back?"

"Do you really think that a housekeeper is going to pursue a doctor over a couch cover?"

"What was your other point about the cover?"

"That you leave it here with us for safekeeping, along with your underwear and the bit of ether cloth."

Afraid of walking alone through the darkened streets to the night bus stop, Dorothy has asked CWCC to call her a taxi. Depressed, bitter and ashamed, she gazes forlornly out the taxi window. *I'm not sure I want to be a doctor, anyway. Long hours, hard work, and some bastard doctor shoves his thing in you! God, I feel terrible! Worthless! I need someone to talk to! It was a smidgen of relief to talk to Naomi – to let it all out! Can't talk to Papa or Momma. Momma will just tell Papa, and he'll be in the police station ten minutes later. The police will make an inquiry, and while that's going on, Wadaki and the hospital will close ranks against me.* She bites her lip. *Who is a credible, mature, neutral female I can talk to? Of course there are therapists, but sometimes I think they have to report cases of abuse.*

I, the One, suggest Hetti Aguta.

Suddenly, Dorothy remembers Hetti. *Yes! She's also powerful, but I think she would respect my choices. What time is her show? Eight to nine. I can call her just after nine.*

Why is it necessary for the One to get that awful Aguta involved? She makes her living by making life difficult for my friends! She's just dreadful!

Quietly, Dorothy enters the house. She has decided to plead illness if her parents wake during her return, but she can hear her father snoring.

Her night is miserable: no sleep, depression bordering on despair and frenzied, disjointed thoughts.

On her cell phone, at nine-fifteen she is calling Channel 24 quietly from her room. Eventually, she hears Hetti's familiar voice. "Dorothy, how good to hear from you! How are you?"

"Hetti, I'm not so well. Have you got some time today that I can see you?"

"Yes, of course! What's the trouble, Dorothy?"

"Do you mind if we talk about it when I see you?"

"That's fine. I can see you in about an hour, or we can have lunch together."

"I'll be there in an hour."

Achieving Superpersonhood:

Dorothy expects to be kept waiting when she arrives at the Channel 24 offices, but Hetti appears almost immediately. There are no questions, but Hetti scrutinizes her, as if the problem will be disclosed in her face and posture.

In a small meeting room decorated with photographs of Channel 24 icons, Hetti pours two cups of tea. "Tell me, Dorothy."

Dorothy confesses: "I've been raped!" and breaks into tearful sobs.

"Oh my God! How awful! Was it Wangai?"

"No, it was a senior doctor at the hospital," and haltingly, she tells Hetti what happened.

"You've been examined professionally?" Dorothy nods. "You know, Dorothy, I was raped by an uncle when I was fourteen."

Dorothy gapes at the older woman. "You were?"

"Yeah. All too often, it happens to some of the best of us."

"What happened to your uncle?"

"In those days, the police didn't bother much with the villages. They left things to the elders, and it was the elders who threw my uncle out. Rumor had it that he tried to settle on the edge of another tribe's village in the northwest. And that he raped the young daughter of a village elder. They say the villagers hacked him to death and threw his body in the river."

"So he disappeared."

Hetti nods. "Crocodile dinner."

For a moment, they consider this outcome.

"Hetti, do you know whatever happened to Wangai?"

"Well, he lost his chairmanship and was defeated in the last general election. Disappeared."

Dorothy gazes out the window as her thoughts unwind. "Hetti, how did you get to where you are now . . ." She gestures around the room. ". . . from where you were then?"

"I've always wanted to be a journalist, but don't get me wrong; it was a pretty hard slog. Sometimes I felt that life wasn't worth living. When I was a girl, women who were raped were considered social outcasts. I was depressed, confused and lonely. But, I'm a bit like emery paper: I don't wear through very easily. I finished school, went on to university, and got my first job as the agricultural reporter for the *Star*. Still, my scars haven't gone away. I have terrible dreams sometimes, even now. I suffer from occasional depression. And when some men come onto me, I slide into a panic."

"I don't know whether I should stay in medicine."

"What attracted you to medicine?"

"I think the main attraction for me was the prospect of making people's lives better."

Hetti smiles. "A bit of an idealist."

Abruptly, Dorothy shoots back: "What's wrong with being an idealist?"

Hetti ignores the question. "So, what happened last night in the real world makes you doubt your idealism."

Dorothy looks wistfully out the window. "Maybe so."

"What else attracted you to medicine?"

"The technology. Understanding the human body: it's so complicated. I like complicated puzzles."

"But last night you were confronted with a very serious mystery: how can a human mind get so distorted?"

"So you think I should just skip over what happened last night." Dorothy makes a flat statement.

"NO! You couldn't skip over it even if you wanted to! I think you should do two things: fight back, hard! And don't let one perverted person change your life and your values. Besides, Dorothy, you have all the personal attributes of a good doctor." Hetti ticks them off on her fingers: "Intelligence – intellectual and emotional, dedication to what you believe in, a caring and likeable personality, and a belief in yourself."

Dorothy studies her clenched hands. "How can I possibly fight back, Hetti? You know what's going to happen . . ."

Hetti holds up a restraining hand. "Whoa! What we need is some expert advice." She picks up a telephone. "Jelani, this is Hetti. Could you join us in meeting room two please?" Turning to Dorothy, she says, "Jelani Akiloye is our corporate lawyer. He clerked for a superior court justice and was county prosecutor before he joined Channel 24."

Akiloye is a handsome man in his mid-thirties with an intense manner, and a tic to his right eye. Hetti briefs him on the 'favor' which Dorothy did for Channel 24 during the Wangai expose, and then on the trauma which Dorothy has experienced.

Akiloye puts his folded hands on the table. "I think Miss Maiyo is right in her concerns about complaining to the hospital and the police." Hetti is about to interrupt until he holds up a hand. "I think there may be another way that involves neither the hospital nor the police, initially. And that would be for Miss Maiyo to ignore legal politeness and file a civil suit, without any warning, against both the hospital and Dr Wadaki, asking for major damages. Hetti, you then could follow this up with an expose of the bullying culture in the hospital and of Dr Wadaki's past indiscretions – assuming that you can find some. This will stir up public indignation and attract the attention of the City prosecutor. You should ask for several million in damages, Miss Maiyo, in order to put both defendants on the back foot, and they'll be worried about paying a huge settlement, but also what might happen in a subsequent criminal trial."

Hetti slaps the table. "Brilliant!"

"But, Mr Akiloye," Dorothy ventures, "my family and I haven't got the financial means to hire a big law firm."

Akiloye shakes his head. "Not a problem. I know several good firms that would take a case like this on a no-win-no-fee basis. The point is that both the doctor and the hospital have deep pockets. The only problem, Miss Maiyo, is that the law firm will take a substantial cut of your winnings."

"I don't care about the money. I just want justice."

Hetti adds, "There's one other advantage besides justice in bringing a suit, Dorothy. You'll get the reputation: 'don't fuck with me!' That can be very handy sometimes."

I like that! I like it a lot. That will make the risk of failure worth it.

It goes without saying that Wadaki is a friend of mine, and as such, I'll do what I can to protect him from legal schemes and shenanigans. After all, if Dorothy had been more sympathetic to his request, none of this drama would be taking place and she would be assured of an excellent next assignment!

* * *

The evening world news is on his TV, but Kamiri is half asleep on the sofa when his cell phone rings.

"Oh, hello, Hassan, how are you doing?"

"I'm OK, Kamiri. I've decided I want to join the army."

"What? Why would you want to join the army? Has something gone wrong at work?"

"No, everything is OK at work. I've been thinking. The army will give me the discipline I need, and the chance to earn some respect from my family."

"I can understand that, but the pay in the army isn't much better than the abattoir. Besides, does the army offer you a long-term future?"

"I've been reading that sergeant-majors make a pretty good living, and they're highly respected. So yes, I'm prepared for the long-term struggle for advancement."

"OK, Hassan, but how can you explain your involvement with the terrorists?"

"I've thought about that, too, Kamiri, and I think I've got a potential solution. My immediate worry is my suspended prison sentence."

Achieving Superpersonhood:

"The suspended sentence must have elapsed by now, but I can check."

"If you would, that would be very helpful, Kamiri. And I have another favor to ask: I have an appointment with the recruiting sergeant next Monday. Can you come with me?"

"Yes, I can come with you." *I don't know about Hassan. Seems like he jumps from one thing into another!*

I, the One, think that jumping 'from one thing to another' is understandable. After all, the world is a complex place, and a young person may not know where his talents and self-realization lie. Uncertainty, family or economic necessity may necessitate the diversion to an available, but less appropriate path – hopefully temporarily. What's important is to believe in oneself while prying open the possibilities. A neutral, honest and perceptive Educator is invaluable in this search and testing process. The Other is a seducer, not an Educator

During his visit to the central police station in City, Kamiri is able to confirm that Hassan Arusei's record has only the old conviction for assault, and the suspended sentence has elapsed – nothing since then.

Monday afternoon: Kamiri has no training scheduled, and Hassan has taken half a day's holiday. Kamiri parks his motorcycle near the government building. Hassan pauses to take in the poster of an impressive soldier in battle dress. "Soldiers are real men."

Inside, they are directed down a corridor to an office with a frosted glass window in the door. It says: COUNTRY ARMY RECRUITING   Staff Sergeant M J Nnamani

Kamiri knocks.

"Enter!"

The office is small with a single desk, behind which sits a man in a starched khaki uniform with gold decorations and campaign ribbons. His head is shaved – like a black bowling ball – and his white teeth show as he breaks into a smile. The walls are decorated with army recruiting propaganda. "Staff Sergeant Nnamani. Please have a seat!" he announces and studies the pair of visitors. His head jerks slightly in disbelief as he scrutinizes Kamiri. "You tired of playing for the Lions, Killer?"

"No, sir, I'm here with my friend."

Nnamain turns to Hassan. "Your name?"

"Hassan Arusei."

The sergeant's head jerks again in disbelief. "You guys playing some kind of a prank?"

"No, sir, I really want to join the army."

Nnamini leans forward. "Are you - by any chance - Kaddour Arusei's son?"

"Yes, sir."

"Then what the hell are you doing here? Why aren't you sitting in some big office with 'CEO' on the door?"

Hassan takes a deep breath. "I guess I'm sort of a black sheep, sir."

"And what do black sheep do, Arusei?"

"Well, sir, when I was in university, a while back, I got a suspended sentence for assault. I decided to take my faith seriously, and . . ."

Nnamini interrupts. "What faith is that, Arusei?"

"Islam, sir."

"So you became a good Muslim and then?"

"I joined Dhul Fakir."

The sergeant covers his forehead with his hand and stares at his desk. "Why would a good Muslim join Dhul Fakir, Arusei?"

"I was studying with an imam who was teaching me about Islam, and he recommended I should join." Nnamini is shaking his head in disbelief. "At first I thought I was going to be a holy warrior in service to Allah."

"Who is this imam, Arusei?"

"I can tell you later, sir."

"So, Dhul Fikar kicked you out?"

"No, sir, I found out that Dhul Fikar is a brutal, terrorist organization, against all the real words of the Qur'an. I deserted."

"You deserted, hunh?"

"Yes, sir. I was on the run for the three days it took to shake off the men who were trying to kill me. Then I found Kamiri and he found me a job."

"Which is?"

"Working in an abattoir."

Nnamini closes his eyes in disbelief: "Why an abattoir?"

Kamiri intervenes. "I used to work in the abattoir, and I knew that Hassan could make a little money there and be in a place where his pursuers would never look."

"Well, that's true enough. Your father know about all this, Arusei?"

"No, sir."

"Why not?"

Hassan hesitates. "Because," Kamiri says, "he'd be ashamed to tell his father."

Nnamani contemplates the ceiling. "So you're a black sheep who's deserted from Dhul Fikar. Why would a black sheep want to join the army?"

Hassan begins speaking with conviction. "I'm the youngest in the family, and I've been spoiled all my life. Being in Dhul, I was regimented; there was a schedule and an objective for every day. I actually found that liberating. Dhul has a purpose." He holds up his hand to forestall interruption. "I know now it's the wrong purpose. But it made me realize that I desperately needed a purpose, and the army has a clear purpose."

"Your father didn't give you a purpose?"

"No, sir." Hassan pauses. "He doesn't have much confidence in me."

There is a long silence in the room. Finally, the sergeant says, "Continue."

"And then there's also the comradeship that I'm sure exists in the Army. I've never had a bunch of close friends. I'm too much of a loner. Right now there's just Kamiri, a guy named Koinet at the abattoir and a girl I fancy."

"You said you were in University. What were you studying and how far are you from a degree?"

"I hope to get a degree in communication. Since I've been at the abattoir, I'm studying by the Internet."

The sergeant studies the ceiling again. "Tell me, Arusei, why would the Army want you?"

"Well, sir, I'm actually a trained soldier, and that's what I want to be: in Country Army. I can also tell you quite a bit about Dhul Fikar."

"Do you know where Dhul Fakir is based?"

"Yes, sir, I knew where my group was based."

Nnamani nods. "Tell me, Arusei, if your father was here right now and I asked him if he would recommend you for the army, what would he say?"

"He would definitely recommend that I join the army."

The sergeant glances at Kamiri, who inclines his head in agreement. "Do you have any questions for me, Arusei?"

"No, sir."

"What branch of the army are you interested in, Arusei?"

"Infantry, sir."

"OK, Arusei, I'm sure you'll understand that your case is quite unusual. I'll have to take it up with my chain of command and I'll let you know. What's your phone number?"

Standing by the motorcycle, Hassan asks, "Do you think they'll take me, Kamiri?"

"I'd say it's about fifty-fifty."

"I know the other fifty; what's the fifty in favor?"

"Well, you come across as an honest person, a dedicated Muslim – that means you have the right values. Your time with Dhul Fikar means you're had some training, but they'll suspect your loyalty. Mainly, the army needs recruits."

"Thanks very much for coming, Kamiri. I think it made a big difference."

"What are you talking about, Hassan? I barely said two words."

"It isn't what you said, it's who you are that makes the difference."

"You mean because I play football?"

"It's not just that. Everybody knows Killer Kamiri, the goal-scoring threat for the Lions."

"That shouldn't make any difference at all in a meeting like this."

"But it does, Kamiri. Because you're a celebrity, what you say must be important, and because you're important and you took the time to come with me, it must mean that you think I'm important."

Kamiri chuckles at Hassan's logic. "You are important to me, Hassan, because you're my friend – not because I'm a 'celebrity'." He pauses for emphasis. "I'm not a celebrity and I don't like the idea of being one. I hate it that I can't go into a little shop to buy a Pepsi without people wanting my autograph and asking me silly questions."

"I think I know what you mean, Kamiri. Everybody who hears my last name thinks I must be important, but I'm not. I'm not even a real Arusei. The difference between what people think I am and what I really am makes it difficult to be what I'd like to be."

"What would you like to be, Hassan?"

"I'd like to be a professional soldier, someone who is looked up to by other soldiers, who is reliable, brave and decorated; someone who has a strong faith to guide him, who knows how to lead."

Kamiri studies his friend for some moments. "That sounds pretty good, Hassan. That's something you can be proud of."

"How about you, Kamiri? What do you want to do after football?"

"After being with my father, I feel like I've pulled up my roots and am not the person I was meant to be. I'm not a celebrity,

I'm a Kikuyu. I'm not comfortable in big crowds. I like to watch the sun rise, and the elephant herd feeding. I like to think about things that matter. I don't know, Hassan. I don't know."

"I got a call from Sergeant Nnamani. He says the army is thinking of taking me, but first they wanted some information about Dhul Fikar."

Kamiri says, "OK, that's easy enough."

"Yeah, I know. I went to a big meeting at army headquarters. There must have been fifteen people there, including two or maybe three generals. The meeting must have lasted two hours. I told them everything I knew."

"Excellent."

"So now they want me to go on a mission with them to find the Dhul camp."

"Do you know where it is?"

"Yeah, I doubt they moved it – too convenient, too well defended. Besides, they think I'm a wimp who wouldn't have the courage to rat on them."

Chapter 18

Litigation

Hassan is sitting in the front seat, next to the driver. Behind him, in the rear seat of the jeep, are the major, a radio in his hand, and the lieutenant. On either side of the command jeep, which is flying the Country flag, is an armored personnel carrier and an army pickup mounted with a heavy machine gun. The major hands the radio to his lieutenant and picks up his binoculars, looking across the two kilometers of open grassland. "I can see only villagers – no one in camouflage," the major says.

Hassan looks at his watch. "They're probably at prayers."

The major orders: "Move 'em up in line with me." And to the driver: "Move ahead slowly about fifteen hundred meters."

Hassan, unnoticed by the other jeep passengers, is shaking his head. *This is crazy! Why are we moving in broad daylight? Why not at two o'clock in the morning, on foot, as I suggested?*

The heavy diesel engines of the APCs are growling a strong bass and sending out gusts of black smoke. Now Hassan can see several villagers looking toward the invaders and pointing at them.

The army vehicles come to a halt. The major stands up to scan the village with his binoculars. From the village, comes the sound of engines starting. Armed men in camouflage are racing out of the village and dropping prone in the grass. The villagers have disappeared. Terrorist technicals (pick-ups with heavy machine guns) are moving across the village, and the standing gunner's fire bursts at the invaders. There is the simultaneous crackle of rifle fire from the grass.

"Commence firing!" the major shouts. There is a groan of dismay and disbelief as he topples over backwards out to the jeep.

A lone terrorist appears from the village and raises a weapon. There is a streak of white smoke, and an explosive boom from the left-hand APC, which is shrouded in smoke and fire. The army machine guns begin a continuous roar of return fire. Two terrorist technicals shudder to a halt, their gunners gone. A third technical flees to the village. The lone terrorist reappears with his weapon. The white smoke trail ends with a boom in the grass just in front of the right-hand APC. Bullets shatter the windshield of the command jeep; the driver is killed instantly.

"Retreat! Retreat!" the lieutenant shouts into his radio. "Pick up the major, Hassan!"

Hassan leaps out, hauls the major to his feet, and pushes him toward the jeep door. The lieutenant drags the commander in. "Go, Hassan, go!" Hassan races around to the other side, yanks open the door, and pulls the driver clear. He slams the jeep into gear and accelerates into a sharp turn to the rear. Soldiers are running from the crippled right-hand APC, piling onto the three operational vehicles. There is a sudden punch and terrible pain in Hassan's left shoulder. His right foot slams down on the accelerator; the three jeeps make a plume of tan dust as they surge away.

"Go to the medical assistance center!" the lieutenant bellows. Hassan hears him shouting into his radio for an army ambulance.

At the medical assistance center, a small white-frame house surrounded by mud-brick houses with rusting roofs, casualties are bustled inside. Hassan and four others are wounded, two seriously. The lieutenant orders the center's battered old ambulance to rush the badly wounded to Coast City Hospital. Hassan and the other are bandaged to by the two nurses and given morphine injections by the doctor.

"There are three dead here," the lieutenant advises his radio. "The major, his driver and one of the gunners. We have five wounded; two sent to the hospital. The entire crew of APC Alpha is missing and presumed dead. Six of the crew of APC Bravo are here; the other four are missing. Therefore, our losses are three confirmed dead, five wounded and fourteen missing. Of the fourteen, at least ten are presumed dead." There is a pause. "It was a hell of a fight, sir. We did the best we could." Another pause. "It's difficult to say, sir. Our gunners believe they killed five." A moment of silence. "No, sir, I don't recommend an air strike. We could see many villagers on site."

The army ambulance arrives, siren blazing. Hassan and the other two are taken to Coast City Hospital, where the blood-soaked dressing is removed from his shoulder. Use of his left arm is almost impossible and very painful. An x-ray is taken. The doctor tells Hassan: "Your left shoulder blade has been shattered and two ribs are broken. Have you been coughing up blood?"

"A little, sir."

"I think there is some internal bleeding. We're going to send you to City Hospital, where there is a larger orthopedic team." Hassan sits glumly and in pain on a bench in A&E. *Damn! What a disaster! Over a dozen of our people killed vs. only five Dhul. Stupid! All to show Dhul how big and strong the army is. We were trounced and my shoulder hurts like hell.*

* * *

I know what my father will say when I tell him I'm going to sue. He'll say, "Are you out of your mind? They'll put you out of medicine before you even get started!" But do I want to stay in medicine if I have this malignancy in my heart?

Dorothy begins to realize that the root of her distress is not medicine but one disgusting man, and pushing him to one side in her mind, with her fatigue and stress, she recalls the exhilaration of discovering a patient's illness or injury and applying her medical and empathetic skills to the healing process.

I, the One, didn't answer her prayer, directly, but I gave her the peace of mind she needed.

She makes up her mind. *He is the cancer that must be excised.* That evening, after dinner, when her sister was upstairs studying, her mother inquires, "How are you, Dorothy? You seem to be getting over that awful stomach bug."

"Yes. I am feeling better. I have something to tell you." As she considers each of them in turn, she feels their concerned glances. "I haven't had a stomach bug. The night before I told you I was ill, I was raped by one of the doctors at work." Her mother opens her mouth to speak, but Dorothy holds up a restraining hand. Her father is stunned into silence. "I have thought about it over the last week, I have taken legal advice, and I've decided to sue the doctor and the hospital."

"But, Dorothy!" Her father overcomes his temporary seizure. "We haven't the money to pay lawyers. You'll most likely lose, and we'll have to declare bankruptcy – not to mention the end of your career as a doctor!"

For several seconds, Dorothy considers him. "Papa, I knew you would say that." There is another pause. "The law firm I have engaged has agreed to take the case on a no-win, no-fee basis."

Her father's face is suddenly flushed. "Damn it, Dorothy! I think you owe us the courtesy of consulting us before taking a major decision like this!"

Her mother gives Joseph a severe frown and a gesture for silence. "Dorothy, dear, are you all right? Were you injured, and are you . . . I mean . . . are you . . . you know . . . "

"No, Mama, I went to CWCC. They took evidence, my statement and gave me a pill. I am not going to get pregnant."

She pauses. "And, Papa, the reason I didn't consult you and Mama is that I knew you would be opposed to the decision I have taken. But this is my problem and my life and I am an adult. If I took your advice, I would merely be a battered doctor. That's not what I want to be! Doing it my way, at least I have a chance to be a respected doctor."

Gently, Joseph asks, "Have you considered going to the police."

"Yes, and Papa, you know perfectly well how that would end: I would be labeled the temptress, trying to better her position. Case dismissed." She pauses for effect. "As it is, we're going to use the media to make the defendants look guilty before they have a chance to react."

"Who is we?"

"The law firm and Hetti Aguta."

Joseph is incredulous. "Hetti Aguta?"

"Yes, she's going to comment on the case and the behavior of the defendants."

"And drag your name into it, so people can point fingers at you?"

"No, she doesn't have to name anyone to get our message across."

"How did Hetti Aguta get involved?"

"She's a friend of mine. I got to know her when she was working with the congressman on the Shepherds' Field scandal."

I heard the One coaching Dorothy during this exchange with her parents. In fact, the two of them have been rehearsing for days. Of course, Dorothy thinks she herself developed all the smart answers. Am I jealous? Yes, a little. But I have similar relationships with my friends.

The day after the lawsuit is filed, Dorothy returns to work at the hospital. A redacted summary of the complaint, omitting evidence and with names blacked out, has already found its way into the evening newspaper. Most of her colleagues are unaware of the complaint, and are inquiring, as friends, about her stomach flu. A few – those who might be classified as busybodies – have read the news, have realized the suit must involve City Hospital, and owing to Dorothy's absence, have theorized that she is the 'junior doctor'. As the rumor mill gathers momentum, there are several ideas as to the identity of the 'senior consultant'.

When Dorothy is asked, "Have you seen the article in the *City Chronicle* about the doctor who was raped?"

Her reply is: "Yes, terrible, isn't it." The busybody colleagues have given up trying to solicit her views after her repeated disclaimers of: "I don't want to feed the rumor mill."

Dorothy's female colleagues seem to be unusually kindly and her male colleagues particularly respectful.

Dr. Wadaki has been noticed only briefly in the distance.

Dorothy receives a call from her lawyer, Disraeli Jelani: "Miss Maiyo, the defense has filed a motion with the court requesting that the media be prohibited from naming the defendants, as this would tarnish their reputations without due process. I'm going to talk to Hetti about this."

Two mornings later, before the judge has issued his ruling on the motion, Hetti announces on her program: "I decided to pay a visit to City Hospital to get some opinions as to who the mysterious 'senior consultant' is in the rape case involving the junior doctor. The consensus is that it is a Doctor Benjamin Wadaki, a consultant anesthesiologist, who is a departmental director at the hospital. Why? Well, the thinking is that Dr Wadaki has had several previous scrapes with the authorities over complaints of harassment of female staff. They mentioned a case of assault on a nurse twelve years ago, the alleged rape of a secretary and an assault on a hospital cleaner. I have been able to determine that these complaints were actually made but were dismissed. There was also a complaint of harassment by a junior doctor which was later withdrawn. I have asked the hospital why no punitive action was taken on any of the cases. Their response was that in each case there was evidence of consensual behavior or lack of evidence of assault." Hetti's face registers surprise as she looks into the camera. "Really?" Another pause. "It couldn't possibly be that cover-ups were necessary to protect the investment they have in a senior consultant? It couldn't possibly be a member of staff with a persistent psychological disorder? I will let my viewers decide."

The hospital is furious; their attorney complains about Aguta's disclosure and admits that the hospital was being 'deluged' with criticism. The judge responds that it was speculation rather than a disclosure, as he is unaware of the relationship between Dorothy and Hetti. He grants the defense's motion, but warns that it was unlikely, given the ubiquitous nature of social media, to be 'airtight'.

Dorothy is called into a meeting with the Human Resources Director of the hospital. "Miss Maiyo, we don't think it's really necessary to sue us. We can promise you steady advancement to consultant if you will drop this suit. And if you wish, we can arrange an apology from Dr. Wadaki."

"An apology?" Dorothy is dumbfounded.

"Yes, if you wish it."

"I would settle for his balls."

"I beg your pardon, Miss Maiyo."

"Have you ever been raped, Mrs. Iweala?"

"No."

"Well, when you are, perhaps we can talk again. Good day."

The following day, on her program, Hetti tells her audience that she was able to confirm from the complainant's attorneys that the reason that the complainant did not go to the police or to senior management at the hospital was the fear of a whitewash. She continues: "This is a rather sad commentary on our judicial system, that before a complaint comes to the attention of the City Prosecutor, it gets whitewashed out of existence."

Later that day, about twenty protestors carrying placards reading 'Justice for the Junior Doctor!" appear, marching and chanting outside the City Prosecutor's office.

Two days later, Hetti goes on the air: "I have a lot of sympathy for the junior doctor. Rape is a horrible experience. I know, because I was raped as a fourteen-year-old!" She goes on to tell the horrified audience what happened to her and of the terrible psychological trauma it caused. She concludes: "Some of you are protesting outside the City Prosecutor's office. I don't think he can hear you."

The next day the protest swells to over one hundred.

Later that week, Hetti interviews the junior doctor, live on her program. The doctor is not identified; she is only a black silhouette facing the interviewer. The name of the hospital and the defendant doctor are not mentioned, nor is the assault itself discussed. Hetti elicits from Dorothy her feelings, both during the assault and afterwards to the present. It was a seminal moment in Country television, with Dorothy expressing her acute feelings of humiliation, worthlessness, and spiritual pain, breaking down now and then into fits of sobbing.

> I, the Other, am aware that there is a great deal of pressure on my friend Wadaki. He is struggling to find him a way out, so I help him with some ideas.

With pressure coming now from MPs, and from a larger, angrier mob outside his office, the City Prosecutor decides to take up the civil case as a criminal investigation.

A week later, Jelani calls Dorothy: "Miss Maiyo, I have a startling piece of news for you. Dr. Wadaki has absconded! He was due in a bail hearing on Monday. He did not appear. The police have confirmed that he left City on a one-way air ticket to Belgrade, Serbia. His wife and children left the next day. His bank accounts have been cleared out."

"Why would he go to Belgrade?"

"I suppose that the Serbian authorities are so desperate for good doctors that they don't bother with references."

"So where does that leave things?"

"It will take about a month to get an official confirmation that he has absconded. At that point the judge will rule against him and the hospital."

"But if he's taken all of his money, how can we get anything out of him?"

"Well, he left a big house and a small flat here in City and a condominium in Coast City on the beach. Plus, he has four or five cars, including a Jag and a Merc. So, we'll get a fair amount of cash out of that. And the hospital will have to cough up a bunch of cash."

Dorothy is back at work. Her female colleagues treat her with warm admiration, and almost none of the anticipated sympathy. One Francophile colleague was even heard to characterize Dorothy as 'our Joan of Arc who wasn't burned at the stake.'

She is called to another meeting with the Human Resources Director, which begins with the offer of a comfortable chair, coffee in a porcelain cup and saucer, and solicitous queries as to her health.

"Miss Maiyo," Mrs Iweala begins, "the board of directors of City Hospital have been following your situation with keen interest." Dorothy is about to pour scorn on Iweala's opening statement, but the HR Director gestures for patience. "Please let me continue, Miss Maiyo. The board asked me for a full report on previous instances of assault or harassment. When I presented that report, I was excused from the meeting. Since that time, as you may have heard, there have been a number of changes in senior management, and an employee ombudsman has been appointed with responsibility directly to the board. She will investigate every complaint about assault or harassment, resolve it and report her resolution to the board."

"Good."

"Miss Maiyo, I have been asked to deal personally with your case." Dorothy says nothing and shifts her sitting position. "City Hospital, its board of directors and its senior management team wish to offer its sincerest regret and apology for what happened. We have issued letters of censure to Dr. Wadaki, with copies to his new employer, and to the College of Anesthesiologists." Dorothy nodded. "We will be offering a financial settlement to you through your attorneys, and we hope very much that you will continue your work and your study at City Hospital. We are confident you will make an excellent doctor."

"Thank you, Mrs Iweala. I'm very pleased for all the women – including yourself, – Mrs Iweala – at City Hospital that bullying, harassment and assault will now be taken seriously."

Dorothy's male colleagues treat her with the deference they sense she is due for causing a cultural revolution at City Hospital: the environment has changed; there is an almost egalitarian sense among the clinical staff, and all sexual innuendo and touching – even the harmless sort – amongst colleagues has ceased. Nonetheless, Dorothy is aware of a vague notion of shame from her male counterparts. *Is it their shame, as men, they are feeling, or mine, as a woman, that they are projecting?*

* * *

Late in the afternoon shift, there is an announcement over the tannoy: "Attention surgical and orthopedic staff: three injured soldiers will arrive in fifteen minutes!"

Achieving Superpersonhood:

Injured soldiers? Three of them? Maybe they were involved in an accident. But the announcement seems to imply that the hospital was advised by the army of the impending transfer. Was there some kind of incident? What's going on?

Dorothy's team is not called into readiness to deal with the arriving patients, but her curiosity remains. She hears the ambulance arrive, but she is treating other patients. One of the porters is heard to whisper, "One of 'em is an Arusei!"

Could it possibly be Hassan? I have to find out!

She intercepts a gurney as it is being moved out of the treatment area. There is a cadre of hospital staff surrounding the bed, but Dorothy recognizes the familiar face of the patient, who is naked from the waist up, his left shoulder swathed in bandages. "Hassan!"

The patient, in struggling to elevate himself, causes the gurney to slow. "Dorothy! Is that you?"

"What happened to you, Hassan?"

"Oh, I've been involved in a bit of a ruckus."

"Where is he going?"

An orthopedic surgeon responds, "He's going to x-ray, doctor."

Dorothy is tempted to follow, but there is more than an hour left in the shift, and several patients waiting, but after participating in the shift change-over, she hurries to the hospital information desk.

"Mr Hassan is on Albert Ward B."

There is a crowd waiting for an elevator; she hurries up the stairs.

Hassan is sitting up in a bed halfway down on the right. His shoulder is still covered in bandages; he looks thin and tired, but otherwise well enough. He is delighted to see her approaching. "Dorothy! I forgot you're working here!"

"Hassan, what was this 'ruckus' you were involved in?"

"I was helping the army in a raid on a terrorist camp."

"So, you've joined the army?"

"Not exactly." He gives her a one paragraph summary of the last month of his life.

She sits at the bottom of the bed, facing him. "Hassan, why would you join a terrorist group?"

"I didn't really know who I was joining; I just trusted the imam."

"Shame on you, Hassan! Has any of this made you a better Muslim?"

He looks out the window, reflecting. "I've learned that I have a lot of growing up to do, and that the road to becoming a better Muslim doesn't pass through any particular sect. That road has to be my personal construction."

"What do you mean 'personal construction'?"

"I mean: it's not about other people; it's what I personally believe and how I behave."

"Bravo, Hassan! And you're planning to join the army?"

"Yes. They've kind of promised it to me. What about you, Dorothy?"

"Well, at the moment, I'm working in accident and emergency as a trainee doctor."

"Is that what you want to be: an A&E doctor?"

"I don't think so – I'm not sure I ought to be a doctor at all."

Hassan's eyes flash in disagreement. "Dorothy, what are you talking about? I don't know anyone who better fits my idea of the perfect doctor!"

"I take that as a compliment, Hassan. But I'm not sure you understand some of the politics of working in medicine."

"I probably don't, but I know that you were considering both medicine and politics for your future."

"My father – who is coaching me in my self-overcoming – suggested that I work, pro bono, for an MP. What I have learned discourages me from politics. There is too much corruption and compromise for me as an idealist."

Hassan smiles. "That makes sense."

I, the One, think that finding one's way in life is like learning to ice skate: at first, you fall for no apparent reason, then, you understand why you fell, and finally, having learned what doesn't work and what's comfortable, you can begin glide along effortlessly.

Dorothy gestures toward his shoulder. "Tell me about your condition, Hassan."

"Well, the bullet passed through my shoulder, breaking one rib and fracturing another. My shoulder blade is shattered, so tomorrow, the surgeons are going to piece it back together with a special plate. They're going to check for any internal bleeding and damage to my lung."

"How long are you going to be here?"

"I don't know. At least a week. . . . Dorothy, do you know if the hospital notifies next of kin of patients like me?"

"Yes. Your parents have been notified. Probably the army has done the same. Is there anybody else you want me to call?"

"Could you tell Kamiri where I am?"

"Yes, of course. Anyone else?"

He shook his head. "No. Thank you very much for coming to see me, Dorothy! You're a special friend!"

"Take care of yourself, Hassan, and good luck tomorrow!"

* * *

A woman dressed head to toe in black with only flashes of gold from her slippers and wrists sweeps up to the information desk, makes an inquiry and disappears into an elevator. She finds her son lying in a bed near the middle of Albert B. He is asleep. A nurses' aide brings a chair and she sits at his bedside. Softly, she whispers: "Hassan?"

His eyes open. "Mama!"

"How are you feeling?"

"A little groggy, but now that I'm awake, my shoulder has a terrible ache."

She gets up, speaks to a nurse and resumes her seat. "What happened to you?"

"I was shot during a terrorist raid."

"I haven't heard of any terrorist raid. Why did I get a call from the army?" He tells her he plans to join the army, avoiding any mention of Dhul Fikar. Frowning, she pushes a wisp of black hair away from her face. "Hassan, what are you withholding?"

"Do you promise not to tell Father?" She nods. A nurse brings two white capsules and a paper cup of water.

The involvement with Dhul Fikar is revealed. "Shame on you, Hassan, for thinking that terrorism is a path to anything other than hell!"

"But Mama, I didn't really know they are terrorists!"

"Who in the Prophet's name did you think they were?"

"I thought they were Allah's soldiers, fighting for the Qur'an."

"Hassan, one of the things you must learn in life is the ability to distinguish between opportunities offered by Allah and those offered by Satan."

> It's not easy to distinguish which of us is priming the consciousness and conscience of a human being. But I compliment Immam Arusei for her recognition of the difference between the Other and me, in Hassan's case. Why isn't it easy to tell? Well, our contest wouldn't be a contest if it were easy to tell. Besides, we never give up on stealing each other's friends.

Hassan's brimming eyes contemplate the ceiling. "Do you think, Mama, that the army is an opportunity offered by Satan?"

"No! The Prophet himself led large armies." Gently, she strokes his right arm. "I think, Hassan, that the army is an opportunity for you to be a man." Her caress continues. "Hassan, you are not an Arusei; you must find a path of your own."

A tear spills down his cheek as he looks away.

"Hi, Dorothy! So nice of you to come and see me! This is my mother. Mama, this is my friend, Dorothy Maiyo."

"How do you do, Missus Arusei?"

"Hello. Miss Maiyo. Are you a doctor?" Dorothy is wearing loose-fitting, green cotton trousers and a matching top. There is a stethoscope suspended from her neck.

"Yes, ma'am, but I'm not responsible for Hassan's care." Nonetheless, they discuss Hassan's case. He has brightened noticeably.

"I'm on duty, so I have to go now, Hassan, but I just want you to know that I spoke to Kamiri."

Imman Arusei watches Dorothy stop at the nursing station for a moment and disappear.

Hassan gazes wistfully after her. "She's really nice, don't you think, Mama?"

"She doesn't wear a headscarf."

"That's because she's a Christian."

"Hmmm."

"I like her a lot!"

"I noticed."

Kamiri is sitting at the foot of his friend's bed. "Tell me what happened, Hassan."

Hassan recounts in some detail the fire fight with Dhul Fikar.

Kamiri clenches his fists. "The army made a complete hash of it. I understand there is an official inquiry."

"Well, what they should have done is move in under the cover of darkness with special forces."

Kamiri agrees: "Or even with regular soldiers who have been thoroughly rehearsed.... Have you heard anything from the army?"

"No."

"I'm sure you will, but I think you ought to apply for officer training."

"Oh, come on, Kamiri, how can I get into officer's training? I'll be lucky to become a soldier."

Kamiri shakes a forefinger at his friend. "I think you ought to be an officer."

"Kamiri, there's no prospect of getting into officer training without a high-powered recommendation."

"How about your father?"

"There's no way my father would recommend me!"

"Mind if I talk to him?"

"Kamiri, with all due respect, he wouldn't listen to you."

"I have a pretty good relationship with your father."

Hassan's puzzled frown turns to an apologetic smile. "Oh, sorry! I forgot. The Lions."

They discuss possible tactics, and Hassan's recuperation.

A chair is brought up alongside the bed. Imman Arusei sweeps in, kisses her son, and seats herself.

"Mama, this is my friend Kamiri; Kamiri, this is my mother."

Kamiri offers his hand. "Hello, Missus Arusei."

She ignores the hand and bends almost imperceptibly at the waist. "Hello. . . . Did you go to university with Hassan?"

"No, ma'am. We played football."

"So you live here in City?"

"No, ma'am, I live in Coast City, but we have a game here tomorrow." He turns to Hassan. "I've got to go, mate, but I'll let you know how I make out."

Imman Arusei turns to watch Kamiri leave. "Who is that man?"

"As I said, Mama, he's a friend of mine. He plays for the Lions."

"Unnh. A footballer, and a villager, I guess."

"Yes, Mama, he's a Kikuyu."

"Hassan, you seem to be socializing with the wrong people."

The judge has made his ruling: Wadaki's property is to be sold to satisfy the judgment against him. And Dorothy has made her decision. *My parents have objected, and I am terrified, but for the sake of women, I'm going to shed some light on the devil's work.*

Achieving Superpersonhood:

Hetti Aguta makes an announcement at the end of her Thursday program: "Tomorrow, my guest will be the junior doctor, who will tell her story. Don't miss it!"

Dorothy keeps telling herself: *by this time tomorrow/by tomorrow at eleven/ in four hours/ in two hours this will be over. My life, my decision, my risk, but I want to change things!*
She is ushered to Hetti Aguta's office, and Hetti's warm, round face provides a degree of reassurance. "I'm nervous, Hetti!"
"Of course you're nervous, Dorothy. If you weren't, you wouldn't be an interesting guest, and, by the way, I still get nervous on my shows."
"You do?"
"Yes, I get nervous when I have a particularly hostile guest, or when the producer is frantically trying to tell me something."
A make-up lady appears with an oversized silver suitcase full of cosmetics. Without comment, Dorothy's facial perspiration is wiped away, a light powder is brushed on and her lips tinted a brighter red.
They move to the studio. Dorothy squints at the intensity of the hot lights. She can see two, no three, large, mobile cameras and several shadowy figures behind them. Hetti seats herself at a kidney-shaped white desk, behind which are two swivel chairs. She makes eye contact, and pats the seat to her right. Opening a folder that has been placed in front of her, Hetti briefly peruses its contents. A man in jeans wearing earbuds and a microphone crouches down to confer with Hetti, who has donned the same audio equipment. A technician fastens a clip-on microphone near the top of Dorothy's white cotton blouse.
"Thirty seconds, Hetti," someone announces. There is a soap commercial playing in the background. "Ten seconds, Hetti." A light 'On Air' flashes red.
"Good morning, Country and welcome to the Hetti Aguta show. . . . I have a guest that I know you want to meet. She is the famous junior doctor who was raped by a senior doctor

while on duty at City Hospital. The senior doctor was found guilty and has absconded from County, leaving most of his property behind. The hospital was found guilty of negligence. You may remember that my guest began her quest for justice with a civil law suit, but with her compelling evidence and your wonderful support, the City Prosecutor initiated a criminal case which resulted in convictions." She paused and faces a different camera, which takes in Dorothy, as well. "My guest, this morning is Miss Dorothy Maiyo, a junior doctor at City Hospital." As the camera rolls closer to Dorothy, she takes a deep breath. "Welcome, Dorothy! I think you are very brave to give up your anonymity!"

Dorothy nods, imitating the style of many interviewees. "I felt that when my case was successful, I could no longer remain anonymous."

"Why is that, Dorothy?"

"Because rape is not an anonymous crime. It involves a real woman who has been severely hurt, and I feel it is my duty to fight against anonymity. The anonymous rape victim has nowhere to turn for the solace she so desperately needs. And if the victim is anonymous, is she really a victim?"

"So, to your latter point, are you saying that if the victim isn't identified, there may be opportunity for the justice system – and society at large – to doubt that a crime has been committed?"

Dorothy's anxiety has evaporated, and she feels as if she is speaking with friends. "Yes, exactly, or the assumption may be that the crime can only be minor if the victim is unknown."

"And you mentioned the issues for an anonymous rape victim. Tell me more about those issues."

"For the anonymous victim, there are several issues. First, if she is anonymous, she cannot speak out clearly on her own behalf. She must be disguised or rely on others to fight for her. Second, if she is committed to anonymity, she cannot unburden herself with her friends. The dreadful hurt she feels is bottled up inside her. And third, if she is anonymous, she begins to think that the crime against her cannot be so bad, which is directly in conflict with her severe feelings of hurt."

"Dorothy, why do you think we have this concept of anonymity for rape victims?"

"It's interesting. I can't think of another crime where society at large actively covers up the victim of an attack. I believe this is a long-standing cultural prohibition. A woman is supposed to feel shame at being raped for two reasons: because she did not take steps to prevent it, and because she has become damaged goods." Hetti smiles, knowingly, and urges Dorothy to continue. "Not taking steps to prevent it," Dorothy goes on, "is absolute nonsense. Rape is, by definition, non-consensual. In my case, I had to be anesthetized. If anyone should feel shame about rape, it is the man for permitting his base instincts to control him."

"What about this idea of a woman becoming damaged goods?"

"I happen to think this is a vestige of our ancient patriarchal culture, where men made up all the rules, some of which, like this one, are self-serving. If a man forces himself on a woman, she becomes undesirable to all other men. What's the logic in that?"

"But is there some reality to the notion of damaged goods?"

"Not in the broad cultural sense. In a physical sense, lasting damage is relatively rare. The psychological effects can be lasting, but the same can be said for many other forms of abuse where victims are not considered 'damaged goods'. As I've said, anonymity does not help the process of psychological healing."

"Do you think that rape victims should not be permitted anonymity?"

"No! We're definitely not ready for that until men take a more enlightened view of rape. But I believe that when the perpetrator has been convicted, the victim should consider going public."

"Dorothy, you've spoken about the 'dreadful hurt' of rape, and you've said that lasting physical damage is relatively rare. Can you help our male viewers understand this 'dreadful hurt'?"

Dorothy turns to face the camera with its light on. "Well, we've all experienced the discomfort we feel when an angry, disagreeable someone puts his face very close to ours." She pauses to allow that feeling of discomfort. "In the case of rape, what a woman feels is discomfort at least one hundred times greater. Partly because of physiology, partly because of the female psyche, it is an intolerable invasion. And I haven't even mentioned the physical pain. Trust me! It's a dreadful hurt!"

"How does one recover from this dreadful hurt?"

Dorothy gives a wistful smile. "Slowly. . . . Talking about it with empathetic people is definitely cathartic. In fact, speaking on this program has been helpful. You have to keep reminding yourself: you're not a lesser person! You're still the same person who's been through a horrific experience. You will be OK!"

"Do you feel that justice has been done for you, Dorothy, relative to your attacker, who has absconded?"

"I don't desire any further punishment for him. He's lost most of his possessions, he has been struck off as a practitioner in Country, and he has had to move his practice to what for me would be an undesirable country. I'm concerned, though, that he will be a repeat offender in Serbia."

"Do you think you could ever forgive him?"

"Not now. Maybe sometime down the road."

"And how about the hospital, which should have taken action against him long ago?"

"The hospital has really taken on board the idea that bullying in any form is not to be tolerated. I have decided to donate their payment to me back to them toward the purchase of a new radiotherapy machine."

"You've granted Channel 24 exclusive coverage of your story. But some of our viewers may be thinking that you've given up anonymity to become a celebrity."

Holding up both her palms, Dorothy faces the camera again. "No, Hetti, I have no interest in becoming a celebrity. For me, being a celebrity means changing who you are to get attention.

Achieving Superpersonhood:

I'm a doctor. Although I can tell you that, for a while, this has shaken my commitment to medicine. But I can also tell you that the very welcome support I've received from my colleagues and from the hospital has been wonderful. I have come to the realization that the evil values of one man cannot be permitted to undermine the great ideals of medicine. I want to put my energy and attention into becoming a very good doctor."

With regard to Dorothy's decision to give up her anonymity, as you've probably noticed, I generally do not like secrets: they get in the way of constructive behavior. The Other promotes secrets as a reliable (?) means of concealing regrettable behavior.

Chapter 19

Sword of Honor

"This is Kamiri speaking. I would like to have a meeting with Mr Arusei sometime soon. It's not about football; it's a personal matter... No, ma'am, Coach wouldn't be able to help... It's a matter involving Mr Arusei's family." There is a lengthy pause. "Yes, tomorrow at five-fifteen would be fine. Thank you, ma'am."

Kamiri's two previous meetings – team meetings, actually – with Kaddour Arusei have taken place at the Lions training center in Coast City. He has never visited the Republic Building, let alone the thirty-third-floor lair of the chief executive of Arusei Industries. The floor-to-ceiling glass, the dark paneling, the music and the white receptionist are all from another, remote planet. When he is ushered into the vital office, Kaddour is speaking on the phone, the sleeves of his crisp white shirt are rolled half way up his forearms, and he is gesturing expansively as he talks. Slowly, Kamiri swivels his chair to take in more of the office: a water buffalo's head on the wall to the left, framed black and white photographs of a pride of lions, gazelles, sun-basking crocodiles, and a lavish safari lodge. *I've heard he also owns a safari camp on the edge of Zamsula National Park.* On the right, a big Lions banner, several trophies mounted on individual wood stands, and more photographs.

"Kamiri, it's good to see you!" Kaddour has finished his phone call, and rises to greet his visitor. "How are you? In good shape for Saturday's game?"

"Yes, Mr Arusei, I'm feeling pretty good."

The chief executive sits in the other swivel chair next to Kamiri. "What is this matter you wanted to talk about, Kamiri?"

"Well, sir, it's about the Arusei name, and how it's recognized as belonging to intelligent people who are among the best citizens of Country."

Kaddour adopts a skeptical, defensive posture. "And what's your concern about my name, Kamiri?"

"It's not about you, sir, it's about your son, Hassan."

There is a groan of frustration. "Go on, Kamiri."

"Well, sir, Hassan is one of my closest friends, and I'm concerned for him."

"So am I, Kamiri. So am I!"

"I can tell you, sir, that Hassan, made a bad choice a while ago, and he got involved with some undesirable people."

"Who are these people?" a frowning Kaddour demands.

"With all due respect, sir, I don't recommend that you know very much about this incident. I can tell you that Hassan is not being investigated by the police, and that he decided to become associated with these people to strengthen his commitment to Islam."

"His commitment to Islam?"

"Yes, sir, he wanted to take some actions that would strengthen his faith."

"So, he joined one of these dreadful Islamic proselytizing groups?"

"Yes, sir, something like that."

I object! I overheard the One making suggestions to Kamiri and Hassan when they were rehearsing this meeting between Kamiri and Kaddour, but it is entirely misleading to suggest that Dhul Fikar is 'like an Islamic proselytizing group'! The only proselytizing that Dhul Fikar ever does is with a gun, and it is wrong to suggest otherwise!

Well, look who's talking about right and wrong! The Islamic proselytizing groups never came up in Kamiri and Hassan's discussions, so Kamiri's response was ad-libbed. It's easy to give vague, evasive answers, and I think they're forgivable as long as no one is injured.

"So what's he doing now?" Kaddour inquires.

"He's working for you, sir."

"For me?" The executive is astonished.

"Yes, he's working at the abattoir."

"What's he doing there?"

"He's a floorman, sir."

"OK, but why is he there?"

"Oh, well I suggested it, because he wanted to make some money, and have a place to stay where he wouldn't be noticed."

Kaddour leans back in his chair to consider the ceiling for a moment. "What is he planning to do next, Kamiri?"

"He wants to join the army, sir."

Kaddour's eyes are closed, and his brow is furrowed. "Why the army?"

"He feels he needs some discipline and the opportunity to grow up a little and . . ."

"Amen!"

". . .and he sees it as a career with opportunities for advancement."

"Well, that's starting to make a little sense." Kamiri and the executive consider each other. "So what does all of this have to do with my name?"

"Well, sir, I thought that because Hassan has several years of college education, it would be better if he went into officer training, rather than basic training. That way he could come out as Lieutenant Arusei, not just Private Arusei."

"How does that make a difference to the Arusei name?"

"Well, sir, the Arusei name is very important, and people are always looking up to it. So when people construct a family tree, they see you at the top as chief executive, and most of your children below as presidents and vice presidents, and then there's this Private Arusei. It doesn't look good, sir."

"Well, why don't you tell him to apply for officer training?"

"He has already checked on that, sir. He was told that officer training is full, but I'm sure you'll agree that a strong word in the right ear can change a situation."

There: I've said it! What's he going to say: maybe 'yes', maybe 'no'?

There is a long pause during which the chief executive contemplates the footballer. "Tell him I expect him to graduate with honors."

"I'm doing pretty well, Kamiri. It's nice of you to call. I think they're going to let me out tomorrow. Then, I have to come in every day for physio for a couple of weeks." He pauses. "Did you speak to my father?"

"Yes. He's going to put in a word for you."

"Thank you so much, Kamiri!"

"Hassan, how are you going to manage working for Mr Kakuyu <u>and</u> getting into City Hospital for physio therapy? That's a time-consuming trip."

"I'm going to ask Dorothy to let me have my car back."

"And you'll be the only floorman who has his own sports car in the car park, next to Mr Kakuyu's VW Passat."

Hassan smiles radiantly. "Yes." A pause. "Kamiri, what did you think of Dorothy going on TV like that?"

"I thought she was very brave."

"Yes, but don't you think it'll spoil her chances of ever getting married?"

"Only with those who don't deserve her," Kamiri says, "I've always liked Dorothy: she's smart, she's pretty and she likes people."

"Yeah, but would <u>you</u> marry her?"

"Hassan, she would never even think of it. I'm miles below her!"

"So, you're saying you would?"

"I'm not ready to get married, but if she asked me - which isn't going to happen – I'd probably say 'yes'. Why all the questions, Hassan? Is the future Lieutenant Hassan thinking about getting married?"

"Oh, well . . . I just think it's amazing that she talked so freely in public about being raped."

"Do you respect her any less for having spoken out?"

"No. No. I admire her a lot, but I wonder what average people think."

"I think that most women will admire her and secretly thank her for criticizing men at their worst. Some men will hate her for denigrating them, some will be afraid of her, but lots will mentally give her a pat on the back."

"I guess that's where I am: the pat on the back category."

Later, as Hassan reflects on this discussion with Kamiri, he gives Dorothy more than a pat on the back: he begins to see her as a morally-correct leader, a woman of importance. This results in him to downgrading his own culturally-inherited bias against 'fallen women', and strengthening his resistance to his mother's bias against Christians.

"I hear you're going to be discharged tomorrow." Dorothy, dressed in her green scrubs, is standing at the end of his bed. "I thought I'd stop by to wish you good luck."

Hassan has suddenly abandoned his newspaper and is sitting up attentively in bed. "Yes. Dorothy. Very nice of you to come by. . . . Umm . . . I've been meaning to ask you about my old car."

"You remember Mr Kemboi, Hassan? You know: the shepherd who said Mine Ventures . . ."

"Oh, yes, I remember him. Said they were stealing his diamonds."

Achieving Superpersonhood:

"Yes, well, we put a tarpaulin over it and it's at his place."

"Do you suppose I can get it back?"

"Yes, of course. I'll give him a call and we can go and collect it."

"Thanks very much for that, Dorothy, and I'd like to take you out to dinner when you have a chance."

She offers an off-hand shrug. "It was no trouble."

"Umm... Dorothy..." She cocks her head slightly. "I just want to say that I think you were very brave to go on TV like you did."

She looks out the window with a snort of doubt. "Brave is one thing; foolish is another!"

"Why do you say it was foolish? I'm sure a great many people learned a lot listening to you."

"I do hope so, Hassan."

They are interrupted by a woman in black who comes sweeping down the aisle.

"Good afternoon, Missus Arusei." There is a brief nod from the lady in black. "Well, I have to get back to work. Take care, Hassan." Dorothy disappears down the corridor.

A nurse brings a chair and Mrs Arusei seats herself at her son's bedside. "What was she doing here?"

"She was just making a friendly visit."

"Hassan, I want you to stay away from that woman. She is the worst kind of degenerate: speaking about her sex acts on national television! Do you understand me?"

The muscles in Hassan's cheek are working. "I heard what you said, Mother, but I don't understand you. Did you watch Dorothy's interview?"

"No. I wouldn't watch filth like that!"

"Then, you don't know what you're talking about, Mother! Dorothy talked about how terrible rape is. She gave a lesson to men. What's wrong with that?"

Immam Arusei's face is determined. "I'll tell you what's wrong with it! Any woman who talks about her sex in public is a degenerate slut!"

"By that standard, a woman can never defend herself against her attacker in court."

"She should not appear, and her lawyer should handle it."

"Mother, how are violent men ever going to get the message that rape is a grievous sin?"

She sits back in the chair and considers her son. "I can see we're not going to agree about this, Hassan, but I strongly suggest you stay clear of that woman. You have a reputation to protect!"

"What reputation? As a terrorist?"

"Nobody knows about that!"

"So is that your answer to every problem: sweep it under the carpet?"

Imman Arusei winces and her lips begin to tremble. She looks out the window as her eyes fill with tears. They sit in silence for a long moment. "What time are we to expect you at home tomorrow, Hassan?"

"I'm not coming home tomorrow, Mother. I'm going back to the abattoir."

"But you need to rest at home."

"You're forgetting, Mother. I have to earn a living."

To be fair to Mrs Arusei, I think it's normal that she has such a strong, instinctive dislike of Dorothy as a degenerate woman who flaunts her sex on television. It's what I call a cultural bias, and it takes a long time and a lot of effort to put in place a robust, lasting bias, which, unfortunately, the One is constantly trying to erode.

* * *

The vacant parade ground that had been covered in a sheen of fine, tan dust yesterday is alive with activity today. Two men are wrestling with cantankerous black hoses to spray the thirsty surface. Following them, a tall, dark-skinned man in a

Achieving Superpersonhood:

black turban is struggling with a creaking roller to pack the wet dust against the hard earth. On the east side of the ground, other men are unloading scores of folding chairs from a truck, and a man in a wide-brimmed pith helmet is standing near the red brick administration building, consulting a sheaf of instructions. The fronds of the palm trees bordering the ground are moving listlessly.

But for the cadre of OAs (officer aspirants) who have returned from their five-mile run, the panorama is exhilarating. Tomorrow is commissioning and graduation day for the seven in ten who have made it through the last seventeen weeks. There has been physical hardship, unyielding discipline, an overwhelming siege of military education, perpetual testing and evaluation. They view the familiar, dusty parade ground with a new sense of joyful anticipation. There is a rumor – there are always rumors – that Mr Mohammad Adesida, Minister of Defense, is to be officiating at the ceremony, and instructors have conceded that Mr Adesida has never previously attended an OA graduation ceremony. To receive one's gold lieutenant bars from Mr Adesida is indeed an honor, but what is fuelling this keen sense of anticipation? It is the question as to who, among the fifty-two graduating OAs is to receive the coveted Sword of Honor, the prize for the OA judged to have been 'best in class and most likely to succeed in his career as an officer'. Three OAs: Sekibo, Biobaku, and Okoye are considered the top contenders, but Sekibo himself is betting on Arusei: "Not because of his name, but in spite of it."

"What do you mean?" he is asked.

"What I mean is he never mentions his name. He's just 'Hassan'. He is a classroom sponge, in great physical shape, and if I were a grunt in his squad, I'd go over the top for him."

Hassan himself has no expectation that the sword will be added to his dress uniform. He is thinking about Dorothy's promise to attend the ceremony. *I'm going to ask her to pin on my bars, and afterwards, will she kiss me? Lots of guys say it's traditional that the new lieutenant gets a kiss. I hope so!*

There is also the uneasiness about his mother's attendance. *Mama said she wants to be here. Father told her he couldn't make it. No surprise there. I've warned Dorothy about my mother – told her she's super conservative. If there's any kind of a scene between them, I'm going to take Dorothy's side.*

Kamiri will be here, too. He's such a good friend; said he would miss half a day of practice. Always says that Dorothy could never be a love interest – too much above him. But sometimes I wonder. Whenever I see them talking, they seem very close. He's tall and good looking, and a celebrity after all. I'm just glad that he's on the coast and I'm in City!

A long dais has been set up on the ground, facing the neat rows and columns of chairs. There is a podium with two chairs on either side. The Country flag flutters from the pole atop the administration building. A twelve-piece brass band is sounding random notes from chairs off to the left. Dorothy and Kamiri are sitting in the center of the fifth row of chairs; Mrs Arusei is seated to their right.

Family, friends and guests are filling the vacant chairs as the hour approaches. A bell in the cupola of the administrative building begins to ring the hour; a file of officials approaches. A colonel and a lieutenant colonel seat themselves to the left of the podium, and two civilians in suits and ties take the seats to the right of the podium.

The colonel stands at the podium, welcomes the spectators, and announces, "I would like to present the successful Officer Aspirants!"

At a nod from the colonel, the brass band rises and begins a spirited march.

A column of khaki-clad young men and six women emerges from the administration building. They are marching in step to the music, proudly swinging their arms, and their infectious grins belie any solemnity of the occasion. The spectators rise to their feet, applauding. The column files into the first three rows; with a crash of drums and cymbals, the band ends the march, and the colonel signals all to be seated.

For several moments, the colonel seems to be savoring the ceremony, then he begins, in passionate oratory, to inform the spectators of the rigors of the training the first three rows have received and their demonstrated competence and zeal for their task of defending the nation. There is polite, expectant applause. "Now," he says, "it gives me great pleasure to introduce the Minister for Defense, The Right Honorable Mohammad Adesida."

The minister is handsome, medium build with cropped graying hair. Neither tall nor stocky, wearing a fine suit and striking blue tie, it is his manner at the podium, not his appearance, which conveys the sense of power. His gestures, his pauses, the phrasing of his unscripted speech hold the rapt attention of the audience. For fifteen minutes he talks about the evolution of Country from a 'beautiful, impoverished tourist destination' to 'a regional economic power with rising levels of personal well-being'. He highlights the role of the armed forces in achieving 'this leap in per-capita GDP' by ensuring the security of Country and by setting the example of good citizenship. "Today, we are all honored to welcome new leaders into Country's Army."

Following prolonged applause, the colonel announces: "Minister Adesida will now present our graduates with their Notice of Commission as lieutenants in the Country Army and their badges of authority. Officer Aspirants, rise!"

In alphabetical order the candidates are called to the platform where each receives a rolled scroll, a blue box containing the coveted gold bars and a handshake of congratulations from the minister. As each name is called there is a burst of applause.

Hassan's is the third name called. As the minister shakes his hand, he says, "Congratulations, Hassan!"

He called me by my first name.

He turns, spots Dorothy, and gives her a joyful wave.

The Notices and blue boxes have been distributed. The colonel says, "We have prizes, now, for our young lieutenants." And he announces winners of the military comportment, physical fitness and army history prizes.

Hassan is rubbing the finish of his new gold bars. *They're not really gold, but I wonder how thick this plating is.*

"Hassan Arusei!" He looks up. Everyone is applauding.

"Come forward, Lieutenant Arusei!"

Oh Allah, this must be the Sword of Honor!

He rises – in a mental fog – and approaches the dais, where the minister is holding what must be a sword and a gold-braided belt. He stands, facing the minister, who reaches around his waist, snaps the buckle in place, and appraises the young man. The minister pats his shoulder: "Well done, Hassan!"

The fog has not lifted as Hassan resumes his seat. His colleagues on either side are whispering congratulations and trying to inspect the sword, which he can now see is encased in a black leather scabbard; the intricate gold hilt has a gold tassel.

"There are refreshments on the lawn to your left," the colonel announces.

"Hey, well done, Hassan!" It is Kamiri, who won't be deterred from enveloping him in an embrace. "Let me see that thing!"

Hassan draws the sword and holds up the shining, stainless blade which has decorative engraving and a citation: 'Lieutenant Hassan Arusei, Outstanding New Officer, Officer Aspirant School'.

His colleagues press around to feel and inspect the weapon. "Do you know how to use it, Hassan?" somebody asks.

"No. I think it's just for ceremony. You wear it with the full-dress uniform."

"Yeah," somebody grumbles, "but the rest of us are expected to buy a cheap imitation to go with full dress."

Dorothy is standing a few feet away, beaming.

Achieving Superpersonhood:

"Dorothy, thank you for coming!"

"Do you want me to put on your new bars, Hassan?"

"Yes, please." He hands her the small blue box.

Deftly, she attaches the bars to his collar. "There!"

Tentatively, he leans forward; she doesn't offer him a cheek; their lips meet. "Congratulations, Hassan!"

"Thank you, Dorothy! Thank you very much!"

He spots his mother at the edge of the crowd, a tea cup in her hand. The minister is speaking with her. Slowly, he approaches, watching the two of them. *They seem to know each other. Of course, with all the dinners she gives, he's probably been to the house half a dozen times.*

"Minister, this is my son, Hassan."

"Yes, Immam. We're proud of you, Hassan."

"Thank you, sir."

"Do you know where you'll be posted, Hassan?"

Again, my given name.

"I think it will be to the third division, sir."

"Ah, the Leopards. They're based in Coast City, are they not?"

"Yes, sir. There were no openings near City, which would have been my first choice, but Coast City is where my friend Kamiri lives."

"Yes, I recognized him. I understand the two of you used to play football."

"Yes, sir, we did. Of course, he's much better than I. But, how did you know that, sir?"

The minister smiles; with an air of feigned nonchalance, he says, "Military intelligence, Hassan."

I want to spend some time with Dorothy. "Well, thank you very much for the sword, sir. I hope I don't have to use it."

I, the Other, am disappointed in the direction that Hassan has taken. I had expected him to continue his career in Dhul Fikar. This would have opened opportunities for him to make an important name for himself, and would have blown a big raspberry at his step-father – his two overriding objectives. Not only did he fail to remember the advice I offered, but he did a complete backflip into the arms of the Army. Moreover, he applied himself so diligently that he has won that silly sword.

Cup of tea in hand, Hassan looks around.

"I gotta go, mate." Kamiri has wrapped an arm around his shoulder. "Congratulations, Hassan, I knew you could do it. Give me a call when you get to the coast."

Dorothy is sipping a cup of coffee and watching the band play. He stands next to her.

"When will you be moving to the coast?" she asks.

"Probably the day after tomorrow. Can you have dinner tomorrow night?"

She smiles ironically. "About twelve fifteen OK?"

"You mean lunch?"

"No. Dinner. I have the afternoon shift tomorrow."

"Damn! Well, I'll let you know when I have my first pass – probably a week from Sunday. I'll drive over and we can have lunch or dinner – whatever works for you."

"OK, but Hassan, I think a pizza would be fine, and it ought to be Dutch treat. We can't afford nice restaurants on our paychecks."

* * *

Joseph is immersed in the *Morning Courier* and his coffee when Dorothy comes down for breakfast. "How was the graduation?"

"It was a nice ceremony. Hassan won the Sword of Honor."

Joseph pushes the paper aside and considers his daughter. "Pretty amazing recovery from what looked like a rough downhill slide."

"Yeah, I'm very proud of him. He was determined to get at least some kind of honor when he graduated."

"Any family there?"

"His mother was there."

"How do you get on with her?"

Dorothy shrugs: "We don't. She doesn't like me at all. She probably thinks I'm bad for Hassan."

"Mmmm . . . What was she wearing, Dorothy?"

"Black. Head to toes, except gold slippers."

"I ask because that gives me an idea of where she sits on the Muslim scale."

"And the verdict is?"

"Pretty conservative."

"That's what Hassan says."

Joseph looks across the room pensively. "Where do you think Hassan sits on the same Muslim scale?"

"I'd say he's pretty liberal."

"Dorothy, am I right in recalling that Hassan went through a very religious stage before joining the terrorists?" She nods. "Does he ever talk about religion?" She shakes her head. "Do you?"

"No, Papa, it never comes up."

"Maybe it should."

She frowns. "Why do you say that?"

"Because you are a committed Christian. He, at one time – at least – was very dedicated Muslim. There may be room for some fundamental disagreements."

Dorothy folds her arms across her chest. "Are you saying that I should stop seeing him?"

"No. I'm just saying, 'test the waters', particularly with a conservative mother, who may have more influence than is obvious."

"I don't think so."

"OK. I don't want to come across as opposed to anything, and I really don't know Hassan, but could I ask you to consider two other factors?" She gives a perfunctory nod. "One is that military officers in this country earn almost nothing until they reach the lieutenant colonel level – at about twelve years of service."

"I know." *But, I, as a doctor, would be making pretty decent money.*

"And the other point is that military people tend to be away from home a good part of the time."

"No, they don't!"

"Dorothy, we're members of the African Union, and at the moment, we have peacekeepers in Somalia, Sudan, the Central African Republic and Sierra Leone. We just had a contingent in Burundi and there's talk about Mali. These guys are typically gone for six months to a year."

"I didn't know that." *That's not so good!*

"As long as there is UN or African Union funding involved, the army is in favor of participating, because it keeps our forces combat ready."

* * *

An intuition has persuaded Hassan to do some research on Mohammad Adesida. He is a Muslim, 54 years old. *A little younger than Mother.* Minister for Defense for the last six years. "Widely regarded as the likely successor to the current president." Married, with three adult children. Educated at City and Cambridge Universities. Served five years as an army officer, the last two as adjutant to the commanding general of the armored divisions. Joined a large, international consultancy firm based in City; became a partner. Was on the board of Arusei Industries for six years. Elected to parliament. Joined the cabinet as Minister for Defense Procurement. *On the board of Arusei Industries for six years. Maybe that's the connection. I wonder why he left the board.*

Chapter 20

Attack

Some months ago, Major el Hashem stopped at a favorite restaurant in the outskirts of Coast City for some green prawn curry, basmati rice and mango ice cream. There were, apparently, a few girls and three bodyguards also present. Their exact identity wasn't important to the DNA technicians in the Anti-Terror Branch; they were instructed to confirm that the major was present at the time the Hellfire missile struck. Warari was in camp then. The major's driver returned, alone, to camp the next morning on a stolen bicycle. The Toyota RAV4 in which he had been waiting – he was actually most likely asleep – had been hit by a blast of shrapnel. Leaking petrol caught fire almost immediately, but the driver escaped with burns, cuts and bruises. He told Warari: "It was real quiet except for Benga music in the distance. Nobody was on the street. Most of the lights were out. All of a sudden this horrendous *boom* nearly knocked me out of the car, but I got out before the fire started. I started to run. Then I looked back at the restaurant. It was gone. Just some smoke and small fires."

"Did you see the helicopter?" Warari asked.

"There wasn't no helicopter. I looked all over the sky. There was nothin'."

Warari pursed his lips. "Somebody must have tipped the Americans off. Do you have any idea who?"

"I'm thinking the same thing, sir. It must have been one of the locals who seen the major going in."

Three nights later, when Anti-Terror Branch and the police had gone, Warari and eight soldiers from Dhul Fikar descended on the area. In an hour, seventeen people were questioned and four men were executed. *It don't really matter whether we got the culprit,* Warari thought, *we made our point: don't fuck with Dhul Fikar!*

With the major's death, Warari decided that he would never appear in public, except on a raid, and even then, with his face shielded by a baklava. *They can know there's a Warari out there somewhere, and they've even got old police mug shots of him. But the guy they see today might or might not be Warari!*

The drone strike and the newly-offered $100,000 bounty on his head worry Warari. *I guess that they've persuaded Kamiri to give a blood sample to use for DNA identification. That's really dirty!*

To which I, the One, responded, "And executing people to make a point is clean?" Has the Other cloned himself as Warari?

Just before he was killed, the major initiated a 'dispersal policy'. Rather than being consolidated in a single camp of about 100 Dhul Fikar soldiers, the new policy was to have no more than twenty-five soldiers in a village, or remote, stand-alone camp. To make this work, the cadre of soldiers would provide economic benefits to the villagers – usually small sums of money from kidnappings, hijackings and robberies, with the promise that the soldiers and their benefits would leave if they became identified to the outside world. A remote, stand-alone camp is the main repository for well-hidden vehicles and weapons. The Country army continues to have evidence of the presence of Dhul Fikar – primarily from attacks – and they know in which geographic area DF is probably based, but general searches have proven fruitless, so far.

Warari doesn't like travelling at night. When he lived in Village, travelling at night was exciting: it meant a rendezvous with a girl in the soft, weeping lovegrass by the dry creek bed. But now, with one hundred thousand US dollars offered for information leading to his death or capture, he is wary.

    Tonight, Warari has been called to a meeting with Nazir al Hamas, leader of the Dhul Fikar faction in northeast Continent. To most of the soldiers of Dhul Fikar in Country, al Hamas seems more fictional than real. They have never seen him – even a picture of him. By reputation, he is a powerful ruler, committed to an unflinching, hard-metal version of Islam, where most Muslims and all but the most conservative imams are excess baggage and all other faiths are poisonous. According to various rumors, al Hamas is in the mountainous northwest, in the City slums, in other countries to the north or south, or in some variable combination of these. The coordinates which appear in the phone message Warari receives after his departure for the meeting indicate a desolate area in the country to the north: the GPS map show nothing but dirt tracks in the area. *If somebody passes these coordinates to the Americans, they will have no worries about civilian presence: just jackals and mice.*

    As the replacement Toyota approaches the designated coordinates, the GPS becomes less reliable. The driver, shifting his attention between the moonlit track ahead and the moving blue map, has seen the checkered flag of the destination slide farther away. "Do you want me to head straight for it, sir? But I should probably turn the lights on."

    "No. Stay on the tracks. No lights. Turn around. We've got to go back and look for a turning we missed." The driver veers off the track to make a U-turn. "Careful! There could be IEDs off the track!"

    The Toyota creeps back along the track. All four of the occupants are straining to see ahead. Irish springs up from his seat. "There! I think it's there!"

    "Where?"

"There! Just ahead on the left!" There is a tall tuft of grass, and just beyond it a patch of bare earth; in fact, two patches. The Toyota draws up to the patches.

"That's it," Warari announces. "Turn in."

Turn completed, the yellow arrow on the screen is pointing directly at the checkered flag. For a time, the Toyota bumps along slowly, but there is no light ahead. The gap between the arrow and the flag is decreasing at a snail's pace.

"Isn't that a tent up there?" Irish is pointing over the driver's shoulder.

"Probably," Warari concedes.

In the dim moonlight, here are five tents. Four small, lighter tents surrounding a larger dark tent. The Toyota stops; its engine is switched off.

"Wait," Warari orders.

Irish and Bad Ass are cradling their AK-47s watchfully.

The only sound is the ticking of the engine as it cools.

A voice from nowhere speaks: "Who are you?"

Warari says: "A visitor as requested by the boss."

"What do you eat for dinner?"

"Boiled rice."

A spotlight illuminates the Toyota. "Get out. Leave your weapons in the car." Warari and his three colleagues approach the spotlight. A man carrying an automatic rifle emerges from the darkness on either side. "Identity."

Warari hands him his Country identity card; his face and the card are scrutinized in the light.

"OK." The spot light is extinguished, and half a dozen small lights appear around the tents. "Come this way." Warari is led to the entrance of the large camouflage tent. "You go in. Others wait outside."

Pushing aside the tent flap, Warari enters the dimly lit space. The floor is covered with overlapping carpets. In the middle, there are two men sitting on large leather cushions: both have long black beards; one man is dressed all in white; the other is wearing dark camouflage fatigues. "Come and sit down, Warari."

Seating himself opposite the two men, Warari studies the faces of the two men. The smaller stranger, dressed in a white dishdasha and turban, has light skin, fine features, dark eyes and a frozen look of disdain. The other's familiar, dark face, bulbous nose and huge cheeks mark him as a man from the interior: Colonel Mbadinuju, the boss in Country.

The guy in white must be al Hamas. An Arab.

Al Hamas silently appraises his visitor. "Tell me about yourself, Warari."

"Well, I'm from a small village west of City. I came to City to have my own business – had some trouble with the law and I joined Dhul Fikar a couple of years back."

"Your business was selling drugs, I understand."

"Yes, it was. I was making good money."

Al Hamas gives an offhand shrug. "But you didn't use the drugs you were selling, correct?"

I hear the Other whispering, "There's only one answer to this: 'No'."

Warari glares at al Hamas. "No."

I, the One, don't suppose the assertion means, 'No, it's not correct. I did use some of the drugs I was selling'. But it seems that al Hamas hears what he wants to hear.

"Tell me, Warari, what kind of work have you done in Dhul Fikar."

"The major was very interested in raising money, and . . ."

Al Hamas interrupts, "You were chief fund raiser?" and to an old man carrying a tray, "You can set it down right here. Don't forget the bread."

"Yes, I took the lead on many fund-raising projects."

"Can you give me some examples?" and to the old man, "You can bring us a large pot of tea."

"I worked on several profitable kidnappings."

"Tell me about the most profitable." Al Hamas selects a face towel and a bowl from the tray, gesturing for the others to do likewise. "This is lamb with some beans and potatoes, but the lamb may be slightly over age." He dips his right hand into the bowl to feed himself.

"I would say it was the North American Oil project. We got just under three million US dollars for a senior vice president."

"What was his name?"

"Wisnewski."

"Ah, yes, I remember. Tell me: how did it work?"

"I heard that he was in Coast City for meetings about a big project with Country Oil. And I thought, we've got to pull this off, so when he left the meeting at the Country Oil building, I arranged for a radio car to follow him. About three kilometers from the airport, two other cars forced his limo off the road. His bodyguard started shooting from inside the limo, but I got behind and shot the guard through the rear window. The driver was reaching in the glove box when I nailed him. We bundled Wisnewski into one of our cars and took off. Waited a couple of days before calling Houston with our demand. When we wanted to communicate with Houston, we'd put him in an old van and drive around Coast City with different mobile phones. We made him think we were gonna kill him if we didn't get the money. Beat him up pretty good; he believed us."

"And how did you get the money?"

"We arranged for a drop from an airplane. When it was in the air, we made radio contact, and we kept giving it different instructions on where to drop. Finally, we sent it to Zamsula National Park, and told it to drop the package on a herd of zebras. We came out of the forest and collected it."

"What did you do with Wisnewski?"

"Dropped him off in a shanty town at two in the morning."

Al Hamas wipes his right hand with a towel and sets his bowl aside. "Were you involved in the hijacking of that Indian ship?"

"Yeah. It was the only one we did. You gotta control the coast to be successful there."

"But you got a couple of million."

"Yeah, but we lost two good men."

"What happened?"

"Well, we got a fast boat, and we intercepted this small cargo ship carrying building materials. Took control of it and ran it aground up the Zamsula River. We held the crew in the forest near the ship, so the army was afraid to attack. Eventually, the owners caved in and made an air drop."

"You said you lost some men."

"The army made an attempt to free the hostages – it was clumsy – we lost two guys and a couple of hostages, but we killed three or four soldiers."

The old man re-appears with the pot of tea and three chipped mugs. The tea is poured in silence. Turning to Colonel Mbadinuju al Hamas asks, "Are we ready, colonel?"

"Yes, we are ready!"

Al Hamas gives a slight nod. "And you, Warari, are you ready?"

It seems to me that Warari is ready to ask, 'for what?', but I hear the Other's rapid intervention.

"Yes, I am ready to carry out my orders, sir."

Al Hamas purses his lips in satisfaction. "It is time for Dhul Fikar to go on the offensive. Allah is demanding that we make ourselves and our message felt in Country. We will ignite fear in the unbelievers. They will tremble at the mention of our name. Many will be destroyed but some will hear the will of Allah and will join us in a caliphate of true Muslims." He pauses to assess the reaction of his listeners. The colonel raises his right thumb; Warari quickly does likewise. "What we have decided, Warari, is an attack on the Coast City Stadium, just as the crowd is leaving a game. You will arrange for a car bomb to detonate by the exits from the home stands. After the detonation, you and your men will move in and kill as many of the survivors as possible before the police arrive."

"Yes, sir, but I will need some technical assistance in the construction of the car bomb."

"Of course. Our bomb maker, Mohammad Nassir, will contact you."

"So how was the meeting, boss?" Irish inquires.
"Excellent! We have a new assignment."
"What is the new assignment, sir?"
"I cannot give you the details yet, Irish, but it involves a major attack on a big public event."
"Will it be in Coast City, sir?"
"Yes."
"Has a date been set?"
"It will depend on the event schedule."

You may think it strange, but I, the One, am still connected to Irish. I have an image of him, in a red cassock and white surplice, as an altar boy in the St Patrick's Church in Donegal Town. He was a beautiful, friendly, red-haired lad who seldom missed a Sunday mass. Life has buffeted him; his choices haven't always been the best, but I think of him as my lost friend.

Bad Ass asks: "What's al Hamas like, Warari?"
"Typical Arab. Arrogant. Thinks he knows it all."
"He's been pretty successful."
There is a snort from Warari. "He owes any success he's had to people like me – and you – who pull off the ransoms and hijackings, and now he wants us to pull off a major event."
"Who else was there, Warari?"
"That idiot Mbadinuju."

"But he's the boss and a colonel."

"Colonel, my ass! He's barely got the brains of a private. All he's got is a mean streak as wide as his ass!"

"How did he get to be colonel, then?"

"It's not so hard. You just snuff a couple of big shots in public. You remember that reporter from CNN?"

I can hear the Other chuckling at this exchange; then he says, "This is your chance to take over from the colonel, Warari." Apparently Mbadinuju has outlived his usefulness to the Other.

I should be the country leader, that's clear! The reward on me should be at least one million. And it may be my chance to get even with my brother.

"That's a good point, Warari; how did your younger brother get so far ahead of you in fame and fortune?" the Other whispers.

Not for long.

* * *

It is a routine Monday morning for Hassan. He has had breakfast, attended officers' call, mustered his squad, given them the plan for the day (training, exercise, noon meal, training, exercise), and he has inspected the barracks. He is on his way to the HQ Building for a meeting called by the commanding officer, a lieutenant colonel named Ojukwu. *I wonder what this is about.*

"I just want you to know," the commanding officer says, "that this brigade is on alert. There is an indication of terrorist activity around Coast City, and we have to be prepared to respond to it. Don't brief your men about this, because there is no further info, and we don't want the general public to be concerned."

As the meeting breaks up, Hassan approaches his commanding officer. "Sir, does this terrorist activity involve Dhul Fikar?"

"Yes, I suppose so, Arusei."

"I know a lot of the Dhul Fikar people, sir, and it seems to me unusual that they are planning activity. They usually did ransoms and hijackings, but not 'activity'."

"The briefing I received this morning mentioned 'attack', but you're right, Arusei; they haven't done an attack before, so I simplified it to 'activity'."

Hassan is chewing on his inner lip. "They have quite a lot of money, so I wouldn't be surprised if they want to build a name for themselves through an attack on the public. . . Do we know any more about this, sir?"

"I don't, but . . . Come to my office, Arusei."

The CO pushes a sheet of paper across his desk.

"This mentions a 'tip-off'," Hassan says, "but it doesn't say any more than that."

"I suppose that army HQ has some detail."

"Would it be possible to call them, sir?"

The CO pauses, then makes a call, during which he explains Hassan's history. "They want to see us."

At first, there are only his boss, Lieutenant Colonel Ojukwu, Colonel Ibori, Hassan and a major in the meeting room, but then half a dozen others arrive, including three civilians in suits with badges, two senior army officers, and a two-star general, who inquires: "What's this about inside knowledge of Dhul Fikar, Colonel Ibori?"

The colonel explains.

"What do you know about this threat, Lieutenant?" Hassan expresses his belief that the threat presages an attack on civilians.

The general turns to a subordinate. "In fact, the original document says 'attack' does it not, Major?"

"Yes, sir, it does."

Hassan puts in: "Excuse me, but did you say there's a document?"

"Yes, a man in dirty fatigues handed a note to a shopkeeper and said, 'Be sure to give this to the police.'"

"Is there any description of the man in fatigues?"

"Yes. The shopkeeper said he was a red-headed white man."

Hassan blurts out: "Irish!"

"What's Irish?" the general demands.

"Irish is a soldier in Dhul Fikar, sir."

The general frowns. "You mean a terrorist, Lieutenant."

"Yes, sir."

"Tell us about this Irish."

Hassan gives a brief summary of Irish, and then asks, "Sorry, Major, but is there a copy of this note I might see?"

The major removes a sheet of paper from his file and hands it to Hassan. Hand-written in bold capitals, it says: "POLICE BE WARNED! DHUL FIKAR IS PLANNING A MAJOR ATTACK ON A BIG PUBLIC EVENT! THE ATTACK DEPENDS ON THE SCHEDULE OF THE EVENT. THIS IS REAL!"

Hassan's head tilts from side to side as if weighing alternative possibilities. "I think the words 'the schedule of the event' are the key, because they imply that the schedule hasn't been determined. But what 'big public event' doesn't have an established, particular date? Therefore, it has to be an event that has multiple dates, like maybe a tennis tournament."

"We don't have a tennis tournament this year."

Someone suggests, "How about football?"

There is a stunned silence. The major is looking at a small card he has removed from his wallet. "The Lions are playing at home on the seventh, the fourteenth, twenty-fourth, and then on the eighth of April. Today is the twenty-fifth of February."

"When do we play the Rhinos?"

"On the twenty-fourth."

"That's got to be it!"

The general clears his throat. "Lieutenant, do you think that the terrorists are prepared now for the attack, or will they have to complete some preparations? For example, if they were going to use a car bomb, do they have one available?"

"I never knew of a large bomb."

One of the civilians says, "They have a bomb-maker who goes by the name of Mohammed Nassir. He's believed to be in Yemen."

"Well," the general says, "that suggests we have a little time. They've got to make the bomb and transport it here from Yemen, but I think we should cover all the upcoming home games."

The colonel suggests, "Sir, when you say we should cover the games, can I assume that you want the army – in addition to the police – to provide the cover?"

"Naturally."

"In that case, sir, may I propose that Lieutenant Arusei and his squad provide the cover?" The general looks around the table.

"Does he have the requisite anti-terror training?" the major asks.

Hassan's CO responds, dryly: "He has quite a lot of experience, and he might well recognize some of his former associates."

This is the third time Hassan and his squad have been on patrol outside Coast City Stadium. It is cloudy, hot and humid. *I don't envy Kamiri playing the Rhinos in this heat.*

His men, a sergeant, two corporals and five privates, are in full battle dress: camouflage fatigues, boots, helmets and flak jackets. Each has an assault rifle slung over his shoulder; Hassan has a Browning Hi-Power nine millimeter in a holster on his hip. Three of his men have been posted on the visitors' side of the stadium; the rest are with Hassan on the home side, where the crowd is at capacity. Scattered about the yard outside the stadium exits are six policemen, three of whom are armed.

Achieving Superpersonhood:

Hassan and his men have been following the progress of the game by listening to the loud cheering, and noting from which side it came. Reportedly, the game is in its eighty-eighth minute with the score tied at three.

As with the two previous games, there has been no hint of terrorist activity. The admission process for ticket-holders has been tightened with metal detectors and bag inspections. *If they're going to do something, it will probably be out here – when the crowds exit.*

There is a sustained roar from the other side of the stadium. A trickle of ticket-holders is exiting the turnstiles. One of the privates is speaking to a departing fan. "Rhinos four three final," comes over the army PPR radio.

"Shit!"

Hassan says, "OK, guys, heads up now."

The crowd is pouring out of the turnstiles. There is a single gunshot from the far end of the stadium. "Sir, there's a car coming."

"Stop it!" Hassan and the sergeant are running. The crowd is screaming and running the other direction.

"Policeman's down!"

A blue sedan comes into view careening toward them.

"Take the driver, Sarge!" Hassan withdraws the Browning and slips the safety off as he runs.

There is a fusillade of shots. The car stops. Someone is running toward the car with an assault rifle. "Bad Ass!" Hassan screams and fires the Browning.

It is bedlam. Screams and shots from every direction. People running and falling. Over the radio: "Ibrim is down!" "Got one!" "Behind you. Rob!"

A shout: "Kamiri!" Hassan turns to see his friend, still wearing his strip, emerge from a door. The shouter is Warari, who has ripped off his baklava.

Hassan yells, "Warari!" There is a burst from Warari's weapon. He turns and flees, firing into the crowd as he goes.

Hassan takes aim, but there is no clear shot.

The shooting stops. Cries and screams. Dozens of people are down. The sounds of several sirens in the distance.

"Help the wounded!" Hassan shouts into his microphone. He turns again to look for his friend. There is a crowd of people. Hassan pushes in. A yellow and black figure on the ground. Two people on their knees attending, wrapping a shirt around a leg. "Kamiri! . . . That son of a bitch!"

"At least he didn't kill me."

Players and an ambulance crew arrive. Injured spectators are loaded in. It takes off, siren blazing.

Hassan turns his attention to the blue sedan. Its windscreen has five crazed bullet holes, steam is streaming from the bonnet, the tires are flat. There is a man slumped in the driver's seat. Another man lies on the ground: Bad Ass.

"Evacuate this area," Hassan orders. "Sergeant!"

"Yes, sir?"

"Casualties?"

"We lost Mwangi, sir. And Maina has been taken to the hospital – stomach wound."

"Police?"

"One gone to hospital."

"Any idea of civilian casualties?"

"I think there are about twelve dead. They're still taking the wounded to the hospital."

"And the terrorists?"

"Just those two dead, sir," he gestures toward the blue sedan. "But there must be several wounded."

I, the Other, am angry: Hassan has actually killed an old colleague of his, when Bad Ass was just trying to complete the plan that Warari and I devised. Damn his impertinence! Then, there'll be talk of a Service Valor First Class award for saving the lives of 'all those people'.

Achieving Superpersonhood:

"Any prisoners?"
"No, sir. Unfortunately."

* * *

Dorothy is in her room at home, preparing to rest: her midnight shift is looming. She has watched the game with her father and sister, Mary, and she is ambivalent about the result. As a child, Dorothy and her family were Rhino supporters, but with Kamiri playing for the Lions, her Rhino-loyalty has evaporated.

"Dorothy," Joseph calls from downstairs, "Kamiri's been shot!"

She hurries down to the living room, where the post-game wrap-up has been replaced by a news bulletin. "We go now to our reporter, Ben, at the stadium."

"Yes, Ippy, there has been a terrorist attack here at the stadium. A number of spectators have been killed by an armed gang of terrorists who apparently tried unsuccessfully to detonate a car bomb. Police and the army have been engaged in a running gun battle which has seen several soldiers and police casualties. For reasons which are unclear, the Lion's left wing, Killer Kamiri, came out of the stadium just as the shooting started. We can confirm that he was shot by one of the terrorists, and he has been taken to hospital, but we have no reports on his condition."

"Oh my God!" They continue watching as the screen shifts back and forth between the newsroom and the stadium. *Oh God, please don't let Kamiri die,* Dorothy prays. *He is so special. Please don't let him die.*

"We go back to Ben now who has an update for us."

"Thanks, Ippy. I've been able to find the Army officer who was in charge here, a Lieutenant Arusei. Can you tell us about the car bomb?"

Hassan is perspiring heavily and the chin strap of his helmet is unfastened. "Well, we can't be sure yet there is a car bomb. The bomb disposal unit hasn't arrived, but I can tell you that an unauthorized blue sedan attempted to drive into the area where spectators were exiting the stadium. When the driver failed to comply with an order to stop, he was shot dead."

"And have you identified the driver?"

"No, but he was wearing a black headband of the Dhul Fikar group."

Mary elbows her sister in the ribs. "So that's your boyfriend."

Dorothy frowns at her sister. "He's a friend, not my boyfriend."

"I don't know why he's not your boyfriend. I think he's pretty dishy." Dorothy raises her chin and stares fixedly at the screen. Mary casts sidelong glances at her sister, seeking provocation. "Well, if you don't want him, maybe I'll go after him." Dorothy looks disdainfully at her sister. Joseph surveys his daughters and bites his tongue. Mary wags her head. "Well what about it, sis?"

"Mary dear, he happens to be Muslim."

"So, what's wrong with that? He also happens to be an Arusei."

"Mary, since when are you a social climber?"

"All right girls, that's enough silly talk."

* * *

"Run it again from the beginning, Corporal," Colonel Ibori directs. A still picture appears on the screen and starts to move. "Who started it, Mr Arusei?"

Hassan walks to the screen. "I believe it was this policeman here, sir. When an order to halt was not obeyed, he drew his service revolver and started shooting at the driver."

"And then your men started shooting."

"Yes, sir, I ordered Sergeant Omondi to take out the driver, and I shot this man, here. He was probably going to set off the bomb."

The colonel turns to a civilian. "What did you say the bomb consisted of?"

"It was about three hundred kilograms of ammonium nitrate mixed with diesel oil and packed with nails and bolts into steel drums. There was a manual trigger operated from the front seat of the car."

"A crude but pretty substantial bomb."

Lieutenant Colonel Ojukwu says, "Surprisingly, after the initial assault, they decided to quit. Probably realized they were outgunned."

"All except that guy there, who shot Kamiri."

"Do you know who he is, Mr. Arusei?"

"His name is Warari, sir. He's Kamiri's older brother."

The colonel shakes his head in disgust. "So he's the leader now. . . . Tell me: why weren't we able to catch any of them?"

"We've recovered some of their weapons, sir, and part of the clothing they wore. They just melted into the crowds, and probably used stolen motorbikes."

"Mr Arusei, was Irish there?"

"I didn't see him, sir."

I, the Other, am thoroughly disappointed with Irish, on whom I was counting to support Warari in his excellent plan, but who faked a severe stomach disorder at the last minute. Nonetheless, Warari executed the plan so as to stamp the terrorist name 'Dhul Fikar' on Country, with plenty of bloody media coverage, evening the score with Kamiri, and with trivial losses of my friends. Warari will be in line for a promotion.

Chapter 21

Surgery

One case of emotional baggage is troubling Kamiri. On the sports pages, ever since an astute sports writer had connected two surnames: Killer's and the chief terrorist's, the speculation seemed endless. The attack is viewed as bitterly personal – not a random act of mayhem. Why would Killer's own brother attack him in a way that could potentially end his career? Career jealousy, a love triangle, a money dispute, warped ideology, and several other motivations were proposed.

In the telephone call with his father, a day after the shooting, Kamiri thought, at first, to anonymize his assailant, but then: *he'll probably hear eventually who it was, and I'll be wrong for not being forthcoming.* His father was furious. "I will have him banished from Village. It is one of the Great Wrongs to injure without just cause."

Kamiri harbors a sense of the shame it has brought on his family and his tribe. He equivocates with a reporter who interviews him in the hospital: "I don't know . . . Perhaps he mistook me for someone else . . . Perhaps it was a mistake . . . I can't think of a reason."

With Dorothy, it would be different: he needs someone he trusts not to gossip, and who has a sense of social justice, to invalidate his personal shame. Who better to test his bitter chagrin than someone who is above village culture and cannot be burdened with it?

Achieving Superpersonhood:

There has been a virtual blackout regarding Kamiri's injuries; the Lions have reported only that his injuries are 'serious'. Dorothy contacts a colleague from medical school who is now assigned to Coast City Hospital: "Henry, can you find out for me how serious Kamiri's injuries are? He is an old friend, and I'd like to call him, but I don't want to disturb him if he's badly injured."

An hour later, there is a beep from her cell phone, and a red 1 on the WhatsApp icon: "Dorothy, Kamiri's injuries are not life-threatening. His left knee is very bad. Otherwise OK."

Dorothy is both relieved and anxious. *He's not critical – thank God! But a bad knee injury? Will he be able to play again?"*

"Hi Kamiri, it's Dorothy. I understand your knee has been hurt."

"Hi Dorothy, nice of you to call." His voice is slow and slightly slurred. "Yeah, the knee's not so good. They're trying to figure out what to do."

"You were shot in the knee. How awful!"

"Yeah, there are a couple of other places on my legs, but they don't seem as worried about them. I'm in a splint and enjoying a lot of morphine."

"I don't understand why you weren't still in the locker room when the shooting started."

"I got a text from my brother. He said, 'I need to see you urgently – come outside now'."

"So he called you out and they shot you!"

"No, he shot me."

Silence on the line. "Your brother . . . shot you?"

"But . . . I'm lucky he didn't kill me."

"I just don't understand, Kamiri."

He recounts his brother's bitterness over his escape to the abattoir from drugs, arranging bail, buying the motorcycle, but most of all for being a popular Lion.

"Oh my God. It makes me feel sick. I'm so sorry, Kamiri, that you have to pay for your brother's deranged jealousy."

"But Dorothy, what Warari did reflects badly on our family and our village. It is a Great Wrong and should never happen."

"It is a great wrong, Kamiri, but neither you nor your family nor your village can possibly take responsibility for a deranged idiot."

"Yeah, well, I've been thinking – praying in a way – hoping – that the devil would let him go."

"I'm afraid there's not much chance of that Kamiri."

A pause.

The One whispering to Kamiri: what about Dorothy's attacker?

"Do you ever think that about the doctor who . . . who hurt you?"

"Think about him? No. I don't forgive him or even think of praying for him. I just hope he doesn't molest other women."

"Isn't that the same thing?"

"What do you mean?"

"Well, isn't praying that the devil lets go of him the same as hoping he doesn't molest other women?"

Dorothy considers. "I guess my focus is on the other women and not on him, but I see your point: if the devil lets go of him, he won't molest."

The line is silent for a moment. Kamiri asks: "Is it possible to pray for someone without forgiveness?"

"Oh Kamiri! You ought to be wearing a dog collar!"

"Why should I wear a dog collar, Dorothy?"

"It's slang for a collar that priests and ministers wear – I just meant I think you should be one."

"No, I couldn't. But about my brother, if I pray that he stops being a terrorist, do you think I should try to forgive him?"

"Prayer I can understand, but forgiveness can wait – for a long time."

"OK, Dorothy, but if I pray <u>with</u> forgiveness I should notice a difference."

"Which is?"

"I'll feel better."

Dorothy releases a sigh. "OK, Kamiri, suit yourself, but please don't take any more phone calls from your brother – even if he is forgiven, and don't blame yourself for your brother's derangement."

As she ends the call, she thinks, *How can I forgive a man who selfishly and brutally attacked me and why should I?*

I, the One, would say to Dorothy: if you're going to pray about Wadaki, it is best for the achievement of peaceful emotions, to forgive, as well.

"You back again, Coach?"

"I've been talking to the doctors." Elim seats himself awkwardly on a chair next to Kamiri's bed. "Your injuries are quite complex, Kamiri, and the doctors here don't think they can fix your knee."

Kamiri struggles to a sitting position. "Oh shit!" This is the eventuality which Kamiri has shoved, repeatedly, from his mind. He trusts his body unreservedly; it always had – it always would – respond magically to his wishes: to see, to hear, to speak, to run, to jump, even to cartwheel on command. In his village, there were amputees, people with crutches, or a club foot, he had seen dozens more who were crippled or deformed. Silently, secretly, he had felt a momentary surge of pity, quickly to be put aside. *Not me. Thank Ngai, not me.*

Now it was upon him like an anaconda.

Elim turns to face him, grasping his arm. "There is – in London – a doctor who may be able to fix your knee. We're going to send you to London for a consultation."

Questions spill through Kamiri's mind. *Who is this doctor? What are the chances? What happens if he can't . . . ? How long will it take? How do I get there?* He takes a deep breath. "How do I get there?"

Elim pats Kamiri's arm in gratitude for the acceptance. "We have a chartered ambulance to take you."

"But how long's it going to take?"

"About six hours, I think."

"Six hours?"

Elim registers his player's disbelief. "It's an air ambulance, Killer, a private jet. British Airlines won't take you, as is. You'll fly to Biggin Hill, south of London, then they'll take you by regular ambulance to the private Cromwell Hospital, where they'll tuck you into a nice comfy bed, and Professor Marsh-Thompson will see you in the morning."

The small, twin-engine jet shrieks down the Coast City runway. Twisting on the narrow bed, against the restraining arm of the nurse, and peering out the window, Kamiri takes in the flying dwellings, collected villages, a panorama of clustered, Coast City skyscrapers, and then a dizzying, tilting blue and white sky. He muses about London and what lies ahead with trepidation and anticipation. In the telephone call with his father, he was assured that "in London they treat you well. You'll be back on the pitch within three months." The example was cited of a Nigerian center forward who suffered a ruptured knee from a red card tackle, went to London, and is now back in Lagos for the starting whistle. *But what if my case is different? Perhaps a bullet can do more damage than a right back.*

There is no sense of motion; there is no view of passing clouds or the ground below, only the hum, as if there were a bee hive behind him in the tail.

In Village, people talked of London as a rich place filled with treasures: wide streets, amazing buildings, people dressed as fashion icons, all in motion; where anything socially, technically and artistically is possible; where real democracy is king; where your deepest wishes are granted. But no one had ever been there. *Yes, I want to see what London is really like.*

Achieving Superpersonhood:

The room is barely lit and the window is still dark when an energetic, brown-skinned nurse in a white head scarf and blue uniform wants his vital readings. She glances up at him while transcribing this data into a tan folder. "How are you feeling this morning, Kamiri?"

"My knee is pretty sore."

"I'll get you some more pain relief." She turns to go.

"Why do you wear that white head scarf."

There is a bemused smile on her face. "Because I'm a Muslim."

"That's what I thought. There are plenty of Muslims in Country, but I didn't know about here. Do you sometimes feel lonely?"

"Not really," she chuckles. "Besides my family, there are another seven hundred thousand of us here in London."

"So, here, it must be like the big cities in Country. A lot of my friends and team mates are Muslim."

She nods agreeably. "The doctor will be in to see you after breakfast."

A portly woman sets the tray down: "We didn't know what you like for breakfast, and you came in after orders closed, so we've given you a full English breakfast. If there's anything else you'd like," she continues earnestly, "just let me know and the chef will prepare it for you."

Kamiri surveys the tray; he looks up. "I'd like some fried sweet potatoes and a small plate of mahamri."

"Umm . . . we can try for the sweet potatoes, but I'm not sure if the chef knows mahamri."

Kamiri is enjoying the encounter. "They're sweet donuts made with coconut milk and cardamom. Delicious!"

"Umm . . . well, we've made baba ganoush for our Arabic patients and gravlax for our Jewish patients, but I don't think the chef knows mahamri."

"Well, tell him if he wants to come up, I'll be happy to give him the recipe and explain it."

"Thank you, sir."

A tall, gray-haired man in a tailored business suit, accompanied by medical staff, enters the room. "Good morning, I'm Mister Marsh-Thompson." (Surgeons in the UK are called 'mister' rather than 'doctor'; in the 18th century, surgeons seldom had a formal degree, while qualified physicians were doctors of medicine. Now, qualified surgeons use 'Mr' as a badge of honor.)

"Hello. I am Kamiri."

There follows some banter about football, the Chelsea club – to which Marsh-Thompson has season tickets – and outlook for the Premier League season.

"Kamiri, I have looked at the scans of your knee, and I think we can get you walking again, but I can't make you any promises, now, about sprinting."

"Well, sir, I'm willing to work hard to regain my fitness."

"That's excellent but the knee is a complex joint and for this reason, when it is quite damaged, it can become somewhat difficult to treat."

"But I have heard of people who have had knee replacements. Doesn't that solve the problem?"

"When people speak of a knee replacement, they are really talking about resurfacing the three major bones. In your case, the damage is considerably more extensive than the bone surfaces."

"Can you tell me, doctor, what is the extent of my damage?"

"Yes." He turns to a junior doctor who is holding a computer tablet. "May I have the scans, please?"

Mr Marsh-Thompson shows Kamiri a graphic of a knee joint which can be viewed 360°. He points out the various ligaments which hold the joint in place. Then, flipping to another graphic: "This is a scan of the front of your knee, Kamiri."

"Oh my God!"

"And this is a lateral view. You can see that the ends of the femur and the tibia have been shattered."

"What are these things here?"

"They're bone fragments. Now, there are two important points on these scans. First, it is impossible to resurface the femur and tibia, because their surfaces no longer exist, and second, the anterior and lateral ligaments have been damaged."

"Yes, but isn't it possible to make up a new metal joint and attach it to the bones?"

"That's what we're planning to do – with your permission, Kamiri."

"OK, let's get on with it."

"Kamiri, it's not quite that simple." He points to the tablet. "These ligaments will need to be repaired to provide stability to the joint."

Kamiri is chewing the inside of his cheek. "How do you do that, doctor?"

"To the extent that a ligament is not badly damaged, we can stitch it back together. Otherwise we can graft in an artificial ligament. I should tell you, Kamiri, that healing from ligament repair can be a lengthy process."

"How long, doctor?"

"Well, I would expect that we can have you walking with crutches within a week, and without crutches in a month. You'll probably have considerable discomfort for three months, which should subside in about six months."

"When will I know whether I can sprint?"

"When the pain is pretty well gone, you can try running – not aggressively. You may find that you just don't have the speed you used to have."

"Why is that, doctor?"

"It will be difficult to pinpoint a cause, Kamiri. First of all, a man-made joint, while strong and stable, may not be able to keep up with the rate at which your muscles want to move it, and second, your repaired ligaments may not provide exactly the positioning of the joint that you would need for top speed. Even natural ligaments don't function perfectly in this regard. Since you are a particularly speedy chap – so I'm told – your natural ligaments seem to have been perfectly formed, and it is extremely difficult to make them perfect again."

"Well, it's not going to get any better like it is, and you're my man, so let's go."

"All right, Kamiri, we have you scheduled to be in theatre at three o'clock this afternoon, and the procedure will take four or five hours. I will see you in theatre and again back here after the procedure. In the meantime, my anesthetist, Doctor Satapathy, will be around to see you."

There is a vacuous feeling in Kamiri's stomach as if he has been stripped naked and forced to swim across a deep, swift river to an unknown land. *I'm not actually afraid, but I've never even been in hospital before, and they're going to take five hours to fix my knee. I think they know what they're doing, but do I know what I'll be like after I wake up and what I'll be able to do – what my future holds?*

Doctor Satapathy wants to know about football – from a real star. His son is a semi-professional cricketer somewhere up in the north of England, and he confesses to watching cricket matches "every weekend, live from India."

Kamiri's suppressed anxiety forces a re-routing of the discussion. "So doctor, you're going to put me to sleep?"

"Yes, and I will wake you up when Mr Marsh-Thompson, who I assure you is very good indeed, has finished the procedure."

"Some of the guys on my team have had operations on their knees while they were awake. Why don't we do it that way?"

"Well, I would assume that the procedures they had were relatively minor and were completed in an hour or so. With a procedure like yours, it's better for all concerned that you sleep peacefully through it."

"But I'd like to know what's going on."

"We can give you a full report afterwards." He considers Kamiri for several moments. "Have you ever watched one of those historic movies about the Royal Navy in battle?"

Achieving Superpersonhood:

"You mean like *Master and Commander: the Far Side of the World*?"

"Yes, and did you notice the surgeon practicing his profession?"

"Yes, pretty awful. Sailors having their legs amputated with no painkiller other than a mug of rum. But, if they had a painkiller for just the leg, in those days, wouldn't they have used it?"

Dr Sanapathy shakes his head. "Not if they had today's general anesthesia. It avoids all the things that patients generally don't like to see or hear, and it makes it so much easier for the surgeon to work on a quiet, peaceful patient."

Kamiri considers this and slowly inclines his head. *I'm pretty sure I wouldn't like to hear a saw going through my leg bone.*

Slowly, Kamiri regains consciousness. He feels like he is floating in some distant space, but gradually, the ceiling, the feeling of the sheets, the nurse leaning over him, and a plastic bag hanging on a vertical rack come into focus. "Yes, I'm OK." There is a question about pain. "No, it's OK; my knee isn't hurting."

"Well, if you start to have pain, you can press this button here."

He dozes.

"How is my patient?"

Opening his eyes, he recognizes Mr Marsh-Thompson. "The operation went very well, Kamiri. You have a new titanium and polymer knee. One of your damaged ligaments has been sewn up, another two have artificial inserts. All the other damage has been cleaned up. There are thirty-nine stitches down the front of your knee, and eleven behind. There is a drain in your knee which will help reduce the swelling."

"OK, thanks, doctor." *He really did a lot of stuff!*

The blessed morphine, the saline and the wound drain vanish and crutches arrive with a drill sergeant physiotherapist. "Very good, Kamiri . . . stand up straight . . . swing your leg . . . put your weight on your hands . . . back down this corridor . . . tomorrow we'll try the stairs."

Friendly yellow pills and ice therapy replace the lovely morphine. The ice box with its electric pump is loaded with ice, and freezing water is circulated through a sleeve around the knee: welcome at first, but numbingly cold after thirty minutes.

Every few hours, a nurse checks the status of the wound and monitors the swelling. The drill sergeant returns twice daily to supervise in-bed exercises and his improving ambulation.

The hospital chef pays him an unexpected visit to discuss the preparation of mahamri, and Kamiri is astonished to find six of the crisp, puffy delicacies wrapped in a napkin on his breakfast tray the next morning.

During the day, there is the possibility of unlimited television interrupted by naps, but the most welcome diversion is the ringing of his mobile phone at the bedside. Dorothy, Hassan, Eddie and Elim have each called twice; many teammates have called, and then there was the call from Kaddour Arusei: "We all hope you're recovering well, Kamiri." *Well, of course he's interested. He's paying for all this one way or the other, and he's spent a lot of money on me, but it would be easy to ask Elim for a report. Instead, he picks up the phone himself.*

Mr Marsh-Thompson says: "I think you're ready to go home, Kamiri. The swelling is down, and the wound is healing nicely. I have good reports from the nurses and the physio, so you're OK to go. I understand there's a seat for you on this evening's flight to City. That all right?"

"Yes."

"I recommend, Kamiri, that you spend plenty of time with the team physio. The secret to a good recovery is regaining the strength and flexibility, but don't push it beyond what's pretty tolerable. It's going to take plenty of time. You can have the staples and sutures removed in seven days. Best of luck to you, and I hope to see you in a major tournament."

The British Airways agent hands him his ticket. "Departure is from gate B35. You can go to the first-class lounge."
First Class! I've heard that this is amazing. I won't have to worry about stretching out my leg.
The private jet outbound was unique but unmemorable: it was marred by pain and uncertainty for the future, but the homeward-bound flight is miraculous: a spacious cubicle with a real bed, limitless cinema, incredible cuisine, and champagne, but the real miracle was Kamiri's new knee. *I'm going to play again!*

Kamiri rides with Eddie every day to the Lions' training camp. It is good to joke with his teammates, to smell the grass of the pitch, and to feel a ball at his feet. His days are spent with the team physio, walking, stretching, straining against restraints, and sitting alone on the bench because he tires easily. Staples and stitches are removed, so his teammates can marvel at the livid pink scar nearly a foot in length. There are moments of great frustration when pain or sluggish response becomes a barrier to improvement. Deliberate walking is not a problem and the crutches have long since been banished, but even a gentle jog is confined to fifteen to twenty meters. A young substitute has been moved 'temporarily' into starting position at left wing. *What if I can't displace him?*

Months pass. The Lions trainer is impressed by the progress Kamiri has made, and particularly laudatory about the dedication and determination of his athlete, who is able now to participate in 'no contact' scrimmages. Lions' management is concerned about the durability of the mechanical knee, at this stage, under a hard tackle. But their main concern is Kamiri's speed of response; as they watch him in practice, executing a deceptive ball control maneuver takes him tenths of a second too long. These tenths of a second are what a defender needs to make an interception. When clocked at forty meters, Kamiri's time has slipped from 4.53 to 5.51 seconds; the first being a team best and the second above team average. Their conclusion is short: Kamiri is no longer the player he once was.

Kamiri is aware of these deficiencies, but he clings to the hope of further improvement. Day by day, though, he begins to accept that he can never return to the player he was.

As a distraction and a gesture of goodwill, he has taken his replacement, Dennis Ngugi, under his mentoring wing, coaching him on tactics and positioning. Young Ngugi has excellent stamina and ball control skills, but he lacks Kamiri's once-great speed and long passing accuracy.

Kamiri understands that, much as he might like it, the current situation will not be permitted to continue indefinitely. He senses that other players are expecting that the coaching staff, who are displaying a tentative attitude toward him, must make a decision.

Elim is faced with that decision: what to do? Making Kamiri redundant would not go down well with Lions fans. It is also observed that making Kamiri redundant would 'give the terrorists what they wanted'. Moving Kamiri to a defensive position would mean displacing a good defender with an inexperienced player who has a speed handicap. Leaving him on the bench for 'just in case' situations would be tempting, but would not be viable in tournament situations where team size limitations apply. Besides, what would Kamiri think? There is one other possibility to discuss with Kaddour: making Kamiri assistant coach of the Lions' under twenty-one team, where a vacancy exists. Elim sees that this option might appeal to Kamiri, who demonstrates, in his voluntary relationship with Ngugi, an interest in working with younger players. It would keep him involved in the game and with the Lions at, admittedly, a smaller financial package, but from experience, Kamiri does not seem particularly money-motivated.

Kaddour, having heard the various pros and cons of the options, agreed that Kamiri should be approached about the under twenty-one coaching position.

Achieving Superpersonhood:

And Kamiri, having been approached by Elim about the position, asks for time to think about it. Over the past months he has come to accept that his body will never again be what it was, yet he is grateful to Mr Marsh-Thompson for giving him near-normal mobility. The continuing connections with the Lions, ongoing involvement in football, and being able to pass his knowledge on to younger players all appeal to him. The money is not what it once was, but *when I think back over what I once had and what I hoped to have, I have been truly blessed by God. But . . . I do need time to think about who I am and who I want to be. Is it really football? Am I a football player by accident?*

* * *

Hassan's company has returned to barracks after a six-month assignment in the Democratic Republic of the Congo. Aside from memories, he has a green and blue campaign decoration, whose bronze medal features the DRC's coat of arms: the head of a leopard wreathed in the words 'Justice, Paix, Travail'. "Well, they got one thing right," Hassan comments to a colleague on receiving it. "They have plenty of Travail, but damn little Justice or Paix."

When he collects his post, there is an official-looking brown envelope for which he has to sign. Inside, he finds two documents: one, a shipping notice announcing the enclosure of the other document: a certificate for ten thousand shares of Arusei Industries in the name of Hassan Arusei. *What is this? Is it real? Where did it come from?* For some time, in his quarters, he scrutinizes the share document from every angle, wanting to believe it is real, but fearful that someone has decided to play an unkind joke on him – a joke which laughs at his very identity. *Who would do that? His siblings? No, they all take the company much too seriously to do something like that. Anyone else? I can't think of anyone who knows me and dislikes me enough to go to the trouble to produce this counterfeit.* Dhul Fikar? *No, they'd rather shoot me.* He examines the shipping notice and recognizes the name of the City stock brokers who appear to be involved. A call to the brokers confirms that they sent the certificate, and that they have an account in the name of Hassan Arusei for ten thousand shares of Arusei Industries.

Hassan asks, "What price are the shares trading at?"

"Just a moment. . . . One hundred and fourteen and a half shillings."

"Can you tell me who the previous owner was?"

"No, sir, we are not authorized to do that."

"Can you tell me what the current dividend is?"

A pause. "It's paying eight thousand shillings per quarter, sir? Did you want to sell?"

"No, thank you.

He put down his telephone. "Thank you, Allah – and whoever did this for me. Eight thousand shillings a quarter will be very welcome!"

But who did this?

My step father? Possibly. Maybe he's pleased that I'm an army officer and no longer require an allowance.

My mother? Maybe. But where did she get the shares? May have had them or she cajoled them.

My real father? Possibly. He may have had shares from when he was on the Arusei board.

My siblings – individually or collectively? Maybe. They're actually speaking to me nowadays.

But who do I thank? If I guess wrong, it may cause a lot of trouble.

This must be anonymous for a reason.

In addition to his memories, Hassan has brought back a sheaf of letters, including two from his mother, four from Dorothy and one from Kamiri. His mother's letters are brief, kindly, no-news responses to his descriptions of a hopeless, peace-keeping mission; in them she expresses her pride in his 'chosen career' and her hope that he returns home safely.

Dorothy's letters are full of medical anecdotes, responses to his mission briefings, and opinions on the political malaise in the DRC, but lacking the personal content he had hoped to prompt with his clear but cautious references to their relationship.

Kamiri's letter voices his pain in the realization of his new physical limitations, his doubts and uncertainty about the future. He says, "I've been so lucky to find my way to what I thought would be a highly-paid job in football. Who would have thought that within a couple of years after leaving my village, I would be on the starting team of the Lions? Now that opportunity is evaporating, and I have no skills other than physical. What can you suggest?"

Hassan responded: "Kamiri, I'm so sorry your injuries have become a career handicap. This is what I'm sure your evil brother – may his soul burn in hell – intended. I'm also sorry that I can't recommend a specific course of action for you, as you did so well for me when I left DF. But I am confident that you will find a new role, just as I have. Can it be coincidence that Dorothy and I have found our careers only after experiencing catastrophes? If not, I'm sure your new career is just around the corner." The letter went on to suggest that they get together on Hassan's return to Coast City.

> I, the One, would suggest that catastrophes do not have a cause-effect relationship with the start of new careers, but catastrophes can force a period of introspection leading to new self-awareness and insights.

In that meeting, over a leisurely Saturday at a burger emporium on the south beach, Hassan suggests that Kamiri should speak to Dorothy's father, who has "lots of connections and knows all about the jobs situation".

On Saturday, Hassan speaks about the hardships involving peacekeeping in the DRC: constant rain, never-ending mud, old leaky tents, bad food, and, unsurprisingly, miserable morale.

"Did you see any combat?" Kamiri wants to know.

"Not combat as most people think of it, which involves sustained fighting. What usually happens is that one of the rebel groups would attack a civilian village. We would get called out, but by the time we got to the village the rebel forces would have disappeared into the jungle. There were two or three firefights in which one or two rebels would be killed."

"Were there any casualties in your company?"

"Two of our guys were wounded."

"Is it possible to wipe out the insurgency?"

"Don't forget that they're based in thick jungle in small groups. Going after them would be hazardous and difficult. There are only several thousand of them."

"How big is the anti-insurgent force?"

"Over twenty thousand – the world's largest peace-keeping force."

"Oh, for goodness sake! . . . In your opinion, Hassan, how can this situation be resolved?"

"I don't know, Kamiri, but I've heard people say that if all the money which has been spent on peacekeeping were spent on development of the east, the problem would disappear."

"Oh, Africa! When will we ever learn?" Kamiri laments. He considers his friend for a moment. "But was it worthwhile for you, Hassan – personally, I mean?"

"Yeah, I think so. The living conditions are poor – about what they were with the terrorists, but there's so much you can learn: about the social and economic situation of the people, but most of all, there's plenty to be learned about leading a platoon under bad conditions: how can you keep your men focused on their assignment when they have too many personal distractions?"

"Sounds like you're a committed soldier, Hassan."

Achieving Superpersonhood:

"Yeah, I feel good being an Army officer. It's challenging, you keep learning, you're always around people, and you're doing something worthwhile for the country. By the way, I'm about to get my captain's bars."

"Congratulations, Hassan! How does your family feel about an army versus a business career?"

"My mother's definitely OK with it. Haven't heard from my father – not that I expected to. But there's an interesting thing: my sister-in-law, my second brother's wife, with whom I've had no contact since her marriage twelve years ago, called me the other day. Don't know how she got my number. She asked if I would talk about the DRC at a women's club she belongs to."

Kamiri cocks his head. "If she invited you, that means your brother must know of the invitation and approve . . ."

". . . of me – maybe." Hassan looks out to sea for a moment. "I've been reading a biography of Muhammad, the Prophet. You know he was kind of a general – fought some interesting battles, which I didn't really know. When you read the Qur'an you don't get much idea of the personality of the man who's telling Allah's story, but in the biography, his determination against the odds and his unshakeable commitment to Allah come through. Aside from being the Prophet, he was a great man."

Kamiri smiles. "I should lend you my biography of Jesus."

"He was a great prophet and also a great man. We Muslims believe that."

Kamiri looks away. *There's no point in arguing about Jesus' true identity with a friend who believes in God and that Jesus was just a prophet: for each of us it's at the core of our faith.*

> I, the Other, think it is essential to get the core truths right. Was He or wasn't he the actual son of God? If there is a bit of uncomfortable controversy, that's the price that has to be paid for authenticity.

I, the One, think that if people – some would call them religious fanatics – who promote arguments about who is right - Christians or Muslims – regarding the true identity of Jesus, devoted their energy, instead, to living by the teachings of their respective prophets, the world would be a kinder place.

"You know, Kamiri, I saw a news release from Mohammad Adesida, Minister of Defense, in which he was talking about our company serving in the DRC. At the end, he mentioned that he has a relative serving in DRC."

"So who's the relative?"

Hassan takes a deep breath. "I think it's me. Not sure, but I think so."

"How would you be related?"

"I might be his son."

"What?" Kamiri is open-mouthed in amazement.

"As I say, I'm not certain, but there are some things I can tell you in absolute confidence." Kamiri signals his assent. "First of all, I have always been an outsider in my family. My father and my siblings treat me differently. This has always made me wonder whether I was secretly adopted. Then, you remember that Adesida came to my graduation. He doesn't normally do that. He gave me the sword of honor and he called me 'son' and by my first name." Hassan holds up a hand to silence his friend. "At the graduation, Adesida and my mother were talking as old acquaintances, and later I found that he had been on the board of Arusei Industries until about the time I was born."

"Circumstantial evidence. I guess you can't ask your mother directly about it. Have you checked whether any Adesidas were serving in the DRC?"

"There weren't . . . not that that proves anything, because he said 'relative' and it could be another name."

Both men look out to sea.

Achieving Superpersonhood:

"Kamiri, if my suspicion is right and it becomes public knowledge, what will people think of me?" Kamiri laughs. "It's not funny, Kamiri. This is serious."

"OK. I think it would make you a bastard love child."

Hassan is exasperated: "Damn it, Kamiri, what would people think?"

"Well, the media will be all over you, and they'll try to make you out as some kind of hero – as an Army officer. If you were still a terrorist, they'd make you some kind of devil."

"And my parents?"

"The media will want to know all the secrets. As an Army officer, the assumptions will be that the secrets are all good secrets; as a terrorist, the secrets will be bad secrets."

"But I'm the same person: Army officer or terrorist."

"No, you're not."

"Well, my parents are the same."

"They have very little to do with who you are."

I, the Other, have to concede that Hassan is a different person. I steered him in a direction I liked, but he chose to go the other way, and now has that awful confidence that that he's got it right. I never give up, but once confidence sets in, it's hard to shake.

The Other is right. Hassan's career has evolved into confidence: not just confidence in himself as an army officer, but more importantly, confidence that he is committing his life to a path that is worthwhile and honorable. A vital evolution requiring introspection, experimentation, dedication and a willingness to take temporary detours. Too often, I find people stuck in an unsatisfactory detour on the way to the life they deserve and need.

Chapter 22

Romance

Nearly every weekend, when he isn't on duty, Hassan gets into his polished red sports car and drives to City. Almost always, there is a 'date' with Dorothy: a casual dinner, a simple lunch, a movie, or a visit to a museum, depending on her schedule – three hours at most. The rest of the weekend, he spends with friends in the university area, going home for the night, where he is welcomed warmly by the staff. Relationships with his family are more problematic. When he first started returning, his mother devoted half an hour to ask him about life in the army, leaving him a sense of her pride in the man he had become. One morning, she asked if he still 'saw anything of that Christian woman doctor'. It was a random, conversational, query: one that could be briefly dismissed, with the distraction of the questioner, before moving on. His response, to the effect that he saw her most weekends, clearly shocked her. Recovering from her stunned silence, she asked: "What are your intentions regarding her? Certainly not marriage, I hope."

"I don't know, Momma. At the moment, we are just friends."

"I trust that your friendship will not extend in the direction of marriage, Hassan. If you choose to expand it in an erotic direction, I would be understanding. There are, it can be said, numerous prominent Muslims who have Christian mistresses - men always seem to want what they don't have – but these men all recognize that to solemnize their relationships would throw their social and business positions into doubt. For us, marrying a Christian would be an act of apostasy."

"But Mother, the Prophet referred to Christians as 'people of the book', meaning that they share with us scripture, history and a belief in the one true God."

"Hassan, the Prophet – the blessings of Allah upon him – was speaking only in the sense that Christians are not the enemy, but he certainly wasn't blessing inter-marriage!"

Hassan knows several Muslims who have married Christians, and they seem to be happy and successful. . . . *But there's no point in arguing with her about this now.*

When he sees his siblings at home, they were, at first, prepared to have a brief chat about what was, to them, his uniquely divergent lifestyle, recognizing its value, and his apparent, unexpected success. This interest opened further after his well-received discussion at the Thursday Mecca Women's Club. But following the confrontation with his mother, interactions with his siblings slipped into brevity and vagueness. There were occasional oblique references to 'your Christian cupcake'. Hassan is puzzled until he realizes that having a 'Christian cupcake' <u>before</u> marriage represents a threat to family virtue.

'Christian cupcake'? Are there also 'Muslim cupcakes'?
Are we slipping back into the know-nothing Dark Ages?
I, the One, say don't categorize to demean; accept that you are diverse!

Hassan has an ill-defined, persistent longing, a feeling of incompleteness, as if the well-regarded Captain Hassan Arusei had unveiled a live self-statue in full dress, which, on closer observation, is lacking an arm or a leg.

For Hassan, Dorothy seems to be the one who could complete that fractionality. She is a person of intelligence, of substance, of character; she is engaging and likeable, pretty – perhaps even beautiful, and they are certainly friends. As Hassan weighs her many virtues, he begins to notice what seems to him her missing piece: sensuality. *Perhaps the experience of rape destroyed her sensuality.* When he thinks of her body, he admits, freely, that it must be beautiful, even desirable, but there is no voltage there, no potential electricity between them. *How can that be? Is it her? Or is it me? I am not bad looking, and I have had lovers who said that I am handsome, one even called me Adonis – I think she meant that I am more than handsome. Perhaps if our relationship changed – if it became closer – her sensuality would blossom.*

They are having lunch at a small, Italian restaurant near the hospital. There is no music, but there are three white flowers in a tiny vase; Dorothy doesn't drink wine before duty, Hassan is having a beer, it is quiet: only four of the dozen tables are occupied. He has struggled to find a plan for opening the topic: like an opening chess move, it should be to the point but vague. He begins by telling her the improved relations with his family, and that he feels accepted for the first time.

"That's excellent, Hassan. I think it's comforting to have a warm family."

"I have a lot of respect for your father. He's a good man."

"My mother's very sweet; she's a worrier. My sister has grown up a lot; she's studying psychology at university."

"Have you thought about having your own family, Dorothy?"

"Yes, but not now. I have another year before I am qualified."

"Aren't some of your colleagues already married?"

"Yes, but that's not for me. To be a good doctor you must learn so much," she looks up with a smile, "and I don't want to be qualified as a half doctor."

"Would you consider a longer engagement?"

She cocks her head to one side. "Is that not quite a hypothetical question, Hassan?"

"No, Dorothy, it's a question about the two of us."

Achieving Superpersonhood:

Dorothy's eyes wander over the distance behind him, searching for a suitable response. "I think ... I think that we are good friends, Hassan, but I don't think marriage would work for me."

"Is there someone else, Dorothy?"

I, the Other, whisper 'Kamiri' to Dorothy, but it is ignored.

"No, I spend nearly all my free time with you, Hassan. I think you know that my Christian faith is very important to me. I believe that in a marriage, two people become one, and their beliefs must be one, as well. When there are children, they must be raised in the common beliefs. I have no right to ask you to become a Christian, Hassan, and I recognize that it would be very difficult for you."

"So the answer to my question is 'no'."

"I'm afraid so, Hassan, but I will always want to be your friend."

Hassan drives slowly, robotically, back to Coast City. He has suffered a crushing defeat. *I am a failure* keeps running through his mind. *I am not good enough for her. Maybe she doesn't like that I'm in the Army ... but she came to my graduation ... maybe she knows my mother doesn't like her ... maybe she wouldn't want to have sex with me ... perhaps there is someone else. I'm just not good enough for her.*

The One asks him gently if he is surprised by what has happened.

Not surprised, actually, no. Deep down I was afraid this was going to happen. I just had to know. I must get on with my life. If she won't have me, maybe someone else will. All this rubbish about Christianity ... why can't she convert? Then we could have a common faith.

The One asks, Would you convert?

Me convert? No. How could I? I have devoted my life to Allah and to the voice of the Prophet. My family would disown me; my friends would disappear.
Perhaps she is right.

But for some months, his mood is low, as if he is engulfed in a dark, sunless mist, his commands have a tentative tone, and he is envious of his drinking colleagues, who wash away their pains.

At her work, *poor Hassan!* seems to perpetuate itself in Dorothy's thoughts. *I shouldn't have said 'No' so quickly. He's heartbroken now. But it wouldn't be fair for me to pretend . . . to pretend that there was something more to our relationship. I should have told him long ago, 'You're just a friend, Hassan', but there was never an obvious time . . . he never pushed before – though I knew it was coming . . . eventually. 'Just a friend' sounds callous, <u>un</u>friendly. Besides, he wasn't just . . . a friend . . . he was a special friend . . . I guess for me he's a sort of Prodigal Son, and I <u>liked</u> being connected to him. But could I ever marry him? Yes, I think faith is an issue, but his dogma is gone now. When I'm with him, I sometimes feel 'hug him!', but I'm always afraid he'd misunderstand and try to take things in a direction I don't want to go. He is good looking, but there's just no spark, no 'have a go, Dorothy!' urge.* She smiles. *When I'm with Kamiri, I have to keep myself on a short leash.*

* * *

"It is for you, Kamiri, to choose your own path." There is a sense of finality in the old man's statement, as if it is wrong for him to give advice.

"I understand that, Baba, but I would be foolish not to consider the counsel of my father, who is wiser than I."

Achieving Superpersonhood:

Mchumba shifts to a more comfortable position on the rustic bench. "I don't understand: what is this final payment from the Lions?"

"If I decide not to take the coaching offer, they are offering a sum of money – how much hasn't been decided yet – which I can either have in one payment, or a payment every month for as long as I live."

Mchumba regards his son doubtfully. "As long as you live? How is that possible?"

"The payment each month would be much smaller than the one payment, but larger than you might think."

Mchumba gives a snort: "Bank magic! What is against taking money every month?"

"Nothing. You just don't get a lot at the beginning."

Another snort. "Getting a lot at the beginning is not always good, particularly if you get more at the end. What is against taking the one large payment?"

"You have to pay the government more in taxes."

Mchumba nods vigorously. "I should have guessed." He considers for a moment. "I think the many payments are better than one, particularly if they pay for food and shelter."

"OK."

"But that's not the only reason. Are you still in communication with your God?"

Kamiri asks, "What does God have to do with this?"

"If you have enough money to survive, you can wait until your God can show you your future."

In the evolving distance, there is an extended elephant family under a large grove of acacia trees; the matriarch flaps her ears to identify the source of the unwelcome noise from Kamiri's motorcycle. Drawing even, though at two hundred meters' distance, he gives her a salute, at which she turns, pushing her family deeper into the grove.

I think my father gave me a plan I like: I can look for work which is right for me, but pays less, yet I can get by with the monthly payment. The big payment makes me feel guilty when I see how my parents and others live in Village.

He remains seated on his motorcycle outside a ramshackle shop, whose sign says: "Get connected! Cheap mobiles here!" *If they sell phones here, there must be coverage.*
"Hello, this is Home Away."
"This is Kamiri; may I speak to Joseph, please?"
"Hi, Kamiri, this is Dorothy. Where are you?"
"Oh, Dorothy, I didn't expect to hear you. I'm on my way into City, and I was wondering whether Joseph has time to see me."
"Yes, of course, Kamiri. When can we expect you?"
"In about two hours, I think."
"OK. I'll tell Dad to expect you. Maybe we can have a bite to eat afterwards?"
"Yes, but don't you have to be in the hospital or in class?"
"My shift starts at four this afternoon. We'll see you soon, Kamiri."

Joseph is skeptical. "I don't think I'm the right person to help you, Kamiri. I can't even come close to finding a match for the pay you've been getting."
"Joseph, you know I'm a rich, poor village kid with a village high school diploma, who used to play football. I was just hoping you could tell me what my options are."
"OK. First of all, have the Lions offered you any sort of position?"
"Yes, they've offered me assistant coach of their under twenty-ones."
"I would say, 'take it'."
"I'm not so sure. I've talked to Eddie, my roommate, and other players about it. They all say that coaching isn't just

coaching, it's about winning, it's keeping the players, their parents and the owner happy; it's about acting like a winner even if you're losing."

Joseph smiles. "So you're a football player, but you can't see yourself as an actor."

"Yeah, I can't pretend to be what I'm not – that's what I'm like. Besides, they say that if the owner isn't happy, he'll send you to look for other coaching in Africa, or Asia, even China. That's not for me; I'm a village kid."

Joseph pushes back his chair. "There are three kinds of work that could earn you a pretty decent living: being a manager in a business, becoming an expert like a lawyer, a scientist or an artist, or owning your own business. Of these, I think to one that could apply to you would be to buy a business."

"You mean like a restaurant, or a shoe shop, or a printing business?"

"Could be most anything."

"But it would involve sitting in some kind of office and fixing things with employees, customers, sellers, banks, city people?"

"Most likely."

"That's not for me, Joseph; besides, money's not that important. Don't forget: I used to live on less than five hundred shillings a week."

Joseph is thinking and the One is helping him. *Outdoors. Village kid.*

"Uh, Kamiri, we talked once about park rangers. Do you recall?" Kamiri nods. "They're doing their annual recruitment at the moment."

"Yes?"

"The job involves a lot of walking with a rifle."

"Walking's not a problem – as long as it's in a park and not the city. Don't know much about guns, but I've got a friend who can teach me."

"The pay is only four thousand, nine hundred and fifty shillings a month, but the Park Service provides accommodation and most meals."

"Can I find out more about it?"

"Yes, I can arrange an interview for you. . . I have to say, though, Kamiri, that the Park Service will wonder why a rich, famous kid would want to work for them."

Damn! I wish I'd worn my white sleeveless top with the pearl buttons. Dorothy is trying to make up for the missing, seductive garment with vivacious interest in her companion. "I think, Kamiri, that the Park Service will be falling all over themselves to convince you to join them – then, they'll probably make you their poster boy."

"What is a poster boy?"

"He would be an individual they use in all their publicity – on TV, in brochures – to get their message across to the public."

"You mean because I used to play football?"

"Yes, you're a well-known person that people trust."

Kamiri is incredulous. "That's crazy! What would I say?"

"Well, you'd tell them about how the Park Service protects animals against poachers and does lots of other things to help us enjoy our parks."

"I could do that. I would like to do that."

Dorothy pushes aside the remnants of her chef's salad. "Did Hassan tell you that he and I have broken up?"

"No, he didn't; I'm sorry, Dorothy."

Dorothy lifts one shoulder negligently. "Well, I don't think we were quite right for each other."

"You mean you weren't really in love?" Kamiri cocks his head attentively, his hamburger suddenly neglected.

"No, not really. . . Have you ever been in love, Kamiri?"

"Well, when I was thirteen, I thought I was in love with a girl called Mary."

"And since then?"

"There seem to be only two kinds of girls. Ordinary girls that you can go out on a date with, but you shouldn't really marry, and special girls that you can't marry."

"Why can't you marry a special girl?"

"Because I'm an ordinary village kid, a Kikuyu."

"For goodness sake, Kamiri, who cares what tribe you represent? Kikuyu is as good as any. What matters is that you're not ordinary, a kid or . . . or . . ."

"A villager? I am from a small, poor village, Dorothy."

Dorothy's head is shaking violently. "You're missing the point, Kamiri! There is nothing small, shabby or provincial about you. You are something different now."

"What is that?"

Dorothy considers for a long moment. "You are someone I respect, Kamiri – a fellow Christian, who honestly values other people, and who has taught himself how to find the right way in the world." She pauses for a moment. "Besides (there is a broad smile) you're pretty good looking."

Kamiri laughs. "I certainly value your opinion, Dorothy, which – for reasons I don't understand – is quite biased."

* * *

Boredom and frustration have overtaken Hassan; he blames it on military base routine in the summer, but he is vaguely aware that he has happily been on the base in previous Julys. But then, there was Dorothy on his not-so-distant horizon, to occupy his vacant moments. Now, too many of his moments are vacant. *I've got to do something – anything!*

He consults the battalion bulletin board. There are 'lift notices' by officers who want, or who have cars and are willing to provide, a ride in a specified direction.

There is the Plan of the Day and the Plan of the Week: boredom submerged in mindless action.

Maintenance Notices: "Hot water in Bachelor Officers Quarters B7 will not be available from 08:00 on the 17th until 18:00 on the 18th. Please use other facilities."

There is an Executive Officer's Notice regarding requests for leave.

Then there is a long list of Requests for Volunteers:

"To provide musical (or other) entertainment at Silver Leaf Home for the Aged."

"To referee boy's football, aged 6 to 8, evenings, locally."

"To present Army Life to students at City University. See Executive Officer."

Yeah! I could do that. I'd like to do that. Drive to City, see the campus again, talk to some kids, get out of here, do something useful.

I, the One, confess to modest receptivity intervention – not complicated, just a light stirring of the subconscious.

Hassan finds Lieutenant Colonel Ojukwu in his one-window office, crowded with multi-colored filing binders. "Sir, I am interested in that volunteer assignment to present Army Life to students at City University."

Ojukwu swings around, mopping his face with a blue bandana, which he re-drapes over the arm of his swivel chair. "Why the interest, Mr Arusei?"

"I like to talk about the Army, sir, and I used to study at City University."

"Sit down, Mr Arusei." The Executive Officer removes his rimless glasses and polishes them with the bandana. "The talk is a PowerPoint presentation prepared by the Army Recruiting Office. I think there's also a short video. It seems Recruiting is a bit under-staffed at the moment. The assignment interest you, Mr Arusei?"

"Yes, sir."

"Very well. You'll be as good at this as anyone. I'll make arrangements. You have your own transport?"

"Yes, sir."
"Naturally, you can submit a claim for the mileage."

Hassan has borrowed a laptop from battalion office, he has viewed the video – *Too rah, rah – need to talk it down,* perused the (rather defensive) Responses to Difficult Questions, and practiced the presentation, without notes, the way he feels it should be presented.

He arrives at Sociology Lecture Hall 2 half an hour before 1 pm. It is cavernous and deserted: an endless tier of wooden seats ascending toward the distant ceiling focused on a lecture table and three huge white boards. Careful examination of the lecture table reveals projector controls, USB connections and power sockets. Within ten minutes the central white board lights up with 'Welcome to the Country Army: Opportunities and Challenges'. As there is no place to sit at the lecture table (lectures are expected to be delivered in a standing position), he seats himself on the lecture table, facing the hoped-for audience, his polished brown shoes and creased uniform trousers floating above the floor.

"Hello, captain. I am Roosevelt Mwangi." He extends a hand. "I'm a student activities co-coordinator." He glances at the white board. "I see you're all ready to go. Is there anything you need?"

"We seem to be missing an audience."

Mwangi glances at his watch. "Yes. Well, I expect some students will be along shortly. They time things down to the last second, you know." He looks down at the precious clipboard he is hugging. "So, I will introduce you, and then, unfortunately, I have to run along. Is that all right?"

"I should think so."

Mwangi finds himself unexpectedly shoved aside by an energetic, pretty young woman wearing a ruffled blouse and tight jeans. "Hello captain, do you remember me?"

Oh dear! Who is she? I should know. The ease he had been feeling is suddenly shattered by this brash and vaguely familiar young woman. "Well," he began, "I recognize your face but I can't think of your name."

She feigns disapproval with a shake of her head. "You came to my house . . ." she continues in a teasing tone, "you met my parents . . ." she pauses for a sign of recognition, "I was about fifteen then, and I was watching TV. . . and . . ."

"Oh, yes! You're Miss Maiyo, Dorothy's sister!"

There is a disapproving tone, "We don't talk about my stupid sister, and, yes, I am Mary Maiyo."

Hassan's tension evaporates in the warmth radiating from this attractive girl. "So are you a student here, Mary?"

"Yes. I'll get my degree in psychology next year, and when I heard that you would be here to give a talk, I thought, 'Well, I have to be there!' I'm a big fan of yours, Hassan."

Hassan, nonplussed, repeats, "A big fan?"

"Yes, of course. I've read all about you. About your graduation with the Sword of Honor. About how you defeated the terrorists at Coast City Stadium and about your tour in the DRC. And now, I get to meet you in person and listen to your talk."

Lamely, he asks, "Are you thinking of the Army after graduation?"

"Oh, no! I would be hopeless in the Army, but after all this time, I . . ." A loud buzzer sounds; she looks around. "So you'll be starting soon, and I'll just have a seat here." She seats herself in the second row, center, crosses her legs and leans forward in expectation.

At the conclusion of Mwangi's introduction, there are about a dozen students seated in the first five rows and three perched high up in the lecture hall.

In spite of Hassan's instruction to "interrupt at any time with questions", the audience remains silent, with facial expressions and body language ranging from keen interest (Mary) to disgust (two in the back and one up front).

"That completes my presentation. I'll take any questions you may have now."

Achieving Superpersonhood:

Mary's hand shoots up. "Captain, isn't it quite frightening to have people shooting at you?"

Hassan explains that training, discipline and teamwork tend to diminish the fear factor in actual combat, and that it is the role of the officers to give their men (and women) confidence in the run-up to actual combat.

A loud voice from the back: "That's just bullshit! My friend says the grunts in front are scared shitless when the officers in back shout 'move up'."

Hassan considers the heckler: tall, thin, very black, unshaven in an unwashed Rolling Stones T-shirt and an angry face. "Well, I don't know where your friend had his experience, but I doubt if it happened in the Country Army."

"Are you accusing me of being a liar?"

Mary springs to her feet, turns around and shouts. "Are you here to learn something or to start a fight about which you know nothing? Why don't you push off?"

"Shut up, bitch!"

"Who is he?" Mary demands of the students around her.

Somebody says: "Kiki Kimani."

Mary begins taking the steps up the theatre two at a time. "OK, Kiki Kimani, if you want to keep your place at City U, you better move your dumb ass out of here!"

The heckler, taken aback by the approaching female fury, sidesteps, slinks down the far aisle and disappears. Several students applaud; others begin to drift off.

Mary and two others continue to ask questions until only she remains. "Are you hungry, Hassan?"

"Well. I . . ."

"Come with me; let's get some lunch."

Hassan has lost his bearings. This headstrong, brash woman, unlike any he ever met or dreamed of meeting – if asked, he would have denied any interest in meeting such a woman – has completely captured his attention; it is as if a swan had found itself in the company of a white peacock. Years of being the runt of the litter have ingrained a sense of self-effacement, and an instant distrust of cocky people. But this one isn't just confident; there are elements of realistic self-denigration, jocularity, and unpredictability, as if she savors her occasionally erratic behavior. She seems able to read people with instinctive accuracy; when he asked her how she knew that the heckler would retreat under her oral and confrontational threat, she says that she made him out to be a bully, and that she learned in class that bullies are usually cowards.

"But what if he had stood his ground and told <u>you</u> to push off?"

"I probably would have collapsed into negotiation mode."

Hassan chuckles with admiration. "So your psychology studies are really important to you." She nods. "And do you see yourself as a practicing psychologist some day?"

"Practicing every day, yes, but probably not with a patient on my couch. For me, psychology is the means of reading people – to get what you want in life."

"What do you want in life, Mary?"

She gives him an appraising look. "I haven't decided, but I can tell you this: it will be good, it will be important, and it will be different."

He contemplates the dregs in his coffee cup. "You say you're a fan of mine; I find that hard to understand. You don't really know me, but you've read – and perhaps heard – about me. From a psychologist's point of view, what about me interests you?"

"Fair question. Courage: very important. If you had been the one marching up the steps to that heckler and if he had held his ground, you would have punched him. Even with a year's karate training, I could never do that. Ambition: vital. You may not have recognized it at the time, but you had to <u>want</u> that sword to win it. Perseverance: very good to have. I understand you went to work in an abattoir while you sorted out your career. Concern for others. I think here we have some common ground: you returning to your Muslim roots out of disgust with Dhul Fikar, and I with my hatred of hecklers." She paused for a moment. "I could go on, but I'm not a fan of swelled heads."

It wasn't a five-course luncheon: just a large Coke Zero, burgers, bajias (fried potatoes), sliced pineapple with lemon sherbet, and tea in a student cafeteria. They sat down at 2:05 and parted at 5:15 with a planned reunion the following Saturday.

* * *

Dedicated to nature, the Park Service has none of the conventional affinity for high-rise accommodation in City. Its offices are a collection of mud and palm-thatched premises in the veldt, two kilometers south of the east-west highway. Kamiri, astride his motorcycle, studies a 'Welcome to Country Park Service' billboard, which includes a map of the 'campus'. His first glance suggests that interviews will be held in the largest, central edifice, but then he notices a large, outlying hut, whose position suggests banishment, with the label: 'Personnel'. He unfolds the letter, and scans it for the title of the person he is to meet: 'Recruitment Official'. *OK, he must be in there.* He parks the motorcycle outside of 'Personnel' when it occurs to him that Recruitment Official isn't necessarily a he. The name of his interviewer is Fanaka Ohiambo. *But Fanaka can be either.* A further examination of the letter offers no clues.

Inside the hut, there is a battered wooden desk, occupied by an old woman with rheumy eyes and a drooping mouth; she is wearing a tightly-wrapped gray turban and a black-maroon kanga. At first, the woman does not respond to Kamiri's request in Swahili; he tries again in Kikuyu.

In Swahili, she drawls: "I heard you the first time," and slowly moves to pick up the phone. Kamiri sidesteps the three rigid black plastic chairs; his feet crunch on the traditional Masai sisal carpet as he turns to examine the native art on the walls, most of which are primitive but colorful depictions of animals.

"Hello, Kamiri." A warm and enthusiastic voice – in English – from a short, smiling barrel of a woman dressed in a sunburst-colored kanga. Her round, polished face is beaming, there are darker tribal scars on her cheeks, and outlandishly large gold bangles tremble from her ears. She extends her hand in welcome then leads him down a narrow corridor.

"I am Fanaka Ohiambo," she says, when seated at her file-laden wooden table. The walls are scattered with large black-and-white animal photographs. "I never expected to meet you in person, and certainly not for a job interview."

"Actually, I had an opportunity to apply for a position here some years ago, but I had already accepted another job."

"Another job?" She scans a paper on her desk.

"Yes, I was working at the City abattoir."

An ominous frown. "An abattoir?"

"Yes, ma'am. When you have no money and nothing to eat, the abattoir is salvation."

"But, it's not mentioned on your CV, and it looks like your career started in football."

"I'm sorry ma'am, I've never done this before, and the paper you have was prepared by Joseph at Home Away."

Scowling, she hands him the sheet of paper. "What else is missing from this, Kamiri?"

He examines it thoughtfully. "Apart from the abattoir, I worked for my brother when I first came to City."

"And what was his business?"

"Drugs."

"You mean pharmaceuticals."

"No, ma'am, I mean drugs."

"Have you got proof of rehab?"

"No, ma'am, I never tried the drugs."

Ohiambo studies him for a time. "Why did you quit your brother's business?"

"I was afraid of being arrested, and I didn't like living with my brother."

Achieving Superpersonhood:

"What didn't you like about living with your brother?"

"He didn't keep his promises and sometimes I had to sleep on the floor when one of his girls came over."

She rolls her eyes and looks at the ceiling. "Kamiri, have you ever been arrested?"

"No, ma'am."

"Kamiri, can you think of anything in your life that you're ashamed of – I mean, if it was printed in the newspapers?"

He considers. "Well, there was the time I was selling drugs for my brother, but it was only a couple of weeks, and I was involved in that protest when they shut down the City University newspaper."

"What happened then?"

"I threw some stones at the policemen."

"Was anyone hurt?"

"No, ma'am."

"Anything else, Kamiri? Any gambling, sex scandals, cheating, theft, that sort of thing?"

He shakes his head. "I'll tell you later why your answers to those questions are important. Now, I'd like to get back to the abattoir."

"You used to work there?" a surprised Kamiri asks.

"No, Kamiri," (somewhat exasperated) "I want to return to the subject. How does working in an abattoir make you feel about animals?"

"Oh, I see what you mean. I think there are two kinds of animals: domestic animals and wild animals. It's OK to kill domestic animals, because they're raised to be slaughtered. It's not OK to kill wild animals, because they don't belong to man."

"What about hunting?"

He shakes his head. "I don't believe in it."

She pauses. "What do you believe in Kamiri?"

"I believe in God, and I believe in His son, Jesus."

"So you're a Christian?"

"Yes, I'm a member of the West End Baptist Church in Coast City."

"Do you have any girlfriends, Kamiri?"
"Well, there's one girl I like and I think she likes me."
"Think you might get married?"
A slight shake of the head. "I don't think so."
"Why not?"
A long pause. "She's a doctor and I'm just a village boy."
Ohiambo leans back in her chair, contemplating her interviewee. "Kamiri, you are not just a village boy; you are a celebrity."
"What do you mean?"
"I mean you're famous." He gives a negligent shrug. "Kamiri, why do you want to join the Park Service as a ranger?"
"Well, you probably know I've been injured and can't play football anymore. The idea of being a Park Ranger came up, and the more I thought about it, the more I liked it, because I like being outdoors, and I like animals – our wild animals are a precious resource – so I believe what the Park Service does is very important, and I was thinking that maybe I could help."
"In what way?"
"Well, lots of people know me, and maybe I could give talks about what the Park Service does and why it's important."
"Mmmm . . . You know that we aren't able to pay anything like what you can make even playing minor league football?"
"Yes, I know, but Ms Ohiambo, you can't . . ."
She interrupts: "Please call me Fanaka."
"Well, Fanaka, I believe that when you feel you're being called – if you know what I mean – you can't allow money to force you to say 'no'. I mean: I've got a sort of pension from the Lions, so I can get by all right, and I have a feeling that I would end up punching myself later if I didn't try for this job. Money is nice, but what's important in life is doing what you like and what you believe in."

I, the One, suggested several weeks ago to the pastor at the West End Baptist Church, that a sermon on the subject of 'being called' would be timely.

Achieving Superpersonhood:

Ohiambo considers for a moment. She picks up her phone. "It's Ohiambo. May I have a word? Hello, Mr Bamgboshe, I've talked to him, and he's fine. OK."

She gets up from her table. "Mr Bamgboshe wants to see you."

"Who is he?

"Our managing director."

I, the One, didn't prompt anything in the foregoing conversation, but in the week prior to the discussion, I added a slight bias to the attitudes of the participants so that each was successful: Fanaka in assuring herself that Kamiri is 'fine', and Kamiri in impressing Fanaka with his honesty.

Kamiri is sitting astride his motorcycle, watching a herd of tail-twitching wildebeests graze on the dry savannah. *I can't believe it. She took me to see Mr Bamgboshe, the managing director of the whole Park Service. Too bad he's not a Lions fan, but he does like football, and he asked me about talks I've given. He said I'll have what he called a screen test, and that if I pass that, they'll pay me twenty thousand for each commercial and ten thousand for each audience talk.*

And Fanaka said I can start ranger training as soon as I pass my physical.

He watches a flock of pale flycatchers settle on the backs of the wildebeests.

I am kind of floating . . . no cares . . . life is good. Strange. When I was accepted by the Lions, I was excited, determined, challenged. Now I feel at peace. I'm happy. I am me. Thank God for His love of me – which is undeserved.

Several of the black bulls turn together to face an invisible enemy.

Probably a cheetah. I can see her tail. Looks like she is giving up. Now, I have to go and thank Joseph.

"Hi Kamiri, my dad says that you got the job."

"Yes, Dorothy, subject to a physical exam, which should be no problem."

"Are you happy about it, Kamiri?"

A soft laugh. "Yes, I am."

"You'll be an armed policeman in the wilderness with animals and friends who will be depending on you."

"Yes, I suppose so. Speaking of animals, I saw a cheetah this afternoon."

"Up close?"

"No, she was about two hundred meters away."

"She?"

"Yes, females carry their tails differently."

Dorothy chuckles for a moment. "Perhaps I can learn something from the cheetahs. I understand you're going to have a screen test."

"Yeah, I don't know what to expect."

"I think what you have to do is to pretend that the camera is a very interested person, and just talk to it as you usually would. You'll be fine, Kamiri. Where are you going to be living?"

"I understand that the Park Service has various shelters which are scattered around."

"Will you be able to keep your motorcycle?"

"I think so."

"That's good. Then you can come and see me." An uneasy laugh from Kamiri. "Seriously, Kamiri, you have some time before you start; why don't we get together later this week? How about Friday?"

They settle on Saturday for lunch.

"What's eating you, Kamiri? Eddie looks over at his flat-mate.

"I don't know . . . I just don't get it." Kamiri, elbows on knees, chin cupped in hands, is looking out the window.

"You made a date; what's the problem?"

"Well, that's just it."

"What, you don't like her?"

"No, I like her a lot. It just seems that sometimes she is chasing me."

"That's easy. Trip, and let her catch you."

"But what happens then?"

"Do I have to draw you a picture?"

"No! I'm just afraid it won't work out."

Eddie contemplates his friend. "What are you worried about, Kamiri?"

"Eddie, she's a doctor – a real doctor! She's educated. She's been to Europe. Her father is a managing director, and . . ."

Eddie holds up a restraining hand. "So you're afraid she'll discover that Kamiri, the good-looking, celebrity football player, is really just a dumb village kid?" A concessionary nod and shrug from Kamiri. "How long have you known her?"

"I met her when I first came to City."

"So you think maybe she's a little slow . . ." Kamiri frowns. ". . . and she hasn't figured out that the dumb village kid she met a while ago has changed: the hungry chick that fell out of the nest has become a falcon?"

Kamiri gives a long sigh; he is sitting up straight. His eyes search the far wall (perhaps the answer is written there).

"Kamiri, you're not afraid of anything. She's challenging you to a duel. Are you going to wimp out?"

For Kamiri, being in the ranger training classroom is like being in a perfect time machine: he is back in his childhood classroom – but it isn't cramped seats and writing surfaces, it's individual desks; it isn't an irritable woman teacher, it's an enthusiastic male instructor; it isn't writing and arithmetic, it's flora, fauna, geography, meteorology, topography, laws and regulations: real adult education, and he slurps it up like a thirsty desert traveler.

And it isn't all classroom, it's outdoor education: plenty of field trips, camping techniques, map reading and navigation, rifle range, dealing with injured animals, with annoying tourists and with poachers.

"Poachers and bush meat hunters are a scourge!" the instructor says. "It is illegal to kill any animal in the park. They belong to Country and all of us as citizens. We all feel a loss when one of them is killed illegally."

A future ranger asks, "What about the foreign hunters who pay a lot of money to kill our animals?"

The instructor nods. "Foreign hunts are very carefully controlled and involve only single animals which are not threatened species. Permits are very expensive and the money goes to support orphaned animal facilities and the Park Service generally."

On two occasions, trainees came across elephants which had been shot and their tusks sawed off. One was a magnificent old bull whose tusks would have weighed at least 80 kilos, valued at about a quarter of a million shillings each. The other was a thirty-year old female, still mourned by her small calf.

"What are we supposed to do when we come across poachers?"

"The first priority is to alert Field Service on your radio, giving them your location, and any information you have on the poachers. You may have seen the photos in the camps of suspected poachers. The second priority, when help arrives, which will be soon, is take them into custody and disarm them."

"Can we shoot poachers?"

"In no case should you shoot first. You may threaten to use your rifle to persuade them to disarm. But you should only return fire if fired on."

Kamiri learns he is to be assigned to Kioko National Park, the largest in the area.

Chapter 23

Ivory Poacher

Kamiri gazes about him with pride and satisfaction. The veldt with its tall seer grass and acacia reaches to the horizon in the north; to the east, a dense grove of locust and quinine trees marks the bank of the Rufiji River; there is a patch of green juniper around the jagged outcropping of rock to the west; but it is to the semi-forested south they are walking: toward the panorama of green muna, ash and khaya and the fire-blackened skeletons of shea trees. It is quiet, except for the crunching of the grass underfoot, the warbling of roller birds and the occasional invitation of a distant cuckoo. A small herd of gazelle is sheltering under a stand of acacia, wildebeests and zebra are scattered in the distance, and there were three young elephants just beyond the rock formation.

Faraji, a middle-aged ranger, makes good company. A small man, he murmurs endless songs, which to Kamiri's ears seem like native lullabies, except he never sings them at night; rather, he wraps himself in a dark cotton shawl, covers much of his face with his floppy ranger hat and falls asleep, snoring gently, almost at once. Faraji is disinclined to small talk, but his eyes and ears are keen: identifying a camouflaged leopard in a tree three hundred meters away, and hearing the cry of a fish eagle before it is visible. He is the married father of seven children who lives with his extended family in a village to the east of the park, and every six months, he joins them for a month's leave. He knows of

Kamiri's prior life as a footballer, but expresses no interest in it. Instead, he will respond, briefly, to Kamiri's frequent questions about the wildlife, viewing it as his responsibility to educate this new ranger in the lore of the veldt.

"Television people are there," Faraji announces.

Kamiri squints in the direction of his gesture, and makes out one – no, two – dark green safari jeeps huddled under the distant locust trees. "They're filming that pride of lions."

Faraji grunts his agreement. "Rufiji pride."

Continuing, they come no closer than a hundred meters from the jeeps, which are occupied by two white men, a blonde woman, and two native trackers. Faraji exchanges hand signals with the trackers. "Not much doing."

They stride on into the semi-forested area, where it is cool, steeped in shadows on the soft green carpet. A covey of plovers takes sudden, noisy flight, twisting through the labyrinth of tree trunks. A pair of kudu stare at the intruders and bound away. Kamiri pauses to admire them.

The forest begins to thin: one can see the barrier of dense green foliage along the river.

"Humph." Kamiri looks up. There is a cream-colored tent in the distance – and a safari vehicle. "We must check."

They find two European couples – probably German – sitting on fabric camp chairs by the river. Faraji speaks to the native guide, who produces the required permission. Kamiri approaches the tourists. "There are large crocodiles in the river, and they come out on land at night," he says in English. "May I suggest that you stay well back from the river at night?"

"Ja, OK."

They continue on their route south along the river. As the sun slips down toward the horizon, the watery blue of the sky overhead darkens to an intense blue before darkness overtakes it; the western clouds become yellow, light orange, pink, red and a somber purple.

They approach a khaki canvas tent built on a three-meter square wooden platform in a clearing well away from the river.

Achieving Superpersonhood:

Within a circle of stones in front, there is a scattering of gray ash and charcoal. A conspicuous padlock hangs from the tent flap. With quiet satisfaction, they bustle about: Kamiri drawing river water, Faraji unlocking the tent and lighting the kerosene lantern. Camp chairs are brought out, and after an inventory of the canned provisions, Kamiri pumps and lights the kerosene stove.

Ham, beans and kale are served on stainless plates, followed by bananas and chocolate biscuits from their knapsacks.

"There is the great she bear," Faraji announces with a motion skyward.

Kamiri leans well back. "And there is the little bear."

"There were bears here long ago," Faraji replies, "but they say that when the great she bear was taken up to heaven, taking her cub with her, the animals died out."

They place their rifles upright against the tent wall. Faraji, having elected the cot on the right, arranges his knapsack into a pillow, gives a nod to Kamiri, and stretches out, encased in the cotton shawl.

Kamiri lingers at the threshold, gazing up at the stars, and listening to the night symphony: crickets, cicadas, an owl, zebras, wild dogs, and a distant lion. He is content to be alive in this ever-changing, sensual assault by countless other unique, living things, beautiful or grotesque, hiding and obvious, noisy or silent, releasing a faint spectrum of strange odors. *There is so much to see, to learn, no end of work . . . a lifetime. I am fortunate, and I owe a great thanks.*

The first television commercial for the Park Service is exciting and daunting: intense, inescapable lighting, too many people milling about, the need not only to memorize a script, but to express genuine feelings – feelings with which a semi-somnolent audience can empathize.

The set has Kamiri sitting in a safari rover with a film projected on the screen behind him so as to give the impression that he is driving through shrub-filled woodland. For him, the difficulty is getting the words and the accompanying emotions just right. There are several consultations with the director.

Kamiri says, "I wouldn't say it that way."

"Kamiri, you clearly understand the message we're trying to establish, and you come across as sincere and caring about your message. In this next take, why don't you put the message into your own words?"

The cameras and film roll once more.

"Ninety-three seconds."

"Kamiri, that presentation was excellent. Take a break for a few minutes. When you come back, let's see if you can shorten in to about a minute, but just as good."

Kamiri can be seen off to the side of the set, looking at his watch and speaking to the wall.

Another take begins.

The director crosses his hands in a 'Finished!' gesture. "We'll use that one."

When Kamiri returns to civilization and mobile phone service from his next assignment, there is a voice mail from Dorothy: "Kamiri, I just heard your public service announcement on channel 5, and I'm afraid you've missed your calling: you should be working in front of a TV camera, full time. Seriously, though, you make the Park Service look like national heroes, and I've talked to a lot of people who were very impressed. They say things like: 'I thought he was just a footballer'. I want to celebrate with a little champagne, so give me a call when you get back."

They leave their camp at sunrise, with Faraji anxious to "have a look around; things happen at night".

They are crossing a wide, nearly treeless area, rich in low-growing thorn bushes. A forested area lies ahead.

A distant shot cracks out.

Faraji grimaces. "Not one of ours . . . at least a three fifty-seven . . . about a kilometer that way." He gestures ahead to the right.

"His truck is on the other side, so he's probably in there somewheres. Usually wears light khaki shirt and trousers and a straw hat."

The 'he' refers to a convicted poacher who has been released from prison, and whose movements the Kioko Park Service particularly wants to follow.

"What do we do if we spot him?" Kamiri asks.

Faraji lifts an indifferent shoulder. "Nothin' much. We just want him to know that the Park Service is interested in what he's doin'."

Faraji's waistband radio crackles with a distant transmission. He turns it down so as to be barely audible.

As they approach the trees, Faraji gestures to his left. "There's some high ground there. Let's have a look."

Threading their way through huge red termite mounds, they push their way through dense thickets and begin the switch-back climb up the rocky outcrop. They are nearly winded when they reach the grassy top with a lone khaya tree and a circumferential view of the forest below. Faraji has his binoculars in hand and is scanning.

An angry whiz and whack into the khaya tree. Faraji drops to the ground. "Get down, Kamiri!" But Kamiri focuses his attention on the direction from which the report comes. There! Between two trees at the edge of a small clearing is a khaki figure with rifle raised. Another angry whiz and quick bang. Instinctively, Kamiri unslings his rifle and points the muzzle at the small figure. He pulls the trigger and drops down beside Faraji, who already has his radio in hand. "Nicholson just took two shots at us. We're three kilometers west of the Rufiji U bend, on top of termite mound rock."

There is an answering cackle.

"OK, we'll wait for them." He hangs a restraining arm over Kamiri's shoulders. "No, he may still be there. We'll wait for the other two teams."

An hour later, there is a warbling whistle from the west. Cautiously, Faraji gets to his feet, and from the shelter of the khaya trunk, returns the whistle. Kamiri gets up, turns his attention to the origin of the attack, but seeing nothing, he borrows the binoculars. Scanning the distant clearing, there is nothing . . . wait . . . what is that? A light brown object . . . not a tree trunk . . . maybe an antelope . . . wrong color . . . maybe it's . . .

It was the white man, Nicholson, lying on his back, one blood-soaked hand clutching his neck, his blue eyes staring skyward. The leaves and grass at his head and shoulders are coated with sticky maroon blood. His hat lies to one side.

Six black rangers stare down at him, incredulous, shuffling their feet and tilting their heads as if a different angle will reveal the solution.

Someone says: "Maybe his tracker did it."

Faraji asks Kamiri: "Was there another shot?"

"No. I shot at him, didn't really aim, just wanted to scare him."

Faraji says, "But he was a good five hundred meters from where we were. You couldn't have hit him if you tried." He keys his radio. "Nicholson is down. Dead. Kamiri fired one warning shot, but it's doubtful that at five hundred meters it could have killed him. We're going to search the area."

Dutifully, Kamiri follows in the path made by Faraji. He is stifled in gloom – unable to bring his mind out of extreme low gear, where it displays images of the dead white man's face from every angle. When he wrenches it up a gear, it spews out hopelessly impossible alternatives: maybe there is another angry poacher, perhaps his bearer turned on him, possibly a suicide, an accident. As each flimsy proposal sinks away, deflated, his stride slows, his head descends on his chest, he hears nothing, and all that he sees is the back of Faraji's shirt ahead. *What have I done? Oh God, forgive me. Let me wake up from this nightmare. How could this happen?*

"Look there," someone shouts

Diverting, they see a huge gray mass – a bull elephant, pitched over on his side, the blood from the single bullet wound in his temple still oozing over an open eye. His tusks have been sawn off, and the vegetation around his head is beaten down.

"Is that bastard Mbugua still working for him?" someone asks.

Faraji says, "Probably."

Another query: "Why don't the Park Service revoke his license?"

"Never got the goods on him," Faraji responds. "Besides, his father's a tribal elder."

In a clearing to the east, they find a pickup truck; a tarpaulin covers the back. Under the tarpaulin are a pair of trophy-sized tusks, miscellaneous tools and a hacksaw.

"Don't touch the saw," Faraji warns, "his prints are probably on it."

Another radio report is filed.

Back at the death site, there are three uniformed policemen and a civilian who identifies himself as a detective inspector. The body has been covered with a tarpaulin.

The inspector holds up two shiny brass objects. "Two shell casings. You say that he fired at you twice?"

Faraji says: "Yeah, twice. Damn near hit me the first time."

"Where were you when he shot at you?"

They climb termite mound rock.

The inspector holds up another shell casing. "This yours?" he asks Kamiri.

Kamiri nods.

Among the termite mounds, the rangers begin to part company. One of them takes Kamiri by the shoulder. "I can see you're worried about this, mate. You shouldn't be. I know you're a new ranger, but you didn't do nothing wrong, and the Park Service will clear you. It was self-defense. That bastard Nicholson had it comin'. He's been killin' elephants for years."

Kamiri nods his thanks.

But the sorrow and regret cling to him. Killing another human being – regardless of justification – is, for Kamiri, an inescapable sin. *If only I had got down right away, like Faraji said, it wouldn't have happened. But then maybe he would have come hunting for the two of us. Better if he'd killed me. But then he would have killed Faraji, too.*

All of Kamiri's thinking changes nothing: he is guilty of a great sin. The only slightly offsetting mitigation is the image of the murdered elephant. *So Nicholson was also a great sinner.*

Unburdening himself with his fellow rangers has become impossible: for his colleagues, Kamiri is a hero: he's the ranger who finally got the one who's been killing our elephants. He considers going to see Hassan during his time off, but his instincts tell him that Hassan will simply repeat the ranger's justifications. He doesn't need someone to tell him that what he did was OK; he needs someone who will listen with understanding to his feelings.

Dorothy.

Over lunch, he reveals the entire story to Dorothy, who silently and attentively takes in the sensations conveyed by his somber words and hang-dog body language.

"What an awful experience, Kamiri." He waits for her to launch a palliative, but she ignores what he did and why it is right. Instead, she wants to discuss his consequent feelings.

"You have really been put through a terrible wringer, and I don't suppose your colleagues were much help."

He shakes his head. "They think I'm some kind of hero for killing another human being."

She gives a staccato snort. "I'm proud of you, Kamiri." She waves away his puzzled frown. "I'm not thinking of what you did – and I don't have a problem with that – rather, I'm proud of your steadfast adherence to your values. You killed a man, you do not believe in killing <u>ever</u>, and you are tormenting yourself as punishment; you don't set about concocting justifications that mean nothing to you. You are really sorry, and probably a little depressed."

"Yeah." Kamiri admits, slumped in his chair.

"Your feelings are the evidence of the kind of person you are: extremely kind, and you are right to feel the way you do. To feel otherwise would be to deny your own identity."

"I hadn't thought of that," he laments.

"All I can say to help with the pain is that over time the pain subsides. I know that from personal experience."

"Yes."

"The other thing I would say, Kamiri, is that while you have strongly-held values, and you should not modify them to suit others, it's important to recognize that other people have different values which lead them to feel very differently about events. Who, apart from God, is in a position to say which values are correct? That's just the nature of the world we live in: a lot of things are very uncertain."

"Do you think that prayer would help?"

"Yes, I think it will be very helpful."

Dorothy pays the bill. He offers her his hand as they are leaving. "Thank you, Dorothy."

She ignores his hand and embraces him. Gratitude overwhelms him, and tears form as he returns her hug. On her toes, she manages to kiss him. "You get through this fine, Kamiri, I'm sure of it."

With a smile and a nod, he mounts his motorcycle and speeds away.

Dorothy stands looking after him. *How I love that man!*

Dorothy, Hassan, his half-brother, Elijah Arusei, who is Vice President and General Manager of Arusei Leisure, and much of the general public read with interest the on-going news reports on Kamiri's involvement in Nicholson's death. Elijah, who has responsibility for the huge Arusei private safari camp, Nyambura, on the eastern border of the Kioko National Park, has professional interest. Nyambura is not immune to poaching of its game. This is worrying enough, but the additional presence of wealthy tourists makes the possibilities of gunshots in the night and the corpses of elephants in the day particularly unwelcome.

The Park Service Review Panel consists of three non-executive directors, a retired judge, a senior police officer, a recent, randomly selected juror, and is chaired by an appointee from the Department of Environment. Where the behavior of an employee of the Park Service is at issue, the Panel has the power to dismiss the employee or make a referral to the prosecutor. The Panel's review of the death of Mr George Nicholson is open to the public and the media. The witnesses called in addition to Kamiri are Faraji, the Park Service manager who had radio supervision at the time and the detective inspector who visited the site.

The detective inspector confirms that the deceased had fired two shots and, based on ballistic evidence, was shot in the neck by a bullet fired by Ranger Kamiri. He also testifies that the tusks which were discovered in Mr Nicholson's truck had been cut from an elephant that had been killed approximately two hours previously, and had been removed with a hacksaw which had Nicholson's fingerprints on it.

The Park Service manager and Faraji then give their accounts.

When Kamiri was called to testify, his hands and lips were trembling. *Oh God, help me.* He sat in the witness chair and looked up at the face of the chairman. Was that perhaps the wisp of a smile? With a deep breath, he began to recount what had happened on termite mound rock that day.

"Kamiri," the chairman asked, "when you say you 'took a shot' at Mr Nicholson, did you raise the rifle to your shoulder, fix him in the sights and pull the trigger?"

"No, sir. I held the rifle like this." He demonstrates by cradling an imaginary weapon. "And then I pulled the trigger. I didn't mean to hit him, sir. I only wanted to say, 'stop shooting at rangers!'"

The chairman scans his colleagues on the Panel. "Any further questions? No?"

He turns to the senior police officer. "Mr Ouma, is there any interest in referring this case to the federal prosecutor."

"There is no interest in a referral, Mr Chairman. We view this as a case of fully justifiable self-defense."

The Panel was polled for their conclusions. "Let the record show that no action is to be taken against Kamiri. The Panel is dismissed."

Mrs Muriel Nicholson, wife of the deceased, and her lawyer sat in the audience. She wants to purge her husband's memory, to 'teach that village footballer a lesson', and separate him from a large portion of the money she is sure he has.

Much depends on the cooperation of Mbugua, her husband's secretive tracker/gun bearer. Her lawyer identified an intermediary who approached Mbugua with an offer of a share in the expected 'prize money' in exchange for his 'assistance' at trial. From Mbugua's point of view, this is attractive: his long-term employer is dead, and his notoriety in the Park mitigates against any referrals to tourists. He says, 'yes'.

The large, official envelope from the Second District Court in City has an ominous look. Kamiri checks the address and turns it over several times, hoping it is mis-addressed. He opens it. Inside, he is informed that he is summoned to give a deposition in the case of Nicholson vs. Kamiri at the City Court House in two weeks' time. On the following pages, it goes on to say that Mrs Muriel Nicholson alleges that her husband, Bruce Nicholson, was wrongfully shot and killed by Park Ranger Kamiri on 12 October, and that Mrs Nicholson demands compensation for loss of consort and livelihood in the amount of ten million shillings.

Oh my God! Ten million will wipe me out.

The Park Panel hearing had dissipated much of his feelings of shame and culpability. Now, they are back with unavoidable force, stinging and biting his self-esteem. *What have I done to offend God?* For hours, he walks alone in the forest, seeking something – anything – to relieve his pain. Time begins to relieve the nausea of self-pity and self-torture. *But what am I going to do? What can I do? I don't know. I need some help.* He thought of Ms Ohiambo, or the Park Service. *They've helped me enough in the hearing. Besides, if I turn it over to them, I'll lose control. Dorothy? I've leaned on her enough. Hassan? Why not? He may have some ideas.*

Hassan's advice strikes Kamiri as embarrassingly obvious: "You need a good lawyer, Kamiri."

"But where can I get one? I don't know <u>any</u> lawyers, never mind the good ones."

"Leave it with me."

On Friday, Hassan is home for the family meal after prayers. On these occasions, he is usually reserved and taciturn, but he sees an opportunity when Elijah begins talking about the loss of two bull elephants, and Kaddour expresses the view that "our rangers have to get tougher."

"It's difficult when rangers get sued," Hassan suggests.

"Who's suing the rangers?" Eli demands.

"Well, for example, Mrs Nicholson is suing Kamiri for ten million."

"You're kidding!" Eli is astonished.

"No, unfortunately, I'm not. He told me about it a couple of days ago,"

Kaddour's open palm strikes the table. "These people are the devil's spawn! We ought to shoot the lot of them."

Elijah ignores his father's outburst; he turns to Hassan: "Has he got a lawyer? He'll need one."

"I know, and no, he doesn't."

"Ask him to come see me on Monday, will you?"

Kamiri knew the Republic Building, and he had been to the thirty-third floor lair of Kaddour Arsei, but this was new: he is going to the thirty-second floor den of Elijah Arusei. He doesn't know why; all he knows is that Elijah has responsibility for the large, private Nyambura Park, among other ventures. Hassan had said, "I don't know. He just wants to see you."

Dressed in his Park Ranger's uniform, Kamiri feels completely out of place, particularly when he is ushered into Elijah's opulent office, where the man himself is wearing a gray silk suit and patterned blue tie. Kamiri reckons him to be about forty, handsome, with a gentle nose and prominent jaw. There is a sharp light in his black eyes.

"Hello, Kamiri, I'm Eli."

There is some small talk about football.

"My old man is pretty fond of you. You made him a lot of money, Kamiri."

"I like your father a lot, and I enjoyed being a Lion."

It occurs to Elijah, as the conversation progresses, that this man is no ordinary villager turned ranger: there is intelligence, social skill and determination, as well as the inevitable subservience.

"I understand that you've had some unfortunate experiences as a ranger. Tell me about them."

Kamiri, less weighted down by the authority of the man across the desk, tells the story with confidence.

"So, you didn't duck when that bastard started shooting. You shot back. I like that."

Kamiri gives a brief description of the Panel hearing and ends with the court summons.

"Do you have it with you?" Kamiri nods. "May I see it?"

For some time, Elijah scrutinizes the document, flipping the pages back and forth. "I understand you don't have a lawyer."

"I don't know where to find one."

Elijah picks up his telephone: "Have you got a couple of minutes, Michael?"

A tall, white man, hazel-eyed, with neat gray moustache and goatee, wearing a rumpled brown suit enters the office.

425

"Michael, this is Kamiri. You know who he is?"
"Of course."
"Kamiri is in a bit of trouble with the Nicholsons." He hands Michael the summons.

Michael Sommerville dons half-moon spectacles and reads with absorption. He looks at Kamiri. "You know this guy Mbugua?"

"No, sir."

"Is there any truth in what he has said?"

"No, sir. He wasn't even present at the time."

"Oh, one of those." He considers the ceiling for some moments. "Juries are hard to predict," he muses. "Tell you what, Kamiri. Can you get me a complete transcript of the panel hearing?"

"Kamiri, this is Michael Sommerville. I've read the transcript. Faraji says that Nicholson's first shot hit the khaya tree. Correct?"

"Yes, sir."

"Has the bullet been recovered?"

"No, I don't think so. There was no reason to."

"Well, there is now. I'm going to have someone from the police department call you. Would you take him to the khaya tree, show him where the bullet hit, and let him remove it?"

"Yes, sir."

When the bark is stripped away from around the bullet hole, the nose of the alloy bullet was found to be embedded in the wood of the tree. The detective examined it and dropped it into a small plastic bag.

"Kamiri, this is Michael Sommerville. I have some good news: the Nicholsons have dropped their case."

"Thank you, sir. Why did they decide to drop it?"

"Well, I had what you might call a 'come to Jesus' conversation with their attorneys. First of all, I said that we had ballistic proof that one of the two shots at you was fired from Nicholson's .357. I mentioned that Bamgboshe is available to provide character witnesses for you and Faraji. And I said that we would tear Mbugua apart in court, so that they ought to think about their corporate reputation in backing a witness who will be guilty of perjury."

"Thank you very much, sir."

For Kamiri, the obscure sounds of the veldt become the voices of familiar friends, the odor of the crushed grass is invigorating, and dreary rain squalls are a cleansing welcome. He is, once again, the owner of a great legacy.

Welcome as Sommerville's news had been, he is struggling to understand how fortune could perform a somersault so quickly. Yes, there were good, logical reasons that the case should be abandoned. But why so quickly, without even a joust in court? *How can I be so lucky? I don't deserve it, but thank you, God!*

> It wasn't difficult for me, the One, to transfer some ideas
> to lawyer Sommerville.

Kamiri presses the number 32 button. He has made an appointment to thank Elijah for freeing him from the curse of termite mound rock. The same white secretary greets him again – in Swahili. *How does a white woman about my age learn to speak Swahili?*

He asks her.

"I grew up on a coffee plantation where English was my second language. You can go in, Kamiri. He's expecting you."

Elijah is pondering something, head down, a pen poised in his right hand. "Oh, hello Kamiri." He focuses his attention on his visitor. "I understand that the Nicholsons have given up their frivolous suit."

"Yes, sir, and I . . ."

"Kamiri, I am Elijah, or better yet 'Eli'."

"Yes, Eli, and I want to thank you and Mr Sommerville for all your help. I think without . . ." He is interrupted with a dismissive gesture.

"I'll let him know. Sit down, please." He cocks his head to one side as if to better evaluate his visitor. "You like being a ranger, Kamiri?"

"Yes, Eli, I do."

"Do you think you could also be a guide, pointing out things to tourists and answering their questions?"

"I haven't thought about it, Eli. Maybe I wouldn't know all the answers."

Elijah is amused. "Some guides, when they don't know the answer, rather than admit it, will make up fascinating answers."

"I could never do that."

"Kamiri, what is the name of the bird that builds hanging nests?"

"That would probably be a weaver bird."

"What color is this bird?"

"Ours are yellow and black."

"And how do they build their nests?"

"They start by weaving a loop around a branch out of bits of grass. Then, they keep expanding the loop until it becomes a kind of cone with an entrance on the bottom, and . . ."

"How did you learn this, Kamiri?"

"I asked Faraji about the birds and then I looked them up in my guide book."

"OK." He catches Kamiri's eye. "How would you like to be a ranger/guide on Nyambura Park?"

Kamiri hesitates. "Well, I don't know, Eli. I haven't been working at Kioko that long."

"Umm. I know Bamgboshe pretty well. I feel pretty sure we could arrange a deal where you work at Nyambura, and I make a contribution toward your public service adverts and talks. There are some advantages in working at Nyambura, Kamiri. First of all, we pay about fifty percent more, because the job involves tourist contact, as well. Secondly, the accommodation is better;

we have a comfortable bunk house. And then, since our kitchen is cooking for tourists, the food is better."

"That sounds very interesting, si ... Eli."

"OK, I'm going to suggest that you go and see Howard Ng'ang'a, who is our general manager at Nyambura."

How is it that the Aruseis are always connected with the good things in my life: first the abattoir, then the friendship with Hassan, which led to the Lions, and now to Nyambura?

I, the One, don't think you should forget the other people who have helped you: Joseph, Dorothy, your father, Warari.

Warari?

Yes, Warari. Sometimes when your nose is rubbed in filth, you resolve to be clean.

Perhaps that's what happened to Hassan.

I have no doubt.

Kamiri leaves his motorcycle alongside four neatly parked Jeep Safaris, and follows the winding path through the oak trees to the clearing in front of a dark wood lodge. There, in front of the building are near-life-size bronze sculptures: three lionesses facing a cape buffalo bull; the bull, head down, one fore-hoof raised ready to paw the ground, the lionesses, hesitant, and torn between the lust for a three-star meal and their fear of a terrible goring. Inside, the lodge is one open space built of dark, native wood on several levels, following the undulation of the ground, and flooded with light from the opposite floor-to-ceiling windows which look down on the swirling, brown Rufiji River. To one side, the tables are set with white linen and glassware;

at the other, there are cliques of inviting couches, arm chairs and low tables, one of which is currently occupied by two older European couples. Brilliantly colored, loosely-woven native carpets decorate the dark bubinga wood floor. In the center is a circular bar, with attendant seating, hundreds of glasses and dozens of labeled bottles on display.

The barman, white towel in hand, looks up. "May I help?"

"I'm here to see Mr Ng'ang'a."

"The office is outside. The building to the right."

Ng'ang'a is about sixty, overweight, with white hair and a sunny disposition. "Yes. Hello, Kamiri, how are you? Eli told me you were coming." He turns to a side door. "Jimbo, bring us some coffee!" He gestures Kamiri toward a seat. "Yes. I am very pleased to meet the star of the Lions, and I hope you will help us tame our lions. Ha-ha!" Kamiri offers a noncommittal smile. "Yes. Well, Eli reminded me of three reasons for sending you. One is that as a famous footballer, our guests will be eager to go on safari with you. Then, there is the matter of the dead poacher at Kioko. Eli thinks we need to take a tougher stance with poachers, and he admires your no-nonsense approach. Finally, this ties in with the retirement of our head ranger."

"I see. Do you have much of a poaching problem?"

"Well, we are losing one or two elephants per month, which is about average." He shrugs. "What can you do? Poachers come at night, and they are gone by the time our rangers go on patrol."

"You mentioned something about a retirement."

"Yes, our head ranger is turning seventy, and he wants to go back to his village. Why don't I turn you over to him for an orientation? His name is Hezekiah Njogu. As far as I'm concerned, you can start right away."

Hezekiah Njogu is found asleep in the bunkhouse, which accommodates up to 30 all-male employees, of which there are currently 24, not including Ng'ang'a, who, with his wife, occupies the general manager's cottage in a clearing off the car park. Njogu appears to be suffering from a skeletal disease – perhaps advanced arthritis – as his mobility is limited. It is soon apparent to Kamiri that Njogu has retired mentally, if not geographically. The chief ranger has little interest in showing Kamiri around the park, let alone the camp, but he willingly sits in the sun outside the bunkhouse and answers Kamiri's questions.

There are a dozen chalets, each accommodating two guests in a king-sized bed draped in white netting and sheltered under an extensive roof. A white masonry wall, a meter and a half high, surrounds the living space, private plunge pool and shower room. Each chalet has a wide panorama of the river and is decorated in rustic Africana. Njogu volunteers the information that each guest pays about three thousand shillings in equivalent hard currency per day for the chalet, three 'real good' meals, morning and afternoon safaris, and use of the lodge with its swimming pool and library. "Only very rich people come here. Europeans, Americans, and some Asians."

Including Njogu, there are eight rangers. Six are always assigned to guide duty each day, on the basis that at full capacity, with four guests assigned to a safari vehicle, six guides are required. In theory, the remaining two "supervise trail maintenance and repairs using casual outside labor."

"Do you ever send your rangers out on patrol?" Kamiri asks.

"No, we don't have the manpower for that."

Kamiri stops by the office where Mr Ng'ang'a confirms the proposed salary. Expressing his continued interest, Kamiri promises to make his decision within a week.

The salary of one thousand shillings a week, better room and board is certainly attractive to Kamiri, but he is hesitating over the assignment itself. It seems that one of the reasons the job has been offered is the expectation of a crackdown on poaching, based on his killing of a poacher without serious consequences. *But I can't go on killing poachers.*

I, the Other, think he should go ahead and kill the lot of them, fabricating self-defense when necessary.

I, the One, suggest there may be a compromise, short of killing, which involves seriously intimidating the poachers.

But that will take patrols, and they seem to be understaffed.

You'll find a way, says the One.

Normally risk-averse, Kamiri decides to accept the offer, based on sketchy patrolling ideas, and, in part, on his desire to remain connected to the Arusei steamroller.

Chapter 24

Marriage

In a letter to his father, Kaddour, during a six-month deployment in South Sudan, Hassan wrote, "It's hard to imagine a more hopeless situation. The rebels, who represent the Nuer tribe, but more particularly the government's Dinka forces, will use any force imaginable against civilians – starvation, rape, pillaging, torture, arson, robbery, slavery and outright murder – to suppress the enemy. The government is a corrupt dictatorship running a lawless state on the proceeds from their oil wells, and they are impervious to international pressure. Recently, I had a run-in with a Nigerian colonel over a decision I took that my company would block any access by government forces to civilians in a UN-backed refugee camp near the Ugandan border. About fifty government soldiers – some in uniform, some not, but all armed – approached the camp at about 0140 hours. I deployed two platoons to block them – also armed. A translator, speaking through megaphone, announced that no entrance to the camp would be permitted. They ignored the announcement and kept approaching. I ordered one platoon to fire a volley over the heads of the government forces, who quickly withdrew. But next day the government complained that their troops were fired on by UN soldiers, contrary to an agreement that UN forces act as peace-keepers, taking no part in combat operations. The colonel was planning to court martial me, until the South African general listened to the story. He said. 'Mr Arusei, if you had <u>not</u> taken the action you took, in my judgment, there would have been rape and pillaging in the camp we were sent to protect, followed by a government white wash'. That kind of commendation goes down well back home."

On Hassan's return, months later, the relationship with Mary has evolved into greater levels of commitment and hormonal electricity. But, Hassan's quarters are strictly for bachelors, and Mary is living at home with 'old fashioned' parents. As far as Mary is concerned, hotel liaisons are sordid, and the use of a friend's premises is 'dirty business'.

"Not that I have any objection to the act itself. On the contrary, I think sex with you – at the right time, in the right place – would be brilliant."

> I think Mary has it totally wrong: sex with anyone, at any time and in any place, is brilliant. I am not fussy: enjoy!

> It seems to me that the Other is excluding Love, which precludes <u>many</u> people, times and places.

Hassan has discovered what he hopes will be a short-lived solution. They are sitting on a blanket, backs against a baobab trunk, in rustic parkland with a view of City skyscrapers. The remnants of a picnic lunch have been stuffed into a paper sack, and the pair are languid after an almost fully clothed but quite satisfactory sexual encounter.

"That's my family's building," Hassan suggests, pointing.
"You mean the Republic Building?" she asks.
"Yes, but they're not really my family."

> I, the One, know that Hassan has been burdened with the consciousness that Mary may not be aware of his parentage, and that her knowledge may strike a fatal blow to the relationship. While I salute his candor, it does seem an awkward way to begin the discussion.

Frowning, Mary turns to face him. "What do you mean, Hassan: they're not your family?"

"Didn't your sister tell you?"

"She would never tell me anything about her friends, let alone her lovers."

"I was never her lover, Mary."

"OK, but she didn't tell me, so you have to."

Hassan recites the many reasons he believes that he is not the biological son of Kaddour Arusei, and that he suspects Mohammad Adesida is his real father.

"You mean the defense minister?"

"Yes."

Mary tilts her head from side to side considering the matter. "I can't see that it makes much difference. They're both pretty powerful men. In fact, it's probably an advantage having two of the most powerful men in the country as your fathers."

"Well, but I'm a bastard; don't you see?"

"Baah! What are you talking about, Hassan? Join the real world. You have plenty of company: probably twenty percent of the people on this planet are mistaken about who their father is."

"Maybe, but all this secrecy and hurt make things difficult."

"Well, we've got to clear up the secrecy and that will take away the hurt."

Hassan recoils, horror-struck. "I can't clear up the secrecy."

She rests a soothing hand on his arm. "We will clear up the secrecy, Hassan."

"How are we going to do that?" His head is shaking 'no'.

Blithely, she announces, "I don't know yet. We'll find a way."

Hassan stares into the distance and exhales deeply. "That's one thing I really like about you, Mary: your confidence. But it's not just your confidence: you have a magical way of making things happen."

"The Jews call it chutzpah; I have plenty of chutzpah. What else do you like about me, Hassan?"

"Well, you're a very pretty, very sexy woman."

"Oh, really? That's good to know. Anything else?"

"You know how the world works – how to move things to your advantage."

"I am a flimflam artist, Hassan." She smiles radiantly. "I take advantage of people against their better judgment."

He hesitates for a moment. "What do you see in me?"

She pulls him close. "I mentioned courage before. When you have your back to the wall, you will fight; I will slink away. I have great confidence before the event; you are cautious – probably because of the uncertainty in your childhood. But confidence and courage together are a great combination."

Hassan nods and strokes her cheek.

"But what I really admire in you, Hassan, is your authenticity. No hidden identity, no mask, no acting. With Hassan, what you see is what you get."

"What's so unusual about that?"

"It's rare and it breeds trust. Most people pretend to be something other than what they really are. This causes confusion and a lot more transactional processing before trust can be extended." She pauses. "Besides, you're a very good-looking man and a splendid lover."

"As you say, that's good to know."

"Hassan, it seems to me that the biggest obstacles we face are not between the two of us, but between us and our parents."

Gloom settles over Hassan. At home, he has been presenting carefree bachelorhood, knowing that announcement of a serious relationship with a very pretty, black Christian woman would arouse virulent objections. "You have a point," he concedes.

"OK, tell me more."

"I don't think my father – that is, Kaddour Arusei – would be particularly concerned about religion, and he never expects to be involved in any marriage arrangement. He would be more interested who the person is, personally, socially, politically. My brothers and sisters would be critical, at first, within the family, based on the long-standing belief that as a black sheep I can't be trusted, but I think they would come around over time. My mother is the problem. Based on her reaction when I was dating your sister, she would make a tremendous fuss."

"Why?"

"My mother is an old-fashioned Muslim woman: it's not so much the faith, but the culture she believes in, the woman's role in the family, the keeper of tradition, referee of social issues, disciplinarian of children, governor of household operations, and invisibly black outside the house. She would expect not only to select my wife, but to take her under her wing so as to be sure the culture is passed on. And as her youngest, she will take a special interest in my situation."

"Did your brothers go through this torture when they married?"

"Yes, to some extent: they were involved in the selection process, but then they immediately moved out of the house."

"Hmmm. I think we ought to start with my parents first. Their issues will primarily about religion, but they'll be easier, I think.

The lunch is completed, the young couple has left – ostensibly to take in a movie – and Dorothy is working a shift. Joseph dries the dishes after his wife, Helen, washes them.

"Isn't it strange," Helen suggests, "how two sisters with identical up-bringing can see the same man and have opposite reactions."

"Well, they're two very different girls: Dorothy is conservative and intellectual; Mary tends to be more liberal, intuitive."

"Perhaps. I remember him when he came here the first time to take Dorothy out to dinner. He was a very nice boy – a little shy."

"Yes. I thought that was surprising, given that he's an Arusei; he wasn't brash."

"Today, he didn't seem shy," Helen says. "He seemed confident, much more mature."

"One thing about the army: it makes kids grow up."

Helen turns to gaze on Joseph. "They seem to care a lot for each other."

"Yes. I wonder what the Aruseis will make of this."

"What do you think?" Helen asks.

"It's hard to say, except that they would probably be looking for the daughter of a rich, important family."

"I just hope that Mary doesn't get hurt. . . Do you think they'll have enough money to live on?"

"Well, a major's pay isn't much, but it does come with quarters, even for married officers, and a minimal food allowance. Mary's always been pretty frugal; she'll be able to get a job when she gets her degree."

"I was impressed," Helen suggests, "the way they're handling the Christianity – Islam issue, They're both pretty religious – particularly Hassan."

"Yes, I agree. It was very surprising when he said he sometimes goes to church with Mary, and she said she's trying to teach him to sing."

Helen pauses, her hands still immersed in soapy water. "I can't imagine what it would be like to sit among the women in a mosque at prayer time. Even with a headscarf, they must know she's not one of them."

"I think it would be interesting to be a fly one the wall."

"But she's not a fly on the wall, Joseph! She's got to recite stuff, and kneel and stand, all at the right time."

Helen unties her apron. "I worry about Mary being able to adjust to army life."

Joseph pulls his wife into an embrace. "Mary's pretty resourceful . . . and determined."

"Like you."

He kisses his wife's forehead. "Don't I wish. Well, fingers crossed."

Hassan has decided to meet with his father in his office, away from the unpredictable interruptions at home. When he called to make the appointment, he told the secretary that the subject was 'personal'. Naturally, he wears his army officers' uniform with gold oak leaf insignia and two rows of campaign ribbons.

Kaddour is on the phone when Hassan is sent in, but he indicates a seat opposite and continues, with gesticulations, to persuade the remote listener. *He's gotten grayer, but I think he's even better looking. More impressive, more in charge. Seems like he's trying to coax somebody about something to do with an acquisition.*

"Hassan! I've heard some good things about you."

"Really, Father?"

"Yes, I understand you may be up for early selection to lieutenant colonel, and your name is mentioned as a possible attaché to an important general officer."

Hassan cannot resist. "Where do you get this information?"

Kaddour has a satisfying laugh. "I have to protect my sources, Hassan, and the information is preliminary, but I think it is correct to say that if you continue down the path you are on, you will have a fine military career."

"Thank you, sir."

Kaddour gives a curt nod. "Right. What is it you wanted to see me about?"

Hassan takes a deep breath. "I came to ask your blessing: I have found the woman I want to spend the rest of my life with."

"Does your mother know about this?"

"No. I wanted to ask you first."

Kaddour pulls his chin in with a jerk; he is dumbstruck. "But . . ." He pauses to reconsider. "Who is this woman, Hassan?"

From his breast pocket, Hassan withdraws a photograph and places it on his step-father's desk. "Her name is Mary Maiyo."

For some moments, Kaddour studies the picture; he puts it down, smoothing the edges. "What can you tell me about her family?"

"Her father is general manager of a charity which provides shelter for migrant men, trains and evaluates them and places them into jobs. Kamiri came through them, and the company has hired a number of their people."

"Is that Home Away?"

"Yes. Her older sister is a medical doctor, and her mother is a freelance psychotherapist."

"Hmmm. They are Christians?"

"Yes. But Mary has attended Friday prayers several times. She wants to better understand Islam."

"If she's attended Friday prayers, I may have seen her."

"Yes, but I don't think you've met her."

"Does the imam know about this?"

"We haven't told him."

"Is she planning to convert to Islam?"

"No, sir, and there is no chance I would become a Christian."

"And the two of you can tolerate this stand-off – for the long run?"

"For us, it's not a stand-off, Father. We respect each other's faith, because each of us has our own faith and can't prove the other wrong. We don't even try."

> This is utter balderdash! If it's different, somebody must be wrong. Only one brand of theology can be right, so speak up!

> The Other knows perfectly well that human theology is a very broad and uncertain intellectual realm. It's like a grand river: the water along the left bank may be very different from the water along the right bank. That does not mean that only one is fit to drink. To insist that only one can be potable leads to conflict. But then, the Other loves conflict.

"I find it interesting and commendable," Kaddour offers, "that you, as a military man for whom conflict is of the essence, have relinquished conflict for the sake of a love relationship."

Achieving Superpersonhood:

"Yes, that is true."
"What is Miss Maiyo doing now?"
"She is in a special master's degree program at the university: writing about psychological politics."
"Good luck to her. It seems to me that politics is the devil's game." He gives a shrug. "I suppose she's had a number of boyfriends before you."
"No, just two and they didn't last very long."
"And how long have you known her?"
"I first met her when she was about fifteen, but we've been dating for the last couple of years."
Kaddour studies the ceiling. "As I understand it, dating means going to bed for most young couples today."
"Not for us."
"Really?"
"Yes, really."
"Why is that?"
"She wants to choose the right time and place."
"Well, good for her. Sometimes, Christianity has its good points." He pauses. "You'll forgive the awkward questions, Hassan. You asked for my blessing, and I want to understand what I'm being asked to bless."
"Yes, Father, I understand."
There is a long moment of silence. "When you go to see your mother, Hassan, my advice is: stand your ground."

Hassan's first meeting with his mother ends in a stalemate: she contending that she has the right to present candidates for marriage to her son; he arguing that she does not have the exclusive right, and that he already has a candidate, to which she replied that he should have advised her of his readiness for marriage. What isn't aired in that meeting is the miasma of mutual distrust over the candidate: she suspecting that the candidate is unsuitable; he suspecting that she will attempt to veto his choice. It was agreed that she would meet the candidate, but that she wanted to make some background checks. He, to have at least a thread of control over the checking process, divulged all the same information he had given his father, who, apparently had not said a word about his meeting with Hassan.

"She's a Christian? She's completely unsuitable!"

What followed was an acrimonious debate about the unsuitability or suitability of Christian brides, and when the verbal ammunition on both sides is exhausted, Hassan stands up, approaches his mother, bends down, kisses her cheek and turns to leave.

"Where are you going, Hassan?"

"I'm going to my quarters."

"But we haven't made arrangements for this meeting." She is on the edge of tears.

"There's no point in having the meeting. You said she is unsuitable."

Her voice is pitched at pleading level. "But I only said that for your own good."

"It's _not_ for my good! You don't even know this woman that you say is unsuitable. You just want to have control of my life!"

She liquidizes into tears. He stands impassively waiting for her to recover. "All right, all right, Hassan. I will meet this woman. I will try to see in her what you see in her. I will withhold my advice until I have met her."

I have been trying to enhance Immam's stubborn streak, to get her to feel that she is right and has the right to move events as she wishes, that she is being taken advantage of. I am aware, though, that the One is urging flexibility and caution. I heard him say, "Express love in what you do. The relationship with your son is more important than traditional righteousness."

The oval table in the Maiyos' living/dining room seats five comfortably when the leaf is inserted. Dorothy has arranged

Achieving Superpersonhood:

her hospital shift to ensure her absence. Immam Arusei has removed her dark blue hijab, allowing her dark auburn hair to cascade over the shoulders of her black abaya, and it is difficult not to notice the quantity of gold bracelets that chinkle at each wrist. Mrs Arusei has never been in a middle-class home; she is bewildered by the size of it. *How can people live in a house this small? And it's so informal. Here I am in the kitchen, drinking a glass of orange juice, while Mrs. Maiyo prepares lunch. They seem normal people, not villagers, but they're obviously quite poor.*

She has already noticed that the table has been set with embroidered place mats (*probably Chinese*), and silverware (*most likely plated*), and glasses (*not crystal*).

Helen is removing a roast leg of lamb from the oven. "I should mention, Mrs Arusei, that this is halal lamb."

"Where did you get it?"

"There is a halal butcher near where Joseph works, and he picked it up."

"I see. Where does your husband work, Mrs Maiyo?"

"He manages a charity for migrants and helps them find work."

Hassan senses his mother's disparaging sentiment and adds, "He's the paid CEO, reporting to the board of directors, of Home Away. We've hired quite a few of their people."

"Who's 'we'?" Immam demands.

"Arusei Industries."

Undaunted, Mrs Arusei turns back to her hostess. "And I suppose you have this house and the children to take care of, Mrs Maiyo."

Plating the vegetables, she responds, "I'm a practicing psychotherapist."

"What does that involve?"

"Well, people come to see me with psychological problems like depression, anxiety, anger management, relationship and sexual problems, and I talk to them, helping them find solutions to the problems."

"So you're a kind of psychiatrist?"

"Yes, but I'm not a doctor and I can't prescribe medication."

"And you do this for free?"

"No, I charge patients by the session, although I do have some charity patients." She smiles at her guest. "I think we can go to the table now."

All heads but the guests bow as Joseph clears his throat. "Bless this food to our use, Lord, and us to thy service, in Christ's name, amen."

"Don't the Jews say something like that before they eat?"

Joseph replies, "I suppose they do, Mrs Arusei."

The lamb, the roast sweet potatoes, kale and carrots are all well-prepared. There are some idle observations about the weather before Immam enquires about the missing daughter. She is informed that the elder daughter is a doctor working in City hospital. "So she's not married yet?"

Joseph says: "No, she seems to be married to medicine at the moment."

Immam turns to Mary. "And what do you plan to do with your time in the future, Miss Maiyo?"

"Well, I'll get my master's degree next year, and I'm interested in the psychology of politics, so I may do some consulting and/or work as a journalist."

"Any plans for children? It doesn't seem as though you'll have much time for children."

"I'd like to have three children, and work part-time at home. That's what my mom does."

"And what are your hobbies? Sewing, cooking, perhaps?"

"I like to spend time with my friends, and with Hassan, of course. I do quite a lot of reading, play some tennis, sing in the church choir. On Fridays, I sometimes go to mosque."

"But it is forbidden for a non-believer to go to mosque."

Hassan interrupts. "No, Mother, it isn't forbidden as long as one shows respect."

Achieving Superpersonhood:

Immam's mood remains argumentative. "Are you thinking of converting, then?"

"No, ma'am, I'm not. Hassan and I want to understand and respect each other's faith."

Angrily, Immam turns on Hassan. "Have you been going to church?"

"Yes. Occasionally. I'm learning to sing – a little."

Mrs Arusei pushes her chair back. She glares around the table. "This is too much! I don't see how it can possibly work."

With a gentle wave of his hand, Joseph says, "Please keep your seat, Mrs Arusei. With all due respect, it is not for you or me or Moses to decide when two people should be together. These two have been good friends for two years, and they – as mature adults – have decided they want to be together for the rest of their lives. We cannot know better than they do."

"But Mr Maiyo, with all due respect, as you say, there are customs and traditions to consider."

"Yes, I agree that they should be considered, but not at the expense of two broken hearts."

There was absolute silence in the room, as the guest chewed her lower lip for a time. "I will think on the matter. In the meantime, I have two questions for you, Miss Maiyo."

"Yes, ma'am."

"First, what are your expectations as to mahr?" (Mahr, in Islam = a mandatory payment from the groom to his bride.)

"I have no expectations, Mrs. Arusei. One shilling would be plenty. What I want is your son."

Immam is startled by the apparent lack of interest in the Arusei money. *My two daughters-in-law each wanted at least a five-carat perfect diamond.* "Second, what are your ideas for the wedding?"

"I visualize two ceremonies: one Islamic at the mosque and one Christian at our church. I think there should be a brief celebration after each ceremony, to be attended by family and close friends. My father is planning to pay for the Christian ceremony and celebration. We think your family should decide about the Islamic side."

"Very well. I will think on this matter." She gets up from the table, the main dish half-touched and the dessert still in the kitchen, expertly winds and tucks her hijab into place, walks out the door with a nod, and into her waiting, chauffeur-driven Mercedes.

En route to the more prosperous suburbs, Immam reflects on the meeting. *The strange thing is that these people are extremely educated for being poor. Mrs Maiyo must have an advanced degree; her husband mentioned his MBA; the older daughter has a doctorate in medicine, and the younger one is getting a master's degree in something about politics. I have a careless high school diploma, and Hassan never finished university – although he is apparently studying part-time. Does it mean that they are smarter than we are? If that is so, why aren't they richer? The other thing: they all – except the younger girl – seem to be engaged in helping other people: the wife helps people with mental problems; the husband has a charity for these awful migrants; the older daughter is a doctor. The younger daughter wants to be a consultant and journalist. . . . But actually, consultants advise and journalists inform others. So this is a family focused on other people. Maybe that's why they're poor. To succeed in life, you have to look out for yourself.*

A few days later, Hassan is summoned to see his mother. "I have decided, Hassan, that you can do much better than this Maiyo girl, and I am going to find some better prospects."

Hassan is about to explode in anger, but as he faces his mother, a distant voice within catches his attention. "Hear her out before you say no."

"How better?" he demands.

"Well, for one thing," she replies calmly, "you need a wealthy wife to live on meager army pay."

Achieving Superpersonhood:

"What in the world gives you that idea? Don't you realize that I have lived on army pay, and not once have I asked you or Father for money? I live frugally; so does Mary. The two of us together in a year spend ten percent of what you spend on your August holiday in London."

"But Hassan, you will need a nice house."

"I don't need a nice house. I am assigned to army quarters and I am expected to use them; Mary, too."

Immam can feel the outer wall of her defenses crumbling, but she continues her attack. "Then, there is this awful problem with Christianity."

"There is no 'awful problem with Christianity' except in your head. Mary and I are entirely comfortable with our respective faiths, and nobody – I really mean nobody in two years – has offered a word of criticism."

"But there is no harm in looking," Immam suggests, "You never know what I might find."

"Mother, there is a lot of harm in looking. Harm to relationships that are important to me: my relationship with you, and my relationship with Mary."

"Oh, come on, Hassan. Don't be so alarmist!"

"Mother, let me be clear. Mary and I are going to get married, with or without your blessing. And if I hear that you are advertising for a wife for me, our relationship is over. Moreover – and I want you to remember this – I expect you to be kind and patient with Mary; look for and appreciate the good in her. Understood?"

Immam, utterly defeated, has subsided into a liquid shelter of tears; she nods.

* * *

Kamiri is beset with an anxiety he has never experienced before: being placed in a position where it seems impossible to succeed. *Half the rangers here are lazy, and the other half are full of excuses. They think my proposals on patrols are impossible, and when I talk to guests about their safaris, they are less than enthusiastic; apparently, there is an idea that it's OK for a guide to talk only when he sees something interesting, but guests seem to want to learn about everything.*

Out of desperation he decides to air the problem with Ng'ang'a, who dismisses the issue with a shrug. "You'll have to fire some people, Kamiri; better talk to the HR people at head office."

His anxiety becomes acute. He visualizes the consequences for a ranger: he goes back home without a job or any real savings. *Won't be able to work as a ranger again: if you're fired from Nyambura, who would take you? The abattoir?*

Nonetheless, he talks to a woman, Mrs Mbungoli, at head office who, sensing his inexperience, lays out the process in smooth, icy steps. *She may have fired hundreds of people, and makes it sound simple, but it can't be that easy: you're ruining people's lives.*

Finally feeling that there is no choice – *Either they leave, or I'll have to* – he begins to take the three biggest problem employees through the process: job description, performance review, warning. Kamiri's acute sense of fairness extends an agonizing process by several months, but during this time he notices a remarkable shift in the attitudes of the remaining four: patrols can be accommodated, guest satisfaction reports improve. Many of the rangers are working harder, *and what is strange, they seem to be good-natured at work.*

Kamiri calls Mrs Mbungoli to thank her for her help. She says, "Sometimes, Kamiri, when you're a manager, you have to be tough and impatient, while still being fair. Employees see that, they respect you for it, and they will follow your lead."

Hanging up the telephone, Kamiri remembers Joseph's advice. *He said that I might be a manager, but I had no idea that being a manager could be so difficult. You can't just be nice and fair: sometimes, as Mbungoli says you have to be tough and*

Achieving Superpersonhood:

impatient. I'm not tough and I'm not impatient, but I'll have to learn to be both of those things. That is my self-overcoming.

During the low season, Kamiri dismisses the three rangers. The task he had dreaded months ago has become more logical necessity than dreadful task.

A good facility with spoken English is a necessity for rangers at Nyambura. Few of the guests do not at least understand English, but this ability is a rarity among the general ranger population. Kamiri knows of one English-speaking ranger at Kioko. He is interviewed and hired. A second candidate is identified at another government park, but his interview is not encouraging and his references even less so. Kamiri turns him down.

Kamiri receives a call from Faraji: "Kamiri, my friend, how are you? I understand that you are hiring good rangers at Nyambura. I am available for hire and as you know, I do excellent work."

"I'm sorry, Faraji, Nyambura will take only English-speaking rangers."

"But Kamiri, my friend, can't you make an exception for me?"

"No, I'm afraid not, Faraji."

"I can learn English."

"When you have learned English, contact me again, and I see if we have a job for you."

For a day or two, Kamiri feels Faraji's hurt at being rejected by a friend, but he understands that the language requirement must be inflexible.

Joseph produces three unskilled migrants with excellent English and Kamiri selects two to attend (at Nyambura's expense) the government ranger training.

The loss of elephants has continued unabated, but Kamiri now has the resources to deal with poachers. For a week running, he selects one of his rangers to accompany him on a dusk-to-dawn patrol, but it is not a geographically random patrol. Rather, on foot, and all night, they accompany the largest of the three elephant herds in Nyambura. Noiselessly, with only whispered conversation and a silent bullhorn, showing no light, but with a portable search light in reserve, and carrying loaded rifles, they walk forty meters from the herd matriarch, wherever she goes. The matriarch is about forty-five, with two-meter-long tusks, and a year-old male calf shadowing her.

When Kamiri and Sami approach the herd at dusk on the first night, she is skittish, but when she smells Sami and the two men get no closer than forty meters, following her movements, she accepts their presence.

Sami whispers, "This is Bella; she knows me."

On the third night of following the leader, Kamiri whispers, "Do you think she knows what we're doing?"

"Yes, I do."

On the fourth night, Bella suddenly stops her rambling, raises her trunk to test the air ahead, ears flapping, and makes a low growling sound.

"There's something up ahead," Sami murmurs.

"A lion, maybe?"

"Bella doesn't care about lions."

The two men stand still, listening and trying to see ahead.

"Somebody's talking up ahead."

"Fire a shot into the tree tops up ahead. Take careful aim, Sami."

The explosive noise causes the elephants to turn and flee.

"Again, Sami. And again!"

There is distant conversation, then a voice cries out: "Stop shooting, Kamiri! Please stop!"

"How do they know I'm here?" Kamiri demands.

"They don't. They know you're at Nyambura. Nobody's ever fired at poachers before. You've shot at poachers, so they think it's you."

Achieving Superpersonhood:

Kamiri raises the bullhorn. "Come out where we can see you. Hold your rifles over your heads." Then: "Put the light on them, Sami."

Kamiri holds his rifle at the ready as two native men, wearing camouflage, rifles above their heads, appear in the light.

The poachers are disarmed and escorted to the lodge, where the police are called. They are charged with trespass, carrying unlicensed weapons, and intent to kill a protected animal (a new law in Country).

Sami comments: "They'll be out in a year, but maybe not so eager to go back to the old business."

Kamiri takes each of his rangers out on a dusk-to-dawn patrol, just so each of them knows what he expects. These patrols are made more interesting by the addition of night vision goggles which reveal a world of nocturnal animals (and potential poachers, in several instances).

There was one event which pleased Kamiri even more than arresting poachers. Sami and another ranger were out on patrol three months later. Sami reported, "When Bella saw us, she came clumping over, ears flapping and trunk raised. We thought she wanted to scare us off, but she stopped right in front of us, made a higher pitched sound and nodded her head up and down. Then she turned and walked back to the herd. We also noticed that every now and then she would check where we were."

* * *

There were several events at the wedding that entered the archive of astonishing episodes in the lore of the Arusei family. Immam enters a Christian church for the first time in her life, and wearing a black, hooded cape, seats herself in front row, right; then, having shed the cape, and wearing beneath it a pale green silk Chanel dress and matching headscarf, shakes hands – for the first time in her life – with a Christian, her new daughter-in-law's mother; but the most startling was when Immam follows the handshake, at the reception, with a brief embrace of the bride.

I, the One, know that prayer and meditation are good for the mind as well as the spirit, and Immam has rediscovered a modicum of inner peace.

The matter of the *mahr* was the subject of a debate between Mr. and Mrs Arusei. Can we forego the *mahr*? No, was the immediate conclusion: the absence of *mahr* would reflect badly on the family. Kaddour argued that it should be of lesser value than that given to their current daughters-in-law, and picking up on the theme, Immam proposed that it be noticeably different than the previous *mahr*. A conclusion was reached: Immam would purchase a three-carat emerald.

When presented with the near-perfect, octagon-cut emerald, Mary is in conflict. On one side she is mesmerized by the beauty of the stone, and grateful for the apparent welcome shown by her future husband's family. On the other, there is the suspicion that this is the first step in the family's attempt to purchase her loyalty and compliance.

Gazing at its glittering luminosity, she muses, "Do you think we should sell it, Hassan, and save the money for our future?"

"Absolutely not! We're going to have it set, and you will wear it at wedding ceremonies and other important occasions."

"Like what occasions?"

"Like the arrival of children, when I make full colonel and general and you are celebrated for your political writing."

"That won't be very often."

"In that case, you can wear it whenever you feel like saying, 'I am Mary Maiyo Arusei'."

"Well, in that case I can wear it all the time."

Following the Christian wedding early on Saturday afternoon, there is a small reception for family and close friends at a nearby restaurant, where drinks (Champagne and fresh fruit juice) and finger food are served. On the buffet table is a discreet little card which says: 'All meat is halal – no pork'.

Hassan, wearing his dark blue, formal uniform, with full decorations and the Sword of Honor, offers a toast of thanks to his father-in-law for "his generosity in giving such a precious creature to a poor soldier."

Dorothy clinks her glass, and stands; her hair is a soft, dark halo. "It is not usually the custom for women other than the bride to speak on these occasions, but as the bride's sister, I feel entitled to do so. Like most sisters, we have had disagreements. We gave up using our fists some years ago, but we still have the occasional oral scuffle." (laughter) "Actually, these altercations always remind us of the love and respect we have for each other. Mary is a special woman. She has intelligence, determination and vision. Vision of the real world, and clarity about people and her role. She has the intelligence to find an important place in the world and the determination to achieve it. Now she has found a man she loves, who can help her succeed. I love you, Mary. Good luck and Godspeed."

Almost immediately, Kamiri gets up, glass in hand and a nervous smile on his lips. "Since I haven't done this before, I have to rely on what I know best, which is football. I was actually introduced to Hassan, who was looking for football players, by Dorothy." He goes on to tell a story about a game between the Eagles and the Buffaloes in which Hassan made a mistake which led to a Buffalo goal, and how, full of determination, he shed several Buffalo defensemen to take a long shot on goal which, miraculously, scored. "For me, this tells you a lot about Hassan: he may make a mistake now and then, but he has the determination and the talent to make things come right. God bless you, Hassan! You're a great friend and I wish you much happiness and success."

The Islamic exchange of contracts takes place the next day in the mosque and is followed by a sumptuous buffet at one of the more exclusive golf clubs. The guest list on the bride's side is taken from Mary's guest list, and some of the relatives are motivated to accept primarily out of curiosity: what is a big Arusei party like? In addition to family, friends, employees, important customers and suppliers, about half of the political and media elite accept the invitation, bringing the total to over three hundred.

Chapter 25

Combat

Warari has moved out of the hidden village northwest of Coast City; however, as chief of Dhul Fikar in Country, he has his soldiers located in three additional covert bolt holes, and he maintains contact and loyalty through coded Internet traffic and monthly night visits. His current venue is a semi-secluded, walled farm outside of Coast City. At one time, it was the residence of a white farm owner, but was appropriated by the government and given to a loyal and incompetent supporter, who let it fall into disrepair and has since died. The house is now a virtual fortress, with hidden CCTV cameras, microphones, barbed wire and two bellicose guard dogs. People living in the area have no cause to complain about the secretive neighbors, but they know better than to trespass.

Living with Warari are Sergeant Kingali, Wassy, Irish, and Mourad, who serves as the cook. There are also three women who consort mostly, but not exclusively, with Warari; they are in their forties, wanted by the police for various offenses, with no acknowledged family ties. At Warari's House, there are always pleasant times: men/women, regular meals, television and downloaded movies, all in the context of a strict routine of 'neo-Islamic' worship.

Food and other supplies are brought in weekly by a gray, widowed woman who has no other income, and who sees only Mourad.

No resident ever leaves the house except when on a 'mission', or to accompany Warari on his monthly night liaisons in an old Jeep Cherokee four-wheel drive. A typical liaison lasts about three hours and includes reviews of recent missions and operations, planning of future events, collection of funds and dealing with any problems that have arisen.

Warari is aware that the Security Service is eager to find him; in fact, there is a reward of one million shillings for information leading to his capture or death. He is amused that the only known photograph of him in circulation (apart from his police mug shot), is at his local school graduation. But he is deeply suspicious of any hint of disloyalty, any lapse in security, or the possibility of defection. Since the escape of Hassan, there have been three other attempted defections. All three potential traitors were shot dead.

Warari has executed at least half a dozen atrocities involving the slaughter of civilians. In addition, there have been attacks on isolated police and army facilities, lucrative kidnappings, robberies, hijackings, and murders of perceived threats.

Eating away at Warari is his awareness that none of this has brought about his vision of a new Islamic state, governed by strict sharia law and by him. He has read the life of Fidel Castro, who, with his 26th of July Movement, came out of the Sierra Maestra mountains to transform Cuba from a corrupt dictatorship to a socialist paradise. He longs for a similar success, but his attacks have changed nothing in Country. Yes, he is recognized by the people and the government as a threat. Yes, he has become famous. But there is no dream realization: Warari as caliph.

For Country, it is business as usual. *There must be a different approach. Something that strikes at the heart of the system and forces change.*

* * *

Achieving Superpersonhood:

Hassan finds it difficult to acclimatize himself to his new assignment. Instead of a predictable, daily routine, there is a chaotic usurpation of shifting priorities. The to-do list he made up yesterday becomes obsolete at eight this morning. In lieu of having three levels of twenty-three officers and two hundred and seventy-one soldiers reporting to him, he has only himself to manage. Before, he had solely the lieutenant colonel to satisfy; now he, himself, is a lieutenant colonel, and in addition to keeping a four-star general – his boss – happy, there are about two dozen potentially discontented others: three-star generals, politicians, the media, and the chiefs of major military contractors. He is asked to be wise, politically astute, tactful, firm and a dynamo at once. There have been times when he mistook the nuances of a discussion with the Army Chief of Staff as an order to take action rather than the intended helpless lamentation, or when he should have realized that a reporter's request for sensitive information or a politician's demand of immediate action could safely be ignored. Hassan has learned to carefully, but promptly, evaluate each situation and calibrate his response with precision between a yawn and reaching for the panic button. What he loves about the assignment is being inundated with change and opportunities to learn; what he likes least are the many opportunities for mistakes and the lack of sleep. (He is expected in the office at seven-thirty am, and frequently returns home after ten pm.)

But home is a genuine oasis. Not just the one-bedroom apartment in government quarters near the Ministry of Defense Building. It is married life that is the balm. Sharing daily failures, trials and successes with an intelligent, critical and loving listener washes away accumulated stress and guides the preparation for the next day's battles. For Mary, the evening revelations – in which she, too, is a confessor – are the bread and wine of her life, particularly when they lead to a grand carnal conclusion in the bedroom.

Highly classified messages frequently cross Hassan's desk. This morning, his overflowing in-tray includes a top-secret message from the US NSA (National Security Administration). It is addressed to overseas allies who share terrorist information, and has found its way to the Army Chief of Staff, who has written on it, "HA, Comments? MK" (MK = Moses Kerubo). The message is four pages long and stupefying in its detail. What it says, in brief, is: There is a 63% increase in network traffic which originates in East Africa, and which includes terrorist language and code words. It goes on to specify the percentages of mobile telephone and Internet traffic as well as the frequency of terrorist words in several languages. It concludes by suggesting that participating allies take particular note of the word 'sword' in local traffic.

What am I to do with this? Our listening people in National Security have already gotten a copy, and they know that 'sword' is associated with Dhul Fikar. They're certainly listening and thinking, so what can I add?

The words *Dhul Fikar* suddenly repeat themselves in his consciousness.

I, the One, offered a little prompting.

Dhul Fikar. Oh, of course! Kerubo sent it to me thinking that I – ex-Dhul Fikar – might think of something.

He goes down three floors to the listening station of National Security. His pass does not admit him. He presses the buzzer and waits. The listening station deputy, a civilian, recognizes and admits him.

"You've seen this message from US NSA?" he asks.

"Yeah, we've seen it. The numbers are a bit off in our case, but we agree with the general picture."

"Where are the numbers off?"

"There are other words that keep popping up in Dhul's case. They're using the dark web for a lot of their traffic, but they don't know that, thanks to the Americans, we have beaten the encryption they're using, so we can read their traffic, most of which is in Swahili, but occasionally in a tribal language.

Sometimes they'll use a code word in place of a key word; for example: '*fedha*' (money in Swahili) becomes '*manyoya*' (feathers in Swahili). We've learned this from context, so when they're talking about *manyoya*, we know they're talking about money. A new word that is cropping up is '*kisiasa*' (political); apparently they haven't thought of a code word for it yet."

"In what context are they talking about *kisiasa*?"

"In the context of operations. It's almost as if they're saying we've got to operate more *kisiasa*."

"That's interesting. Keep me informed, will you? I may be able to help. In a prior life I knew quite a lot about Dhul."

"OK, Colonel."

Mary also finds *kisiasa* an interesting word in the lexicon of Dhul Fikar's vocabulary, but she, like Hassan, cannot think of a relevant meaning. "I doubt that they're planning to run terrorist candidates in the next general election."

During dinner, she gives Hassan a report on her activities today at the university. "There's a lot of interest in this whole redistricting issue, and I'm thinking of writing a paper on it from a psychological point of view."

"You think it's a psychologically charged issue?"

"Yes. There are many sources of anxiety: there are political party issues: the opposition is afraid of losing seats to the Republicans, smaller tribes are saying that they will lose seats to the larger, more powerful; and urban interests are worried about loss of influence to the rural areas. Parliament has agreed that an independent commission should be established to recommend a solution. As I understand it, a consensus has been forming on a Swede who is an ex-UN official to lead the commission."

Mary arrives home with interesting news: "Your step-father has offered Nyambura Camp as a site for senior politicians to meet, facilitated by the Swedish chairman, and agree who is going to be on new redistricting commission."

"Well, that's nice. When's the meeting going to take place?"

"It hasn't been decided yet. Probably in the next couple of weeks."

"Are you going to be there?"

"Don't I wish! I don't think they're even going to let any of the media in."

Days later, walking to the office, at seven-thirty on Monday morning, Hassan stops at a news stand to buy the *City Herald*, a quality broadsheet. At the bottom of page 1, there is a brief item under the title Redistricting Commission Meeting, "The lodge at Arusei game park has been confirmed as the site for the meeting on Wednesday of next week for select members of the Redistricting Commission. Kaddour Arusei, the Swede Olle Engström, and leaders of the political parties will be attending. Mr Ng'ang'a, park general manager, commented, 'We've had to find alternative accommodation for our regular guests in case the meeting goes into Thursday'."

Well, sounds like they're making progress, thanks to Father.

At six ten pm the following Wednesday, Hassan receives a call from the deputy at National Security, Listening. "Colonel, if you have a few minutes, I'd like to go over some stuff with you."

Hassan locks his safe and takes the elevator down.

"What I wanted to show you is some new Dhul intercept material. They're still talking about *kisiasa*, but now they're connecting it with words like '*ushindi*' (victory)."

"*Ushindi*?"

"Yes."

"Anything else?"

"Well, you know how the Dhul communications are. They're full of rambling discourse about the Prophet and Allah's service, and paradise, and martyrdom and being good soldiers. They never seem to come to the point. Here's one from this morning." He hands Hassan a well-used sheet of paper on which there is Swahili text, numerous editing marks and yellow highlighting.

Hassan reads the text and then goes back to see what the editing and the highlighting reveal. Nothing. He reads the text again. One word seems odd: *'Jumanne'. What has Tuesday got to do with anything else here?* Toward the end there is the word *'bustani'. What has Dhul got to do with a garden?*

For another fifteen minutes, he talks to the deputy, whose appraisal is "They're up to something."

In his office, Hassan returns to reading a procurement report, but there is a distinct sense of unease: the weighty presence of unfinished business. He sets the report aside, leans back in his chair and stares at the sound-proofing tiles on the ceiling. *Bustani – garden or park, park or garden. Park. Could they possibly mean Nyambura Park? And Tuesday? Why Tuesday? The meeting is Wednesday. Because they have to leave and get into position on Tuesday. Great Allah!* He snatches up the communication copy and sprints down the corridor.

An armed sentry stands outside the door. Two secretaries are still busy at six-fifty-five. The younger one looks up, "Yes, Hassan?"

"I have to see him. It's very urgent."

"He's talking to the defense minister."

Hassan pauses to consider. "Would you let him know it's very urgent?"

She picks up her telephone, presses a button, and says: "Colonel Arusei. Very urgent." She hangs up. "You can go in, Hassan." The sentry steps aside. Inside, Hassan salutes. The gray-haired man with four gold stars on his collar and tired eyes returns a perfunctory salute. "Yes?"

Hassan places the Dhul message on the general's desk and explains his suspicions; he notices that what begins as casual interest becomes outright consternation. "Those bastards!" As is his habit when confronted with bad news, the general clasps his forehead in his left hand as if smitten with a sudden headache, swivels his chair and scowls at the windows. "I just had Adesida on the line. He should know about this." He presses a button on his telephone console. "Mohammad, sorry to bother you again, but we've picked up a Dhul intercept, and it seems they're going to invite themselves to next week's meeting." Listening, he drums the desktop with his fingers. "It is actually Colonel Arusei's interpretation . . . He's right here. I can put him on." The general reaches for a button on his console.

The minister's voice fills the room. "Hello, Hassan, how are you?"

Hassan is aware of the general's astonishment at the minister's use of his given name.

"I'm very well, sir. Thank you."

"Tell me: what's going on?"

Hassan reads through the communication, points out the key words and his interpretation of them.

"Minister," Kerubo suggests, "It may be wise to re-arrange next Wednesday's meeting."

"The problem with that, Moses, is that the media will speculate on the reasons for the re-arrangement, and people will suspect that the real reason for the change is some sort of political shenanigans, and if we tell the truth, we'll be giving the impression of being weak and giving in to terrorists. No, I think we've got to go ahead, but I'd like you to arrange for heavy special forces coverage of the event. Not too obvious, please. That would distract from the problem-solving spirit we're trying to create."

"Right, minister." He ends the call. Hassan hears the Army Chief of Staff muttering: "Heavy but not too obvious. Typical ministerial directive."

* * *

Warari has finished his theologically dense and inaccurate speech about the necessity for good Muslims to defeat the

Achieving Superpersonhood:

infidels, who seem to include all but the 'devout soldiers' of Dhul Fikar. He can give two dozen versions of this rant, seemingly straight from the heart, without prompting, and without believing (or understanding) most of it. *It is necessary for my position a leader, and to retain the financial support of rich fanatics, that I be seen as a great jihadist. Who cares what I say as long as my own position and power advance?*

I, the Other, must say that Warari has learned the way along my path to greatness. He is most attentive to my suggestions.

Warari continues: "Now, let me cover the strategic objective. It is to create a new, holy region where Allah is king, and where Dhul Fikar are his princes. A place subject to our sharia rule and where there are no unbelievers. To do this in Country, we must create a profound uncertainty in the power of the government. We will capture and hold for ransom the President and the leaders of the establishment. We will demand that the captives order the army and the police to take no action against us. We then will assume control of government broadcast channels. A jihadi imam and I will address the people about the establishment of a new caliphate and mandatory conversion to Islam."

He pauses for a moment to accept the delight of his warriors.

"I will now outline our action plan. The A and B teams will assemble on the north bank of the Rufiji River, where two boats will await us, on Tuesday. On Wednesday morning, we will not use the power of the boats. We will paddle silently downstream to Nyambura Lodge. Sergeant Kingali and the B team will land first on the north bank immediately west of the lodge. The B team will storm up the river bank and take immediate, external possession of the lodge. I and the A team will land just below the lodge to the east. We will immediately join the B team and together we will storm into the lodge, where all present will be taken prisoner. Wassy will head team C which, on my command, will take over the government broadcast facilities."

* * *

Kamiri, a rifle slung over one shoulder, is sitting in the bright sunlight on the bench outside the office of Nyambura Camp. For Hassan, it is important that he be here: both his fathers are in the lodge, from which comes a murmur of discussion, and his best friend is sitting next to him. It was necessary to plead with Kerubo for Hassan to be granted permission to attend, with two conditions: that he remain outside the lodge and that he not interfere in the command of Major Wanjala, who has brought with him a two-squad platoon of special forces commandos. The major, a rangy, sinuous man with a perpetual frown, had his troops install a vehicle barrier on the road five hundred meters from the lodge. The barrier will rupture the tires on any vehicle attempting to pass over it. Four commandos, two carrying rocket propelled grenades and two with SA80 assault rifles are stationed with the barrier. Four other commandos are hidden just outside the entrance to the car park. The major and three others are in the oak grove along the path from the car park to the lodge. The balance – a dozen commandos – are distributed along a five-hundred-meter perimeter whose center is the lodge. In this way, the major has established a full-perimeter defense against the postulated attack from the north. Moreover, should any terrorists breach the five-hundred meter barrier, are the major and his three near the lodge, as well as the park's rifle-carrying rangers, who are out of sight in the trees along a hundred-meter perimeter.

Sami is leaning against a tree, day-dreaming about his girlfriend, a sultry and willing sixteen-year-old, his second (or is it first?) cousin in the village. His parents (and hers) are opposed to the liaison. It is necessary now to meet in secret: in the little abandoned hut, where the dirt floor can be covered with burlap and an oil lamp can be lighted so that he can see her naked beauty, taste her skin, hear her murmurs of pleasure . . .

What was that noise? It was over there, down toward the river. Something big broke a branch.

He hunches down to see better through the brush growing above the river bank just west of the lodge. *There! A black face. A human face. Gone now.*

"Who's there?" he calls.

No reply.

"Answer me or I'll shoot!"

No reply.

Now he can make out a human form, dressed in camouflage. He fires a warning shot. There is shouting from the bush: "Take him out!"

"They're here!" he yells as he takes aim and fires at the elusive shape.

Suddenly Sami's world extinguishes.

Hassan hears the challenges, the shouting, the two single shots and the burst of firing; he is on his feet running. There ahead of him is a dark, burly figure surging toward the lodge; well behind the figure of Sergeant Kingali is the rest of Team B. A whistle shrieks... shouting from the car park. Suddenly, Hassan is aware of the service pistol in his hand: safety off point, fire. The figure staggers and bursts through the lodge doors. Deafening gusts of fire off to his right...Hassan smashes through the door... a blaze of shooting inside – he fires a burst at the figure ahead: weapon falls; figure crumples.

Hassan wheels toward the door – no one; magazine nearly empty. He sweeps up the fallen weapon and faces the doors, ready.

A familiar figure charges in: Major Wanjala.

Kamiri is on his feet, rifle at ready. He looks right – a group of black-clad men firing, not at him. Some fall; others arms raised... more repeated bursts farther right: all are down.

He turns left – shouting and crashing there. Instinctively, he raises the rifle to the firing position as if anticipating a hidden rhino's charge. A figure bursts out of the bush, rifle in hand.

"Halt!" Kamiri shouts. The figure pulls off his baklava; it is Warari, paused, but weapon at the ready.

"Put it down, Warari. Your men are dead."

Warari catches sight of the dark figures sprawled in the clearing; he raises his rifle. A close warning shot from Kamiri tears through the bush, then another shot, closer. Astonished, Warari turns and crashes back into the bush, shouting orders at his men.

Inside, the major takes a sweeping look at the horror, sees no more invaders, and keys his radio: "Control from Lodge. Send helicopter. Many casualties. Urgent." He rushes outside to check on the external fighting, which has gone quiet.

Hassan's senses are overwhelmed: men down everywhere, some moaning, others crying out, some still, others moving tentatively. There is blood everywhere: on the men, on the floor, on the chairs and couches, many of which are overturned. An odor of cordite, and the smell of blood. Shell casings and broken glass litter the carpets; the windows along the river have been shattered. Wherever he turns, imploring men reach up to him. Kamiri is beside him. "Kamiri, get some help! We need bandages." But rangers, commandos and employees are pouring into the lodge, tearing up tablecloths, comforting and bandaging the wounded.

Hassan is outside looking for the major: "Mr Wanjala, we need more than one helicopter for the wounded."

"I'm sorry, Colonel, that's all we have."

"There were two assigned. Where is the other one?"

"Pursuing the escaping terrorists."

"No! Reassign it here immediately. That's an order!"

"Colonel, you were not to interfere."

"I am overriding my instructions. Redirect the helicopter."

"Yes, sir." A salute and then a radio transmission.

Back inside, Hassan finds Kaddour first. He is lying on his back, pressing a blood-stained napkin to his belly, his lips quivering and his eyes searching the ceiling. "Father, hang in there, the helicopters are coming."

"The pain is very bad."

Hassan looks around. "I'm afraid all I can offer you is spirits by mouth."

There is a weak smile from Kaddour; he shakes his head. "See to the President, Hassan."

Scanning the scene of many wounded men and carers, he is unable to spot the President. "Where is the President, Kamiri?"

Hassan looks in the direction of Kamiri's gesture. There, stretched out face-down on the carpet and partly covered with a table cloth is a familiar short, stocky body.

The Minister of Defense is sitting on a chair, his right arm in an improvised sling and a bloody napkin on his shoulder.

"How are you, sir?"

"Well, I have been better, but I could be a lot worse." He coughs and wipes his mouth with a blood-splattered napkin. "Your entry was timely, son – er – Hassan. That bastard was just getting started." He looks around. "Do you know if anyone has been killed?"

"I know only that the President is dead."

The minister grunts. "Terrible. Carry on, Hassan."

The first helicopter arrives and the most severely wounded are loaded on board: Kaddour, Olle Engström and five other members of Parliament. The second helicopter appears minutes later and carries Mohammad Adesida and seven parliamentary colleagues, some fully ambulatory, to Coast City Hospital. The nine uninjured attendees, most of whom were seated at the back of the room, watch the helicopters depart, sorry for the evacuees and the President, but relieved not to be among them.

Two other bodies are brought out of the lodge, awaiting the arrival of a surface ambulance, and laid alongside the

President's: Ng'ang'a's and one of the waiters. Another waiter – a relative perhaps, kneels at Ng'ang'a's side, holding the dead man's hand and tells anyone who stops to offer sympathy, "He and the President were standing up and shouting at the terrorists, while the rest of us were throwing ourselves down."

Hassan, driven by curiosity, is scanning the bodies of the dead terrorists. *I've got to see who I know.* He has already considered with satisfaction the body of Sergeant Kingali. *He, like Warari, was a ne'er-do-well, self-centered bully.* Three others he recognizes, including Irish. *I wonder if he tried to warn us again this time. Probably worth checking to see if we missed the tip-off.* He turns away. *Four of them are so damn young – barely twenty years old. They could have been good carpenters, or plumbers or mechanics. Shame.*

But good carpenters, plumbers and mechanics are not what I, the Other, want. They're two to the penny. I want the committed disruptor with a vision of a me-first world without all this soppy love.

Kamiri is counting his rangers. One of them is missing: Sami. "Where is Sami?"

"He was stationed over there," a ranger says, pointing to the forest west of the lodge. A dark gloom of foreboding sinks down on Kamiri as he enters the forest, calling. He searches systematically, left and right, then ahead without success. The gloom begins to lift. *He must be somewhere else.* To his right a scuttling noise attracts his attention. *Must be an animal there.* He goes to investigate, and pushes into a small clearing where the body of Sami is lying at the foot of a tree. "Ah, no, Sami, not you!" He falls to his knees beside the mutilated body and weeps.

Major Wanjala is calling his report into special forces HQ, with Hassan at his side: "I have two men wounded, not seriously;

Achieving Superpersonhood:

they're on their way, surface, to hospital. On the political side, one dead, the President, and fifteen wounded. The wounded have gone to hospital by helicopter. You can get status from the hospital. The park has three people dead: the general manager, a ranger and a waiter. The terrorists came in two boats. The first boatload of eight terrorists has all been shot dead. The second boatload has escaped downriver." He listens to a question from HQ. "Yes, sir, there were two helos reserved for pursuit of escaping terrorists. I diverted one to pick up the wounded. The other was intended to capture or kill escaping terrorists, but the lieutenant colonel countermanded my order, and both helos were ordered here." Sour-faced, he listens to another question. "No, sir, it would not have been possible to get all fifteen wounded on one helicopter. . . . from here it's about a three-hour drive to Coast City." Hassan moves closer to catch the questions from headquarters.

"Do you think, Major Wanjala, that members of Parliament would look quite so favorably on our funding requests if they had to endure a bumpy, three-hour ride while wounded when a helicopter was available?"

"No, sir, I suppose not, but what about the terrorists?"

"The terrorists will continue to be your assignment, Major; it's called 'job security'."

* * *

Mary listens to Hassan's account of the battle at Nyambura. She takes out a sheet of paper and draws a map on it. "So you were here . . ." She marks the spot with an X. "And you ran after the terrorist, here, as he ran toward the lodge, here."

"Yeah, that's about right."

"But you didn't see there were a whole bunch of terrorists over here, and more coming up over here."

"Yeah, when you're in a fire fight, you usually don't know exactly where the bad guys are."

"OK, but these guys here could have shot and killed you." In her anxiousness, Mary slashes several bullet paths which intersect at the X marked Hassan.

"Well, those guys were fully occupied in a fire fight with the commandos."

"Thank God for the commandos." She takes a deep breath. "And then you chased the terrorist into the lodge and killed him."

"I was a little late in getting to him. He had already fired half a clip."

"What's it like to kill someone, Hassan?"

He raises his shoulders and shakes his head. "There is a hell of a lot of noise and the guy falls to the ground. You don't think about him. You protect yourself; thinking: where's the next one?"

"But when it's over, do you think about the man you killed?"

"I don't think anything about him; he's just a problem that's been solved."

Mary exhales audibly. "Whew. I could never do that! I mean, you actually knew that Kingali."

She marks two new X's in the map. "How come Kamiri didn't just kill that bastard, Warari?"

"Well, don't forget, they're brothers."

"I know, and Warari shot him in the knee, ending his football career. It should have been payback time."

"So you think he should have shot him in the knee?"

"No, I would have shot him in the balls, and then in the chest. But, it probably wouldn't be fatal because he has no heart. That man is a reptile."

"It is a little strange that two sons of the same parents have turned out so differently."

"So the President is dead," Mary says. "Do you think your father, Adesida, will get the job?"

"He'll certainly be a contender when Parliament votes on it, but political leadership is such a slippery slope to climb."

I, the One, try to add traction for a good, deserving leader.

Achieving Superpersonhood:

I, the Other, try to add traction for one of my friends.

* * *

Kamiri is more troubled by the loss of Sami than by the escape of Warari, a set of priorities that Dorothy does not understand. During their phone call, she asks, "Did you think about just shooting him?"
"I didn't really think like that. I thought I had to give him a chance. I fired two warning shots, and if he made a move to kill me, I would have to kill him. Wouldn't you have done the same – if it was your sister, for example?
"That's hard because I love my sister. You don't love Warari."
"That's true, but my reflex was to fire the warning shots. Then I realized that if he got past me he would be killing people in the lodge."

It wasn't really Kamiri's 'reflex' as he says. I, the One, touched his instantaneous decisions and triggered 'warning'.

* * *

Warari has returned to his lair with one fewer of his anti-acolytes: Irish. *If my people weren't such damn cowards, we would have landed the boat on schedule, and I could have been at the lodge in time. I can't understand how two fair-size crocodiles in the landing zone got them behaving like women. Wouldn't paddle in. Wanted to shoot them. I threatened to shoot any man who picked up his gun instead of his paddle. We drifted down river. Had to paddle furiously to get back to the landing. Crocs swan off, but we were late.*
Then there was that fucking Kamiri – threatening to kill me. No doubt he would have. Still mad about the knee. By that time, Team B was gone. Did some good, though. Got the President.

William Peace

Bunch of people in the hospital. Some won't make it. Dhul Fikar is on track to reach our goal: my caliphate.

Within the limits of my capabilities, I, the Other, will always take care of my friends. I have a job to do, and while there are people who believe in me without knowing it, or are in a hateful corner, self-imposed, or imposed by others, I will do it.

Chapter 26

Settlement

At Mary's urging, Hassan is waiting for the elevator at Coast City Hospital when his mother, in black, steps out of the lift. After an embrace, he asks her, "How is he doing, Mother?"

"They're both doing all right. I understand we have you to thank that they're alive."

"The thanks need to be with Allah."

She nods. "Allah be with you, my son."

She kisses his cheek and drifts away.

What a strange woman she is.

Kaddour appears to be sleeping. A beeping green monitor above his head is tracing his heart, and a clear saline solution drips steadily into his hidden vein.

"Father?"

Kaddour opens his eyes. "It must be family day today."

"How are you feeling?"

"No too bad. They had to sew up a few holes inside me, and I can have nothing but broth for a while. Sit down, Hassan. How are you? Have you collected that medal they owe you?"

"No, no medal. It's quite enough to see you recovering."

Kaddour gives a snort. "After all the grief I've given you, I would have expected you to administer the coup de grace."

Hassan hesitates for a long moment. "Any grief you gave me was never undeserved, and frequently, though I resented it, it did me good." He sees Kaddour studying his face, trying to anticipate what is coming and what is intended. "Your role was never easy, Father, and I was a difficult, insecure brat. Having a cuckoo – even a small one – in the nest, must have been very difficult."

Evenly, Kaddour asks, "What are you talking about, Hassan?"

"I am talking about my two fathers."

Sharply, he asks: "Who told you that you have two fathers?"

"No one told me. I figured it out."

"Did your mother tell you?"

"No."

After a long pause, Kaddour says: "Go on."

"Father, I understand that it was best kept a secret, but secrets wear thin after a while, particularly in a family. I think it's best for the principals to deal with things as they really are, kindly and without recrimination – as much as may be possible. I can see no need for other than the four principals in this case to be aware of any particulars."

Kaddour is chewing the inside of his cheek. "What are you proposing, Hassan?"

"That I continue to call you 'Father' and think of you as my father. That I call Mohammad 'Uncle' and think of him as a different sort of father."

"He may want to call you 'Son'."

"In a private and personal environment that would be all right."

"Have you spoken to him about this?"

"Not yet. I wanted to speak with you first."

Kaddour's eyes travel around the room and return, brimming, to his step-son's face. "OK."

"Thank you, Father."

Kaddour boosts himself up in the bed. "You look very smart in that uniform, Hassan. I'm proud of you."

"You look like an invalid in that bed, Father. You need to get out soon and return to running the world."

"Speaking of running the world, you know that your uncle is likely to be our next President?"

Achieving Superpersonhood:

"I heard a rumor about it."

For Hassan, this will be the first time in his life he's had an actual, one-to-one conversation with his biological father, and though he is well rehearsed, he is suffering from dry-mouth, light-headedness.

Mohammad is sitting up in bed, reading the *City Herald.* Hearing a cough, he looks over his reading glasses and the *Herald* to find Hassan at his bedside. "Well, hello, Hassan, what are you doing here?"

"I came to see you, of course."

"That's very kind. I should be out in a day or two."

"That's good." A pause. "May I sit?"

"Yes, of course." He looks around. "You can take that chair there." Mohammad is uneasy, but he says nothing.

"I came to wish you well, and to ask if I might call you 'Uncle'."

"'Uncle'? Why would you want to call me 'Uncle'?"

"Because, under the circumstances, I can't very well call you 'Father'." Hassan dispenses Mohammad's search for words of protest with a gentle gesture. "I have just spoken to Kaddour and he has agreed. I made the point that while I recognize the need for the truth to be hidden, generally, the four of us, for the sake of our relationships with one another, need to deal in reality."

A look of cautious acceptance appears on Mohammad's face. "Who told you, Hassan? Was it your mother?"

"No. She kept her pledge of secrecy. I put the circumstantial evidence together."

"What was the evidence, Hassan?" Hassan merely shakes his head. Mohammad is intensely occupied; he glances down at the *Herald* and sighs several times. "You don't know, Hassan, how long I have yearned to call you my son and to hear you call me 'Father'. My longing was particularly intense when I presented you with the Sword of Honor."

"I sensed it, Papi."

Mohammad is startled. "'Papi', now there's a name I like."

"I can use it when we are alone and when I think of you. At other times, you will be 'Uncle' and people will assume that there is a special relationship similar to what Christians call 'godfather'."

Mohammad smiles wistfully. "I should tell you, son, that you are a real love child, contrary to what you may have felt."

Hassan digests this sweet/bitter observation. "It must have been very difficult for you and Mother."

"It was."

In a reflective mood, Hassan says, "I wonder what it means to be a love child."

"Does it not feel good?"

"I'm not sure, but it doesn't diminish the intense feelings that conceiving a love child can arouse in the parents."

"Yes, and you know I had intense feelings of pride when you won the Sword of Honor. Those feelings displaced all my doubts and concerns over the years, and I thought, 'This young man is going to amount to something."

"Thank you, Papi."

I, the One, prompt Hassan with the question.

"Papi, I'm wondering whether you know anything about some shares in Arusei Industries I've received?"

There is a prolonged silence while Mohammad considers. "Yes, I sent them to you." Hassan opens his mouth to put a question, but the patient waves his hand. "I felt . . . I felt very proud, and I wanted to <u>do</u> something. I never did anything . . . it's too easy to say I couldn't do anything. And . . . and I was feeling sorry for myself. Then I remembered the Arusei shares I had accumulated from my time on the board. And I sent them."

"You were feeling sorry for yourself? Why?"

Mohammad looks away. "You don't really want to know, Hassan."

"Yes, I do. No secrets."

Slowly Mohammad begins: "Do you remember – I suppose you were at university – there was a scandal about the purchase of some army helicopters?"

"Yes, and the student newspaper threatened to publish the details."

The patient tilts his head. "I don't know what they were going to publish, but I was worried. And then there was the shock of the Wangai affair – being caught with all that money. My wife confronted me; I told her to mind her own business. I almost got a second divorce. And then my daughter. She had some very hard words. She never spoke like that to anyone. I ... I didn't know what to do, and I thought *this life isn't worth living*. Then, I read that you had been arrested and given a suspended prison sentence for the protest. Something inside me just broke. I wrote out a check. Gave it to the contractor ... and I asked them to hide it in the contract adjustments." There is a long pause. "I didn't have the courage to check whether the Army ever got its money back. But I tried to make it right."

Hassan is looking down the ward. "Tell me, Papi, what are you going to do if you become president?"

"You mean about corruption?"

"Yes."

"Well, I'm not going to touch any of the press, or Hetti Aguta, and I'm going to leave the anti-corruption tsar in place. There's no way I would touch another shilling, but I'm not going to start a witch-hunt. You have to understand, Hassan, that politics is a tricky business. To stay in control, and do what's best for Country, one has to have allies, and it's also important to understand that today, in Country, among the political elite, there's a culture of entitlement – a belief that the country doesn't pay us very much – nothing like what we're worth – so we're going to take top-ups whenever they're offered." Hassan frowns, but Mohammad continues, "If a president tries to wipe out that culture, he would lose all his allies, so one has to close one's eyes to holidays in the Seychelles, new Jaguars, and kids enrolled in the best English boarding schools, but where there is <u>evidence</u> of a big personal gain balanced against a questionable decision, one has to act, and that's what I'm going to tell my cabinet, if they elect me."

"I guess that's the best one can do."

Mohammad offers the trace of a smile. "Over time the culture may become more British, but I don't think even Britain is as pristine as it pretends."

Hassan gets to his feet. "Get well soon, Papi, and thanks for the shares."

* * *

His immersion in the shame of Warari's involvement in the massacre at Nyambura, attending Sami's funeral, searching for a replacement, and trying to be interesting and cheerful with guests who have returned to the re-conditioned lodge, consume all Kamiri's attention. He does not notice that Elijah has installed himself in the park office.

When the office clerk tells him, "Elijah would like to see you," he answers, "When?"

"Now, Kamiri, is there a problem?"

"No, but I'm scheduled to take the French party out this afternoon."

"Kamiri, Elijah is in the office now."

"Oh, OK."

Elijah closes the door of the general manager's office. *Uh-oh, he's going to fire me for not killing Warari.*

"You don't seem very cheerful, Kamiri."

"No, sir, uh, no, Eli, I'm not. I've been thinking about Warari, and . . ."

Elijah makes a dismissive gesture. "Don't worry about him, Kamiri, we'll get him sooner or later." He clears his throat and picks up a manila folder. "I've been looking at your personnel records. It says here you've got a high school diploma, and that you've been taking a number of university-level correspondence courses."

"Yes, I've completed Mathematics 1, Economics 1, and I'm almost finished the world history course. Then, I thought I would learn French."

"I think Spanish might be more useful." Elijah flips though the folder. "Kamiri, as you know, the position of general manager here is open, with the passing of Ng'ang'a."

"I was very sorry about that, Eli."

"Yes, well, would you like to be considered for the position, Kamiri?"

The chief ranger's mouth opens in astonishment, but nothing comes out until the squawk: "Me, sir? I don't know anything about being a general manager."

Elijah leans back in his chair. "As far as I am concerned, there are just five elements to the job: encouraging the happiness of individual guests, inspiring the staff, serving good food well on time, organizing interesting safaris, and assuring that the premises are kept neat and tidy. The only two of these that you don't have direct experience of are food service and premises management. The food service is in the hands of our excellent head chef, Jonny, and premises management is mostly just a matter of regular inspections and listening to clients."

"But I don't know anything about the money side of things."

"Bookings and payment are handled by head office, as are salaries and payments to suppliers. Shaaban takes care of signing off on supplier invoices and taking last-minute guest payments." Elijah considers Kamiri for a moment. "The main reasons I think you're a strong candidate are that the staff like and respect you, and guests write good things about you – by name – in the visitor's book. This is a good camp, but the staff just do their job. They aren't inspired, and inspiration is contagious: guests get infected, too. I think you could inspire the staff, excite the guests, and turn Nyambura into a first-class destination."

"Thank you, Eli; that's very kind, but I'm still learning what it means to be a manager."

"I know. Ng'ang'a told me that you had to learn that management is not all fairness, kindness and patience."

Kamiri's lips are compressed. "Yes. I understand that sometimes a good manager must be impatient and tough."

Elijah smiles. "Yes. I think you can do the job; take a couple of days to think about it. I should tell you that you are the only internal candidate. A search firm is looking at external candidates." *There! That should arouse his competitive instincts.*

Kamiri's immediate call to Dorothy goes to voicemail. He prepares next week's ranger rota, keeping one eye on the telephone beside him. Forty-five minutes later, Dorothy returns the call, and listens to his agitated recap of the meeting with Elijah. "That's fantastic, Kamiri! When do you start?"

"I'm not sure I can get the job. He's looking at outside people – probably specialists in this kind of job."

They discuss, in detail, the job requirements, Kamiri's skills, and Elijah's attitude toward the position. Dorothy develops the conclusion that the obstacle to Kamiri saying 'yes' is his lack of confidence in meeting the new management challenges. *Without the experience, he will need a professional support system.*

Dorothy, having talked to her father about Kamiri's situation, and having developed a possible remedy, calls Kamiri. "I have an idea for you, Kamiri. There's a starting level, but quite comprehensive, course in hotel management that's offered by City University, either as a full time, live-in course for six months, or as a part-time, correspondence course for a year."

"But Dorothy, by the time I complete the course, Elijah will already have appointed someone."

"No. I suggest that you tell Elijah that you will accept the job on the condition that the company sends you to City University, where you can get your certificate in hotel management."

"But he won't accept that, Dorothy."

"I think he might, because it will be telling him that you're very keen to learn the best practice in hotel management, and at the same time you'll be attending class at the university one day a week and talking regularly to the professors and other students."

"Where can I find out more about this course, Dorothy?"

"It's on the university website under hotel management."

Kamiri is apprehensive about the meeting with Elijah. He has downloaded, printed in the office and carefully studied the course in hotel management.

He says, "I would like very much to accept the general management position, Eli, if you offer it to me, but I'm afraid of letting you down, because I don't feel well qualified. If I could take this course in hotel management while I'm working on the job, I'm pretty sure I'd be all right."

Elijah holds out his hand to inspect the prospectus; he reviews it carefully, page by page. "This looks like a good course. Some of our other hotel managers could benefit from this."

He swings his swivel chair and looks out the window. "OK, Kamiri, you've got the job on two conditions. One: that your day at the university will count as one of your days off. In other words, you get only one day a week off – apart from your two weeks' holiday – for one year. And, second, that if you fall behind in your studies, your contract can be terminated."

Kamiri has a huge grin. "I accept."

Slightly exasperated, Elijah says, "We haven't discussed the salary yet."

"No, sir, we haven't."

"The job carries an F grade in the Arusei hierarchy, and I propose to start you at the minimum for the F grade, which is thirty-two thousand, five hundred shillings per month. OK?"

"Yes."

Hurriedly, Elijah adds, "You'll have a ten percent bonus at the end of the year, based on performance. The company will pay your tuition fees at university. You'll have the use of the general manager's cottage here, and meals are included as before."

Dorothy has made a lunch reservation at Neptune for a table for two by the windows. Kamiri is expected momentarily. Beyond the windows are piles of white, cotton-candy clouds, each with a flat bottom, as if no cloud should venture below that altitude. *The first time I came here, it was with his best friend. That didn't work out. Who knows what will happen this time?*

Kamiri notices, when Dorothy stands up to greet him, that she is wearing a pale blue cotton dress decorated with sunflowers, not her usual dark blue track suit. Moreover, she kisses him on the cheek. He, however, is wearing a Nyambura polo shirt and jeans.

When the waiter arrives, champagne is poured into the tall, narrow glasses. "Congratulations, Kamiri." She raises her glass.

"Thank you, Dorothy. You look very nice."

"Well, I thought we ought to have a proper celebration. Are you still happy about the job?"

"Yes, over the moon, as they say, and I want to thank you so much for finding that course for me."

"You're welcome. Speaking of finding things, there is an opening for a doctor at the clinic in Park Town, and I thought I would take it."

"Wow, Park Town is just outside Nyambura, and we'll be able to get together much more easily."

"Yes. In fact, I was thinking of staying at the general manager's cottage at Nyambura."

Kamiri cannot conceal his astonishment. "Wow. . . . I mean: that's a good idea, but I'm not sure the company would allow it."

"I think the company would allow it if we were married."

Kamiri stares at Dorothy, open-mouthed. "If we were married?"

"Yes, if we were married." Then, with a smile: "It is legal in this country."

"But . . ." No other words come out. "I mean . . . do you think we should?"

"Yes, I do. What do you think?"

"I . . . I like you an awful lot, Dorothy. I mean, more than I ever thought was possible. But, well, what would your parents think?"

"They would be very happy. What would your parents think?"

"They would be very surprised that I might be marrying a beautiful doctor from City."

Dorothy is unable to suppress a laugh. "Kamiri, I have the impression that you have the same sort of feelings about getting married as you did about taking the general manager's position." He nods, his eyes locked on the table cloth. "Well, as far as I know," she continues, "there isn't a course that leads to a good husband certificate, but you are very well qualified, believe me, to be a good husband and a father."

"A father?"

"Yes, that's part of the package." She reaches across the table and takes his hand. "I love you, Kamiri."

"I didn't know that." He takes a deep breath. "I love you, Dorothy."

> One of my USPs (unique sales propositions), as they say these days, is that only I, the One, can offer the rapturous tenderness almost universally craved. So, if you want it, talk to me about it. The Other can't match my offer.

"We can have a wonderful life together, Kamiri. We'll have children and some big Western hotel chain will look at your track record and snap you up in preference to white alternatives, and the children and I will come along."

"Will you be able to do that?"

"For sure. Do you know of a Western country that doesn't want qualified black doctors?"

* * *

Mary comes home with a late edition of the *Herald.* She sets it down carefully in front of her husband, who is reading some papers he has taken from his briefcase. "Did you see the news, Hassan?"

"Yes. It's not really news, Mary."

"Well, I think it's pretty important news for us: your father – uncle – has been elected President. Your two fathers are the most powerful men in Country." She wriggles into his lap. "We make a great team, Hassan. We're going to go places!"

> I, the One, will try to teach Mary, in particular, that satisfaction is more liberating than desire; therefore, choose service over power.

* * *

"Now that they're both married," Helen suggests, "I think we should ask the girls, and their husbands, for a Sunday lunch. Hopefully, it will be the start of a Maiyo tradition."

Joseph says, "Their husbands are good friends: no problem there. I just worry that Dorothy and Mary will find reasons for an unnecessary cat fight."

"Believe me, Joseph, there's nothing now for them to fight about."

The table is set with a Chinese embroidered tablecloth, the best cutlery and a low centerpiece of native red and white carnations. The wine glasses still have a centimeter or two of the estate-bottled Chianti, except Hassan's which is half-full of Heineken's zero alcohol.

Achieving Superpersonhood:

Kamiri scoops up his last morsel of pineapple cheesecake. "This was a delicious lunch and an excellent occasion. Thank you very much."

Dorothy adds, "Yes, well done, Mom!"

Helen says, "It was my pleasure that I hope to have quite often."

"It is really nice to be together," Mary says. "Hassan and I don't see Dorothy and Kamiri, now that they're living with the elephants, and I'd particularly like to say that I miss my sister."

"You do?" Dorothy asks in surprise.

"Yes. I feel that we're at a different level now, with a whole new set of experiences to talk about."

"You mean we've grown up?" Dorothy prompts.

"Yes, but more than that: we've found what we want in life – what makes us whole – no more wondering and wandering."

"You've all become 'supermenschen,'" Joseph suggests.

"I don't like that term, Dad," Mary protests. "It's too Germanic and exaggerated. For me, it's about being fully challenged and satisfied at the same time. You know it when you get there."

Dorothy says, "I would add that it's not easy getting there."

Mary holds up both of her thumbs to her sister. "Yeah, and you've done it, Dee! You've transformed yourself from an impatient idealist into a practical, patient-centered doctor. There are even national newspaper articles about you."

Dorothy shrugs. "The publicity is better than some I've had."

"Yeah, but the media experience you had, while soul scorching, focused your attention on what really matters for you."

There are murmurs of agreement.

Hassan says, "I'd just like to say that you, Mary, now that you have a political column in the *Observer*, are turning out amazing stuff."

"You mean instead of being a bomb-throwing lunatic?"

"Well, you're still considered by some to be a bit crazy, but a lot of people – even my father - read your column."

There is a reflective pause at the table.

Dorothy says, "Mr Arusei must be very proud of you, Hassan."

"Well, I'm still invited to Friday lunch."

"But Hassan," Dorothy says, "if we're going to talk about this 'getting there' process, you're the one with the greatest leap: from lonely, rejected, rich kid to a decorated Army officer."

"Well, but I had an unfortunate detour on the way."

"But for you," Mary says, "that was part of the re-focusing process."

"And I think there was also some confidence-building" Kamiri suggests. "Maybe it was your faith that helped with that."

"Yes, it's true. Somehow, Allah's love rubbed off on me. Perhaps you've had the same experience, Kamiri."

"For me, it's been a bit different. I've been enormously lucky, for example: to be here with my wife, Dorothy . . ." There is a fond glance between the two. ". . . at this table with all of you. It's amazing – remembering where I started out. So I think that my good fortune is surely a demonstration of God's love."

"But you haven't just ridden God's coattails, Kamiri," Mary offers, "your satanic brother ended your football career, and George Nicholson did you no short-term favors by dying. You had to respond!"

Joseph says, "From my perspective, Kamiri deserves particular praise for adopting what was, for him, a thoroughly foreign, but essential management style."

Kamiri smiles. "Yeah. I call it 'kick ass now!'"

The table lapses into reflective silence and into one-on-one conversations.

Joseph clinks his wine glass. "I'd like to read you a prayer which I'm told is the Christian version of an old Masai prayer: 'Oh, Father God, please help me polish my latent talents, and

Achieving Superpersonhood:

reveal to me my hidden culpability so that I will be pleased to help these many citizens and be a good and worthy instrument in Your household.'"

The End

Review Requested:

If you loved this book, would you please provide a review at Amazon.com?

Lightning Source UK Ltd.
Milton Keynes UK
UKHW01f2007200918
329247UK00001B/264/P